When Nick went into the paper shop, Gran Emerson, who was a card, and Ivy, her daughter-in-law, who was a saucebox, both brightened up. Nick was a nice young man.

'When's yer sailor dad comin' 'ome Nick?' asked Gran.

'Not till his ship does,' said Nick.

'What's the name of 'is ship – only Wally's got a friend that's in the Navy.'

That's done it, thought Nick. No-one in the family had ever worried about giving Pa's non-existent ship a name.

'It's slipped me mind for moment,' he said. 'I'll ask Ma.'

Ma said, later, 'Tell 'er the *Iron Duke*.'

'Suppose it was sunk in the Great War?'

'Tell 'er the Navy went and refloated it.'

Nick managed to get away with it next time. But as Gran's questions became more pressing he found he was weaving a web that constantly tripped him up.

If only Pa would hurry up and get out of gaol . . .

PRIDE OF WALWORTH

Mary Jane Staples

CORGI BOOKS

PRIDE OF WALWORTH
A CORGI BOOK : 0 552 14291 3

First publication in Great Britain

PRINTING HISTORY
Corgi edition published 1995

Set in 11/12pt Linotype Plantin by
County Typesetters, Margate, Kent

Corgi Books are published by Transworld Publishers Ltd,
61–63 Uxbridge Road, Ealing, London W5 5SA,
in Australia by Transworld Publishers (Australia) Pty Ltd,
15–25 Helles Avenue, Moorebank, NSW 2170,
and in New Zealand by Transworld Publishers (NZ) Ltd,
3 William Pickering Drive, Albany, Auckland.

Reproduced, printed and bound in Great Britain by
Cox & Wyman Ltd, Reading, Berks.

To PIP and STEVE, JUDY and NIGEL

Chapter One

Ma Harrison of Browning Street, Walworth, was a
trim-looking woman. She dressed neatly and wore
her brown hair with a parting down the middle and
tidy buns cosily nestling around her ears. An
energetic and perky character at forty-two, she had
a son and three daughters. Nick was one month
short of twenty-one, Alice was seventeen, Amy
thirteen and Fanny eleven. Nick worked for an
insurance company in Holborn, and Alice had a job
with Galloway's, manufacturers of cough syrup, in
the Walworth Road. She did clerking and filing.
Amy and Fanny were still at school, at St John's in
Larcom Street.

They all went along with Ma's funny little ways,
which had come about on account of the misfortunes of their dad, Pa Harrison. Whenever she
was talking about him to interested parties, it was
obvious she had a cross to bear.

'Is yer old man still away, then, Mrs 'Arrison?'
Female neighbours were interested parties, and
were always asking that question of her. It was a
fact of life in Walworth, the interest female neighbours had in other women's husbands, much as if
they were thinking of offering to swap.

'Yes, he's still away in the Navy,' Ma would reply
with a sigh.

'My, all this time and all, you poor woman.'

7

'Yes, 'is ship's still in the China Seas.' Ma would then take on the look of a wife and mother suffering prolonged separation from the family provider as bravely as she could. It was very suffering when it was at a distance of thousands of miles. Ma couldn't think of any distance farther than the China Seas. It meant the neighbours couldn't suggest Mr Harrison ought to be able to pop home for the occasional weekend leave. 'It's all them chronic Chinese pirates,' she'd add, 'there's no end to them. Albert's often saying in 'is letters that there's a hundred born every minute.'

''Orrible. It's like five 'undred while yer doin' an 'ard-boiled egg. It's a real shame for yer, Mrs 'Arrison, and for Mr 'Arrison too.'

'Yes, Albert's suffering 'imself,' Ma would say, 'but he 'as to do 'is duty as a sailor. I just 'ope them pirates don't capture 'im and hold 'im to ransom, because where would I get the money from, even if they only asked five pounds for him?' And so on.

Actually, Pa Harrison had been known to the Hackney police as Knocker Harrison on account of his tendency to knock off wallets that didn't belong to him. But he'd never done time for this particular lark because the coppers had never caught him in the act or in possession of the goods. All the same, he was now in Marsham Gaol, although not for lifting wallets. It was for knocking off an American lady's jewels from her suite in a posh London hotel in May, 1930, well over three years ago. This kind of caper being above his usual line of operation, fate had struck him a blow for overstepping himself. It contrived to place the lady in the suite at the time, which was not only a surprise to him, but an embarrassment as well.

She came out of the bathroom just as he was shovelling the sparklers into a smart little attaché case he'd nicked the day before. He blushed a bit and panicked a bit. Well, who wouldn't have? The handsome and statuesque American lady was in a ravishing white corset, eye-blinking French knickers, and black silk stockings. Instead of leaving the jewels and doing a sensible bunk, he did something daft. While she was temporarily struck dumb, he pulled off the bedcover, flung it over her head and smothered her in it. Helpfully, the lady swooned. He placed her on the bed, completed the theft and scarpered. He left the hotel the same way he'd entered, by the back stairs. When he appeared in the street, he looked a gentleman of leisure in a tailored suit, a Homburg hat, and a public school tie. Carrying his attaché case and his walking-stick, he merged with the crowds.

But he was copped all the same. The outraged American lady was able to give a correct description of him. His suit and hat were familiar to the Hackney police. He'd had the suit made up for him by a Shoreditch tailor who was still waiting to be paid, and he'd found the hat on a peg somewhere. It was in this outfit that he'd take up his walking-stick and go out, usually to the races. He was probably the best-dressed pickpocket in the business. Ma kept on at him about getting a job, sometimes with the aid of her frying-pan, but she'd always end up saying, well, I suppose I've got to have some money to feed us all, so let's see what you've come back home with. Ma had to be practical.

However, she thought it criminally daft, getting himself copped for a jewel robbery. The judge gave him five years hard labour, first because he'd done the job, second because he'd done bodily assault on the American visitor, and third because the law hadn't recovered the loot. To pile it on, the affronted lady said in court that she'd suffered the outrageous indignity of having a lousy Limey thief catch her in her best fancy underwear.

Showing no hard feelings, the police let Ma and her son Nick see Pa after he'd been sentenced, whereupon he at once assured Ma it had been an unfair cop on account of accidental circumstances. Ma, looking as if she wanted to spit, asked what accidental circumstances meant. Well, said Pa, that aggravating American female wasn't supposed to be there at the time. I was slipped the wrong information, he whispered. You silly old bugger, said Ma, you let someone put you up to it. And it wasn't accidental circumstances, it was getting too big for your boots. Why you let someone talk you into doing a jewel robbery, I'll never know. Why couldn't you have stuck to honest pickpocketing? Now see what you've done by getting above yourself, you've left your family without a father for five years. Yes, five years hard labour, Albert Harrison, like a common criminal. You want your head seeing to. When you come out, I'll make sure you get a proper job, like driving a coal cart. What, said Pa, more hard labour on top of five years?

Ma told him not to give her any lip. He'd upset her enough as it was, she said. Just earn yourself good conduct marks and they'll let you out a bit early. Suffering Punch and Judy, said Pa, out early to drive a coal cart, what sort of a future is that? Don't talk saucy to me, said Ma. Actually, Pa had acquired a gift for talking like a gent, even though he'd been born a cockney. Ma said I suppose you

10

realize me and the children will have to move from Hackney on account of all the neighbours knowing what you've done, and more especially knowing what you did to that American woman when she wasn't decently dressed? Nick can't hardly look his friends in the face, can you, Nick?

Nick, sixteen at the time, asked Pa what the American lady's underwear was actually like. Well, real black silk stockings, for a start, said Pa. The policeman present caught that and grinned. Ma didn't think it amusing herself. She told Pa not to answer questions like that, and she told Nick not to ask them.

Pa said he still felt it was an unfair cop. Not that he'd ever had a fair cop in mind, he said, just a nice neat job that would keep the family in comfortable style for a bit. Ma again looked as if she wanted to spit. Pa patted her shoulder and told her someone would keep a charitable eye on her. He didn't say who or why in case the copper overheard, but he did give Ma a wink. Nick guessed that whoever had the jewels had the responsibility of being charitable to Ma. Nick agreed with her that Pa had overstepped himself by not sticking to honest pickpocketing. Nobody in Hackney minded a neighbour taking up that kind of career. But a jewel robbery and doing bodily harm to the female victim in her underwear meant Ma couldn't stay in Hackney without having all the neighbours asking if ladies in underwear made Pa jump them. Horrible details of the court case would bound to be in the *News of the World*, and the whole family would get looked at and talked about. Ma would definitely want to move.

Her next words to Pa were to emphasize his need to reform himself while doing his time, and to go straight when he came out. Mind, if a friend of his did offer to help her, she wouldn't say no, as she hadn't got anything coming in. It was fortunate Nick had left his grammar school at Easter, she said, and was hoping to get himself a respectable clerking job on account of being well educated and honest. Pa grimaced. He was taking his five-year sentence like the gent he was, but he wasn't too keen on his only son being a clerk. Pardon me, he said, but there's no need for that, not when Tosh Fingers could teach Nick some very useful tricks. Tosh Fingers was a bloke whose real monicker was lost in the mists of Hackney Marshes or somewhere else of a foggy nature. Ma said she wasn't going to have any of her children taught any kind of tricks by a bloke who was a second Charlie Peace, thanks very much. See where useful tricks have got you, she said.

Pa was taken away then to begin his sentence, and Ma and Nick went home, only to find neighbours inside and outside the house. It took Ma an hour to get rid of them, which made her determined to move right out of Hackney.

The following day a bloke in a black belted overcoat and a brown bowler hat paid Ma a visit. He had a large moustache and a large mouth. Whenever he smiled he showed large horsy teeth, and looked as if he'd just eaten last year's Derby winner, bones and all, and thoroughly enjoyed it. A well-known figure in Hackney, being the local moneylender, he was called Mister Horsemouth. His real name was Monty Cooper. Cooper was derived in his case from Kupper, the name of his German grandfather, an immigrant. He had a private talk with Ma and Nick in the parlour, and a week later the family moved south of the river to Walworth, to a three-storeyed house in Browning Street. Ma was a bit peeved at having to leave friends and neighbours she'd known for years, but it had to be done.

'We've got to put behind us the shame of your daft Pa turning 'imself into a convicted felon and bein' sent to prison like a common criminal, which was never what 'e was born to be.'

She perked up once the family had settled in, however. After all, her new neighbours didn't know a thing about Pa or how he'd landed himself in jug. Ma was able to look everyone in the face, and she soon put it about that Pa was away in the China Seas with the Royal Navy. 'Of course, it's a long way away,' she'd say, 'but we're all proud of 'im.' Nick, Alice, Amy and Fanny all backed her up. The girls had a very affectionate regard for Pa, and had never complained about him being a pickpocket instead of one of the workers. As for the jewel robbery, they all took an instinctive dislike to the American woman for having landed Pa in the soup.

Nick was aware that Mister Horsemouth was the friend keeping a charitable eye on Ma, making her a monthly allowance that paid the rent and helped her scrape a living for them all. Which meant, of course, that Mister Horsemouth and his runabout hireling, Tosh Fingers, had put Pa up to snaffling the jewels. Anyway, it was certainly Mister Horsemouth who called on Ma once a month to dispense his charity.

Nick managed to secure himself his job with the old-established insurance company soon after the family moved to Walworth. And Alice, when she left school at fourteen, managed to get herself accepted at Galloway's a month later, which perked

Ma up no end, because then Alice and Nick both contributed to her housekeeping. Amy and Fanny had enrolled at St John's Church School in Larcom Street, which had pleased Ma very much. She said a church school was just right for the daughters of a Royal Navy sailor, and would help them grow up religious and respectable.

'Hold on,' said Nick at the time, 'you're pushing it a bit, Ma. They're hardly daughters of an able seaman.'

'Watch your tongue,' said Ma, 'they've been your sailor Pa's daughters since we moved 'ere.'

'You sure?' said Nick. 'I thought Pa had been daft enough to get—'

'Never mind what you thought,' said Ma. 'I hope you're not goin' to be contrary just because you've been wearin' long trousers for a bit. Now, what's your Pa in?'

'The Royal Navy.'

'And where is he?'

'In the China Seas doing battle with Chinese pirates.'

'There,' smiled Ma, 'you said that quite easy, and it didn't 'urt, did it?'

'Hardly any pain at all, Ma.'

'Good,' said Ma.

That was how it was going to be with Ma and her family until Pa came out.

It was now well over three years since Pa had begun his sentence. Nick was well established in his job, and so was Alice at Galloway's, while Amy and Fanny were doing well at school. Alice at seventeen was like Ma, slim, neat and trim. She was very particular about her appearance, and could get very cross with herself if she discovered the seams of her stockings weren't straight. She made her clothes last by taking extra care with them, since there wasn't much money available for new outfits. She favoured simple blouses and skirts for going to work, and none of the blouses ever showed a wrinkle. She had nice looks without being as pretty as Amy, and fair hair with natural waves, together with blue eyes like Pa's. It was Pa's blue eyes that made him look a trustworthy gent, as well as a personable one. Nick and Alice both thought that if he hadn't panicked when the American woman caught him snaffling her sparklers, that if he'd smiled at her, used his blue eyes on her and come up with a yarn about only doing the nicking job in order to feed some starving orphans, she might have said something like OK, Robin Hood, just take my diamond brooch and give us a kiss.

Thirteen-year-old Amy and eleven-year-old Fanny both had straw-coloured hair and hazel eyes. Amy was as pretty as a picture, and Fanny had a piquant little nose in the middle of a saucy face. Local boys quite fancied Alice and Amy, but Ma vetted all boys who came knocking and so far hadn't approved of any of them. She said Amy was far too young, anyway. Further, as all her girls were daughters of a Royal Navy sailor, it was her duty, she said, to see they didn't get taken up the park by scruffy Walworth boys. She was doing her best after three years to let neighbours think the captain of Pa's ship was considering promoting him to sergeant. Nick had to point out there were no sergeants in the Navy, only petty officers. Ma took umbrage at that. Your Pa might have his faults, she said, but he's never been petty, just unlucky.

And a bit daft, said Nick. Well, a bit, conceded Ma.

She went to see him once a month, on Sundays, and most times Nick and the girls went with her. For some reason, the prison governor allowed Pa the privilege of being able to receive his whole family. Alice said the reason was easy to guess. Pa had chatted the governor up. Pa liked to see how his offspring were coming along, and if any of them were showing a bit of talent. Nick thought he always looked fit, as if his hard labour provided him with healthy exercise. At forty-five, he had a handsome look, even in his prison garb, and was never less than cheerfully optimistic about earning generous remission. But he still wasn't happy about Alice and Nick doing office work. He didn't think that was anything but a waste of their talents. He suggested during one visit that they could go into partnership and try their luck as a double act by selling Buckingham Palace to a rich American visitor. Ma threatened to brain him if he made any more suggestions like that. Such suggestions were always whispered, of course, because warders present had notoriously large lugholes.

Ma followed up her threat to do him a fatal injury by pointing out that a sailor's children had got to grow up respectable. That made Pa grin, for he knew all about how he was supposed to be in the China Seas with the Navy. Ma informed him Alice had the makings of a lady and might very likely marry a wealthy gentleman when she was old enough. As for Nick, she said, I'm hoping it won't be long before he turns into a proper young gent in a bowler hat and a rolled umbrella. Pa told her not to say things like that out loud in case his fellow inmates heard her. He said he hoped he wouldn't live to see the day when Nick went to work in a bowler hat just to earn a pound a week. Nick, he said, could already be earning a couple of quid six times a day by selling gold watches down Petticoat Lane and suchlike markets.

Alice asked what gold watches, Pa? Pa said Tosh Fingers could supply them at five bob a time, and Nick could sell them for fifty bob each. Ma nearly clouted him with her handbag. I thought I told you to reform, she said, I thought I told you to think about honest work. Well, said Pa, in his habitually discreet voice, what's more honest than someone getting a gold watch for fifty bob? You mean thinking he is, said Ma. Well, if it makes him happy, said Pa, what's more honest than that, old girl? Lord give me patience, said Ma, you still don't have no sense of family respectability.

Most visits to Pa were like that. But he had his loyal subjects, his three daughters. They adored him, and believed he really had been unfairly copped. Just after the third anniversary of his committal to prison, Alice said to Nick that that catty American woman ought to have been thrilled at having a handsome man like Pa admiring her best fancy underwear.

'Eh?' said Nick. Alice may have been only seventeen, but he had no idea, of course, how the mind of a female worked at any age.

'Well,' said Alice.

'Well what?' said Nick, tall and personable.

'Never mind,' said Alice, 'you're too young.'

'You're even younger,' said Nick, 'and I don't suppose you even need to wear egg-cups yet.'

'Here, d'you mind, you lanky lump of a dog's

dinner?' said Alice. 'I happen to have been wearin' what's necessary for ages.'

'All right, compliments to your blouse,' said Nick, who talked like Pa, who'd always been able to put on the style. The whole family were cockneys, having been born in Hackney, but Pa had taken naturally to posh speech, and Nick had taken after him. The girls too could put it on a bit. Ma, however, dropped aitches by the dozen, but being a practical woman she didn't think they were necessary, anyway. 'Look,' said Nick, 'I know we agree that Pa could have sweet-talked the woman, but I can't see she'd have been thrilled to be caught in her knickers. When that kind of thing happens, don't women blush and scream and die a death?'

'Oh, lor', you poor dear,' said Alice, 'you've got a lot to learn. There's any amount of women that would enjoy having a handsome man like Pa see what their best undies look like.'

'Pardon?' said Nick.

'That's all,' said Alice, 'now go and play with your train set.'

'Like a tickle, would you?' said Nick.

Alice, who went mad when she was tickled, bolted for her bedroom. Nick went after her.

Ma came out of the kitchen a minute later and called, 'What's goin' on up there?'

'Nick's tickling Alice on the landin', Ma,' called Fanny.

'Oh, is that all?' said Ma. 'I thought she was 'aving a fit.'

'She's 'aving fifty, Ma,' called Amy amid the shrieks of suffering Alice.

'Well, let me know when she gets to a hundred,' said Ma, 'and then I'll come up with me frying-pan.'

18

Alice, escaping, yelled at Nick, 'Oh, I hope you break both legs playin' your next football match.'

'That reminds me, there's a committee meeting this evening,' said Nick.

Chapter Two

The football committee meeting took place, as usual, in Ma's parlour. Early on in the proceedings, Nick thought his ears were deceiving him.

'That's it, then, I ain't goin' to lend the team me football no more,' said Chrissie Evans, otherwise known as Chrissie Dumpling or just Dumpling. She was eighteen, worked in a factory for ten bob a week, a wage common to factory girls in 1933, and could be said to be round all over. She had an uncle who'd once played soccer for Millwall, and he'd given her a new football on her birthday last August because she supported Millwall and also fancied herself at the game. Nick supposed some people found that hard to credit, a fat girl fancying herself as a footballer, but with potty females like Lady Nancy Astor going about saying anything men could do women could do as good or better, even girls like Dumpling were going off their chump. What Dumpling was after was getting herself into the local team, Browning Street Rovers. Most of the team lived in or off Browning Street. 'I mean it,' said Dumpling earnestly, 'if you don't let me play on Saturday, you ain't gettin' a lend of me football no more.'

'What?' asked Freddy Brown, shaken. Freddy was nearly nineteen and lived in Caulfield Place, just round the corner from Nick's home. He was the team's right half, slim, supple and nifty.

'Dumpling, you ain't serious, are yer?' asked Danny Thompson, twenty years old and right back for the Rovers.

'Course I'm serious,' said Dumpling, and Danny looked pained. His black hair seemed to droop. A decent young bloke, he actually fancied Dumpling. It was true that a lot of short women went barmy about tall men, and that some blokes were partial to plump females. Since Dumpling really was roundly plump, Danny was extremely partial to her. Dumpling thought him daft every time he asked her to go out with him. She had only one interest, and that was football. Also, she had only one love, and that was Browning Street Rovers.

Nick, Freddy and Danny made up the team committee, with Dumpling as a co-opted member because she let the team use her top quality football. Nick was captain, secretary and treasurer, since he was able to read, write and add up in superior fashion and was also pretty good at ordering people about. Further, although not the oldest member, he was visibly the tallest and also a commanding centre half. The Rovers played against other Walworth street teams on Saturday afternoons on a hired pitch in Brockwell Park. The hire cost five bob, and each team contributed half a crown. Every member of the Rovers, including their one reserve, paid a subscription of threepence a week during the season. That left a tanner a week to go into team funds, which just about looked after the cost of replacing the occasional shirt or shorts. Any cost relating to football boots came out of the pockets of individual members. There was never enough money in the kitty to buy a new football. A decent one cost fifteen bob. The previous ball had come apart, and the one owned by Dumpling was the team's lifeblood. Unfortunately, the committee had promised Dumpling that in return for her regular loan of it, she could step in if ever they were a man short. And they were a man short for Saturday's game. So Dumpling was standing up for her rights.

'Now look here, Dumpling,' said Nick, 'this is a man's game—'

'Well, 'Erbert Briggs ain't a man yet, nor much of a footballer,' said Dumpling, tossing her tangled brown curls about. ''E played 'orrible last Saturday, and we nearly got beat by Brandon Street United. Fancy nearly gettin' beat by that cissy lot. I went 'ome almost cryin' with shame for yer. Well, now that 'Erbert's got flu and Charlie Cope's got chronic gumboils, the team's only got ten men for Saturday against Manor Place Rangers, and the committee as good as swore on the Bible that I could play whenever you only 'ad ten men.'

'Now look here,' said Nick, 'it's—'

'Don't keep sayin' now look 'ere,' complained Dumpling, usually a very jolly and cheerful girl, 'I am 'ere, ain't I?'

'Well, of course you are, lovey,' said Nick, 'you wouldn't be sitting there if you weren't. You're always here, Dumpling.'

Dumpling, in fact, never missed any committee meeting, nor the chance to speak in turn, out of turn and mostly all the time. She considered it such an honour to be on the committee that she'd have given up Christmas rather than miss a meeting.

'Nick can't 'elp sayin' now look here,' said Danny, ''e's got a desk job and a grey suit.'

'Well, nobody forced it on 'im,' said Dumpling.

22

'Why couldn't 'e 'ave got a decent job, like navvying or lookin' after the council's dustcart 'orses? Then 'e wouldn't keep sayin' now look 'ere like 'e was a bank manager.'

'Dumpling,' said Nick, 'to me eternal sorrow, I'm going to have to smack your bum in a minute.'

'Crikey, did you lot 'ear that?' said Dumpling, round eyes rounder in her plump face. 'Did you 'ear Nick say to 'is eternal sorrow? Where's 'e gettin' it from?'

'From his clerkin' job,' said Freddy. 'Me brother-in-law Sammy Adams told me once that clerkin' companies are always sayin' to their eternal sorrow they can't do something or other. Still, a job's a job, and you can't always pick and choose. I'm lucky meself.' Freddy worked in a Southwark brewery owned by his brother-in-law. His dad worked there too. 'We can't blame Nick for being in clerkin'.'

'No, but 'e don't 'ave to talk like someone readin' the wireless news,' said Dumpling. 'I'm only askin' for me rights that was promised me, and me rights say you've got to let me play on Saturday. I do a lot of kickin' about with the blokes behind the fact'ry at dinnertime after I've ate me sandwiches, and I've been paid 'igh compliments regardin' me dribbling and shootin'.'

'Well, blokes,' said Nick, 'she does have her rights, so we've got a situation that's a bit desperate. What it means is how can we fit a girl into a team of fellers without the other team weeing their shorts?'

''Ere, I heard that,' said Dumpling, her well-stocked blouse alive with indignant quivers. 'I didn't come 'ere to listen to vulgarities.'

23

'No, of course you didn't, Dumpling,' said Nick, 'you're a nice girl, a credit to your mum and dad, but you've got to face the fact that if we put you in a football jersey and shorts, Manor Place Rangers will either fall about like drunks or wee themselves.'

'Serve 'em right if they do,' said Dumpling, 'they won't like playin' in wet shorts. We'll beat 'em easy.'

'We've got to beat 'em, that's certain,' said Nick. Manor Place Rangers were the Rovers' greatest rivals. Manor Place was opposite Browning Street.

'Well, Dumpling does 'ave the right to play,' said Danny.

'But in what position?' asked Freddy.

'Me? I can play anywhere,' said Dumpling.

'All right, in goal,' said Nick.

'Beg yer pardon?' said Freddy.

'In goal?' said Danny dubiously.

Nick knew they were thinking of the better part – well, the roundest part – of Dumpling in Charlie Cope's goalkeeping jersey. But it had to be. The Rovers had to supply the ball for this particular match, and Dumpling didn't seem shy about fitting herself into the jersey. If she could. She was beaming about it, and a beam on Dumpling's face was like a sunray.

'As goalkeeper,' said Nick, 'she'll be as far away from the Rangers as we can get her.'

'And not get noticed a lot?' said Danny.

'Eh?' said Freddy, and made a survey of Dumpling, a hopeful one. It didn't help. Dumpling was a noticeably bonny girl from any angle. And she was so cheerful and good-natured that the whole team couldn't help liking her. She was their mascot.

'Listen,' said Freddy, 'what about if the Rangers

win a lot of corners? They'll crowd Dumpling then.'

'I'll knock 'em all flyin',' said Dumpling, 'I'll be yer best goalie ever. Crikey, Nick, I ain't half proud of you for askin' me.'

'Pleasure,' said Nick, 'but look, about changing. You won't be able to do that in the hut with us, so you'll have to put the kit on at home. You can travel on the tram wearing a coat. Your dad's coat. And tuck your hair up in the goalkeeping cap. And if anyone in your family's got a false moustache, stick it on.'

''Ere, leave off,' said Dumpling, 'I ain't stickin' any false moustache on, I'll look daft. Listen, I don't mind I'm a girl, yer know, and me dad's proud I am.'

'All right, Dumpling, we're proud too,' said Nick.

'Girl and a half, you are, Dumpling,' said Danny.

'Twice over,' said Freddy.

'Oh, I do appreciate yer kind sentiments,' said Dumpling happily, 'I never 'ad any blokes nicer to me than the Rovers. It makes me feel just like one of you.'

'Well, do your best on Saturday to look like one of us,' said Nick. 'Try not to look like a girl.' He coughed. 'Stick a stiff sheet of cardboard up the jersey.' Danny and Freddy coughed as well then. Dumpling just looked puzzled. She never took any notice of her plumpness. Nick thought she probably didn't see herself as having a bosom at the moment. She probably thought girls couldn't officially own one until they were women. She probably thought hers was still a chest. 'You listening, Dumpling?'

'Yes, but I don't know if I 'eard you right,' she said. 'I mean, what do I want to wear a sheet of cardboard up me goalie's jersey for?'

'Good question,' said Freddy.

'Er well,' said Danny, who admired all Dumpling had and could admit she had a lot of it.

'It's to square you off, Dumpling,' said Nick, 'and make you look manly. And to protect your chest if the ball hits it.'

'I don't want to look manly,' said Dumpling, 'I'm a girl. Besides, if the ball does 'it me, it won't 'urt me. I've got a robust chest like you blokes 'ave.'

That was it. Dumpling really did think that what she'd got at the moment was a chest, not a bosom. Nick hid a grin.

'What was that she said?' asked Freddy faintly.

'Yes, me dad says so too,' smiled Dumpling. 'I like me dad, 'e's one of me best mates, and 'e won't half be proud I'm goin' to be goalie for the Rovers on Saturday.'

'Not if you let any goals in,' said Nick. 'Your dad won't even see you again, not unless he digs you up out of the pitch.'

''Ere, that ain't very kind,' protested Dumpling.

'Nick's the captain,' said Freddy, 'he can't afford to be kind, he has to chuck 'is weight about or the team gets sloppy.'

'Well, 'e'd better not chuck it at me,' said Dumpling, 'not now I'm goin' to keep goal. Mind, I don't say I don't honour 'im for bein' captain, but I ain't a weak and fearful girl, yer know, I can stand up for meself.'

'Y'er a lovely girl, Dumpling,' said Danny, 'I could sit in the back row of the flicks with yer all night.'

'I don't know what you want to talk daft for,' said Dumpling, but in a friendly kind of way, so that Danny wouldn't take offence. 'Nick, you goin' to write the team sheet out now?'

Nick, using a sheet of notepaper, began to inscribe the names in team formation, starting with C Evans, goalkeeper.

'There you are, Dumpling,' he said when he'd finished, and she looked at her own name in misty pride.

'Oh, don't it warm me heart?' she said. Nick smiled. Good old Dumpling. Being barmy about football, he supposed she should have been born a boy, except that fat boys came in for even more stick than fat girls. 'I'll take it to Ashford's sweet shop on me way 'ome tomorrer, and get Mrs Ashford to put it up in 'er shop window, like always. Crikey, everyone'll see me name, all me friends as well. Oh, I ain't 'alf happy.'

The meeting broke up, and as Nick was seeing his visitors to the front door, Ma appeared in the passage. Freddy and Danny said hello to her.

Dumpling said, 'Oh, would yer believe it, Mrs 'Arrison, I'm playin' for the team on Saturday. I'm playin' goalie.'

'Bless me soul, Chrissie, you in their football team?' said Ma in astonishment. 'I never 'eard of a girl playin' before. You sure it's natural?'

'Oh, it's me life's wish,' said Dumpling, 'and I've been natural ever since I was born. You can ask me mum and dad. Oh, is Nick's dad still away?'

'I'm afraid so,' said Ma, producing a little sigh.

'Well, it's a shame,' said Dumpling, 'Nick and 'is sisters ought to 'ave their dad around a bit. We'll all have to 'ope that Mr 'Arrison comes 'ome soon, so's he can see one of our football matches before the season ends – 'ere, what's goin' on?'

''Night, Mrs 'Arrison, so long, Nick,' said Freddy, and he and Danny hauled Dumpling out of the house and into the misty October night. If the Rovers couldn't afford a new football, at least they had Dumpling as their cheerful chatty supplier of a first-class one. In 1933, not many street teams could have asked for more.

'That girl's got some funny ideas,' said Ma.

'Harmless, though,' said Nick.

'I hear Danny's got a special likin' for her.'

'Yes, it's a special liking for her shape,' said Nick.

'I can't think why she's shaped like that,' said Ma. 'She doesn't get it from 'er mum and dad, and none of 'er brothers and sisters is a bit fat. Now you sure she won't do 'erself an injury, playin' football?'

'If anything's injured, it'll probably be Charlie Cope's goalkeeping jersey,' said Nick. 'Chrissie could damage it permanently, if she can get herself into it.'

Ma nearly giggled. Nick winked, then remembered the Rovers were committed to Dumpling as their goalkeeper against Manor Place Rangers. The Rangers had a large, beefy and kill-on-sight centre half who could hospitalize an opposing centre forward with a twitch of his hips, and scare the living daylights out of any goalkeeper. What he might do to Dumpling if he found out she was a girl could mean she would never be the same again. Ruddy hell, what've I done, thought Nick, I forgot about that tank of a centre half.

He followed Ma into the kitchen, where his sisters were sitting around the table. The range fire was alight, the kitchen warm, and the girls were enjoying hot cocoa. Upstairs, cold bedrooms awaited them and so did the cold linoleum that covered the floors. On winter mornings, the lino was like ice beneath bare feet. It was no wonder old people wore bedsocks. It was either bedsocks or chilblains.

Nick was careless enough then to come out with the news that Dumpling was going to be the Rovers' goalkeeper on Saturday. His sisters fell about, of course. Hysterically.

'That's it, have a good time,' he said. 'Don't mind what the prospect is doing to me. I'm only your brother being as good as a father to you.' They all had louder hysterics. 'Hope you all wet your drawers.'

'Oh, crikey, don't,' gasped young Fanny, the one with the small nose in the middle of a saucy face. She was turning red.

'Nick, I 'ope I didn't hear what you just said,' remarked Ma.

'Chrissie Dumpling tied us all up in knots,' said Nick. 'We had to let her play. In goal.'

'Oh, me head,' gasped Alice, 'Chrissie playing in goal, Ma, did you 'ear that?'

'Oh, don't,' begged Amy.

'Never mind young Chrissie,' said Ma, 'I won't 'ave Nick bein' vulgar.'

'Listen, Ma,' said Nick, 'when everyone knows Dumpling's playing in goal, the whole team could have an accident.'

'Oh, 'elp,' cried Fanny, and her hysterics got the better of her. She jumped to her feet, rushed out of the kitchen and up the stairs.

'Hope she gets there too late,' said Nick.

'She'd better not,' said Ma, 'or I'll clip someone's ear. I don't know what you two girls are laughin' like that for.'

'But, Ma, Chrissie Dumpling playing in goal, I ask you,' said Amy amid splutters.

'Well, I did tell 'er it's not natural,' said Ma.

'Nick, couldn't you play with just ten of you?' asked Alice, a supporter of the Rovers along with Fanny.

'What, without a ball?' said Nick. 'She wasn't going to let us use it unless we included her. I thought the best bet was to put her in goal before she started to talk about playing centre forward.' Alice fell about again, all over her chair, and Amy sounded as if she was drowning in gurgles. 'It's not that funny,' said Nick.

'Well, I'm not goin' to miss it,' said Alice.

'Here, you're not coming to watch, are you?' asked Nick. Alice and Fanny attended every game, being quite keen football fans. Fanny always looked after the little job of supplying slices of lemon to the team at half-time. 'I don't want you and Fanny racketing about having hysterics on the touchline.'

'Well, hard luck, ducky, Fanny and I aren't goin' to miss watching Chrissie perform in goal,' said Alice.

'I'm goin' to come and watch as well this time,' said Amy.

'Now look here—'

'All right, give us a tanner and I'll stay away,' said Amy.

'That's blackmail,' said Nick.

'We don't want none of that, Amy,' said Ma, 'it'll upset your Pa.'

'No, it won't,' said Amy, 'he likes us to use our

talents, 'e's always sayin' so. Still, all right, I won't ask Nick to pay me for stayin' away, I'll come and watch.'

'Watch what?' asked Fanny, reappearing.

'The football match, with Chrissie in goal,' said Amy.

'Oh, crikey,' gasped Fanny, 'don't start that again.'

'Got dry ones on now, have you?' asked Nick.

'Honest, who'd have a brother?' said Amy.

'Oh, if you do 'ave one,' said Alice, 'you just 'ave to try and believe there's some people worse off.'

'Can't think where,' said Amy.

'Nick, is Chrissie goin' to wear Charlie Cope's goalkeepin' jersey?' asked Fanny the terror.

Nick decided not to answer that. He knew the girls were picturing what Dumpling would look like in the goalkeeping jersey. It was bright yellow. He decided to put the kettle on and make some tea. Ma would share it with him. He took the kettle off the range hob and put it on a gas ring in the scullery. The girls watched him.

'Nick?' called Alice.

'I'm listening.'

'Good,' said Alice. 'Nick, is Chrissie goin' to wear the goalkeepin' jersey?'

Nick decided not to answer again. But Ma called, 'Nick, Alice is talkin' to you.'

'Well, good old Alice,' said Nick, 'if there's one thing that bucks me up more than Sunday crumpets, it's having Alice talking to me. Wally Rogers at the office has two sisters who never talk to him at all. Well, what's the use? He's got ears like blotting paper, poor bloke, but all the same—'

'Nick?' called Amy.

'Is that Amy talking to me now, Ma?'

'What're you actin' daft for?' asked Ma, who plainly couldn't see what all the fuss was about, even if she did think it wasn't natural for Dumpling to be in a football team.

'It's not daft waiting for the kettle to boil,' said Nick.

'Well, while you're waitin',' said Amy, 'could you tell us if Chrissie's goin' to wear Charlie Cope's goalkeepin' jersey on Saturday?'

'No, her dad's nightshirt,' said Nick.

'What?' demanded Ma, ignoring the fact that her daughters were falling about again. 'What was that you said?'

'I said Dumpling's going to wear her dad's nightshirt to keep goal in!' bawled Nick. His sisters shrieked. The kettle boiled, he made the tea and brought the pot to the table. Ma spoke her mind.

'Now you listen to me,' she said, 'I'm not 'aving you take young Chrissie up to Brockwell Park in her dad's nightshirt.'

'Well, if I make her stay at home, Ma, she won't lend us her football,' said Nick.

'You're not goin' to 'ave her play football in her dad's nightshirt, d'you 'ear me, my lad?' said Ma.

'All right,' said Nick, 'just in her winter vest and her football shorts.' It was Amy's turn to shriek and to rush upstairs. 'Now Amy's got laundry problems,' said Nick.

'You shouldn't get them all 'ysterical,' said Ma, 'just remember they're young girls and what 'ysterics do to them.'

'Tell you what,' said Nick, pouring tea for himself and Ma, 'if we manage to beat the Manor Place scruffs on Saturday, I'll treat all of you to the Clark

Gable film at the Prince's Cinema in Kennington in the evening. How about that?'

'It'll be a chance for me to wear me best Saturday evening 'at,' said Ma.

'Lovaduck, Clark Gable, swoony,' said Fanny.

'Lovaduck, Chrissie in a goalkeepin' jersey,' said Alice.

'A bright yellow one too,' said Nick, and that nearly did for Alice, even though she was all of seventeen.

Chapter Three

The next evening, Nick answered the door to Frankie Hughes, the team's left back. He was eighteen, worked in a factory and had an Adam's apple like a gobstopper. He'd come, he said, to ask Amy if she'd like to go for a walk on Sunday afternoon.

'You sure?' said Nick.

'What d'yer mean, am I sure?' said Frankie.

'Are you sure you know what you're doing, I mean,' said Nick. 'Amy's only just out of her cradle.'

'Get you,' said Frankie, 'she's been walkin' about for years, ain't she? And she's been growin' up a treat lately.'

'All right, it's your funeral,' said Nick, and called Amy, to whom Frankie made his request.

'Beg yer pardon?' said Amy.

'To tell yer no porkie, Amy, I'm startin' to fancy yer,' said Frankie. 'I used to fancy Alice a bit, yer know, but I'm pleased to inform yer I've transferred me affections to you, like. You don't tell a bloke to push off like Alice does.'

'Yes, I do,' said Amy, putting on a bit of Pa's style. Fourteen in a few months, she was beginning to feel her feet. 'I happen to have told nearly every boy in Walworth to push off in recent times on account of their sauce. What d'you mean by coming round here and telling me you fancy me with my brother Nick listening?'

'Don't mind me,' said Nick.

'Look,' said Frankie, 'I'm only askin' if you'd like to come for a walk on Sunday.'

'I suppose you know I'm still at school?' said Amy, sounding as posh as Pa could. 'If my carin' mother knew you were on our doorstep saying you fancy me, she'd come forth and give you a piece of her mind. I don't go out with any boys yet, and besides, I'm choosy. Well, I have to be, I'm a sailor's daughter.'

'Well, I'm the Rovers' left back, yer know,' said Frankie, Adam's apple working overtime. 'I ain't somebody's nobody.'

'Yes, but you're not anybody's somebody, either,' said Amy.

'Browning Rovers count for a lot round 'ere,' said Frankie, 'and probably more than a sailor's daughter. Mind, I say that kindly.'

'Just as well,' said Amy, 'or me mum would set about you. Anyway, football's boring, and only scruffy blokes play it.'

'Borin'?' Frankie couldn't believe his ears. 'Turn it up, Amy. Also, I ain't scruffy.'

'You will be if me mum sets about you,' said Amy. Actually, Frankie didn't stand a chance, not with his thin neck and his galloping gobstopper. Nick conceded he was a good left back, but that didn't count with Amy.

'You ain't sayin' Nick's scruffy, are yer, Amy?' said Frankie.

'No, he's just boring,' said Amy.

'Don't mind me,' said Nick again, 'treat me as if I'm not here.'

35

'Well, you're boring about football,' said Amy, 'and so's Chrissie Evans that everyone calls Dumpling. Blimey, fancy a girl likin' football.'

'She's always liked it,' said Frankie.

'She's playin' in goal for you on Saturday,' said Amy.

'Eh?' said Frankie, Adam's apple suddenly paralysed.

'Yes, Nick told 'er she could,' said Amy, and left her brother to explain how that horrendous decision came about.

Frankie had a fit on the doorstep.

Saturday morning

In a Kent quarry not far from Marsham Gaol, Pa Harrison, otherwise known as Knocker, was breaking stone with a sledgehammer in company with a number of his prison kind, the hard labour fraternity. The heavy work might have been dispiriting to Pa, he being a gentleman crook, but he was an eternal optimist and every tomorrow held its hopes. Hopes, for instance, of generous remission on account of good behaviour. Accordingly, he always swung his hammer or his pickaxe more cheerfully than the other men. Taking note of the working convicts were watchful warders, some on duty in the quarry and some patrolling round its lip. The October morning was an autumn gold, inducing Pa to make vigorous assaults on stone boulders.

An elbow nudged him, and a whisper came out of the corner of someone's mouth.

'Message for yer, Knocker.'

'I'm all ears, old chap,' said Pa, and kept swinging.

'Knocker, yer talk poncy. But Brains sends yer 'is regards.'

'So he should.'

'Wants yer to know 'e's still keepin' a kind eye on yer missus. Goin' to give 'er a lodger at ten bob a week some time. 'Opes you'll 'ave an 'appy weekend.'

'Much obliged,' said Pa.

'Hey, you, Johnstone!' A warder was shouting. 'Get on with your work! Harrison, down tools. The Governor wants to see you.'

'Is it remission?' asked Pa, when he was on his way with the warder.

'Now if you'd asked me if it was Christmas, I could've told you it wasn't,' said the warder. 'But as to remission, all I know is that it still ain't Christmas.'

'Never mind, Mr Blakey, you're still a good sort,' said Pa. 'How's your trouble-and-strife and the little ones, might I enquire?'

The warder grinned.

'Kind of you to ask, Knocker, but it still ain't Christmas till you cough up information on the loot.'

The corridor rang to the sound of clumping boots as Pa said, 'Wish I knew, Mr Blakey, believe me, but as I informed the law, I dropped it on my way out of the hotel, didn't I? That's what comes of being in too much of a hurry, which was what the willing lady said to the sailor when he fell off the bed.'

'Well, hard luck, sailor,' said the warder. 'Here we are now, Governor's office. Show some respect, Knocker. Which means don't try to lift 'is watch and chain.'

The Governor, an austere and awesome character, viewed Pa from under lowered brows.

'Harrison?' he said.

'Good morning, sir,' said Pa, 'pleasant weather we're having outside.'

'No lip, Harrison,' said the warder.

'I'm still wondering, Harrison,' said the Governor, 'when you're going to be sensible enough to disclose the whereabouts of those jewels. Leniency in regard to your sentence is still on the cards in return for volunteered information.'

Pa knew that. The law didn't like law-breakers having a nest-egg to go home to, and he could earn generous remission if he pointed the authorities in the right direction. But if he did so, his life wouldn't be worth living when he did get out. He was stuck with the hope that good behaviour would knock a few months off his five years.

'Wish I could do some helpful volunteering, Governor,' he said, 'but I'm in the unfortunate position of the unlucky, due to dropping the case in my hurry to get out of the hotel, as previously stated at the time and also thereafter.'

'Harrison, there are large numbers of idiots in this world, but I'm not one of them,' said the Governor. 'Like other representatives of the law, I ask myself why you didn't pick the case up.'

'Well, it hurts me to say so, sir, but the fact that I didn't makes me one of the idiots,' said Pa with credible gravity. 'There it was, just behind me, and what did I do? I just kept going. It's given me very painful recollections, but it's taught me something I should have known, that I ought to have stuck to an honest way of life.'

'Harrison,' said the warder, 'I told you to show the Governor respect. Telling 'im fairy stories is impudence.'

'Hand on my heart, Mr Blakey—'

'Harrison, spare us an oratorio without music,' said the Governor. With a slight twitching of his lips he changed the subject and asked Pa if he was literate enough to spend one day a week, perhaps two, working in the prison library. The books available in the library were for the benefit of prisoners who had good behavioural records. Pa said he'd read every Dickens' novel twice. Actually, he'd just skipped through *Pickwick Papers* once. He preferred Edgar Wallace, but thought he'd keep quiet about that.

'Twice? Is that so?' asked the Governor.

'Pleasure, I'm sure, Governor,' said Pa.

'What did you think of *Bleak House*?'

'Educating, Governor, couldn't put it down,' said Pa. 'You could say I owe most of my intellectual learning to Dickens.'

The Governor's lips twitched again. The warder grinned.

'A pity, Harrison, that your intellectual learning led you to crime,' said the Governor.

'Might I be permitted, Governor, to point out I was known for my honesty before sore temptation downed me?' said Pa, doing what he could to look ashamed of himself.

'It's not something I knew,' said the Governor. 'However, since you've been a model prisoner and have read all Dickens' novels twice, we'll arrange for you to work in the library. One day a week to begin with.'

'I'm touched, Governor,' said Pa, 'and warmly appreciative.'

'So, I dare say, are the Marines,' said the Governor.

In the back room behind his office in Hackney, Mister Horsemouth smiled at a weedy-looking man known as Tosh Fingers. It wasn't, however, precisely the kind of smile Tosh liked. It held the threat of a sack of bricks accidentally dropping on his loaf of bread if anything went wrong. Mister Horsemouth was still sore about Knocker Harrison being incorrectly informed that a certain female hotel guest was absent from her suite on the occasion when he was being given the chance to elevate himself to the role of a cracksman. Mister Horsemouth failed to see that it had just been bad luck caused by Tosh's need to go for a quick Jimmy Riddle. The perishing female had got back to the hotel while he was in the public convenience. He'd only been away two minutes, and Knocker had arrived on schedule ten minutes later.

'So, the gee-gees are at the post, are they?' said Mister Horsemouth.

'Ready for the off, guv,' said Tosh.

'Good, very good,' said Mister Horsemouth. 'If I can believe it.'

'Course you can, guv, course you can,' said Tosh.

'The first of six jobs to be pulled. No more, no less.'

'Right, guv. And I got yer full team lined up. All clean, no records, and the rozzers ain't even got their dabs.'

'Two for tonight's job,' said Mister Horsemouth through his large moustache, 'plus one to keep his peepers skinned.'

'All arranged, guv, all arranged, and nobody's got a record.'

'Names for tonight's job?'

'Flash Ferdy—'

'George Simmonds.'

'As ever was, guv. Also, Bone Idle.'

'Alfred Bone.'

'You got it, guv, same bloke. Ain't exactly idle, though. Then there's me, with me on-the-job peepers.'

'They'd better be on the job, you runt. Or else.'

'Now would I let yer down, guv, you that pays me rent and keeps me in meat, veg and kippers?'

'You let me down once,' said Mister Horsemouth.

'Desp'rate call of nature, guv, and a bit of bad luck. Gawd, yer nearly broke me leg for it, which 'urt me feelings as well as me leg, considerin' I didn't fail to 'and yer the loot – 'ere, watch it, guv.' Tosh just managed to slip a heavy-handed swipe from his boss.

'Don't give me any bleedin' lip,' said Mister Horsemouth.

'Not me, guv, not me. Is the job on?'

'It's on,' said Mister Horsemouth. 'Just keep it clean. No damage, no fingerprints.'

'I got yer, guv,' said Tosh.

The offices of Adams Enterprises Ltd, a little way up Denmark Hill from Camberwell Green, closed at twelve-thirty on Saturdays. Robert Adams, the general manager, known as Boots to his family and friends, was still at his desk at twelve-forty. Everyone else had gone. He turned as the door to his office opened, and in glided an elegant woman in a brown coat with a fur collar, and a fur-trimmed hat.

'Hello, old sport, wondered if you were still here,' said Polly Simms, eternally vivacious. She was a few months younger than Boots, who was thirty-seven. He wore his years in easy fashion. She wore hers as if several of them had never happened. 'Were you waiting for me?'

'Why, did we have an appointment here, then?' asked Boots.

'Good question,' said Polly, 'considering we've never had an appointment in all the years we've known each other. Have you ever thought what that kind of ungenerous attitude can do to a woman like me?'

Boots, coming to his feet, said, 'I think we've had an appointment or two, Polly old girl.'

'Listen, you bounder, I'm speaking of appointments behind closed doors, and you know it.'

'I had an idea there'd been one meeting of that kind, although not behind closed doors,' said Boots.

Polly's brittle smile came and went. She was a long-standing friend of Boots and his family, and his mother frequently invited her to Sunday tea. But over or after Sunday tea, what could a woman do with a man who was someone else's husband? There had been just one occasion when, in a country hotel near Guildford a few years ago, he might have made love to her, but no, the guarded devil had turned the opportunity down, leaving her as frustrated as ever. She knew he cared for her, but when it came down to having him love her she might as well have been a doorpost. All she had ever had from him was friendship. For him to expect a woman like her to be merely a friend was maddening. She demanded to take a reasonable place in his life as his mistress. But Boots said no, he was not the kind of man to keep a mistress. Polly, heated, said he was the kind of man whose major role in life was to be a stuffed shirt. Only a stuffed shirt, she said, could say no to a woman who loved him. Well, said Boots, this stuffed shirt is also a husband and father. And a prig, said Polly. Boots said is that your temper showing, Polly? Bloody hell, said Polly, how would you like my fist in your eye? Not very much, said Boots. I'll begin to hate you one day, said Polly. Well, you're still a sweet woman, said Boots, damned if you aren't.

What could a woman do with a man like that? Polly could only hope.

'It's something to know you care for me, I suppose,' she said now.

'Especially as it's something we should push under the carpet,' said Boots.

'You're an idiot if you think I can do that,' said Polly.

'What's brought you up here, anyway?' asked Boots.

'You, of course,' said Polly. 'I was about to pass by. Then I thought I wonder if my darling old stuffed shirt is still in his office? If he is, perhaps he'll make love to me under his desk. Or even on top of it, bless his eager heart. So here I am. You choose, I'll get undressed.'

'Same old Polly,' smiled Boots, guarded as always.

'Same old reluctant lover,' said Polly, brittle as always. 'How's Emily, blow her.'

'Trusting,' said Boots.

'How sweet,' said Polly. 'But isn't it about time she settled for fair shares?'

'What fair shares do you have in mind?' asked Boots.

'Well, old darling,' said Polly, 'if I'm willing to

43

share you with her, she should be willing to share you with me. What's fairer than that?'

'Ask me another,' said Boots.

'Fat lot of good that would do me,' said Polly. 'You never give me the kind of answers I need and deserve.'

'Have we got problems, Polly?'

'I have,' said Polly, 'and you're all of them. If I've got to wait until I'm ninety before you make love to me, I might as well join the French Foreign Legion and look after their camels.'

'Lucky old camels,' said Boots.

'Camels bite,' said Polly, 'and so do I. See my teeth?'

'Yes, very nice,' said Boots. 'Regular brushing, I presume, Miss Simms?'

'We are not amused,' said Polly, but she laughed all the same. 'No, listen, dearly beloved, come down the chimney into my bedroom on Christmas Eve, and I'll play Sleeping Beauty to your Santa Claus. D'you like the idea?'

'I'll think about it, naturally,' said Boots.

'That'll be the day,' said Polly. 'By the way, my father would like to see you some time, to talk to you about Hitler and his Stormtroopers. You know about his Stormtroopers, don't you?'

'I know they'll be his battering ram in the event of a war,' said Boots.

'What a frightful curse,' said Polly, 'the madman of Munich now the Chancellor of Germany. On top of that horrendous appointment, when Hindenburg snuffs it, old chum, as my father says he will soon, Hitler will take over the Presidency as well. He'll become the dictator of Germany. What does that thought do to you?'

44

'It gives me a headache,' said Boots, 'and will probably make me forget to come down your chimney on Christmas Eve.'

'Oh, I'll phone you just before I get into bed,' said Polly. 'How's Rosie, and how's Annabelle?'

'Rosie's doing some reading before going up to Oxford,' said Boots, 'and Annabelle is collecting boyfriends by the dozen and turning them all into slaves.'

'Very right and proper,' said Polly. 'A girl as bewitching as Annabelle should have slaves by the dozen. Well, it's been exciting seeing you, lover, even if you didn't drag me under your desk. So long, old darling.'

She kissed him. She did not intend to depart without at least claiming that. She pushed her mouth moistly and dewily to his. Boots, guard dropped, returned the kiss. Polly's slender body surged. Boots put his hands on her shoulders and held her off, shaking his head at her.

'Hoppit,' he said.

'Sweetie, what a wonderful way you have of telling me you love me,' said Polly.

'All my own work,' said Boots.

'My God, don't I know it?' said Polly, and went out laughing. For all that he was the most frustrating devil in a world that abounded with all kinds, he was still the one she wanted all to herself.

Chapter Four

Saturday afternoon

The day was still crisp and bright, and the Browning Street Rovers were travelling to Brockwell Park on the upper deck of a tram. Chrissie Dumpling, goalkeeper for the day and therefore one of the blokes, was up there with them. Nick's three sisters were down below, together with Cassie Ford, Freddy Brown's girlfriend and a living breathing example of how to send a feller off his chump without hardly trying. Cassie was nearly eighteen and very imaginative. She was also precocious, and as she owned long raven-black hair of a lustrous texture, wheedling brown eyes and a facile tongue, Freddy had little hope of ever asserting himself. He tried. In fact, he'd been trying for over seven years, but all to no avail. Cassie was always one too many for him, and Freddy sometimes wondered if he'd live to come of age. Not that Cassie didn't have important feelings for him. She did, and if she ever had to go through fire and water, she'd make sure Freddy was with her.

Dumpling sat with Danny Thompson, much to his pleasure. He couldn't help himself, he was gone on her. He accepted there was a lot of her, but he was fond of all of it. Skinny girls made his eyes water.

Dumpling was wearing her hefty dad's overcoat,

fully buttoned up by order of Nick. Dumpling, being what she was, a respecter of a football captain, wouldn't have dreamed of not obeying him in regard to everything concerning a match, even if she did exercise her right in committee to argue the toss with him. She'd let everyone know that underneath her dad's overcoat she was clad in her own football shorts and Charlie Cope's goalkeeping jersey. On her head was his large-peaked goalie's cap, her wayward hair tucked up inside it. On her feet were her footballing boots. To the team she still looked like Chrissie Dumpling of plump renown, and the Rovers could only hope that the Manor Place Rangers would see her differently, as a plump bloke. She could hardly wait to get to the park and for the match to begin. It was going to be her very first game for her beloved Rovers. General Petain's stirring admonition to the French troops at Verdun during the Great War had been, 'They shall not pass.' He'd been referring to the attacking German forces. Dumpling was now thinking in the same terms about the attacking forwards of the Manor Place team.

The Rovers had accepted there was no option but to let their mascot keep goal. On the whole, the blokes felt nature had been a bit unfair to her in shaping her like a balloon. Her mum said it was only puppy fat that was staying around a bit longer than it had a right to, but that she would lose it eventually. Her dad, however, confided to the team once that Dumpling would always be a jolly bouncing girl. Danny said as far as he was concerned, that was a happy prospect. Well, keep at it, Danny, said Mr Evans, she might come to see you're worth your weight in football boots. Such encouragement from the right quarter was music to Danny's ears.

The tram reached Loughborough Junction.

'Crikey, ain't you excited, Nick?' asked Dumpling at that point. 'I mean, it's goin' to be Manor Place Rangers.'

'Yes,' said Nick, 'and I'm saying a few prayers for the team.'

Someone ought to say some for me, thought Freddy, seeing I've got a feeling that when Cassie gets to be what they call a full-blown woman, she's going to be my full-time problem.

'Nick, we don't need no prayers, not for beatin' Manor Place Rangers,' said Dumpling. 'Me Uncle Gus, who gave me me football, told me once you only need prayers if you accident'lly fall off an elephant and there's a lot of other elephants comin' up behind.'

'I ain't specially devoted to sayin' prayers meself,' said Frankie Hughes. His Adam's apple had a sharp wintry edge to it. 'I'm more devoted to me fretwork set.'

'Well, I will say that if Dumpling reckons we don't need prayers to beat the Rangers,' remarked Danny, 'I take that as a serious and informed comment.'

'Well, blokes,' said Nick, 'sometimes we all need a bit of help from God. Like this afternoon. It might be appropriate for Dumpling to say a prayer herself, never mind what her Uncle Gus said about elephants.'

'Oh, all right,' said Dumpling cheerfully, as the tram entered Milkwood Road. She began. '"Our Father, which art in 'eaven, hallowed be thy Name—"'

'My life, what's goin' on up in front there?' called Abel Goldsmith, a follower of Moses. The Rovers had nicknamed him Starving Crow because he looked all bones and flapped his arms about whenever he was excited. But he was a speedy left winger. 'I should be 'earing prayers?'

'Course yer should,' said Dumpling, 'Nick says so. "Thy Kingdom come, thy will be done, as it is in 'eaven—"'

'Not out loud, you daft baggage,' said Nick.

'Oh, all right,' said Dumpling blithely. 'Only I was tryin' to make sure the Lord 'eard me. Mum says she thinks he's a bit deaf sometimes. Never mind, I'll say it under me breath.' She was quiet for all of twenty seconds before she spoke again, with the tram careering and clanging towards Herne Hill station. 'There, I finished me prayer, Danny.'

'Well, I like yer for it,' said Danny.

'Honoured, I'm sure,' said Dumpling, patting her football, which was on her lap. 'Nick, you ain't remarked 'ow I look in Charlie's cap.'

'Point is, how'd you look under your dad's overcoat?' said Nick.

'Oh, I'll show yer,' said Dumpling, and began to unbutton it.

'No, leave it,' said Nick, quite sure it was best for the yellow goalkeeping jersey to remain unseen. 'Tell you what, Dumpling, keep the overcoat on all the time.'

'What, all the time I'm keepin' goal?'

'Good idea,' said Freddy, 'best one you've had yet, Dumpling.'

'Me?' said Dumpling.

'Well – er – it's not a bad idea, Dumpling,' said Danny. While he knew she'd look a joy to his own eyes in the yellow jersey, he was prepared to admit the opposition wouldn't see her quite like that.

'I'll tell the Manor Place lot that you feel the cold,' said Nick, as the tram stopped at Herne Hill station.

'But ain't I goin' to show meself in me goalie's jersey?' asked Dumpling.

'Not this afternoon,' said Nick.

Despite her respect for his status as captain, Dumpling said, 'Well, I can't think why not.'

'It's an order,' growled Nick, chucking his weight about.

'Oh, all right,' said Dumpling, cheerful again, 'you're the captain. You're easy the best bloke for the job, bein' naturally bossy and 'aving a clerkin' job.' The tram crossed the lines into Norwood Road. 'Crikey, we're nearly there. I can't 'ardly wait for the kick-off.'

'I can't 'ardly wait to get back 'ome to me high tea,' said Frankie, sure that Dumpling in goal was going to be a disaster.

'All off, you lot,' called Starving Crow, 'and I should worry about who's playin' goalie and who ain't? My life, I should.'

The tram pulled up opposite the park gate. The four girls down below were off first. The team followed. Everyone crossed the road and entered the park, taking the path to the hired football pitch. Dumpling bounced along in the van, bursting to get into the fray. Nick's sisters and Cassie were with her. They were all warmly wrapped up, woollen hats cuddling their heads. Nick, bringing up the rear of the little procession, could hear Fanny giggling. And Cassie was in stitches, having been so since Freddy told her that Dumpling was playing in

50

goal. Freddy was a lot of fun to her, even if she did boss him about. He had taken her on as his mate seven and a half years ago. They'd been through a thousand verbal carry-ons together, but he still looked on her as his mate, and called her that. It made Cassie tell him to stop sounding like a plumber. Only plumbers had mates, she said, and I'm your one and only girlfriend, don't forget. I don't want to forget it, said Freddy, I'm nearly getting fond of you.

'It feels funny, walkin' in me football boots,' said Dumpling.

'Well, it had better not feel funny while you're in goal,' said Alice, well up on the finer points of football.

'Oh, in goal I'll spring about like a tiger,' said Dumpling. 'They shall not pass,' she added.

'What?' asked young Fanny.

'Oh, I read it somewhere,' said Dumpling.

They approached a netball pitch. Two teams of girls were playing. They all looked active, healthy and glowing, and Nick suddenly realized he was short of what most blokes of his age were enjoying, a steady girlfriend, a girl of fun and laughter. But while Pa was in clink, he couldn't take up with a girl, any more than Alice could take up with a young man. Too many lies would have to be told. Well, he couldn't see himself telling the truth to a steady girlfriend. My old man's doing hard labour, d'you mind, Priscilla?

He went on with the team, and when they reached the football pitch, he told Dumpling to go straight to one of the goals. Off she went, dropping her football and booting it forward. Brimful of enthusiasm, she fell over. Up she bounced and on she went. Manor Place Rangers were already in the changing hut. The Rovers entered their own section, and trotted out several minutes later. The Rangers were having their kickabout. Dumpling, standing between the opposite goalposts, beckoned the Rovers on. Nick ordered Frankie and Danny, his backs, to guard her with their lives.

'I'm prepared to lay mine on the line,' he said.

'Got yer, Nick,' said Danny.

Dumpling kicked the ball to the team and they began to test her. As she'd promised, she sprang about like a tiger. She fell over.

'Don't do that!' bawled Nick, putting thoughts of a steady date out of his mind for the sake of all that was at stake in this particular soccer match. 'Get up and stay up!'

'It's me dad's overcoat,' said Dumpling, back on her feet. 'Can't I take it off?'

'No,' said Nick, well aware that his sisters and Cassie were waiting to split their sides, and that the Rangers would fall about. Up ran the referee, someone's volunteer dad.

'Here,' he said, 'your goalkeeper's not playin' in his overcoat, is 'e?'

'Yes,' said Nick, 'he's nearly got a dose of flu, so he needs to keep wrapped up.'

'I don't know about that,' said the ref, 'rules of football say goalkeepers 'ave got to wear a green or yellow jersey, yer know.'

'But there's got to be another rule for overcoated goalies trying to beat flu,' said Nick, and the ref scratched his head.

'I'll see what the Rangers' captain says.' He ran back down the pitch to speak to the large and brawny centre half, while Freddy banged a shot at

Dumpling. She punched it back to him with her gloved fist. Just like that. Freddy hit another shot. Dumpling caught it and fell over.

'Top-'eavy, that's 'er trouble,' said Frankie gloomily.

'Course she's not, she's built lovely all over,' said Danny.

'Oi, Rovers! Oi!' The Rangers' centre half was hollering. 'Yer goalie can keep 'is coat on. Tell 'im me 'eart's bleedin' for 'im.'

'Nick, d'you 'ear that?' asked Dumpling, upright again.

'Yes, best if they think you're a bloke,' said Nick, 'otherwise they might have your coat off and your jersey as well.'

'Like to see 'em try,' said Dumpling, stopping a shot from Starving Crow with her overcoated knees, 'I'll show 'em something.'

Starving Crow and Freddy had coughing fits. Dumpling didn't always realize what she was saying. The ref blew his whistle, and Nick ran down the field to shake hands with his opposite number, Bonzo Willis. The Rangers' walloping centre half was twenty-two and well-known to the Rovers.

'Watcher, Nick mate.'

'Watcher, Bonzo. I'll call heads.'

The ref spun the coin and it came down heads. Nick said the Rovers would stay as they were. Bonzo said it wouldn't make any difference to the licking the Rovers were going to get, and the teams formed up.

'Come on, Rovers!' yelled young Fanny, an ardent supporter.

'Doesn't Freddy look nice in 'is shorts today?'

53

said Cassie. Nearby, Rangers' supporters hooted. Cassie said things like that. She had no verbal inhibitions.

With two keen lads acting as linesmen, the ref blew his whistle and the Rangers kicked off. Deadly rivals went at each other. What a game. Nick thought he'd never forget it. His heart was in his mouth whenever the Rangers attacked. He liked to be on the attack himself, to get up with his forwards, as a good centre half was supposed to, but he had to stick around a lot more than usual between Danny and Frankie, knowing who was keeping goal. Dumpling. A ruddy girl and a round one at that. He liked Dumpling, the whole team liked her, but not as their goalkeeper.

Bonzo Willis, of course, was a thundering menace, bringing the ball through and slinging it to his forwards. Dumpling had a terrible time, but somehow the ball never got past her. She kept sticking her gloved fists in the way, her feet in the way and her overcoat in the way. She also kept falling over. Each time she bounced up beaming, as if falling over was the jolliest part of her role. Bless her, thought Nick, she's giving me heart failure, but she's a sport and a trier.

The Rovers conceded a corner. Nick told Dumpling that if she fell over this time the whole team would jump on her.

'Crikey, what yer fussin' for, Nick?' she said, planting herself solidly on the goal line. 'Get out of me way.' Most of the team were packing the goalmouth to protect her. Her face was pink and shining, and some of the Rangers kept looking at her. Nick hoped they'd think she was a Walworth version of Billy Bunter. The corner came over, and

54

she took off. Two opponents collapsed as she ballooned into them, fell on top of them and flattened them, the ball hugged safely and joyously to her robust chest.

'Bleedin' blimey,' gasped one of the flattened Rangers.

'I hate fat goalies,' groaned the other.

Up sprang Dumpling, and she booted the ball clear. The battle went on. No quarter was given, and Cassie almost died a death at what the large lump called Bonzo Willis kept doing to Freddy.

'Kill 'im, Freddy!' she yelled. 'Oh, look at that, Alice, he'll injure all Freddy's prospects.'

'What prospects, Cassie?' asked Alice with a straight face.

'Well, his future ones,' said Cassie, who had her own as well as Freddy's all mapped out, even if Freddy wasn't aware of what he was in for. Alice smiled. She knew what Cassie was about.

Ten minutes before half-time, the Rovers' centre forward, given a chance to score, ballooned the ball over the crossbar.

'Rubbish!' yelled young Fanny.

'Go home, Ronnie!' cried Cassie in disgust.

Fanny thought it tragic, a chance to score missed close to half-time. She watched as Nick took the ball forward a few minutes later, then held her breath as the walloping Manor Place centre half charged thunderously at her brother. Nick side-stepped and Bonzo Willis barged into empty air. Down he went and the ground shuddered.

'Oh, good on yer, Nick!' yelled Fanny in delight. 'Sometimes,' she said to Cassie, 'I don't mind 'aving him for a brother.'

Half-time arrived with no score. By dint of

springing about like a tiger and putting herself in the way of everything, Dumpling had so far kept a clean sheet. Up came the team to the touchline, looking for their traditional slice of lemon. As always, young Fanny supplied them, Nick giving her tuppence from funds to cover a penny for the lemon and a penny for doing the job.

Up came Dumpling to talk to her captain.

'Nick, ain't I done wonders, not lettin' any goals in?' she said.

'Proud of you, Dumpling,' said Nick.

'Yes, good on yer, Dumpling,' said Freddy, and gave her a partial cuddle. Well, it was difficult to get an arm fully around her. He shouldn't even have given her a partial cuddle, however, because Cassie at once gave him an unseen but well-felt kick. In Cassie's book, he wasn't allowed to cuddle any girl except herself.

'Sufferin' legs, I've just been bitten,' he said.

'Course you 'aven't,' said Dumpling, 'you only get bitten in the summer. Anyway, what're you goin' to say about the second 'alf, Nick? You usually talk to the team at 'alf-time. Come on, blokes, Nick's goin' to tell us how to win the match.'

Nick felt a pep talk was necessary, so he addressed the team. 'Hang on for all you're worth, blokes. On top of that, I want our inside forwards to mark their walloping carthorse, Bonzo Willis. He's getting too much of a free ride. Do what you can to break his leg.'

Amy, not a great football fan, blinked a bit.

'Did I 'ear that, Alice?' she asked. 'Cassie, did he say break someone's leg?'

'Oh, it's all in the game,' said Cassie.

56

'Not 'alf,' said Dumpling. 'Break 'is leg and slow 'im down a bit. That's in the game.'

'I don't want that football enemy number one barging his way right through,' said Nick. 'We've got our goalkeeper to think about.'

'That's me,' said Dumpling proudly, just in case Amy hadn't noticed.

'He's capable of blowing a hole in Dumpling's overcoat if we let him unleash one of his cannon-balls,' said Nick. Amy giggled. 'I'll get cross,' said Nick, 'if we have to carry Dumpling home with a cannonball in her chest. As for your goalkeeping, Dumpling, don't do any more falling over. Lean backwards a bit if you have to.'

'Nick, would yer mind not insinuatin' Dumpling ain't all there up top?' said Danny.

'Might I point out Dumpling doesn't need a lot up top?' said Freddy. 'She's got plenty everywhere else.'

'Freddy!' shrieked Alice, while Amy spilled giggles and Dumpling took no offence at all.

The ref blew for the start of the second half, and Nick went back on to the pitch with his Rovers. Bonzo Willis spoke to him as the teams changed ends.

'We don't like yer fat goalie, Nick.'

'Sorry about that, Bonzo.'

'We're goin' to flatten 'im out a bit.'

'He won't like that,' said Nick.

'Do 'im good,' said Bonzo.

'He won't think so.'

'Yes, 'e will, it'll be ruddy bliss for 'im when the pain leaves off.'

The second half began, Dumpling bouncing about in goal and the Rangers' supporters taking the mickey. The Rovers' supporters were joined by one man and his dog. Up and down the field the teams swept, with the Rovers' inside forwards doing their best to mark thunderous Bonzo in a way that would do him a sporting injury. His response was to bundle them over and tread on them. And he had it in for Dumpling all right. He kept charging through, intent on ruining her afternoon person- ally. Nick kept trying to stop him, and the shuddering impacts caused young Fanny a lot of umbrage.

'Oh, blimey,' she breathed, 'I know Nick's only me brother, but I don't want to have to take what's left of 'im home in a sack. It wouldn't 'alf upset Ma.'

Danny and Frankie came repeatedly to the rescue of Nick, while Dumpling frustrated the Rangers and their captain by continually getting in the way of the ball. Bonzo hollered that he'd never seen such bleedin' fluky saves. Nick made him holler more by upending him twice with crafty trips. On the other side of the coin, Starving Crow went on a dizzy run down the left wing, cut in and delivered a shot that flew only inches wide.

With only five minutes to go, there was still no score. Then disaster struck. Bonzo roared through in rampant fashion and made straight for Dumpling and her goal. Dumpling, bless her, accepted the challenge. She rushed from her line and kept going. Rampant Bonzo aimed to strike. Dumpling ran into him. Nick conceded that she quivered a bit from the collision, but what it did to Bonzo was unbeliev- able. It staggered him and felled him. Thunder rolled as he crashed on his back. The ref blew a piercing note on his whistle and pointed to the spot.

'Penalty!'

'Eh?' said Freddy, as Dumpling kicked the ball clear.

'What?' said Danny, eyeing fallen Bonzo.

'A ruddy penalty, that's what!' bawled fallen Bonzo.

'That's done it,' sighed Alice.

'What a rotten ref,' said Cassie.

'Oh, me gawd,' said Dumpling, which made a Ranger ask why the fat goalie's voice hadn't broken yet. Bonzo got up, breathing hard, and placed the retrieved ball on the penalty spot. Four minutes to go now, and it looked like the only goal of the match was coming up in favour of the Rangers. Nick whispered to Dumpling, who was having some natural palpitations.

'As soon as he hits the ball, jump to your right.'

'Crikey, I didn't know there was goin' to be any penalties, Nick. That ref's got blind eyesight.'

'Come on, come on,' growled Bonzo.

The ref moved everyone back except Dumpling and Bonzo. Dumpling gritted her teeth. Up ran Goliath, his right foot swung and he hit the ball hard. It didn't rise more than twelve inches as it travelled straight for the left-hand corner of the goal. Dumpling, obeying her captain, jumped to her right all right, but then fell over. Mother O'Grady, she fell on the ball. The Rovers yelled with delight, and the Rangers stood aghast. Up bounced Dumpling and booted the ball, a real balloon of a kick. Alice yelled, Fanny shouted hooray, and the man's dog barked.

Now as it happened, Starving Crow was the only Rover way down the field, with just two opposing backs between him and their goal. He gathered the ball and set off, arms flapping in excitement. Rangers poured back after him. On he went, then cut inside and darted straight between the two closing defenders. He let go a beauty, and it beat the goalkeeper all ends up with only a minute or so to go.

It won the match for the Rovers. Young Fanny did a bit of a rapturous swoon, Alice did a bit of a dance, Cassie did a knees-up and Amy said something to the barking dog. Danny rushed up on Dumpling, hugged her and gave her a reckless smacker on her flushed cheek.

''Ere, come off it, yer soppy date,' said Dumpling.

'What a girl, what a goalie,' said Danny. Other team members arrived and Dumpling received hugs from all.

'Cor bleedin' blimey,' said a disgusted Ranger, 'what a load of ruddy fairies, they're kissin' their fat goalie.'

Dumpling practically disappeared amid delighted Rovers.

'You lot goin' daft?' she gasped. Another hug and kiss arrived. 'Oh, yer soppy lumps.' Even so, they chaired her off the field and all the way into the Rovers' section of the changing hut. ''Ere, give over,' she yelled, 'I can't come in yer dressin'-room.'

Fortunately, the Rangers were only then beginning to trail despondently off the field, otherwise they'd have heard her and known that none but a girl could have a voice like hers.

'Put her down, blokes,' said Nick, and they put her down.

Happy and flushed, she said, 'Can I take me dad's coat off now, Nick?'

'All right, just for ten seconds, so that the team can see you looking proud,' said Nick.

'Oh, yer a real captain, Nick,' she said, and forthwith took the coat off to display her goalkeeping self. The fellers rolled in the aisles. Well, thought Nick, who wouldn't have? Dumpling in a goalkeeper's bright yellow jersey a little too small for her was a knockout.

Alice, Amy and Fanny were all a bit miffed that they hadn't seen Dumpling perform in her yellow goalkeeping jersey, and they voiced their complaints over a high tea of bacon, scrambled eggs and fried bread. Ma said she'd never heard such silly talk. Amy said indignantly that she wouldn't have gone to the boring old match if she'd known Chrissie was going to wear an overcoat all the time. Nick told her that when she was old and wrinkled, she'd be able to tell her grandchildren she'd been present at the greatest football match ever, when Browning Street Rovers beat Manor Place Rangers by a last-minute goal. Amy said some hopes, she hadn't seen the goal, she'd been talking to the man's dog at the time. Nick said there was something funny about women. What other human beings would be talking to some man's daft dog at a moment when the winning goal of an historic football match was being scored?

'Yes, and she missed seein' Chrissie save the penalty as well,' said Fanny.

'Amy needs half an hour's good tickling to wake her up,' said Nick.

'I'll scream the house down,' said Amy.

'We don't want anyone screamin' the house down, Nick,' said Ma.

'All right, Ma, let's all go to the pictures instead,' said Nick.

'Like you promised if the team won?' said Fanny.

'Yes, my treat,' said Nick.

'I'll wear me best Saturday evenin' hat,' said Ma.

They all enjoyed the film. It featured Wallace Beery as well as Clark Gable. The girls said Clark Gable gave them goosepimples. Ma said she thought she liked Wallace Beery best. She said he reminded her of Joe Hubbard, their hearty and helpful dustman.

'I don't know that your Pa wouldn't of done better for 'imself and 'is fam'ly if he'd been a dustman,' she said on the way home.

'Not Pa,' said Alice, 'he's a gent.'

Freddy and Cassie also went to the pictures. Cassie said he'd got to take her or she wouldn't forgive him for not scoring the winning goal himself. Oh, all right, said Freddy, I'll only get all thin and haggard if I'm not forgiven. I can live with some things, he said, but not with the thoughts of being unforgiven.

That made Cassie smile sweetly. Her ready smile always seemed to be sweet and pacific, but underneath she was a real cockney caution. Woe betide any girl reckless enough to make eyes at Freddy. Cassie would pounce, tread on the girl's foot or pinch her, and she'd do so with her smile at its sweetest.

She had recently told Freddy to make his fortune by the time she was twenty, then they could think about getting married. Freddy said he couldn't see any fortune coming his way, just a continuation of his good steady job at the brewery. So don't talk barmy, he said. Cassie said don't answer me back or I'll do you an 'orrible injury. Freddy said look, just because we've always been mates doesn't mean we've got to get married. Getting married is serious, he said. Yes, I know that, said Cassie, especially getting married to me, and my mind's made up about it. It can't be, said Freddy, not at your age. He shouldn't have said that, because Cassie trod on his foot. Here, said Freddy, what was that for? My Aunt Connie, the one that nearly married a butler, told me to always do it to boys who answered back, said Cassie. She told me that half the trouble in the world comes from boys and husbands answering back. Well, said Freddy, if that's what I'm going to get when we're married, I think I'll stay single. He shouldn't have said that, either, because Cassie trod on his foot again. That is, she would have done if he hadn't taken his foot out of the way. Stand still when I'm trying to tread on you, said Cassie. Not likely, said Freddy, think I'm dozy, do you? Cassie smiled sweetly and gave him a kiss.

They, too, saw the film featuring Clark Gable and Wallace Beery. On the way home, Cassie said Clark Gable was smashing. Freddy asked her if she'd like to go to Hollywood and marry the bloke.

'How can I when I'm promised to you?' said Cassie.

'I don't mind releasin' you from yer promise, Cassie.'

That was one more thing he shouldn't have said, because Cassie kicked him on his best footballing leg.

Chapter Five

On Sunday morning, the paper boy popped the *News of the World* through Ma's letter-box. Ma didn't think much of that. The family always had the *Sunday Express*. In Ma's opinion, the *News of the World* was dead common, and its reports on lurid court cases were an uncomfortable reminder of that part of Pa's trial that had also been lurid.

'What made the paper boy drop that thing on our mat?' she asked over breakfast.

'Just a mistake,' said Nick, 'I'll take it back later and change it for the *Express*.'

'But we could 'ave a look at it first,' said Amy. 'There might be something in it about that woman in Peckham who had two husbands, one at 'ome and one in New Cross.'

'I don't want anyone in this fam'ly readin' about women like that,' said Ma.

'Where's it gone, anyway, the *News of the World*?' asked Alice.

'I'm sittin' on it,' said Ma, 'and I'm stayin' sittin' on it.'

Nick took it round to the paper shop later. The shop was run by Gran Emerson, a widow, and her daughter-in-law Ivy. Gran was a card, and Ivy was a saucebox. She had a flirtatious twinkle running about in her eyes. The Sunday morning rush had died down when Nick arrived.

'Morning, Gran,' he said. Everyone called Mrs Emerson that. 'Morning, Ivy.'

''Ow's yerself, Nick?' asked Gran.

'Yes, 'ow's yer thrilling leg muscles, lovey?' asked Ivy.

'Bearing up under the strain of carrying me about,' said Nick.

'Like a nice lie-down and some leg liniment, would yer, ducky?' said Ivy. 'We've got some Sloane's up in the flat, and a sofa as well, and I've got ten minutes to spare.' Ivy at twenty-five was a good-looking saucebox. 'Fancy it, Nick?'

'Not half,' said Nick, 'but it's Sunday, and if I go around smelling of Sloane's all day, it'll put Ma and the girls off their dinner and tea.'

'Oh, you can eat with us,' said Ivy, 'except Wally might create a bit.' Wally was her husband, Gran's son.

'Might even smack yer bottom,' chuckled Gran. 'Anyway, what can we do for yer, Nick?'

'Packet of ten Players, and a change of paper,' said Nick.

'Change of paper?' said Gran.

'Yes, we got the *News of the World* this morning instead of the *Express.*'

'It's that blessed paper boy,' said Gran, ''e does more whistlin' than lookin'.'

Ivy, inspecting the returned paper, said, 'It's all sorry for itself.'

'Well, Ma sat on it.'

'What for?'

'To keep it dark,' said Nick. 'She's like that about the *News of the World.*'

'Still, it don't like to be sat on,' said Ivy.

'Well, if you don't change it,' said Nick, 'Ma'll come round and sit on you.'

''Ello, cheeky this morning, are we?' said Ivy.

'Nick's always lively,' said Gran. 'When's yer sailor dad comin' 'ome, Nick?'

'Not till his ship does,' said Nick.

'What's the name of 'is ship?' asked Gran. 'Only Wally's got a friend that's in the Navy.'

That's done it, thought Nick, no-one in the family's ever worried about giving a name to Pa's non-existent ship.

'It's slipped me mind for a moment,' he said, 'I'll ask Ma. How about my ten fags and the *Sunday Express*?'

''Ere we are,' said Gran, handing him a copy. 'And 'ere's yer Players.'

'Ta, Gran,' said Nick, giving her a tanner. 'If I've got time when I next pop in, and if Wally's too busy, I'll smack Ivy's bottom myself.'

'Can't yer make time now, lovey?' asked Ivy.

'Well, no,' said Nick, 'I've to sweep our yard out.' He left to the sound of Ivy laughing. When he was back home, he pointed out to Ma that she'd never thought of giving Pa's ship a name. Gran Emerson had just asked what it was.

'Tell 'er the *Iron Duke* if she asks again,' said Ma.

'Suppose it was sunk in the Great War?' said Alice.

'Well, Nick can tell 'er the Navy went and refloated it,' said Ma.

Over Monday morning breakfast, Ma took only a brief look at the front page of the daily paper before expressing outrage.

'Well, I can't 'ardly believe it,' she said, 'it's disgraceful.'

'What is, Ma?' asked Alice. Amy and Fanny weren't down yet. They didn't have to leave for school until ten to nine.

'I don't like keepin' on about how unlucky your Pa's been,' said Ma, 'but there he is, 'aving to spend years away from us on account of just bein' a bit daft, while some real common criminals do a big jewel robbery up in 'Ampstead over the weekend, and the police 'aven't caught any of them.'

'It's a bit soon,' said Nick.

'Well, it was a bit soon all right for your Pa, but I suppose it'll be late or never for these common burglars. It's only unfortunate men like your Pa that get arrested like he did, and then it only 'appened to him because that spiteful American woman told the police exactly what 'e looked like and how 'e was dressed.'

'A bit much that was, when she was half undressed herself,' said Nick.

'That was when Pa really was daft,' said Alice. 'He should 'ave sat her on his lap and treated her to a cuddle.'

Ma blinked.

'What, when she was in her underwear?' she said.

'Well, Pa was entitled to his own treat,' said Alice.

'You bet,' said Nick. 'Treats ought to be mutual.'

'What's that mean?' asked Ma.

'Well, we saw her in court, Ma, and she was a handsome bit of stuff,' said Nick.

'You're gettin' ideas, my lad,' said Ma. 'I suppose it's on account of your growin' manhood.'

Alice choked a bit on toast.

'Don't say things like that, Ma,' she implored.

'I don't know what you mean,' said Ma. Her perkiness was edged by a frown. She was really cross about the possibility that common jewel thieves would get away with their crime while Pa was still doing hard labour just for having a rush of blood to his head.

At the insurance company's extensive offices in Holborn, Nick dealt with claims of a simple kind, like funeral expenses. Lots of people paid a penny or tuppence a week to ensure their funeral expenses were provided for. Then there were claims from people who'd lost their watches or broken a limb or damaged their spectacles. Nick didn't deal with burglaries, theft, fires or earthquakes. Not yet twenty-one, he was still regarded as a junior, and was paid twenty-two-and-six a week.

On Wednesday morning, the claims department manager, Mr Pollard, a serious gent in a serious profession, had the grave goodness to inform Nick that consequent on attaining the age of twenty-one in November an increment of two shillings and sixpence a week would be awarded him. Nick was suitably grateful, refraining from asking the manager if he could make it five bob. Just as well he didn't, for Mr Pollard then expressed a hope that he'd prove himself worthy of such a handsome increment.

Just after twelve-thirty, he was coming out of the men's cloakroom on the second floor of the building when he heard a girl call.

'Excuse me?'

He turned and saw her in the lift at the end of the corridor. She was visible through the openwork metal gate.

'What's up?' he asked.

'D'you think you could help me get out of this contraption?'

'Coming,' said Nick, and walked up to the lift. Through the gate, swimming brown eyes begged for assistance. 'What's the problem?'

'I'm stuck, that's the problem, but nice of you to ask,' she said. 'The gate won't open, and the lift won't move. It's a relic.'

'It's a trap as well,' said Nick. 'Half a mo'.' He gave the gate a kick, and pulled on the brass handle. The gate slid open.

'Crikey,' said the girl, 'are you the son of Houdini?'

'No, just a bloke who knows that when this lift gets stuck, the gate won't open until you give it a kick. A clever engineer comes to put it right every so often, and two days later it starts playing up again. But a kick usually does the trick.'

'Well, thanks.' She stepped out. She was wearing a round hat of dark green felt with a curved brim. It sat on top of glossy chestnut hair. Her winter coat of matching green was very good-looking. So was she. Prettier even than Amy, and just about seventeen, he thought. A peach. 'It hasn't got a notice,' she said.

'What notice?'

'About giving it a good kick.'

'You're right,' said Nick. 'I'll make one out and stick it on. Someone ought to. D'you work here?'

'No, I'm just visiting the fourth floor, but this piece of old iron won't go up any farther,' she said.

'Let's see,' said Nick. He stepped in with her, closed the gate and pressed the fourth floor button. The lift stayed still. He pressed again. Nothing happened.

'That's clever,' said the peach, 'now we're both stuck.'

'We can't be,' said Nick, 'it's against company rules for a feller to get stuck in this lift with a girl.'

'Why? Aren't girls safe with you?'

'Safe as a lamb with its dad,' said Nick. He gave the gate a good kick and pulled it open. They stepped out and he closed the gate. 'I'm not even a danger to a bunch of flowers, let alone a girl.'

'Oh, I expect you'll improve,' she said.

'Yes, I'm hoping time will turn me into someone like Clark Gable,' said Nick. 'But I'll get a flea in my ear if I'm not back at my desk soon. Look, the stairs are over there. Wait a minute, you sure you want the fourth floor?'

'Positive,' she said.

'Well, I suppose you know what you're doing,' said Nick, 'good luck.'

'Wait a moment,' she said, 'you can't just leave me here on my own, I have to find someone.'

'Why, have you come to be interviewed for a job?' Nick wasn't finding it a problem to linger with this extraordinarily attractive girl, even if he should have been back at his work well before now.

'No, I've come to see Mr Douglas.'

'Pardon?' Nick blinked.

'Mr Douglas. D'you know him?'

'I've only heard of him.' Mr J M Douglas was the awesome chairman of the company. 'He's God. He's up there somewhere on the fourth floor. Watch how you go, or you'll be struck by lightning.'

'Oh, lor', will I really?' Little imps danced in her brown eyes, or so it seemed to Nick, fascinated by their colour.

70

'Not half,' he said. 'Good luck again, I've got to—'

'Oh, don't be a funk, you can take me up and show me where his office is, can't you?'

'The fourth floor is all his office, but all right, come on, this way.' Nick took her to the staircase.

'Where'd you work here?' she asked as they began to climb the stairs.

'Minor claims department.'

'What's your name?'

'Nobody, really.'

'Don't be soppy, no-one can be nobody. What's your name?'

'Nick. Nick Harrison. What's yours?'

'Annabelle. Annabelle Somers.'

'Pleased to meet you, Annabelle. Here you are, fourth floor.'

It was hallowed territory. Below them, the building hummed with the sound of busy bees. Here there was only hush and quiet. The landing was large, the corridor wide, the floor carpeted.

'Thanks,' said Annabelle. She was self-assured but very nice, her blossoming figure shaped by her well-fitting coat. Nick already liked her enough to wish she lived next door and that there were no problems with Pa. 'Which door is it?'

'No idea,' he said, 'this floor is out of bounds to everybody except the most important people. Are you important?'

'No, I'm just me,' she said.

'You're not having me on, are you?' said Nick, thinking the quiet had a sort of holy atmosphere to it. 'I mean, nobody's allowed up here unless God's summoned them.'

'Oh, God's my great-uncle,' said Annabelle, 'and

I've come to see him by arrangement. He's treating me to lunch at some posh restaurant.'

'Oh, me gawd,' said Nick. Annabelle, who had her own sense of humour, laughed. 'It's not funny,' said Nick.

'Yes, it is, and so are you,' she said, and laughed again. 'All that stuff about the lift and God.'

'No wonder you asked for my name,' said Nick, 'I think I'm going to get the sack.'

'Blessed cheek,' said Annabelle, 'd'you want a biff in the eye?' Shades of Cassie, thought Nick. 'I'm not that kind of girl, I'll have you know.'

'Sorry,' said Nick. 'Look, I'd better go, or it's a cert I will get the sack.'

'Yes, all right.' Annabelle smiled. 'And thanks, really.'

'Goodbye,' said Nick, and scooted down the stairs, back to the claims department on the second floor. Mr Clewes, senior clerk, asked him where he'd been. Cloakroom, said Nick, and then someone, a visitor, got stuck in the lift.

'Didn't you call the porter?'

'Well, I should have, Mr Clewes, but I thought I'd have a go myself first. I managed it in the end.'

'You just need to give the gate a good kick,' said Brian Godfrey, one of Nick's fellow junior clerks.

'Resume your work, Harrison,' said Mr Clewes.

Nick resumed it, but had little regrets floating about in his mind. She really was a peach. Ruddy goalposts, though, God's great-niece of all girls. Imagine having to tell someone like her that Pa was doing time.

Later, about half an hour after he'd had his lunch of sandwiches, he was called into the manager's office. Mr Pollard had papers in front of him and was frowning at them.

'Yes, Mr Pollard?'

'What's this?' asked the manager.

'Pardon?'

'Funeral expenses claim relating to a Mrs Potter of Clapham. You've passed a claim of twelve pounds, thirteen shillings and sixpence.'

'That's correct, sir, is it?'

'The premium of a shilling a month, Harrison, allowed for a maximum claim of ten pounds.'

'Help,' said Nick, knowing his mind couldn't have been on it.

'What?' said Mr Pollard.

'Sorry, sir, I don't usually make mistakes like that.'

'Fortunately for you, the mistake was noticed or a cheque would have been sent amounting to a settlement excess of over twenty-five per cent. Twenty-five per cent. Mistakes like that, Harrison, could cost the company dear.'

'Must have been the effect of my forthcoming rise, Mr Pollard,' said Nick, 'must have gone to my head.'

'Indeed it must,' said Mr Pollard. 'Make sure such mistakes never happen again, whatever goes to your head.'

'Right, sir.'

'Take the claim with you, then, and adjust the figures.'

'Thanks,' said Nick.

That was by no means the end of events for the day. At three-thirty, he was called into the manager's office again. This time he found Mr Pollard gazing at his desk telephone as if it had bitten him.

He lifted his head quite slowly to look up at Nick.

'Harrison?' He sounded a little hoarse.

'Yes, sir?'

Mr Pollard blinked.

'Harrison,' he said in disbelief, 'you're to go up to the fourth floor.'

'Beg your pardon, sir?' said Nick. It was what was called unheard-of. No clerks ever went up to the fourth floor. Nor did most other employees. Mr Pollard himself had never been. The chairman rarely interviewed anyone who wasn't a director.

'At once,' said Mr Pollard, hoarser.

'You sure, sir?'

'There's no mistake.' But Mr Pollard actually looked as if he was up against a monumental error. 'Go up immediately.'

Nick went up, wondering, of course, if he was still going to be alive at the end of his working day. The fourth floor, with its wide carpeted corridor, was charged with frightening quietness. Nick thought of calm before a storm. The huge oak door of an office was open. He tidied his hair, polished his shoes on the back of each trouser-leg, and went in. He found himself in a spacious ante-room. He knocked on the inner door.

'Come in.' The voice was deep and vibrant.

Nick entered. God's sanctum was huge. An enormous painting adorned one wall. It looked like a picture of some historic board meeting with bewigged City merchants sitting at a long table, everyone eyeing the viewer. The carpet was thick, its colour a kind of mushroom. But the only furniture was a cabinet, four upright leather-padded chairs, and an enormous desk, all in oak. At the desk sat God in the shape of Mr J M Douglas. Nick had never seen him before, but there he was, looking just like the Almighty with his mane of iron-grey hair, arrestingly craggy face, broad shoulders and dark glinting eyes. He said nothing as Nick approached his desk. He looked him up and down in complete silence. It was at least half a minute before he spoke.

'Your name is Nicholas Harrison?'

'Yes, sir.'

'You're a clerk in the claims department?'

'Yes, sir.'

'By God,' said God, 'you're the one, are you? You're the young swine who had the unmitigated gall to trap a young relative of mine in the lift, are you? Explain yourself.'

'I'd like to, sir, as it wasn't quite—'

'Hold your tongue,' growled God. That's coming it a bit, thought Nick, considering he asked me to explain. 'I'd have you transported if that salutary punishment hadn't been done away with by a feeble-minded Parliament. As it is—' God paused, deliberating, no doubt, on what form of execution to impose. Nick, seeing he was going to get the chop in one way or another, took advantage of the pause to speak his piece.

'I've got to say, sir, that the lift stuck with the young lady in it. After giving the gate a kick, which released it, I then tried—'

'I don't want any damned excuses,' said God. He looked Nick up and down again, without finding anything he seemed to like. He was glowering. Nick's impression was that thunder was writ large on his brow. 'I'm tempted to open this window at my back and throw you out of it. As it is, you're dismissed for the rest of the day. You're to take my

75

niece to tea at the Exchange Teashop. You're to behave your impertinent self and to speak of it to no-one in this building. Is that clear?'

'Yes, sir, but are you serious? I—' Nick stopped. What a lunatic I am, he thought, I'm asking God if he's serious.

'All questions in this office, Harrison, are asked only by myself,' said the Almighty. 'Now do as I instructed you.'

'Yes, sir, but the young lady—'

'Is waiting outside on the pavement. Get down to her at once.' God flipped a strong hand and dismissed Nick. Nick went down to his department, collected his raincoat and his City boater, and told Mr Clewes he was under orders from the fourth floor. Mr Clewes didn't believe him, of course, and hastened to the manager's office. Nick hastened out.

There she was, standing on the pavement a little way up from the entrance, her coat hugging her figure. The afternoon was sharp.

'Well, thank goodness,' she said, 'I thought you were never coming. I've had to put up with pipsqueak messenger boys giving me the eye. That's not a very good start.'

'Now look here—'

'Now what? Cheeky devil. Never mind, come on, this way.' Off she went across the road, weaving blithely in and out of slow-moving or stationary traffic. I need help, thought Nick, I think I'm supposed to be in charge of her. What happens if I have to go back and tell God she walked under a beer dray? He caught her up as she reached the pavement.

'Listen, how did this happen, me going to tea with you?'

76

'You don't mind, do you?' said Annabelle, walking on.

'I'm overcome, believe me I am, but could I ask you not to have an accident? I'll have one myself if you do, I'll get chucked out of the fourth floor window.'

'Never mind, perhaps you'll just bounce,' she said, and turned into Fetter Lane. The Exchange Teashop was a little way down. It was an old-established place used by City gents, superior City messengers and Fleet Street blokes who were on the wagon. Nick had never used it himself. One couldn't have just a cup of tea there. It had to be a pot, a silver pot, which cost a horrendous tenpence. The waitresses wore dark blue dresses with white lace-trimmed fronts and what looked a bit like nurses' caps. 'I suppose you feel you've been put in charge of me,' said Annabelle.

'All I'm sure of is that if I fall over my feet, I'll be tried and shot.'

'Oh, dear, poor you,' said Annabelle. 'I can imagine what happened. Never mind, you still look as if you're in one piece, and you're not against having tea with me, are you?'

'Mad about it,' said Nick.

'What d'you mean, mad about it? You've only just met me.'

'Yes, I daresay I have, but this is a lot better than pens, claim forms and blotting paper.'

'Is that what you do when you meet a girl, decide if she's worse or better than blotting paper, or about the same?'

'Nobody's ever asked me that before.'

'Here we are,' said Annabelle, and they left the bustle of the pavements to enter the Dickensian atmosphere of the Exchange Teashop, which despite its name served coffee as well. Also, from twelve until two, old-fashioned English lunchtime dishes were available. The decor was in various hues of brown, but the tables were laid with snowy white cloths, and the cutlery looked like silver. A few City gents were present, doing business in a sociable way over tea.

'I'll take your hat and coat, sir,' said a waitress.

'Do I get them back?' asked Nick.

'Of course, sir.'

'Well, that's fair,' said Nick, and Annabelle smiled.

They were given a table for two in a corner. Annabelle kept her hat and coat on, but she unbuttoned her coat to reveal a jersey wool dress of an oatmeal colour. Nick, taken with her looks and her brunette colouring, thought he hadn't seen too many girls like her walking down Browning Street.

Annabelle, catching his smile, said, 'Yes, isn't this fun? I'm a working girl of seventeen and I love toasted crumpets.' She wrinkled her nose and looked ecstatic. 'I can smell them. They specialize here.'

'Tea and toasted crumpets, is that what we're having?' asked Nick.

'Well, I am. Two. Thanks ever so.'

Nick thought about the money in his pocket. A little over three bob. A pot of tea for one was tenpence, a pot for two, one-and-eightpence. How much were the toasted crumpets? Tuppence? Blimey, not in here. More like fourpence.

Up came a waitress.

'Yes, sir?' she said.

Nick wasn't a gauche young man, he'd seen a lot of life in Hackney and Walworth, the seamy side of it as well as its cockney gusto, but it was one thing to be called sir and another not to be able to pay the bill. A slate appeared then, neatly chalked words detailing the menu. He found out later that slates had been used in this fashion for about a hundred years. He picked out the price of toasted crumpets. Fourpence each. He had just enough money to pay for the tea and two crumpets each, plus tuppence for a tip.

With relief he said, 'We'd like crumpets, please, and a pot of cocoa.'

'Cocoa?' said the waitress.

'Did I say cocoa? I didn't, did I?'

'He's a bit funny in the head today,' said Annabelle to the waitress.

'I meant tea,' said Nick.

'Pleasure, sir,' said the waitress. 'How many crumpets?'

'Can you manage two each?'

The waitress smiled.

'I think I can say yes, sir.'

'We'll let you know later if we want any fruitcake,' said Annabelle.

Fruitcake? How much was that? Too late, the slate had gone. I'd better start praying, thought Nick.

It didn't feel quite real, being in a select City teashop with God's great-niece. What did feel real was his shortage of money. A request for fruit-cake was going to give him a headache. Did she need cake when she'd had lunch with God?

'Didn't you have much lunch?' he asked.

'Well, no, I didn't,' said Annabelle, stripping off

her gloves. 'Just some soup and poached salmon without vegetables. I'd already made up my mind I'd like some toasted crumpets later.' She looked a bit impish as she asked, 'What did you think of God?'

'Look, I wouldn't have talked about him like that if I'd known he was your great-uncle. And I've got to say, Miss Somers—'

'Ugh to Miss Somers,' said Annabelle. 'Don't be stuffy.'

'I've still got to say I didn't think you'd do it on me, that you'd tell your great-uncle I trapped you in the lift with me.'

'Oh, I always tell him the truth,' she said, 'and the truth was you did get me stuck in the lift with you. What a scoundrel, Uncle John said, and I said don't call him that, Uncle John, he was very kind and helpful, and he didn't trap me deliberately. I told him that was how we met, because of the wonky lift. Are you pleased?'

'Pleased?' said Nick. 'What about?'

'That we've met, of course.' Annabelle, outgoing and fond of fun, teased him with her smile.

'Listen,' said Nick, 'I can tell you who isn't pleased, and that's your god-like relative. Talk about thunder and lightning, I'll either get the sack or stay a junior clerk for ever. I might as well give notice now and try for a job as a council navvy. It beats me why he didn't sack me on the spot instead of ordering me to take you to this teashop.'

'I told him to,' said Annabelle.

'You told him to tell me to bring you here?'

'Yes, why not?' said Annabelle. 'I mean, if a girl meets someone who can give a lift gate a rattling good kick, why shouldn't she let him take her out for tea and crumpets? And you like me, don't you? You looked at me as if you did.'

'I like you, yes,' said Nick, 'but I shouldn't.'

'Why shouldn't you?' she asked.

'I'm not daft,' said Nick. 'It's a cert that if your uncle thought one of his junior clerks had had the sauce to take a liking to you, he'd chop him up. Do me a favour and don't tell him.'

'Excuse me, but how old are you?' asked Annabelle.

'Twenty-one next month,' said Nick.

'Well, you shouldn't still be a junior clerk,' said Annabelle, 'it's downright disgraceful, treating a young man like you as not much better than an office boy. Just wait till I get back to the offices.'

'Don't talk like that,' said Nick, 'you'll cause a riot.'

The waitress reappeared then, carrying a laden silver tray which gave off the aroma of toasted crumpets liberally buttered.

'Mmm, famous,' said Annabelle.

'It's a nice change,' said the waitress, setting everything out on the table. Teapot, hot water jug, milk jug and sugar basin were all silver, and so was the salver containing the hot crumpets.

'What's a nice change?' asked Nick.

'Serving young people,' smiled the waitress.

'I don't know about that,' said Nick, 'I'm going grey today.'

'He's still having funny turns,' said Annabelle, and the waitress smiled again and left them to themselves. Annabelle poured the tea, and then she and Nick began to enjoy the crumpets.

'Are you your uncle's favourite?' asked Nick, dispensing with the 'great'.

'I'm his favourite discovery,' said Annabelle. He was, she said, the brother-in-law of her dad's father, and he'd made a name for himself in the City, where he'd started as an office boy. He ended up living in a different world from her dad's father, who had a grocer's shop in Herne Hill. She herself didn't even know he existed until two years ago, when he sort of turned up out of the blue and nearly frightened everyone to death because he looked and talked like – well, like—

'Like God?' said Nick.

'Don't be cheeky,' said Annabelle. 'Yes, like God. But he must have thought me one of heaven's angels, because he began to make a fuss of me. Me an angel, can you believe that? Don't answer if you're going to be cheeky again. Anyway, he insists I come to the City to have lunch with him once a month, and I'm given time off for that. I work for our family firm at Camberwell Green. Aren't these crumpets luscious?'

'I'll say. D'you like being an angel?'

'No, I like having fun. My dad's in the City too, in the wine trade. What does your dad do?'

Suffering cats, thought Nick, why did she have to ask that?

'He works hard, I can tell you that,' he said.

'Well, I'm glad for you,' said Annabelle. She was talking as if they were old friends. 'All dads should be a credit to their families. No wonder you look honest and fearless.'

'Pardon?' said Nick.

'Well, you do,' said Annabelle, who was well into her second crumpet.

'Who's having a laugh?' said Nick, wondering if

her healthy appetite meant she was going to ask for a slice of fruitcake.

'I'm not laughing,' she said, but she looked as if she was ready to. Nick thought her distinctly a peach. She had no side, and if her doting great-uncle spoiled her at all, it wasn't evident. He watched her as she refilled his cup and her own, then topped up the teapot from the hot water jug. The place, fairly busy when they arrived, was quietening down.

'I don't see myself as – here, who's pinched half of the last crumpet?'

'Me,' said Annabelle.

'I thought all of it was mine,' said Nick, 'I've only had one.'

'Oh, dear, naughty me,' said Annabelle, 'I cut it in half when you weren't looking. Are you miffed?'

'No, I can see you're a growing girl.'

'What d'you mean, growing? I'll be eighteen next year. Are you trying to swank because you're nearly twenty-one? What's your family like?'

'It's a struggle for me,' said Nick, 'I've got three sisters.'

'Well, three's a lucky number,' said Annabelle, intent on finding out lots about him. 'You didn't say what your dad does.'

Blow that, thought Nick. But what did it matter? He'd never see her again.

The lie came out.

'He's in the Navy.'

'My word, now I know why you look saucy as well as fearless,' she said, and a little laugh escaped.

'Saucy?' said Nick, who couldn't help a large grin.

'Well, you're the son of a saucy sailor, aren't you? And all sailors are saucy, from captains downwards, aren't they?'

'Leave off,' said Nick, and got her away from the subject of sailors and Pa by asking the fatal question. Did she want a slice of fruitcake?

'No, thanks, but you have a slice, if you want,' she said, 'I had half your second crumpet.'

'No, I'm fine, thanks,' said Nick, 'I was lucky enough to get the other half. D'you have many friends?'

'Yes, nice ones, funny ones and toffee-nosed ones,' she said, and talked about the funny ones. They sounded more like hooligans to Nick, the things they got up to. He liked looking at her and listening to her. She was as vivacious as Amy, and kind of very nice like Alice. And she had some of Fanny's cheekiness. She seemed to like talking. He asked her if she had a great-aunt. 'Well, yes,' she said, 'there's my great-uncle's wife, she's my great-aunt. But I call them aunt and uncle, of course. My aunt gardens, climbs ladders and prunes apple trees. Well, she's only sixty-one. I think the reason why they fuss me is because they've never had any children of their own.'

'Well, your aunt's a game old girl if she climbs ladders and prunes trees at her age.'

'That's my respected Aunt Alice you're talking about,' said Annabelle. The teashop was very quiet now. Most customers had left, and no new ones had come in. Nick felt that at their corner table, he was on a little island with this engaging girl. 'Would you like some more tea?'

'Thanks,' said Nick, and she poured him a third cup. She also refilled her own cup. 'Did you say you come up to have lunch with your uncle once a month?'

'Yes,' she said.

'Well, look here, then, why did you act as if you didn't know where his office was?'

'Because you were so funny about everything. D'you like your job?'

'I like having one,' said Nick frankly.

'What d'you do exactly?'

'Check minor insurance claims,' said Nick, and told her of the mistake he'd made in passing a funeral expenses claim for over twelve quid when the premium only guaranteed a maximum of ten quid. Annabelle wanted to know whose funeral it was. 'An old lady from Clapham, Mrs Potter,' said Nick.

'Well, I think that was very nice of you,' said Annabelle, 'and I'm sure the poor old lady would have thought the same. Ugh to your manager for not letting it go through.'

'Mistakes like that could ruin the company,' said Nick.

'Wait till I tell Uncle John that,' said Annabelle.

'Would you do that?'

'Not after you gave me half your second crumpet,' she said.

'You nicked it, you mean.'

They kept talking. The waitress came up and said the teashop would be closing in a few minutes, at five o'clock.

'Help,' said Annabelle, 'I told Uncle John I'd be back by five at the latest.'

Nick asked the waitress for the bill, and she went to get it. Annabelle opened her crocodile handbag. She said it was up to her to pay. Nick had never heard of girls paying. Even less than fellers could they afford to. This girl was different, of course, she had to be well off, but even so Nick felt it was up to him.

'No, I'll pay,' he said.

'But should you?' she asked, smiling.

'Pleasure,' said Nick. The bill was for three bob, and he gave the waitress three and thruppence. That left him with a penny in his pocket.

'Thank you, sir,' said the waitress, 'I hope you enjoyed the tea.'

'Lovely,' said Annabelle, buttoning up her coat. Nick's boater and coat were returned to him, and when he and Annabelle left, the October twilight was hovering about and the traffic was thicker. Some workers, those who finished at five, were on their way home. Nick's time was five-thirty, which meant he'd dodge being seen with Annabelle by an outpouring of insurance company employees.

On the pavement, her coat collar turned up against the cold air, she said, 'Thanks ever so much, I did enjoy it. Goodbye now.'

'I'll see you across the road,' said Nick.

'There's really no need.'

'I think I'd better,' he said, and when they reached Holborn he took her across to the other side. 'There you are,' he said.

She laughed.

'What d'you mean, there you are? I'm not just out of the nursery, you know.'

'No, but you're still our chairman's favourite relative.'

'You're funny,' she said. 'Goodbye again, and thanks again.'

'Goodbye,' said Nick. He watched her go. She

had a quick, easy walk. He watched until she disappeared amid home-going workers. Not having to go back to his desk, he began to walk home. As he had only a penny in his pocket, he walked all the way, thinking, of course, about God's great-niece.

He said not a word about her to his family. He was sure the awesome J M Douglas really would chop him up if he went around bragging he'd had tea and toasted crumpets with her. As he'd been forbidden to mention it to anyone in the company, he decided to keep it to himself generally.

'You did what?' said Mrs Lizzy Somers.

'I had tea and toasted crumpets with him,' said Annabelle, a girl who always recounted details of exciting events to her parents. 'Uncle John rumbled and growled a bit, but in the end he gave Nick time off to take me to the teashop.'

'Nick?' said Lizzy.

'Yes, I told you, Mum, that's his name,' said Annabelle.

'Had you met this boy before, then?' asked Lizzy.

'Boy? He's not a boy, he's a young man, I told you that as well. Mum, have you been listening?'

'Yes, and it's been confusin' me,' said Lizzy. Thirty-five, Lizzy was blessed with an Edwardian figure that she fitted daily into a lightweight corset or basque with the confidence of a woman who, despite her humble beginnings, had always known how to dress herself to the best advantage. Her husband Ned could still show her an appreciative eye, even though they'd been married for nearly eighteen years. They had four children, Annabelle who was seventeen, Bobby who was thirteen,

Emma eleven and Edward nine. They were all well-behaved, give or take the occasional little fall from grace, and accepting that Annabelle was so outgoing and impulsive she needed to be checked now and again. Lizzy sometimes felt her elder daughter might very well bring home a tramp one day, and ask for him to be fed and housed for a week. 'Annabelle, I wouldn't like to think the way you met the young man meant you let him pick you up.' Lizzy was very much like her mother in some respects. Such as speaking proper and behaving proper. Not in all her years in Walworth had Lizzy ever allowed herself to be 'picked up'. It made a girl look very common. 'Your dad and me don't mind any of you bein' a bit modern, but girls have got to have respect for themselves, or they won't get respect.'

'Bless you, Mum, I wouldn't let myself be picked up,' said Annabelle. 'But I couldn't be toffee-nosed to any young gentleman who helped me get out of a stuck lift.'

'Yes, but then gettin' your Uncle John to let him have time off from his work so that he could take you to a teashop, well, wasn't that a bit fast of you, lovey?'

'Of course not, Mum,' said Annabelle blithely. 'As he'd been so kind, and as he liked me, I thought I'd treat him to the privilege of having tea and toasted crumpets with me.'

'How'd you know he liked you?' asked Lizzy.

'I could see he did. His eyes went sort of dizzy with liking for my health and beauty.'

They were in the kitchen, with Annabelle's sister and brothers elsewhere, and her dad not yet home from work.

Lizzy, preparing supper, said, 'I don't like vanity in a girl, Annabelle. But never mind, I suppose it didn't do much harm, lettin' the young man take you to the teashop. I expect he was fairly respectable, or your Uncle John would have said no to you. Anyway, it was just the once. All over now, so I won't say any more about it, except girls should be careful about makin' casual acquaintances.' Lizzy had high hopes for Annabelle, such a lovely girl who'd make a very nice wife later on for someone like a doctor, say.

'Oh, I'm very careful about that kind of thing, Mum,' said Annabelle, who didn't have just once on her mind herself. 'Uncle John sent his kind regards, by the way.'

'Oh, lor', I hope that don't mean he's thinkin' about a visit,' said Lizzy. The appearance of Ned's awesome uncle in the family circle when hardly anyone, except for Ned and his parents, knew he even existed, had put Lizzy in a flutter. Well, he really was awesome, and didn't go in for small talk. But he'd taken to Annabelle all right, and he couldn't have doted more on her if she'd been his granddaughter. Fortunately, Annabelle didn't think him a bit fearsome, and she'd even been known to pull his leg.

'No, he didn't say he and Aunt Alice were coming over, Mum,' said Annabelle.

'Well, that's a relief,' said Lizzy frankly.

Chapter Six

Ma, of course, was tickled to hear her one and only son was in line for a rise. The family weren't too badly off at this stage, but Ma would have liked something for extras, such as new clothes for Amy and Fanny. Even more, she would have liked enough extras for the family to enjoy a week's summer holiday at Margate. She quite fancied Margate, it sounded as if it had more class than Southend, and a sailor's family was entitled to a bit of seaside class.

Nick gave her seventeen shillings out of his weekly wage of twenty-two-and-six, and Alice contributed eight shillings out of the twelve-and-six she earned at Galloway's. Then there was the monthly handout from Mister Horsemouth, the dubious character the family suspected of having sent Pa into the lions' den. It was a cert that the jewels had finished up in his mitts, although at the trial Pa hadn't said a word about any accomplices.

Mister Horsemouth had gradually cut down on his handout on account of Nick and Alice both earning. It still looked after the rent, but there was a balance of only a few bob. Pa hadn't liked hearing about reductions, but they'd happened, all the same.

Anyway, as a family of five they were hardly well off. Most of the furniture was their own, but it had all seen better days. Somewhere in Queen Anne's time, said Alice. Ma said the stuff was good for a few more years, and that if they got really hard-up they could sell the piano.

'Sell it?' said Amy. 'Who'd buy it?'

'You couldn't even give it away,' said Alice.

'Yes, you could,' said Ma, 'there must be 'undreds of people that would fall over theirselves to 'ave a piano like ours. It's a valuable antique, don't forget, it's not any old piano.'

'It looks like any old piano to me,' said Nick.

'I bet all we'd get for it would be one-and-tuppence and two jamjars,' said young Fanny.

'I'll 'ave all of you know it's been in your Pa's fam'ly for goodness knows how long,' said Ma, born like most perky females to have the last word. 'I think your Pa said it's got Queen Anne's birthmark on it somewhere.'

'Yes, I mentioned about Queen Anne,' said Alice, lifting her skirt and toasting her slip in front of the kitchen fire. The fireguard prevented her action from being suicidal. 'But you sure Pa said birthmark, Ma?'

'Well, something like that,' said Ma. 'Mind, I don't remember any Queen Anne meself, but I do remember your Pa tellin' me just before the police came lookin' for him that it was a fam'ly heirloom.'

'You can't sell it, then,' said Amy.

'Not unless Pa says so,' complained Fanny.

'We'll 'ave to see,' said Ma.

'Amy won't be able to play us any tunes on it if it's sold,' said Fanny.

'We'll 'ave to see,' said Ma again. 'Of course, we could take in a lodger for the upstairs top.'

The terraced houses in this part of Browning

Street were three-storeyed. The family's top floor was furnished but not used. Mister Horsemouth had originally said not to have lodgers. Lodgers, he said, could be nosy and interfering, and could hear what they weren't supposed to hear. Ma agreed. Pa's misfortunes had to be kept dark.

'We don't want any lodger,' said Fanny.

'Lodgers get drunk and fall down the stairs,' said Amy.

'Lodgers look through keyholes,' said Alice.

'If any lodgers looked through my keyhole,' said Ma, 'he'd 'ave to ask the vicar to come and give 'im his last rites. Still, we could let the upstairs top for ten shillings, what with there bein' three rooms and its own lav, and a gas ring in one room.'

'I'll leave home,' said Alice.

'Now, Alice,' said Ma, 'you can't leave 'ome till you're twenty-one or married.'

'Well, I can't get married till Pa's out, can I?' said Alice. 'I don't want a bridegroom whose dad-in-law is a convict. I don't suppose Nick's keen, either.'

'Not on a bridegroom I'm not,' said Nick.

'I know all about that,' said Ma, a bit short for once, 'and kindly remember I don't like anyone usin' that word, Alice. Walls 'ave ears, don't forget. What was I saying? Oh, yes, your Pa's 'elpful friend was 'ere Friday afternoon, when 'e said 'e might be recommendin' someone as a lodger.'

'Now I know why you talked about sellin' the piano,' said Alice, 'it was a way of leadin' us up to 'aving a lodger. Old Horsy told you we've got to have one, of course.'

'I thought he was against lodgers,' said Nick.

'That was out of the goodness of 'is heart,' said Ma.

'His heart?' said Amy. 'Where's 'e keep it, in his bowler hat?'

'Now, Amy, he didn't want us to 'ave any lodgers at first so that we could sorrow for Pa in private. It's what you call human sympathy.' Ma looked as if she was struggling valiantly to believe it. 'Mind you, I'm not saying he don't owe us the 'elp he gives us, seein' it was your Pa that 'ad to go off to the China Seas, and not 'im. Anyway, no-one can say a lodger's rent money wouldn't be useful. Fanny, don't make faces, you might get struck like it. We've got to think about a lodger's rent and about bein' obligin'.'

'Hands up all those that don't want to be obligin',' said Amy.

'Me,' said Fanny.

'I'm not 'aving that,' said Ma, 'it's like mutiny. What an example to set your sailor Pa.'

'Ugh, we're goin' to 'ave a lodger,' said Fanny. 'I might as well be sick now.'

'Not in the kitchen, if you don't mind,' said Ma. 'Go and do it in the yard lav, and don't forget to pull the chain. Anyway, it's not certain about a lodger. Your Pa's 'elpful friend just mentioned it in case it came to pass.'

'Well, if it does come to pass,' said Alice, 'we'll all be sick, not just Fanny.'

The house suited the girls as it was. It was just the family's. They liked the house and the street. Browning Street was always full of life.

Supper for the Harrisons that evening was Ma's version of a Lancashire hot-pot. That meant it was put together very economically and had a lot of gravy to it. Ma was tops at gravies, especially when she cooked a roast. Walworth was the right place for kitchen gravies. Posh people said that the French excelled at all kinds of gravies and sauces, but that it took them all day just to dish one up. Ma and other Walworth mums could put a rattling fine gravy on the table in no time at all. The French got all the credit, however, because a breed of people called gourmets went off their chumps about cooks who took all day over anything. Nick refrained from telling Ma this in case she took umbrage and sorted out the nearest gourmet by pouring a panful of hot thick beef gravy into his trousers. Here, see how you like this for flavour, she'd say, and if it's hot enough.

'Heard anything more about a lodger, Ma?' asked Amy.

'What lodger?' said Ma. 'Oh, yes,' she said, 'no.'

'What d'you mean, oh yes no?' asked young Fanny.

'I 'aven't 'eard any more, that's what I mean,' said Ma.

''Ooray,' said Fanny.

'That's all very well,' said Ma. 'but like I mentioned before, what about a lodger's rent? We could do with that, then I might be able to buy new Sunday dresses for you girls. I'd like you all to look nice on Sundays and be a credit to me and your Pa.'

'I already look nice on Sundays,' said Alice, who did, and by dint of taking great care of all her clothes.

'I don't want to sort of rubbish Pa,' said Amy, 'but what about 'im bein' a credit to us?'

'Yes, we love Pa,' said Alice, 'but we've done a lot of sorrowing for 'im.'

'We've earned medals sorrowing for Knocker Pa,' said Nick.

'Crikey,' said Amy, 'listen to him bein' cheeky.'

'Yes, Nick's got a bit of 'is Pa's devilry in 'im,' said Ma. 'Mind, I'm not saying I didn't like some of your Pa's devilry – well, never mind that, let's 'ope Nick's devilry don't land 'im in the same boat as your Pa.'

'If it does,' said Alice, 'they both ought to be chucked overboard.'

'Like a tickle after supper, would you, Alice?' said Nick.

'Oh, me gawd, no, I wouldn't,' said Alice.

'Now, Nick, I don't want Alice screamin' the house down with the neighbours listening,' said Ma.

'It's 'is devilry, Ma,' said young Fanny.

Dumpling came round later, along with Freddy and Danny, for the usual Wednesday evening committee meeting.

And Cassie came too. She'd called on Freddy and told him she had to address the committee.

'What d'you mean, address it?' asked Freddy, who had gradually acquired the kind of looks Cassie thought a developing young man should have.

'That's what my knowing dad said it was,' declared Cassie, quite a vision in a cherry red coat that kept out the chill of the autumnal night. She worked in a florist's shop in Kennington for ten shillings a week, and saved most of it for clothes.

'Yes, I think I've heard of people addressin' committees,' said plump and placid Mrs Brown.

'I've 'eard of 'em chuckin' rotten cabbages at council committees,' said lean and wiry Mr Brown, 'which I suppose ain't exactly the same as addressin' them.'

'I'm good at addressin',' said Cassie, 'I inherited it from me dad. Well, he used to work at Clapham Junction railway station.'

'I suppose I shouldn't ask,' said Freddy, 'but what's that got to do with addressin' a football committee?'

'Well, me dad used to address the stationmaster, didn't he?' said Cassie.

'You're a laugh a minute, you are, Cassie,' said Mr Brown, enjoying a pipe of tobacco by the kitchen fire.

'Potty as well,' said Freddy. 'Never mind, she's still me keenest football admirer.'

'Freddy, stop talkin' as if you had no head,' said Cassie. 'Anyway, put your cap and scarf on, and we'll go round to Nick's together so's I can address the committee.'

'All right,' said Freddy, who never quite knew why he always resigned himself to doing what she wanted. When he arrived with her on Nick's doorstep at the same time as Dumpling and Danny, he explained she had some idea about including herself in the meeting.

Nick said, 'Now look here, Cassie—'

'He's off,' said Dumpling, 'he's doin' 'is look 'ere bit. Still, 'e did play 'eroic on Saturday. So did I.'

'I've come to represent the supporters,' said Cassie.

'Oh, they've got a point to make, have they?' said Nick.

'Well, of course they 'ave,' said Cassie, 'or I wouldn't be here, would I?'

'All right,' said Nick, 'come and join in.'

The meeting began with Cassie sitting in. After the minutes had been read, Dumpling had her usual wordy say about everything touching on last Saturday's game, and nor did she forget to make a speech about her inspired performance as goalkeeper.

'Reg'lar marvel you were, Dumpling,' said besotted Danny.

'Yes, did yer notice the whole team gave me kisses and cuddles afterwards, Cassie?' said Dumpling. 'Not soppy stuff, of course, more out of admiration for me savin' the penalty.'

'It was really touchin',' said Cassie, 'you gettin' all those cuddles, Chrissie. I don't get many myself. Just about two a week.'

'Well, hard luck,' said Nick, 'write to *Peg's Paper* about it. We'll get on with the meeting.' As treasurer, among other things, he was able to announce the team had four shillings and tuppence in the kitty. He proposed that that could go towards the cost of a brand new football of their own, and that they could double the weekly subscriptions until they had enough to make the purchase.

Dumpling was against it, and said so.

'What d'yer want to go and buy a football for when there's mine that'll last for ages? It's daft. And the kitty's supposed to be kept for buyin' new shorts and shirts, it's in the rules.'

'Well, Nick's proposed a change,' said Freddy.

'It ain't been seconded,' said Dumpling.

'All right, I'll second it,' said Freddy.

'I ain't accepted the proposal,' said Dumpling, 'so I don't 'ave to ask anyone to second it.'

'Dumpling, what're you talkin' about?' asked Danny.

'It's my turn to be chairman,' said Dumpling. 'We all 'ave to take turns so that it's fair. That's in the rules too, and it's my turn this week.'

'Wait a bit,' said Freddy, 'how d'you know so much about the rules? You weren't on the committee when we started the team two years ago.'

Dumpling pointed out that when she did get on the committee, she found Nick had only scribbled the rules on a piece of notepaper. So she copied them all out in her best handwriting in an exercise book she bought for a penny out of her own money. She said there was one rule about all committee members taking turns to be chairman, and that they'd all been sloppy about it except herself, which was why she knew it was her turn to be chairman this evening.

'So it's me duty not to accept any proposal to buy a new ball out of money that's against the rules,' she said.

'I second that,' said Cassie.

'Do what?' said Freddy.

'I second what Chrissie said,' smiled Cassie.

'Cassie, you're goin' to make me old before me time if you don't stop playin' Alice in ruddy Wonderland,' said Freddy. 'You can't second anything, you're not on the committee, and even if you were you could only second something that's been proposed.'

'All right,' said Dumpling, 'I propose we don't buy a new ball against the rules.'

'I second that,' said Cassie.

'Danny,' said Nick, 'chuck both these girls out.'

'Me?' said Danny, shaken at the thought of chucking Dumpling anywhere.

''Ere, nobody's goin' to chuck me out,' said

Dumpling, 'that's against the rules as well. The rules say—'

'Dumpling, d'you want to live to see Christmas?' asked Nick.

'Yes, course I do, we've got matches ev'ry Saturday,' said Dumpling.

'Then stop hogging the meeting,' said Nick. 'Now, about a new football. Double subscriptions would help us buy a couple of the best quality.'

Dumpling quivered all over.

'But what about my football?' she asked.

'Well, let's be frank, Dumpling, we wouldn't need it any more,' said Freddy.

'So I wouldn't be on the committee?' said Dumpling. 'That's it, break me 'eart. It don't matter I've given the Rovers nearly two years of me lifeblood and saved a penalty against the Rangers. Go on, chuck me out, then, so's I don't 'ave anything to live for.'

'I'm not secondin' that,' said Cassie. 'Crikey, it's like sendin' Chrissie to the Tower to have her head chopped off.'

'All right, let's settle that one,' said Nick. 'I propose Dumpling be made a permanent member of the committee.'

'Eh?' said Freddy.

'Me?' gasped Dumpling.

'I'll second that,' said Danny lovingly.

'Up to you now, Madam Chairman,' said Nick.

'Oh, blimey,' said Dumpling faintly, but pulled herself happily together. 'All in favour of me bein' permanent, show yer 'ands,' she said. All hands went up, including Cassie's. Cassie was kind of lovable in that she never allowed herself to be left out of anything. Freddy rolled his eyes. Well, what was the use of saying a word? His best girl had always been slightly off her rocker. But as his brother Will was married to her sister Annie, he felt obliged to keep an eye on her and her potty ways.

'Right, all in favour, Dumpling,' said Nick. 'Now you can say passed unanimously.'

'All right, passed unanimous,' said Dumpling, beaming. 'I'll put it in the minutes when I do them for yer, Nick. I don't 'alf feel proud, bein' on the committee permanent. Does that mean till me dyin' day?'

'Yes, why not?' said Nick.

'Oh, y'er me fav'rite football captain ever,' said Dumpling. 'If you're still alive when I pass on, Nick, could yer see me football's buried with me?'

'And the rules book as well?' suggested Nick.

'Crikey, what an honour,' said Dumpling rapturously. 'I'll go to me grave as 'appy as a lark. Could yer think of something to put on me gravestone, Nick, you bein' a bit more educated than me?'

Nick thought, while Freddy and Danny did some coughing, and Cassie sat looking angelic. Then he came up with, '"Here lies good old Chrissie, who as a goalie was pretty, but better than that, as a matter of fact, she was on the Rovers' committee." Will that do, Dumpling?'

'Oh, ain't you clever, Nick? I never 'eard anything more heart-warmin' for me epitaph.'

'I second it,' said Cassie, and Freddy rolled his eyes again.

'Dumpling, I couldn't be more pleased for yer,' said Danny, 'I could go 'appy with yer to yer grave.'

'Sounds like a mournful cuddle-up,' said Freddy. 'I suppose we couldn't get down to pickin' Saturday's team, could we?'

'Wait a minute,' said Cassie, 'I've got to speak up for the supporters first.'

The Rovers boasted six supporters, namely Dumpling, Cassie, Alice, Fanny and the girlfriends of Charlie Cope and Ronnie Smith.

'All right, Cassie, let's hear you,' said Nick.

'Well, thanks,' said Cassie, 'I hardly ever get heard at all usually.'

'Has anyone noticed that?' asked Freddy.

'Not much,' said Danny.

'I was talkin' to Alice on Saturday,' said Cassie, 'and we both agreed supporters ought to 'ave their just rewards, like the team payin' our tram fares and treatin' us to bars of chocolate at every match. We don't mind just tuppenny bars. Would you put that in the minutes, Chrissie?'

'Well, no, I can't, Cassie, Nick wouldn't let me,' said Dumpling. 'It ain't been proposed, nor seconded.'

'Oh, I'm proposin' it, and Freddy's seconding it,' said Cassie.

'Yes, but yer see, Cassie, it's got to be proposed by a committee member,' said Dumpling.

'All right, Freddy can propose it,' said Cassie, 'and you can second it.'

'If Freddy proposes it, I'll boot him through the window,' said Nick.

'Can't someone let Cassie know that tram fares and chocolate bars cost money?' said Freddy.

'Let's get this out of the way,' said Nick. 'I propose we treat the supporters to a bar of chocolate each and that Danny tans their bottoms if they ask for more.'

'Seconded,' said Freddy.

''Ere, I ain't acceptin' that,' protested Dumpling.

'You've got to,' said Nick, 'it's in the rules. Those in favour?' He and Freddy raised their hands. 'Those against?' Cassie and Dumpling raised their hands. 'Not you, Cassie,' said Nick, 'you're ineligible.'

'Here, d'you mind?' said Cassie. 'Me and my dad both agree I'm eligible enough for the Prince of Wales 'imself, especially as Dad's Aunt Mildred 'ad blue blood, due to her mum bein' found in bed with a royal duke one Bank Holiday.'

'Chuck her out, Freddy,' said Nick. 'What about you, Danny, you in favour of the proposal or not?'

'Well, I'm in favour of buyin' the chocolate bars out of the kitty,' said Danny, 'but I ain't in favour of tanning any bottoms, specially not Dumpling's. I ain't ashamed to say Dumpling's is sort of precious to me.'

''Ere, leave off,' said Dumpling. 'What I'm sittin' on is me own, and it ain't precious to anyone except me meself.'

'Danny's abstaining,' said Nick, 'so the proposal's passed by two to one. Put it in the minutes, Dumpling.'

'What, about Danny 'aving to – 'ere, I ain't goin' to write that down in any minutes,' said Dumpling indignantly, 'it wouldn't be fit to be read.'

'Well, I've got to tell you you'll 'ave to force yerself, Dumpling,' said Freddy, 'it's all been passed. Tuppenny bars of chocolate for you supporters and Danny to tan yer bottoms if you ask for more.'

''Old on,' said Danny, 'I ain't tanning Dumpling's bottom, I just said so. Nor Cassie's.' Cassie smiled sweetly. 'I was brought up to respect girls.'

'I can't remember if I was,' said Freddy, 'so I'll do it for yer, Danny.'

'I ain't writin' that down in Nick's minutes, d'you 'ear?' said Dumpling. 'It ain't decent.'

'I second that,' said Cassie. 'Some hopes Freddy's got of smackin' my bottom, and I don't know what the supporters are goin' to say about not 'aving their tram fares paid. I wouldn't be surprised if we didn't all go on strike.'

'Do it now, Freddy,' said Nick.

'Do what now?' asked Freddy.

'Smack Cassie's bottom.'

''Ere, that ain't allowed, nor ain't it in the rules,' protested Dumpling, 'not at a committee meetin'.'

'Oh, all right,' said Freddy. 'Sorry, Nick, can't be done, not 'ere.'

'Somewhere else, then, and before the evening has got as far as Cassie's bedtime cocoa,' said Nick.

'Well, yes, all right, Nick,' said Freddy, 'even if it 'urts me more than Cassie.'

'It will,' said Cassie.

'Let's pick the team,' said Danny. That was hardly a headache, just a question of deciding whether or not to give the standing reserve another game now that the Rovers were back to full strength. They agreed they would. Dumpling asked if they wanted her to play in goal again. Only a blank silence was heard. Dumpling sighed audibly but resignedly, then accepted the silence like a man. After all, there was still the bliss of having been made a permanent member of the committee until her dying day.

Freddy accompanied Cassie to her home in Blackwood Street, off the East Street market. Cassie, of course, gave him what for in respect of it not being good manners to talk about smacking girls' bottoms. Freddy decided not to listen. He interrupted her.

'Cassie, I've been thinkin',' he said.

'Oh, it can 'appen to anybody,' said Cassie.

'Yes, I've been thinkin' about your idea of us gettin' married later on,' said Freddy, 'and it's just come to me that as me brother Will is married to your sister Annie, that makes you me sister-in-law.'

'Course it doesn't,' said Cassie, warm breath escaping into the cold night. Winter was lying in wait off places like Clacton and Margate, girding itself to sneak into Walworth and freeze a few chilblains. 'It's Annie that's your sister-in-law.'

'Yes, and you as well, Cassie. We've got to face it, I can't marry me sister-in-law. It's not legal. Still, we can always be best friends.'

He shouldn't have said that, because Cassie let out a little yell of rage, and it behoved Freddy then to hop it. She flew after him, up through King and Queen Street. She caught him outside her home. Freddy took a wallop. What a life, he thought, who'd have a friend like this? However, it was only a playful wallop, although it was followed by Cassie's declaration that if he didn't stop calling her his best friend, she'd put her dad on to him. She made her dad sound like a fearsome Alsatian. Freddy said he was only pointing out what he thought he ought to.

'All right, I forgive you,' said Cassie, and then let him know that if he had enough money saved up by the time she was nineteen, he could buy her a diamond engagement ring.

'That sounds like I've got to propose to you on yer nineteenth birthday,' said Freddy.

'Yes, and I second it,' said Cassie.

'Cassie, you sure you know what you're sayin'?' asked Freddy.

'Yes, and after we're engaged, you can start makin' your fortune so as to keep me in the manner to which I want to get accustomed,' said Cassie.

'Anything else?' grinned Freddy.

'Yes,' said Cassie, 'don't forget to put it in the minutes.'

On his way home on Friday evening, Nick called in at the paper shop. Gran said hello, and Ivy said would you like to meet me in the moonlight? Nick said he would, but wasn't keen on having Wally, her husband, knock his head off. His head was something he needed, he said. Gran said stop your teasing, Ivy.

'What can we do for yer, Nick?' she asked.

'Six tuppenny bars of Nestles milk chocolate,' said Nick.

'Six?' said Ivy.

'One each for six girls,' said Nick.

'Well, you're a dark one, you are,' said Ivy, 'six girls all at once. It's yer fatal charm. You and me won't get a look-in now, Gran.'

'Nick's a joker,' said Gran.

'Like 'is smile, don't we?' said Ivy, putting the six chocolate bars into a paper bag, and taking a shilling from Nick. 'Listen, Nick, why don't you 'ave a steady young lady?'

'I'm just taking my time,' said Nick.

'Well, don't take too long,' said Ivy, 'or you might get left in the lurch.'

'If I do, I'll come and help you behind your counter.'

'Under it, more like,' said Ivy.

'Not if I can 'elp it,' said Gran. 'Oh, I saw yer mum today, Nick, and was sorry to 'ear yer dad's not got any chance of comin' 'ome yet. I asked 'er about 'is ship, and she said the *Iron Duke*, so Wally's goin' to try and find out from 'is Navy friend if it's got any chance of at least bringin' yer dad back by next Easter.'

'Good of Wally,' said Nick.

'Well,' said Gran, 'what I say is that seein' that Parliament ain't much use to anyone except itself, we've all got to do what we can to 'elp each other. When me old man was alive, 'e went up to Parliament once to complain about what wasn't bein' done that should of been, and one of them MPs with a bald 'ead came out and told 'im everything was bein' done that 'ad to be done. Bert, me old man, said he 'adn't come there to listen to bleedin' lies, and 'e bounced a paperweight on the bloke's bald 'ead. The bloke fell over, and as the copper wasn't there at the time, me old man picked the bloke up, sat 'im on a bench and then came 'ome to 'is dinner. I asked 'im what he did that for, and Bert said it was natural for 'im to give anyone an 'elping 'and, even a baldheaded MP.'

'Sorry I never met your old man, Gran,' said Nick.

'So am I,' said Gran.

On arriving home, Nick spoke to Ma.

'That's it, then, Ma, you've put Pa aboard the *Iron Duke*, according to Gran Emerson.'

'Well, I 'ad to put 'im on some ship,' said Ma.

'Then let's hope the *Iron Duke* isn't floating about up in Scapa Flow,' said Nick.

'Scarper where?' said Ma.

'Scapa Flow, northern naval anchorage,' said Nick.

'Oh, well,' said Ma, 'as long as that's somewhere near the China Seas, it won't matter.'

Ma's perkiness was as constant as Pa's optimism.

As for Annabelle's uncle, he had made no attempt to summon Nick up to the fourth floor to put him through some kind of holy inquisition before having him burned at the stake. The episode over, God obviously preferred to let the matter rest.

Chapter Seven

After his Saturday morning office stint, Nick reached the front gate of his house just before one o'clock. A voice accosted his ears from behind as he opened the gate and walked through.

'Well, if it ain't young Nick, a chip orf the old block. 'Ow yer doin', matey?'

Nick turned. Where the bloke had come from was a mystery. He hadn't been aware of anyone on his heels, but there the bloke was. He was the kind of character who could do just that, pop up in front of one's eyes out of thin air. A lean whippet of a man, he had shiny black hair and a grinning look, and seemed as if he was just about to spring away in pursuit of a rabbit. Actually, he was always instinctively poised for a quick getaway from the cops. He wore an old black bowler and an old black mackintosh, summer and winter. Everyone in Hackney reckoned he was Mister Horsemouth's errand boy. Nick thought he was a bit more than an errand boy. He was known as Tosh Fingers.

'What're you doing on our doorstep?' asked Nick, who was looking forward to the afternoon's match against East Street Albion. If the Rovers didn't beat them by four clear goals, Nick would knock a few heads together.

'I've come to see yer, Nick, you and yer Ma,' said Tosh. 'Swelp me, ain't yer got an 'andsome mansion 'ere? I'm standin' 'ere admirin' of it. 'Ow is yer Ma, still perky?'

'What's your business?' asked Nick.

'Something to yer Ma's advantage, bless 'er,' said Tosh.

'I'm against something to her advantage,' said Nick, and Tosh winked.

'Course you are, Nick, course you are,' he said, his grin perpetual. 'You bein' in insurance, as I hear, you naturally feel something to yer Ma's advantage ain't in the small print. Well, I can tell yer it's straight up and no bent corners. She'll like it. I'll step in and 'ave a word with the two of yer, shall I?'

'All right, we'll give you ten minutes,' said Nick.

He and Ma entertained their caller in the parlour, while Alice took over the responsibility of getting the midday meal ready. Tosh Fingers vowed he was overcome at making Ma's acquaintance again, and Ma responded by telling him she hoped her neighbours didn't know he was in her house. Kindly get on with what you've come to say, she said.

'I'm wantin' to, Mabel,' he said.

'Mrs 'Arrison, if you don't mind,' said Ma, fairly certain, as Nick was, that Tosh had been in on the job that landed Pa with five years hard labour. 'I'm partic'lar about who calls me Mabel.'

'Course you are, missus, course you are,' said Tosh, 'which is why I'm proud to count meself an old friend.'

'Don't come it, just get on with it,' said Ma. 'No, wait a minute, I read in me paper last Monday that there'd been a jewel robbery in 'Ampstead. Was that something to do with you and them fingers of yours?'

''Ere, leave orf, Mabel,' protested Tosh, 'would I come 'ere with me pockets full of illegal sparklers and the rozzers on me tail? Course I wouldn't. What I've come for is to bring you good tidings.'

'Good what?' asked Ma.

'You got it,' said Tosh, bowler hat tipped forward to give his face a chance to hide itself, as was customary with his kind. 'First, me guv'nor that's been an 'elpful friend to yer unfortunate Albert asked me to let yer know yer lodger's movin' in tomorrer.'

'Oh, he's comin', is 'e?' said Ma. 'But on a Sunday? I never 'eard of any lodger movin' in on a Sunday.'

'No worries,' said Tosh, 'he ain't bringing a pantechnicon with 'im, just 'is bits and pieces.'

'I'll 'ave to get everything aired,' said Ma, looking bucked on account of the rent she'd be gathering in.

'I know yer will, Mabel,' said Tosh, 'but the guv'nor don't want yer to put yerself out. Albert's better 'alf is a lady, he said, so tell 'er she ain't expected to do any skivvying.'

'I'm obliged, I'm sure,' said Ma tartly.

'What's the bloke's name?' asked Nick.

'Toby Lukavitch,' said Tosh.

'Toby what?' asked Ma.

Tosh spelled it for her, then said, ''Is monicker ain't 'is own fault, yer know, it come from 'is parents.'

'Still, I never 'eard of any Loovakish before,' said Ma, ''ave you, Nick?'

'Not till now,' said Nick.

'Well, 'e's a Polish gent, yer see,' said Tosh. 'Missus, might I ask if you 'appen to 'ave a bottle of beer that I could wet me whistle with?'

'No, I 'aven't,' said Ma. 'It's been me life's work so far, makin' sure me son and daughters don't take to drink, like some I've seen in Hackney.'

'Only asked, missus,' said Tosh, 'no 'ard feelings, eh?'

'I must say I didn't expect a Polish lodger,' said Ma.

'Course yer didn't, Mabel, course yer didn't. No worries. Toby's a quiet-livin' gent that won't give no trouble. 'E'll rent all yer upstairs top at ten bob a week, and pay yer monthly, like, at two quid a time. Now, with me 'and on me jam tart, 'ere's the second bit of good tidings. It'll warm yer cockles. The guv'nor's got a kind eye for Nick 'ere and is willin' to give 'im a chance to learn the profession.'

'What profession?' asked Ma sharply.

'The earning one, Mabel, the earning one,' said Tosh, tapping the side of his nose. 'It grieves the guv'nor, yer know, that Albert's only son is only scrapin' a livin' as a pen-pusher, which won't get 'im nowhere. Anyone can see 'e looks as much of a gent as 'is Pa does, and that he ought to be in the same profession. He only needs a bit of smart coachin', and the guv'nor, whose name I won't mention—'

'Well, I will,' said Nick, 'you're talking about Monty Cooper, known as Mister Horsemouth.'

'Well, course I am, Nick, but not out loud,' said Tosh. 'It ain't done in the profession to talk out loud. Any rate, the guv'nor likes the way you've grown up a gent, 'aving 'ad the pleasure of sometimes seein' you on 'is 'elpful calls, and 'e'll look after yer expenses while yer bein' polished up.'

'I can't believe what I'm listenin' to,' said Ma.

'I grant yer that what the guv'nor is willin' to do for partic'lar friends can bring a lump to yer throat,' said Tosh.

'Who's going to teach me the profession and polish me up?' asked Nick.

'The guv'nor's give me the honour,' said Tosh. 'I'll take yer to the races first—'

'Excuse me a minute,' said Ma, and made a brisk exit.

'Where's she gorn?' asked Tosh.

'We'll find out in a moment,' said Nick.

Back came Ma, carrying her broom. With it, she set about Tosh. She bashed his bowler with it, thumped his breadbasket with it, and pushed it into his hooter. Spring-heeled Tosh, caught napping for once, took a hiding before he came to and vanished. He disappeared with one bound, his fixed grin racked with disbelief.

'If he comes back, knock 'is head off, d'you 'ear me?' said Ma.

'Pleasure, Ma.'

'I'm not 'aving a common criminal like 'im learn you 'is kind of profession,' said Ma.

'I'm not having it myself,' said Nick.

'You'd better not,' said Ma, 'or you'll get worse than me broom, you'll get me puddin' saucepan. Still,' she said, perking up, 'there's a silver lining. We're goin' to get ten bob a week from a lodger. I'll do me best to put a bit aside every week to buy the girls Sunday frocks and p'raps a bowler hat and umbrella for you.'

'I'll leave home if you do,' said Nick.

Browning Street Rovers entered Brockwell Park at a quarter to three for the game against East Street

Albion. There were six supporters with them, Dumpling, Cassie, Alice, Fanny, Julie Hurst and Meg Miles. The latter two were the girlfriends of Ronnie Smith and Charlie Cope respectively. Dumpling's hearty dad, Mr Evans, was also there. It was the Rovers' turn to supply a referee, and Mr Evans had volunteered, as he often did. Dumpling herself was to be a linesman. She was always willing to perform any kind of service for the Rovers, as long as it didn't mean entertaining Danny in her mum's parlour with the light out. Dumpling was dead against that kind of thing. She considered it a waste of time compared to football, anyway.

A few minutes before the match began, the captain of the East Street lot raised an objection to having Dumpling as one of the linesmen.

'Get 'er orf,' he said, 'we ain't in favour of no female.'

'Why, you're not shy, are you?' said Nick.

'What d'yer mean, shy? Course we're not shy. We ain't 'aving a fat female linesman, that's all.'

Dumpling, warmly clad in a woollen hat, outsize jumper, skirt and sheepskin waistcoat from Petticoat Lane, showed the objector a plump fist and asked him if he wanted his hooter turned into mashed potato. He took a good look at her fist, blinked at it, then grinned.

'All right, Fatty, keep yer shirt on,' he said.

'Watch your cakehole,' said Dumpling, and her dad gave Nick a wink.

The game opened with East Street Albion kicking off. The Rovers at once set about them amid vociferous encouragement from their supporters. The girls had each received a chocolate bar, a treat in these days of low wages and limited pocket money, and accordingly had elected not to ask for more, although not because of any threat to tan them. They were all old enough to dismiss that as hot air, and spirited enough to half-murder any bloke who tried it. In any case, Dumpling had refused to enter it in the minutes. She always wrote the minutes for Nick, and reckoned that any non-entry made a proposal illegal.

Up and down the touchline she galloped, flag in her hand. Danny, quite a nice bloke, with a down-to-earth cockney honesty, watched her bouncing movements with fondness and admiration.

'Go it, Freddy!' shouted Cassie. Her dreamy nature never toned down her exuberant tonsils whenever Freddy was in full cry on a football pitch. He was in full cry now, the ball at his feet. He beat an opponent with ease and then hit a rattling good pass to Nick. Nick collected it, made rings round the East Street centre half, and slipped the ball through to his left winger. Up went Dumpling's flag.

'Offside!' she yelled, and her dad blew his whistle for a free kick to the East Street lot.

'Who said offside?' bawled the culprit, Starving Crow.

'I did!' shouted Dumpling.

'My life, can I believe it?' said Starving Crow. It was all right for Dumpling to be an impartial linesman, but not as impartial as that.

Not that the free kick did much for East Street Albion. The Rovers went at them again. Nick had ordered his team to win the match by four clear goals. Dumpling had seconded it. In a kind way, Danny said he didn't think she could second that. Well, I have, said Dumpling, so you'd all better get on with it. The Rovers did just that, Nick playing

114

an attacking game with gusto and a lot of natural flair.

They were two goals up after half an hour, and five minutes later Nick scored their third with a cracking shot from the edge of the penalty area. Dumpling beamed in temporary forgetfulness of her impartial role. Coming back to the centre line with her flag, she said to Cassie, 'Did yer see that goal of Nick's? What a beauty.'

'Yes, Nick and Freddy are the best players in the team,' said Cassie, and Dumpling bounced back to her duties.

'Cassie, I 'eard that,' said Meg Miles. Meg was special to Charlie Cope, the Rovers' goalkeeper. Charlie had what every goalkeeper needed, a safe pair of hands, although Meg told her mum once that they didn't make her feel safe herself. Well, you'd better stop sitting in the parlour with him on Sunday afternoons, then, said her mum, which was typical of the protective mums of Walworth. Still, Charlie always assured Meg he'd respect her honour, so she said loyally to Cassie, 'Don't forget Charlie's easy the best goalie in Walworth.'

'Oh, I couldn't agree more, Meg,' said Cassie, 'Nick and Freddy are always sayin' the team feel safe in Charlie's 'ands.'

Meg giggled.

'Meg's gigglin',' said young Fanny.

'Well, she knows her Charlie,' said Cassie. Fanny said it was funny that the Rovers were the only team with a lot of girl supporters. Julie Hurst, Ronnie Smith's girlfriend, said that was because the Rovers were the best-looking blokes with the best-looking knees. Freddy had lovely knees, she said, any girl could fancy them. Cassie trod on her foot.

'Here, Cassie, mind what y'er doin',' said Julie.

'Oh, sorry,' said Cassie sweetly.

Alice smiled.

With the Rovers swarming all over the Albion, Fanny said, 'Cassie's Freddy's best friend.'

'Well, I can't begrudge 'im his good luck, even if he 'as got some funny ways,' said Cassie. 'Well, you 'ave to resign yourself to most boys not bein' all there. An aunt of mine told me once that it's their growing-up pains, that you 'ave to take them in hand. She said you 'ave to rattle their brains a bit. Everyone knows I've done my best to take Freddy in hand for years, but 'e's still got funny ways. D'you 'ave anyone like Freddy that you're takin' in hand, Alice – hi, foul, ref!'

'Send 'im off!' yelled Fanny. Nick had just been tripped and trodden on by a frustrated East Street opponent with no manners. The ref, Dumpling's dad, gave him a talking-to. Nick took the free kick himself. He struck the ball hard and only the crossbar prevented another score.

The ref blew for half-time, and up came the footballers for their slices of lemon, hair a bit wind-blown, jerseys breathing warmly around robust chests, knees muddy here and there. Fanny, who always brought the slices of lemon in a sealed jamjar, unscrewed the lid and the Rovers dipped their fingers in. Cockney chit-chat took place.

'Bless yer, Fanny, and yer Monday washin'.'

'Come up trumps ev'ry week, you do, Fanny.'

'I'll be knockin' for yer in a few years, Fanny.'

'Can't wait, can I?' said saucy young Fanny.

'Cross me 'eart, Fanny, y'er me fav'rite bird already.'

'My life, Fanny, ain't you got meltin' peepers?' said Starving Crow, who had a loving Yiddish heart for football and his gentile team mates.

'Crikey,' said young Fanny, 'you don't all 'ave to go potty, not all of you.'

Dumpling, her face and garments all wearing a beam, butted in. 'Three goals up, you girls. Ain't the blokes performin' miraculous? We're famous, us Rover supporters, yer know, bein' all girls together. Mind, I'm like one of the blokes meself, bein' a footballer like they are. When you're a bit older, Fanny, you'll 'ave to watch some of them at Christmas, they call round on the girls with mistletoe, and Julie told me that what can 'appen under the mistletoe with a Rover would make Santa Claus fall off 'is sleigh. Mind, I think that sort of thing's a bit soppy meself.'

'Crikey, what a bit of luck I'm not old enough for it,' said Fanny.

'Nick's old enough,' said Meg, 'but he still doesn't 'ave a girl.'

'Well, he's like me,' said Dumpling, 'he doesn't go in for all that daft stuff. Football's best, and Nick's got a natural captain's way of puttin' it first. But no-one minds, you 'ave to 'ave a captain that don't go in for bein' soppy. I'm goin' to listen to 'im now tellin' the team 'ow to slaughter the East Street lot in the second 'alf.'

'Tell Freddy to start scorin' some goals,' said Cassie.

Five minutes into the second half, Freddy did his best mate proud by scoring the Rovers' fourth goal.

'Bless 'im,' said Cassie.

'And all his funny ways,' said Alice.

'Why doesn't Nick go out with a girl?' asked Cassie.

'He's waitin',' said Alice.

'What for?'

'Someone special, I suppose,' said Alice.

'Well, I think we're all special,' said Julie.

'I'm more special than anybody,' said Cassie, 'you can ask Freddy.'

'Go it, Rovers!' yelled Fanny, jumping about.

The vigorous Rovers were running the East Street lot off their feet, the girl supporters on a high note of enthusiasm. Even so, Ronnie Smith, the Rovers' centre forward, with an open goal in front of him, ballooned the ball over the bar.

'Rubbish!' yelled Fanny.

''Ere, d'you mind?' said Julie Hurst, Ronnie's steady date.

'Is it my fault he's got two left feet?' said Fanny.

But the team polished off their opponents by running out winners six goals to one. Dumpling, her impartial role as a linesman over, bounced about in rapture and actually gave Danny a cuddle for his performance at right back.

'Could yer manage a kiss as well?' he asked. Dumpling's rosebud lips were plump and dewy.

'No, course I couldn't,' said Dumpling, 'me life's devoted to the team, not to daft kissin'.'

'You could break a bloke's 'eart, you could,' said Danny.

'Oh, all right,' said Dumpling, 'you can sit next to me on the tram goin' 'ome.'

'Bless yer,' said Danny.

'Now go and get changed,' said Dumpling, and off he went with the rest of the team. 'I don't know,' said Dumpling to the girls, 'don't blokes get

118

barmy ideas about us? Fancy always wantin' to kiss us.'

'I think it's a bit more than that, Chrissie,' said Alice.

'Yes, I've 'eard what a bit more is,' said Dumpling, 'but they ain't gettin' it from me.'

The girls shrieked.

On their home-going tram, the Rovers were in high spirits, with Dumpling receiving praise from her hearty dad for her good work as a linesman.

'Oh, I never like to let meself down on a football pitch, Dad,' she said. 'And what a team we've got, don't yer think?'

'Nippy,' said Mr Evans, 'and likewise slick.'

'I'm the reserve goalie, yer know,' said Dumpling, 'and a permanent member of the committee till me dyin' day.'

'I'm honoured to be sittin' next to 'er, Mr Evans,' said Danny.

'I don't mind you feelin' honoured,' said Dumpling, 'but just watch that arm of yours, it's tryin' to cuddle me.'

''Elp yerself, Danny,' grinned Mr Evans, who liked Danny and encouraged him in his pursuit of Dumpling.

'Yer a born cuddle, Dumpling,' said Charlie Cope.

'I don't tell a lie, Dumpling, Solomon would fancy yer 'imself,' said Starving Crow.

'Who's 'e?' asked Dumpling.

'My life,' said Starving Crow, 'ain't I heard that the Queen of Sheba was a fav'rite cuddle of his?'

'Well, soppy old Solomon, then,' said Dumpling, 'and I don't think much of 'er, either. Fancy all that daft cuddlin' when they could've been playin' football.'

On the upper deck of the tram, the victorious Rovers fell about.

Chapter Eight

The Polish gent, Mr Toby Lukavitch, arrived at ten the next morning, with a large trunk. A bloke with an old-fashioned look, driving a pony and cart of East End vintage, delivered passenger and trunk to Ma's door. When she heard the knock, she took Nick with her to answer it, feeling sure the expected lodger was on her doorstep. Being uncertain of Polish gents, she felt safer having Nick beside her.

Opening the door, she saw a lean gent of middling height, with a five o'clock shadow and neat black eyebrows. He wore a grey trilby hat, an unbuttoned grey serge overcoat over a blue serge suit, and polished black shoes. A luggage trunk stood on the doorstep beside him.

'Ah, good morning, madam,' he said, raising his hat. His smile revealed slightly irregular white teeth.

'Good mornin',' said Ma, 'are you Mr Loovak-ish?'

'Lukavitch, madam, Lukavitch.'

'Yes, that's it,' said Ma in her perky way. 'I'm Mrs 'Arrison and this is my son Nick.'

''Arrison?'

'Harrison,' said Nick.

'Ah, pleased to meet you, Mrs Harrison,' said the Polish gent. 'And your son Nick.'

Nick shook hands with him.

'Come in,' said Ma, and Nick helped him deposit the heavy trunk in the passage. Mr Lukavitch looked around and smiled happily.

'You know it's three rooms on the upstairs top at ten bob a week?' said Nick.

'Ah, yes, good, eh?' said Mr Lukavitch.

'It's all self-contained, like a nice little flat,' said Ma, looking him over. Deciding he didn't have the appearance of a lodger who'd get drunk and fall down the stairs, she said, 'We'd best take you up and let you see for yourself.'

'You bet, eh?' he said.

Ma led the way up the stairs, Nick and the Polish gent following, carrying the trunk between them. When they reached the top landing, Mr Lukavitch said he liked the look of the house, and that perhaps it was free of bugs and fleas. Ma let him know at once that she didn't allow things of that kind to share her home, she never had and never would.

'Ah, that is pleasing, don't you think?' he beamed, and he then made an inspection of what was on offer. The large front bedroom overlooked Browning Street, and the middle bedroom and the living-room both overlooked the backyard. The living-room had a compact range and a gas ring, and on the landing was the lav, with a handbasin. Mr Lukavitch gave everything a nod and a smile, and kept saying, 'I like, madam, I like.'

Ma asked Nick in a whisper why the gent kept calling her madam. It made her feel like a French madam, and she'd never been one of those. Heaven forbid, she whispered. Nick said Polish gents probably called all ladies madam.

'Suit you, Mr Lukavitch?' he said, when the inspection was over.

Mr Lukavitch, smiling, said, 'Bloody good, eh?'

'Beg your pardon?' said Ma, slightly shocked despite being broadminded.

'I am in England many years,' said Mr Lukavitch. 'I come in 1919, after the bloody Bolsheviks killed many Polish people. Now I speak the London language well, eh? I know there is bloody good, ruddy good and bleedin' good. Also how's your father, how's your canary, up the apples and pears, and corblimey, mate. I also speak London upper class language, like I say, old chap, tophole, bless my soul, how'd you do and dear me, have a banana. Also, who was that lady I saw you with last night? You see, not bad, eh?' His smile asked for approval.

'Well, I must say you're a surprise to me,' said Ma.

'Ah, yes, bleedin' good, eh?'

'If I might mention it,' said Ma, 'I don't want too much language. I've got three growin' girls that can speak very nice, 'aving been taught by their dad not to sound common.'

'Strike a light, there are three?' said Mr Lukavitch, hat in his hand and a little bald patch showing on the crown of his head. Nick judged him to be about forty-five. 'I am happy for you, madam.'

'I don't know about madam,' said Ma cautiously. 'Well, I'm not French, Mr Loovakish.'

'Not French, no,' said Mr Lukavitch. He gave it some thought, then smiled again. 'Of course, yes, I know English like old girl, old lady, old biddy and how are you, old cock?'

'Well, you're up with us cockneys, Mr Lukavitch,' said Nick, hiding a grin, 'but it'll be best if you call my mother Mrs Harrison or missus.'

'Missus, yes, I know missus. Also Mrs Harrison.'

Mr Lukavitch beamed at Ma. 'Pleased to meet you, missus, yes, good morning, eh?'

'Mutual, I'm sure,' said Ma.

'Not 'alf,' said Nick. 'Where've you been living, Mr Lukavitch?'

'Where it's called Mile End. You know? Bleedin' fleas and bugs.' Mr Lukavitch gestured with his hat. 'And bleedin' kids, eh?'

'And a lot of language, if I know anything about Mile End,' said Ma. 'Anyway, are the rooms all right, did you say?'

'You bet. One for sleeping, one for living and one for working, all ruddy good.'

'Workin'?' said Ma. 'What work?'

'I make little things that shops sell as small gifts,' said Mr Lukavitch cheerfully. 'I am good at it, but not rich. Never mind, I'm at home in London very much. My other lodgings were in a house falling down. Corblimey, mate, you should have seen.'

'Well, we're not fallin' down, so you'll be all right 'ere,' said Ma. 'Oh, by the way, me 'usband's in the Royal Navy.' She got that one in without batting an eyelid.

'Royal Navy?' Mr Lukavitch looked delighted. 'Ah, the Royal Navy that goes where the sun never sets, I think, eh?'

'Yes, and me 'usband's in the China Seas just now,' said Ma. 'I don't know about the sun never settin' there, but I do know something ought to be done about the Chinese pirates 'e has to fight.'

'I sympathize, missus, you bet,' said Mr Lukavitch. 'Now I will unpack, but first I must pay some rent. I know it must be in advance, and for a month this first time, eh?' He fished around in his coat pocket and brought out two pound notes. Ma, looking extremely perky now, took the money and said it was very obliging of him. Nick said a rent book would have to be supplied, and Ma said she'd see to it, and then they left the lodger to his unpacking.

Down in the kitchen, the girls wanted to know all about everything, and Ma told them Mr Loovakish had turned out to be quite a nice Polish gent. Mr Lukavitch, said Nick. Yes, said Ma, and he's come from lodgings in the Mile End and picked up a bit of Mile End language. They'd all have to excuse him.

'What kind of Mile End language has he picked up?' asked Alice.

'Bleedin' good, ruddy carbolic, gorblimey O'Reilly and how's your canary,' said Nick.

'What, when he's Polish?' said Amy.

'Well, it's something like that,' said Ma.

'Well, fancy that,' said young Fanny. ''Ow's yer canary, Ma?'

'To show we're 'ospitable, I think I'll make 'im a cup of tea,' said Ma.

'Corblimey, 'ere we go,' said Alice.

In the afternoon, the family went to visit Pa in Marsham Gaol down in the wilds of Kent. They wore everyday clothes, not their Sunday best. They never did wear their Sunday best on any visit to Pa. Ma felt that if they did, they'd look a bit too posh, which might make the prison authorities think they'd dug up the missing sparklers from somewhere and were living a life of luxury. Actually, Ma had never asked questions about where the loot had finished up. No doubt Mister Horsemouth could have told her, but Ma didn't want to know.

She wanted to be able to look the law in the eye as the innocent and aggrieved wife of a man who'd been unfairly copped.

'Afternoon, Mrs Harrison,' said a warder, when the family alighted from the special bus inside the prison gates. 'How's things with you and yours on this 'appy day?'

'We're bearin' up,' said Ma. 'Mind, it's not easy, seein' Mr 'Arrison has been more unlucky than unlawful. Is he bearin' up 'imself?'

'Well, he's still in the swing of things, Mrs Harrison, as you might say.'

'Beg your pardon?' said Ma.

'With 'is pickaxe,' said the warder, unleashing a broad grin.

'It's criminal, all that hard labour for a gent like me 'usband,' said Ma, 'and what I want to know is if he's gettin' good marks.'

'Straight up, Mrs Harrison, it's all good marks and no black ones. He's workin' in the prison library once a week now, and might be twice a week soon. Got something for him in that shoppin' bag, have you?'

'Six Chelsea buns and a treacle tart,' said Ma.

'I'll have to have a look,' said the warder. Other warders were examining what other visitors were carrying.

'You and your suspicious noses round 'ere,' said Ma. The warder grinned again. He inspected the contents of her shopping bag, which contained a treacle tart in a tin and six Chelsea buns in a cardboard box.

'Pass, friend and fam'ly, with tart and buns,' said the warder. Ma and her family always induced good humour in the staff.

'Wait a bit,' said Nick, 'do all hard labour cases get a chance to do library work?'

'Not bleedin' likely,' said the warder, 'the governor's stretched the rules for your old man, especially as he still 'asn't coughed up the unfound proceeds. Pity about that, he's not a bad bloke. He offered to get me a gold watch at a knock-down price when he's done his time.'

'What?' said Ma, bristling a bit.

'You're right, Mrs Harrison, you wouldn't think he'd try that one on in here, would you? In you go.'

Marsham Gaol was like a grey stone fortress on the outside. On the inside, it was all monotonous tiled walls. But the spacious room where visiting relatives could talk to inmates was quite cheerful, mainly because several windows, although barred, let in a flood of light. October sunshine was almost caressing the room today. Various visitors were already there, sitting at tables and conversing with men who'd been daft enough to do crooked deeds and get themselves copped and convicted.

Everyone turned their heads to look at the Harrison family. Ma was a picture of neat respectability, and the girls entered without hanging their heads. Although they regretted Pa's wrong-doing, they weren't ashamed of him. As for Nick, he was taken up with the possibility that Pa's obvious good behaviour might earn him several months off his full stretch. As it was, he still had a year and five months to go. If that came down to a year, thought Nick, I could start looking at what Ma would call pleasurable prospects next autumn, say.

Pa came in when they'd seated themselves at a vacant table under one of the windows. He was wearing his convict's clothes, but somehow he never seemed to look like a convict. He always looked more like a handsome gent wearing prison garb for a fancy dress party. Well, he'd always taken a pride in his appearance, and even if he didn't like being shut up inside stone walls at night, his daytime hard labour had given him a quite healthy colour. Other men had a prison pallor.

He arrived at the table clean-shaven and cheerful, his hair brushed and his blue eyes as clear as a saint's.

'Hello, sailor,' said the girls in concert as he sat down. That made him grin, and it also made him lively. He told Ma she was getting younger every day, and he told the girls they were all looking like Christmas fairies. It's only October, said Amy. Can't help that, said Pa, you all look like fairies on a Christmas tree. He said Nick was looking manly, but hoped he wouldn't turn into a wet weekend through working in an insurance office. Work in an office or a factory is all right for some people, he said, but not for young chaps with inherited talent and a bit of ambition. All you need, Nick, is a West End suit and a handsome titfer. Then you could sell diamond rings to Her Majesty herself.

Ma went for him, of course. Not that she shouted. She never did. She wasn't a shouting woman, especially not in this place, where common criminals would hear her. Further, there were always two warders present, not only to keep order but to make sure nothing illegal went on, such as visitors slipping forbidden items to prisoners, like files for sawing bars, or dynamite for blowing the prison up. Ma went for Pa in a low cutting voice.

She told him she couldn't believe he was still daft, and that he was showing his whole family that he hadn't learned any sense. Don't you encourage Nick to dress in flash suits to try and sell your kind of diamond rings to our beloved Queen, she said. It's not the first time you've tried to give him the wrong ideas. I've a good mind to take this cake tin out of my shopping bag and knock your head off, she said.

'Take the treacle tart out first, Ma,' said Nick.

'Treacle tart?' said Pa happily. 'Mabel, me dear old Dutch, you're a blessing to a man down on his luck, Lord love your caring heart.'

'There's Chelsea buns as well, Pa,' said young Fanny.

'May the soldiers of the Lord jump on the devil,' said Pa, 'that's uplifting news straight from heaven.'

'Bless you, Pa,' said Amy.

'Don't start blessing 'im, not till he's reformed,' said Ma. 'Albert 'Arrison, you won't get the tart or the buns if you don't get your brains sorted out.' She went on to tell Pa that even if he was doing hard labour on account of accidental circumstances, that didn't mean he'd got to hold a grudge against the law and not do honest work when he came out. And what d'you mean, she said, by offering to get a gold watch for that warder Mr Brinkley? Pa said it was only as a favour. Ma said she didn't want any of his fairy stories. We all know where them gold watches come from, she said. From that grinning Flash Harry who calls himself Tosh Fingers. I might tell you, she said, that he had the sauce to show up yesterday offering to teach Nick how to make a living without doing any work.

'I think I heard he was going to offer his services,' said Pa. 'Well, his heart's in the right place, I suppose.'

'Yes, in 'is overcoat pocket, with 'is gold watches,' said Ma.

'I'll say this much,' observed Pa, 'Nick's grown the right kind of looks for cutting a dash with people who've got a useful amount of loose change in their pockets.'

'Pa, you terror,' said Alice.

'I think I also heard there was a lodger on his way to you, Mabel,' said Pa.

'Yes, he moved in this mornin',' said Ma.

'Rent?' said Pa.

'Ten bob a week,' said Nick.

'That should help,' said Pa. 'What's he like?'

'He's Polish,' said Nick.

'Ma told us he talks funny English,' said Fanny.

'Common to Polish geezers, Fanny me pet,' said Pa, 'and of no account compared to what ten bob a week can do for your Ma.'

'Yes, but suppose he gets drunk and falls down the stairs?' asked Alice.

'I trust a certain acquaintance of mine won't have landed you with a lodger who can't hold his drink,' said Pa.

Ma said she had a suspicious feeling that Pa still had an acquaintance with a law-breaking Hackney lot, and that if he didn't give them up his life wouldn't be worth living when he came out. Pa assured her that when he was back home he was going to use some savings to set up a business in the Portobello Road market. Ma wanted to know what savings he had in mind. Pa said confidential savings. Ma said she'd never heard of confidential savings. Pa said he couldn't go into details here, but not to worry, she could look forward to him setting up the aforesaid business, which would be selling Old Masters in the Portobello Road.

'What's Old Masters?' asked Amy.

'I've heard of them,' said Alice, 'I think they're paintings.'

'What, paintings of old schoolmasters?' said Amy.

'Whatever they are, I don't like the sound of them,' said Ma. She was sitting up straight, as she always did in this place. It dissociated her from the other visitors, whom she thought either blowsy or common.

'Old Masters are valuable,' said Nick. 'Who's going to paint yours for you, Pa?'

Pa, trying to look hurt, said what he had in mind were highly prized pictures that gentry would pay hundreds of quids for. Old pictures, he said, Old Masters. Nick asked him where he was going to get them from.

'Glad you asked, Nick,' he said. 'It so happens that Tosh Fingers—' He stopped. Ma's eyes were like fixed gimlets. 'What was I saying?' he asked.

'Don't come it,' said Ma.

'Well,' said Pa, 'I'm not saying the bloke isn't slightly dubious—'

'He's a crook,' said Alice.

'All oily,' said Amy.

'Ruddy common,' said young Fanny.

Pa said he was surprised to hear Fanny using language. Ma said Fanny had got it from Nick, who'd got it from their Polish lodger only this morning. Pa said have a word with the gent. Anyway, he said, he wouldn't get his Old Masters from Tosh Fingers, no, certainly not. He had legal sources in mind. Ma said we know about your legal sources, Albert Harrison, and you can forget whoever it is, or I'll send Nick round to give him a nasty headache. Just be grateful, she said, that you've got an honest son already able to knock people like that Mr Fingers into the middle of next week, and also being as good as a comforting father to the girls.

'Don't you mean bossy, Ma?' said Alice.

'Now, Alice, mind your manners,' said Ma. She and her son and daughters all seemed oblivious to the true meaning of this place, and to the presence of several inmates visibly hard-bitten. They always directed their attentions at Pa alone for the most part. And for the most part, Pa acted much more like a guest than a prisoner. Alice truly believed that if he'd made up to that American woman instead of chucking an eiderdown over her silly head, he wouldn't be here.

When their visiting time was nearly up, Ma took the cake tin and cardboard box out of her shopping bag. One of the warders was on the spot immediately. He inspected the contents of the tin and box.

'Well, well, what've we got 'ere, Harrison?' he said. 'Looks like treacle tart and Chelsea buns. You sure he deserves 'em, Mrs Harrison?'

'Don't you try purloining them,' said Ma, 'or I'll have the law on you.'

'So will I,' said Fanny.

'I'm shakin' in me boots,' said the warder. 'All the same, I've got to admit I'm partial to Chelsea buns.'

'Well, all right,' said Ma, sensible enough to know it was a help to Pa to sweeten his gaolers, 'if Mr 'Arrison says you can 'ave one, I won't argue.'

'And I'd be failing suffering humanity if I couldn't part with one bun,' said Pa. 'No, take two,

Mr Robertson, take two, and if ever Mrs Robertson fancies a silver bracelet, just get in touch with me. No rubbish, I guarantee.'

'He's a natural comic, your old man, Mrs Harrison,' said the warder, helping himself to two buns, 'and I'm Simple Simon when I ain't pickling heads.'

'Pickling heads?' said Alice.

'Right first time, miss,' said the warder, 'it 'appens to be the best thing for most of the heads we've got in Marsham.' Off he went with his buns, which gave Ma a chance to berate Pa for doing his gold watch lark again. Silver bracelet, actually, said Pa. Same thing, said Ma. Pa said the offer had slipped out absent-mindedly. Time was up then. Just as well, said Ma, or I might just 'ave done something absent-mindedly myself, and left you with a nasty headache.

Pa said goodbye with a cheerful smile, and most of the way home by bus and train, the girls talked about how well he was bearing up. Young Fanny said it was corblimey awful that he had to be in a place like that. But by the time the family were back home, Ma had put him in the Royal Navy again. Well, a neighbour stopped them in Browning Street and asked the usual questions about him, and Ma supplied the usual answers.

That evening, Ma thought the lodger had better meet the girls, so that he could see they were being well brought up. She'd heard that some daughters of some landladies, being a bit fast, didn't at all mind being chased up and down the stairs by lodgers when their mums and dads were out. Ma thought it would be a good idea to let Mr Lukavitch know she didn't allow any of her daughters to be fast.

In response to her invitation, Mr Lukavitch came down to the kitchen in the evening. He looked comfortably casual in belted trousers and an old striped flannel shirt. His black hair was slightly ruffled, his ready smile brightening his dark eyes. Ma, not disapproving of his informal look, since it seemed to indicate he was already making himself at home in the upstairs top, introduced him to Nick's sisters.

'This is Fanny, Mr Loovakish. She's me youngest and me snowy lamb.'

'Ah, Fanny?' Mr Lukavitch shook hands with her, and Fanny's saucy eyes looked him over. 'How'd you do, eh? Pleased to meet you, cor-blimey, not half.'

'Same to you,' said Fanny, giggling.

'And this is Amy, me middle girl,' said Ma.

'Ah, middle?' said Mr Lukavitch. 'I know, middle for diddle, eh? Pleased to meet you, Amy.' He shook her hand. 'My word, bleedin' pretty, I think, don't I?'

'Crikey,' said Amy.

'Language, Mr Loovakish,' said Ma. 'And 'ere's me eldest daughter, Alice, that's got an office job.'

'She's the ticklish one,' said Nick.

'Ah, Alice, eh?' said Mr Lukavitch, and took in her neat and attractive look. 'Ruddy tophole,' he said. 'You're liking a tickle or two? Up and down the apples and pears with your young man?'

'Excuse me,' said Ma, 'but we don't 'ave any of that in this house. All my girls are 'ighly respect-able.'

'I am happy for them, missus,' smiled Mr

Lukavitch, 'and very pleased to meet Alice.' He shook hands with her. 'You are in the pink?'

'Yes, I'm quite well, thank you,' said Alice, looking as if she wanted to laugh.

'What good luck for me,' said Mr Lukavitch, beaming. 'I am in the house of a fine family, I think, don't I? All pretty girls too. Mrs Harrison, I'm allowed to give them a small gift?'

'Well,' said Ma, satisfied he understood her girls weren't to be chased up and down the stairs, 'I'm sure they won't say no.'

'Good,' said Mr Lukavitch. He dug into his trouser pocket and brought out four strings of polished coloured beads. 'All my own work, you see? If you please, one for Fanny, the young lady.'

'Lovaduck,' breathed Fanny in delight as she received a string, 'ain't they swish?'

'And one for Amy, the middle girl, yes?' said the lodger, and Amy received her gift rapturously.

'Crikey, thanks a lot,' she said.

'And now one for Alice, the old girl, eh?' said Mr Lukavitch, handing a string to her.

'They'll do our old girl proud,' said Nick.

'Corblimey, you bet,' said Mr Lukavitch, 'they will suit how young you are as the old one, Alice.'

'You said that just in time,' said Alice, 'but thanks ever so, they really are nice.'

'Yes, I'm bloody good at making them,' said Mr Lukavitch. 'And now, this last one for your mother. Mrs Harrison, allow me.' He placed the necklace in Ma's hand. She looked quite overcome.

'Well, I never did, I'm honoured, I'm sure, Mr Loovakish, and so are my girls. What lovely beads, and all your own work.'

'Ruddy tophole, eh? I shape and polish and put

together like an artist, don't I? Bleedin' right I
do.'

'Mr Loovakish, if you could just moderate your
language a bit in front of the girls, I'd be obliged,'
said Ma.

'Moderate is fine, eh?' Mr Lukavitch beamed
again. 'I'm happy to speak such good London
English with your girls. Ah, see how pretty the
beads look.'

The colourful necklaces adorned the girls, and
Ma's looked really fancy.

'Imagine you made them yourself, Mr Lukavitch,' said Amy.

'Good, eh?' he said. 'But no, not Mr Lukavitch
now we are friends. In Poland, I am Toblisch.
Here, everyone calls me Toby. What d'you think,
eh? Toby?'

'Well, I don't know it wouldn't be too familiar,
callin' you that when they've only just met you,'
said Ma. 'Their Pa, bein' in the Navy, don't 'old
with them bein' familiar.'

'Any old time, eh, Mrs Harrison?'

'Yes, any old time after we've got to know you,'
said Nick.

'Ruddy good,' said Mr Lukavitch. 'Now I must
leave you, don't I? Up the apples and pears to my
rooms, eh? Goodbye, young one, middle one and
old one, we shall meet again, don't you think?
Goodbye, old cock.' He gave Nick a friendly pat on
the shoulder, and he gave Ma a smile. 'Goodbye,
Mrs Harrison.' He departed upstairs.

'Well, I don't mind havin' a lodger now,' said
Fanny.

'Not when he gives presents like these,' said
Amy.

'I'm in two minds, not havin' been called an old lady before,' said Alice.

'I suppose some women get to it a bit quicker than others,' said Nick.

'And some fellers get a bash over the head a lot quicker than others,' said Alice.

'I must say it's nice 'aving a kind gent as a lodger, and not one that falls about drunk,' said Ma.

'There's still time,' said Alice, 'he's not been here a full day yet.'

But altogether she and the girls seemed pleased they didn't have a lodger who looked as if he'd fall about drunk and break the furniture, even if he did speak his own kind of London English.

On Monday morning, a piece of front page news in the daily paper really got Ma's goat.

'I could spit,' she said. That was strong for Ma. 'They've done it again, would you believe.'

'Who've done what again?' asked Alice.

'Them common criminals,' said Ma, 'they've got away with another jewel robbery, at a house in Park Lane, right in the middle of London. They did it Saturday night, the 'ome of a widowed countess, poor woman.'

'She's probably still a rich one,' said Nick.

'That's not the point,' said Ma, 'and I don't 'old with bein' envious, anyway. I'm not sayin' I wouldn't like a bit of what the rich have got, but not all of it.'

'Well, Pa's always felt the same,' said Alice, 'and he's spent years doin' what he could to get his bit.'

'Well, 'e did bring home a few wallets, I'll admit,' said Ma, 'but 'e was never a common burglar, not like them that's doin' these robberies. It's fair upsettin' me that they're gettin' away with it. I've a good mind to go round to the police station this mornin' and give them what for, but I've got the washin' to do. You're both off to your jobs now?'

'Yes, Ma,' said Alice.

'Well, when you're on your way, give some thought to your Pa and what he's sufferin' on account of bein' unfortunate.'

'It's rough out there in the China Seas,' said Nick, and thought about Pa on his way to work. And that made him think of the fix he and Alice were in. He couldn't take up with a girl and Alice couldn't encourage any young man while Pa was in clink, doing hard labour like a common criminal. That in turn made him think of a girl who liked toasted crumpets and had the kind of looks Mr Lukavitch would probably call tophole. But what was the point of thinking of her? She'd appeared, just for an hour or so, and then she'd disappeared. Just as well under the circumstances.

On his way home from work, Nick called in at Gran Emerson's shop for a packet of fags. The shop didn't close until six, and he arrived with several minutes to spare. Gran and Ivy greeted him in their usual individual ways, Gran cheerfully and Ivy flirtatiously. They sold him his packet of Players, and then Gran said that her son Wally wasn't sure about the *Iron Duke*.

'It's a battleship,' said Nick.

'Well, it ain't a rowing-boat, that's for sure,' said Gran. 'Only Wally, who's got this friend of his in the Navy, said 'e wasn't sure if the *Iron Duke* was still bein' used.'

'Well, I hope it's not been sunk,' said Nick, 'or Ma will want to know if Pa was sunk with it.'

'Oh, y'er a laugh, you are, Nick,' said Ivy.

'So long, girls,' said Nick, and made an exit before the conversation got a bit complicated. He reported to Ma, and Ma said they'd have to think of the name of another ship and say Pa had been transferred to it.

'What about the *Jolly Roger*?' asked Amy.

'That's a pirate ship,' said Alice.

'Well, Pa's fightin' pirates,' said young Fanny.

'I've just remembered,' said Ma, 'there's one called the *Royal Eagle*. That'll do, and it sounds posh as well. Your Pa bein' a born gent, it sounds right 'im servin' on a posh ship. Yes, we'll say he's been transferred to the *Royal Eagle*. Only if anyone asks, of course.'

'You can forget that, Ma,' said Nick, 'the *Royal Eagle*'s a pleasure boat that sails from Westminster to Margate.'

'Well, that's very inconvenient, I must say,' said Ma. 'Still,' she said, perking up, 'perhaps we could all 'ave a ride on it to Margate one day. As for Pa, we'll think of some other ship.'

'The *Invincible*,' said Alice.

'Yes, that'll do, that sounds nice,' said Ma.

Mr Lukavitch settled in quickly and without fuss. Going out on Tuesday morning to do a little shopping for himself in the market, he met Ma in the passage.

'Everything all right, Mr Loovakish?' enquired Ma.

'Ruddy tophole, Mrs Harrison, bleedin' lovely, I might say.'

'Language, Mr Loovakish.'

'Yes, not bad, eh, Mrs Harrison? Goodbye for a little while.'

Cassie went round to see Freddy in the evening, catching him before he went out and dodged her. She caught him, in fact, at his door, and wanted to know where he was going. Oh, somewhere, said Freddy. Well, you needn't bother now, said Cassie, I've brought me dad's Sunday shoes round for you to put new leather soles on. It's very unfortunate, she said, but me dad sprained his wrist on the railways today, so he can't put them on himself, so I said you'd be pleasured to. Me dad wouldn't put his trust in any old body to see to his Sunday shoes, but he went ever so cheerful when I said I'd bring them round to you.

'I'm complimented,' said Freddy.

'Yes, I thought you would be,' said Cassie. 'Me dad's very 'ighly regarded by the railways.' Her dad was a ganger with the LSER. 'Where's your foot iron? In the scullery?'

'All right, Cassie love, come through,' said Freddy. 'If I'm goin' to do some cobbling, you can pass me the nails.'

'Yes, all right, Freddy dear.'

'Cassie, I don't think blokes get called dear round this part of Walworth,' said Freddy.

'Never mind, you mustn't fret,' said Cassie. 'You're still dear to me after all the years you've been in love with me.'

'Well, that's nice of you, Cassie,' said Freddy, and gave her a generous cuddle as he took her through to the kitchen. Since it was generous enough to include her bosom, Cassie actually blushed a bit.

Sitting at the fireside with her husband, Mrs Brown looked up as the young people entered.

'Hello, Cassie,' she said in her equable way. 'My, you get prettier every day.'

'Yes, I was born like it,' said Cassie.

'You were that,' said Mr Brown, fond of the quaint girl.

'You're a bit pink tonight, lovey,' smiled Mrs Brown.

'Yes, I bumped into someone, I'm a bit accident prone at times,' said Cassie. 'Oh, Freddy's goin' to put new leather soles on me dad's Sunday shoes on account of me dad spraining his wrist.'

'Well, Freddy's quite good at little jobs like that,' said Mrs Brown.

Freddy did the job in the scullery, Cassie kneeling on a mat and passing him the nails.

'Freddy, I suppose you realize you'll have to marry me now,' she said.

'Well, I'd like to, Cassie, but you bein' me sister-in-law—'

'Never mind that, it's what you did to me in the passage,' said Cassie. 'I think when I'm nineteen will be just right for our weddin', don't you?'

'It's all this hammering, Cassie, I can't hear a word you're sayin'. Still, how's that?'

One new sole was in place, and Freddy slipped the other shoe on to the foot iron. Cassie exhaled breath.

'You smell of peppermints,' said Freddy.

'Oh, would you like one?' asked Cassie, kneeling close beside him.

'Well, thanks,' said Freddy.

Cassie leaned and kissed him on his lips. Her

mouth parted and she let her pepperminty breath escape.

'There, and would you like another one?' she asked.

'Sometimes, Cassie,' said Freddy, 'I just don't know what I'm goin' to do with you.'

Cassie rolled the peppermint around in her mouth and then shared its flavour with Freddy for a second time.

'What's 'appening out there?' asked Mr Brown.

'Oh, Freddy and me's just enjoying some peppermints,' said Cassie.

Chapter Nine

Another Saturday went by, so did another football match, which the Rovers won handsomely by four goals to one. Dumpling was ecstatic on the tram going home.

'I bet the Rovers are goin' to be easy the best team in Walworth this season,' she said, 'I bet no other team's got more 'eroic players than Nick and Freddy – oh, and you, Danny.'

'Honoured, Dumpling,' said Danny, enjoying the treat of sitting next to her.

'Mind, all you others played quite 'eroic as well,' said Dumpling.

'Honoured, Dumpling,' said some of the others.

'Oh, that's all right,' said Dumpling, 'credit where it's due, except I don't want to 'ear you answerin' our captain back on the field, Frankie, like you did in the first 'alf.'

'Me 'umble apologies, Dumpling,' said Frankie, 'I dunno what came over me. Must've been Nick chuckin' 'is weight about.'

'Well, he's got to, or you'd all get sloppy,' said Dumpling. Up came the conductor then to collect fares, and in an excess of enthusiasm, Dumpling said she hoped he realized what an honour it was to have the Browning Street Rovers football team on his tram, specially as they'd just walloped the opposing team by four goals to one.

'Well, yer don't say,' said the conductor, 'I'm overcome. I've 'ad His Majesty the King on board occasional, and I've been patronized frequent by lords and ladies, but this is the first time the Browning Street Whatsits 'ave done me the honour of usin' me vehicle. Wait till I tell me old Dutch and me kids.'

''Ere, not the Whatsits, if yer don't mind,' said Dumpling. 'It's the Rovers.'

'Beg yer pardon, love, I'm sure,' said the conductor, 'and I don't 'ardly know 'ow to break it to yer, but I'm up here to collect yer fares.'

'What a liberty,' said Dumpling.

Alice's eighteenth birthday came round, and Ma did her proud with a slap-up tea party, to which Alice invited two girlfriends from work. Nick thought that at eighteen, Alice ought to have had the natural pleasure of sharing the occasion with a steady young gentleman friend. To Nick, his eldest sister had the air and manners of a young lady, so that he associated her with a young gentleman, not a bloke. Alice, however, simply wasn't going to get associated with any kind of feller until Pa was home. It's a wise sister who can follow the example of her wise brother, Nick said to Ma. Don't come it with vain talk, said Ma, it's me that's making you and Alice see you've both got to wait before you can start enjoying social relationships. Nick said like a little bit of what we fancy? I'll take me broom to you if you talk like that, said Ma.

She invited Mr Lukavitch to the tea party, and the Polish lodger was touched. Freddy and Cassie were also present. The parlour was used, and after tea Amy played the piano with the kind of thumping flair and gusto that provoked everyone into doing what she was after them doing, a rumbustious knees-up. The exceptions were Ma and Mr Luka-vitch, who sat and watched.

'Oh, dear me, have a banana, what bleedin' tophole legs, eh?' said Mr Lukavitch, beaming.

'Language, Mr Loovakish, if you don't mind,' said Ma. 'It's Alice's birthday, remember.' Every-one had given Alice a present, and so had the lodger, a bead bangle. 'My, me parlour floor.' The floor was vibrating, Amy banging away at the ivories and thumping the pedals.

'It is a dance I've seen before, don't I think?' said Mr Lukavitch, happily impressed by the perform-ance Alice's two friends were putting on.

'It's a knees-up,' said Ma, 'but oh lor', them friends of Alice's, it's clothes up with them, the saucy pair.'

'Ah, a Polish dance, that's the bleedin' thing, Mrs Harrison,' said the enchanted lodger.

'What's a Polish dance?' asked Ma amid the noise of revelry.

'It is called the mazurka. When Amy has finished, allow me to play.'

'Oh, a pleasure, I'm sure,' said Ma.

So Mr Lukavitch took Amy's place at the piano a little later, and played with a lot of Polish flair in exhilarating fashion.

'Come, dance,' he said.

'They don't know any Polish dance,' said Ma.

'I will show them,' said Mr Lukavitch, and got Amy to play again, a lively tune that was good enough for him to demonstrate the steps in company with Alice. That done, he took over once more at the piano, and Alice's birthday party became riotous.

'Oh, me gawd, it's worse than that French cancan,' breathed Ma.

'Bloody good, eh?' beamed Mr Lukavitch, turning his head, his feet going it on the pedals.

'Not 'alf,' said Freddy. 'I'm totally admirin' of yer Sunday smalls, Cassie.'

'Oh, help yourself, I'm sure,' said Cassie, not so ingenuous that she didn't know how to make him honourably desirous of proposing to her, and madly keen to as well. In other words, she was giving him saucy eyefuls, and Freddy was rocking a bit in dizzily admiring fashion.

Mr Lukavitch treated the company to a prolonged feast of piano music, some of which they hummed to, and some of which they danced to. Ma asked him if the mazurka was French, not Polish.

'Bleedin' French?' he said. 'Gorblimey, no. Polish.'

'Well, I don't think you girls had better keep on dancin' it,' said Ma, 'it don't look decent. Best go back to a knees-up, if you still feel a bit lively.'

Lively they were. So was Mr Lukavitch at the piano, giving Pa's heirloom the time of its life, keys and pedals dancing up and down.

It was a good old cockney birthday party, and when Freddy took Cassie home he said he was having serious thoughts about her own party next year.

'What serious thoughts, Freddy?'

'Well, serious thoughts about you doin' a real French cancan,' said Freddy.

Cassie trod on his foot, but only in a loving way, so that the pain was temporary.

* * *

November arrived, sneaking in moistly and greyly, and looking as if it was prepared to throw a blanket of fog over Walworth if any of its cockneys spoke out of turn. November had always been touchy about its unpopularity, and there was a belief among suspicious cockneys that it listened in at keyholes to hear what families were saying about its weather. It's always hearing something, said Mr Higgins, a neighbour of the Browns. And why, might I ask? Don't look at me, said his trouble and strife. I'll tell yer, said Mr Higgins, it's always hearing something because hardly five minutes go by around here without some silly cow talking about the bleedin' weather. Oh, yer bugger, said Mrs Higgins, where's me rolling-pin? No, I didn't mean you, me love, said Mr Higgins hastily. Too late. Wallop. It served him right, anyway. He should have learned to choose his words more carefully after so many years of coming to conversational grief with his predictable missus. Still, he had a point. If touchy November ever listened at the Higgins's keyhole, it wouldn't have heard Mrs Higgins saying anything nice about it. In the minds of the citizens who believed the thin-skinned demon of November kept an ear open for aggravating talk, complaining neighbours like Mrs Higgins had a lot to answer for whenever the month dropped cubic yards of fog on everyone.

'The law still 'asn't laid its hands on them common jewel robbers yet,' said Ma at breakfast on a Friday morning. She was still ratty about it. 'It fair makes me blood boil, your Pa bein' arrested like he was and him a born gentleman in 'is way. He might've gone to Eton and 'Arrer if 'is dad had been rich instead of just a lamplighter.'

147

'I like lamplighters, especially in November,' said Alice, 'they come round with their long poles and the lamps go pop, and there's one more glow after another to cheer us up. You ought to make up a ditty about a lamplighter, Nick.'

'All right,' said Nick, swallowing a mouthful of crunched toast. 'There was once a young lady well-bred, who met a lamplighter called Fred. Because it was night, she wanted a light, so he made use of his pole, did Fred.'

Alice spluttered crumbs of toast.

'Is that supposed to be funny?' said Ma.

'No, it was a bit of a shock, poor woman,' said Nick. 'She was all in the dark, Ma.'

'I'm not in the mood for common talk when there's criminals out there not bein' caught,' said Ma.

'The cops will get 'em eventually,' said Nick. 'How's our lodger?'

'Oh, I asked 'im down to share a pot of tea with me yesterday afternoon,' said Ma, 'just to show a bit of 'ospitality. He was very agreeable.'

'I think he's got a little bead-polishing machine up there,' said Nick, 'I've heard it humming.'

'Yes, 'e told me 'e polishes a lot of beads,' said Ma. 'Mind, he does use a bit of 'is Mile End language, but it's not 'is fault, 'e picked it up without knowin', like. Bein' a Polish gent, he'd be ignorant of how common some of them Mile End people are. Well, you two 'ad better get off to your work, I suppose, while I get Amy and Fanny out of their bed.'

'Good idea,' said Nick, 'and while we're at work, Ma, don't do anything you shouldn't do.'

'I 'ope I didn't hear you say that,' said Ma.

'Oh, he said it all right, Ma,' remarked Alice, 'it's his devilry comin' out again.'

'Tickle you tonight, Alice,' said Nick, and went off to work grinning.

'Mornin' to yer, Mrs Brown,' said Mrs Higgins, meeting Freddy's amiable mum down the East Street market later that day. 'How is yer good self?'

'Oh, I can't grumble, Mrs Higgins,' said Mrs Brown, who never did.

'Don't like the look of the weather,' said Mrs Higgins. November, all ears, listened touchily. 'All this fog and all.'

'Well, it's not so bad, just a bit misty, like,' said Mrs Brown, 'and it's nice that it's always cheerful here in the market, it makes it a pleasure to come and spend a bit of money.'

November lightened.

'If you ask me,' said Mrs Higgins, 'November never ought to 'ave been invented. It never did no-one any good, except chimney sweeps.'

November scowled.

By the time Nick left the offices at twelve-thirty on Saturday, Camberwell and Walworth were suffering the effects of a thick creeping yellow blanket.

If it got any worse, this afternoon's football match would be off. However, the day wasn't wholly depressing, for his promised rise had been confirmed and public transport was still running.

He dropped in on Gran Emerson and Ivy.

''Ello, and 'ow's yer manly self today, Nick?' said Gran. 'Brought some more fog in me shop, I see.'

'I don't see at all,' said Ivy. 'You sure it's Nick, Gran?'

'Well, it ain't Gloria Swanson,' said Gran.

'It's me all right,' said Nick.

'So it is,' said Ivy. 'What can we do for yer? Like to come up to the flat and see me saucy seaside postcards?'

'It's a bit foggy for that,' said Nick. 'I'll settle for a pound box of Milk Tray.'

''Ello, got a young lady, 'ave yer, Nick?' said Gran.

'No, I've got Ma and three sisters,' said Nick, 'and I'm treating them.'

'My, I like yer nice ways, Nick,' said Gran.

'Not 'alf,' said Ivy, taking a box of Milk Tray off a shelf and placing it in a paper bag. 'He can treat me to some of 'is nice ways on Sunday, if 'e likes. There, one-and-thruppence, Nick.'

Nick paid up.

''Ave you 'eard yet when yer dad's comin' 'ome from the China Seas?' asked Gran.

'Yes, as soon as he gets word of Ivy's saucy postcards,' said Nick. Another customer came into the shop from out of the fog as he left, with Gran delivering a parting line.

'Wally ain't forgot about askin' 'is sailor friend to find out about the *Iron Duke*, Nick.'

'Tell him not to worry,' said Nick, stepping into the fog. The shop door swung to behind him. That sailor might be a friend of Wally's, he thought, but he's no friend of ours.

Ma and the girls were delighted with the chocolates he'd bought them in celebration of his promised rise. Young Fanny said she could live with having a brother, after all.

Ma said things were taking a nice turn, what with Nick's wage increase and the lodger being a very sociable and untroublesome gent. She'd shared another pot of tea with him yesterday, she said. Fanny grimaced and said if he got too sociable, she'd have to tell Pa. Ma said I'll tell him myself, it'll show him he shouldn't have got himself five years hard labour for getting too big for his boots. Besides, she said, I need to enjoy a bit of sociableness with a gent now and again. I'm not a woman for nothing, she said, and if your Pa's not here to be sociable, then I've got to make do with entertaining the lodger. Of course, I wouldn't make do with anyone who wasn't a gent. Mind, I had to tell him to moderate his language a bit.

'Steamy, was it?' asked Nick.

'What d'you mean, steamy?' asked Ma.

'Well, did it steam up the windows?'

'Not on purpose,' said Ma. 'Mr Loovakish just can't 'elp not knowin' what he's sayin' sometimes on account of what he's picked up in the East End.'

'Pa's never steamed up any windows,' said Amy.

'Pa's a gentleman,' said Alice.

'Cor lovaduck,' said saucy Fanny, 'our Nick might turn out to be a gent if 'e brings us any more choc'lates.'

'I might turn out to be disappointed if this fog gets any worse and there's no football this afternoon,' said Nick. 'By the way, Ma, we'd better think about getting Pa transferred to the *Invincible*. Gran Emerson said that her son Wally hasn't forgotten to mention the *Iron Duke* to his sailor friend.'

'Oh, lor',' said Ma, 'I wish some people wouldn't stick their noses into Pa's whereabouts.'

Amy said the best bet, if Gran Emerson mentioned the *Iron Duke* again, would be to say that Pa had just been transferred to the *Mauretania*, as she liked the sound of that better than the *Invisible*.

Nick, studying the fog that was obliterating the backyard, said, '*Invincible*, not *Invisible*, gormless. And the *Mauretania* happens to be an ocean liner.'

'Well, Pa would like that,' said Fanny.

'Ugh, look at that fog, it's sickenin',' said Alice.

The backyard fog scowled.

The day was merely misty in the quarry down in the wilds of Kent. The hard labour men were swinging pickaxes or sledgehammers under the supervision of armed warders. Pa was working with Tiny Angel, so called because he was as big as a house and specialized in lying in wait for rich West End gents and bashing them over the head to make it easier for him to lift their gold watches and chains. He never said much. He enjoyed bashing far more than conversation. The nearest warder having turned his back, Tiny executed a bashing movement with his sledgehammer. The heavy head landed an inch from the toe of Pa's right boot.

'Ruddy hell,' breathed Pa, 'what was that for?'

'You been saucy, you bleedin' fairy,' said Tiny Angel, which was as much as he'd said all week.

Pa knew what that meant. He had let the grapevine know he was taking umbrage at Ma's monthly handout being gradually cut down. The warning bash of Tiny's sledgehammer was to let him know in return to shut his cakehole.

Right, thought Pa, I'm a reasonable case, all things considered, but I'm not another Tosh Fingers. I'll have to reconsider my future, and Ma's legal dues. Further, I'm against being discharged with one foot missing.

November saw to it that there was no football that afternoon. The fog was too thick. It ruined Dumpling's day for her, so Danny went round and offered to cheer her up in her parlour. Doing what? Dumpling asked the question suspiciously. Well, I wouldn't mind doing some cuddling meself, said Danny hopefully.

'Oh, yer daft lump,' said Dumpling, 'you know I don't go in for that soppy stuff, I'm goin' to do some serious leg exercises to keep me footballin' knees in trim.'

'I'll join yer, Dumpling,' said Danny.

'Not likely you won't,' said Dumpling, 'I do me exercises on the floor with me legs up in the air.'

'Ruddy bliss,' said Danny, 'I'll sit and watch.'

'What, me with me legs and drawers showin'? You got a hope,' said Dumpling.

'Well, some of us 'ave always got 'opes, Dumpling. I've got me own, yer know.'

'Well, I don't want them 'anging about on my doorstep,' said Dumpling, 'they might do an injury to me self-respect as a footballer. I'll 'ave to ask you to 'oppit.'

'What, in all this fog?' said Danny. 'Dumpling, you ain't sendin' me off to get lost in it, are yer?'

'Oh, all right,' said Dumpling, 'we do 'appen to 'ave the fire alight in the parlour. Would yer like to play some parlour games?'

'Corblimey, not 'alf I wouldn't, Dumpling, it's me chief ambition,' said Danny in bliss.

'Come on, then,' said Dumpling, showing her first happy beam on this foggy day. Danny stepped in, closed the door, and Dumpling took him into the parlour. It was full of her brothers and sisters.

'Now then,' she said ''ere's Danny. 'E wants to play parlour games, and 'e don't want to be disappointed.'

Her brothers and sisters yelled with delight and jumped on Danny, more or less. As he disappeared, Dumpling left the parlour, closed the door to shut out the sounds of bedlam, and went back to the kitchen to help her mum with the Saturday afternoon baking. Well, a girl who was as good as one of the blokes and whose one love was football, didn't want to spend a foggy day doing soppy cuddling.

'Chrissie,' said Mrs Evans, a remarkably thin woman considering her first-born was remarkably fat, 'what's goin' on in my parlour?'

'Oh, just some games, Mum,' said Dumpling, busy filling Viota paper cases with a bun mixture.

'Games? What's all that crashin' and banging, then?'

'It's games with Danny, Mum.'

'Oh, me gawd,' said Mrs Evans, 'you 'aven't put Danny in with them little cannibals, 'ave yer? They'll tear 'im to bits.'

'Mum, 'e said as it was foggy, parlour games was just what 'e was lookin' for.'

'No, 'e didn't, not with them little devils, I know,' said Mrs Evans, mixing ingredients for a large batch of rockcakes. 'He'd be better off takin' you out and gettin' lost in the fog with you.'

'Me?' said Dumpling. 'I don't want to get lost in any fog with 'im.'

'Well, I would if I was your age,' said Mrs Evans, 'a nice young man like Danny and all.'

'But I've got me footballin', Mum.'

'Well, that won't make an 'ome and fam'ly for you, not if you 'ad it for fifty years and more,' said

Mrs Evans. 'Chrissie, you want your 'ead examined, you do. Danny's nearly twenty-one and you're over eighteen, and it's time you let 'im start walkin' you out nice and steady. Oh, Lord bless us, is that 'im callin' for 'elp?'

''Elp!' bawled Danny from the parlour.

'I'll murder them kids, even if they are me own,' said Mrs Evans. 'Chrissie, go and drag them off 'im and send them up to their bedrooms. Then go and sit in the parlour with Danny, and I'll bring you cups of tea in a while.'

'Mum, 'e'll want to cuddle me and do soppy kissin',' protested Dumpling.

'Well, some girls are lucky,' said Mrs Evans. 'Go on, go and do as I say. I can't ask yer dad, 'e's round at the workingmen's club.'

Dumpling did what was required of her, although there were five minutes of new bedlam in getting her brothers and sisters up to their bedrooms. That accomplished without any actual blood-letting, she gave Danny some first aid and then, when he was fully repaired, she sat in the parlour with him. Five minutes later, Mrs Evans heard her first-born yell.

'Mum! 'Elp!'

Mrs Evans smiled, put a batch of rockcakes in the kitchen oven, and decided she wouldn't make cups of tea yet.

Freddy and Cassie were in another parlour, Mrs Brown's. The fire was glowing, and they were playing cards by cutting the pack. Whoever turned up the higher card received a penny from the other. Freddy was losing the cut often enough to be one-and-tuppence down, and while being sporting about it, he did suggest it was beginning to hurt, and to look suspicious. Cassie said all right, let's play that if you lose you have to kiss me, and if I lose I have to kiss you. All right, said Freddy, it's something to do on a foggy afternoon. We'll do six cuts, said Cassie, then settle the owings. So they did six cuts each, and Freddy lost them all.

'Crikey,' said Cassie, 'that means you've got to kiss me six times. I'll be overcome. Still, I did say, so I'll have to risk it.'

They were sitting on the sofa together, facing the table and the fire. Cassie, a dreamy smile on her face, offered her lips. Freddy kissed them. Cassie accepted the owings as her due, and more than that. She pressed her mouth ardently to his, closed her eyes and hung on. Blow me, thought Freddy, this is nearly as good as playing football. Cassie gulped and unwound herself. Freddy blinked. It looked to him as if his best friend was actually blushing.

'What 'appened?' he asked.

'How do I know?' said Cassie. 'I fainted, didn't I?'

'That's funny,' said Freddy, 'so did I.'

'How many kisses was it?' asked Cassie.

'Just the one,' said Freddy.

'Well, you still owe me five more,' said Cassie.

'You sure?'

'Yes, and I don't mind faintin' again.'

'That's funny,' said Freddy, 'nor do I.'

Cassie giggled. Freddy kissed her. Her giggle became a gurgle. Her eyes closed again and she made each kiss last. In between she accused him of overcoming her. Some hopes, said Freddy, I couldn't overcome an empty paper bag, not in my

156

condition. Well, if you do overcome me, I'll have to tell my dad, said Cassie. What for? Well, she said, like when you squeezed my pomegranates that time, you'll have to marry me, and my dad'll have to know. Cassie, I wouldn't overcome you, even if I could, said Freddy. Why not, said Cassie, don't you want to marry me later on? Cassie, you're me best friend, said Freddy, and me mind's made up, I'm not going to overcome you, not in me mum's parlour nor anywhere else. Cassie went for him and Freddy fell on the floor.

'Get up,' said Cassie.

'I can't,' said Freddy, 'I've fainted.'

Cassie shrieked with laughter.

Dumpling, meanwhile, was trying to give Danny a good hiding. But Danny, having tasted her plump rosy lips, was fighting back in his enthusiasm for more.

'Oh, yer daft lummox,' gasped Dumpling, 'look what yer doin' to me jumper.'

'I like it, it suits yer chest,' said Danny, 'but it ain't yer jumper I'm after, Dumpling, just some more kisses.'

Dumpling yelled, all in vain. A real smacker arrived on her lips. Oh, the soppy devil.

'Mum!' she yelled as soon as she could. Another smacker arrived. 'Oh, me gawd,' she breathed some seconds later, 'I'll break yer legs in a minute.'

'Dumpling, y'er a lovely cuddle,' said Danny.

'Course I ain't, yer loony, I'm a footballer.'

'Just one more kiss?' said Danny.

'Oh, all right,' sighed Dumpling, 'it ain't my fault all you blokes 'ave got barmy ideas about girls.'

She was yelling for her mum again two minutes later, for the soppy devil was getting soppier.

The fog shifted irritably about on Sunday as if the hounds of heaven were worrying its tail. It lifted in a sulky and reluctant way in the afternoon, when Mrs Higgins observed to her better half that if it couldn't make up its mind what it was going to do, November ought never to be allowed on a Christian calendar. It would be more in place on a heathen one, she said. So down it came again, thick and yellow with umbrage, and the chimneys of Walworth belched black smoke into the heart of it. November didn't like that, either.

Mr Lukavitch knocked and put his head round the kitchen door in the evening. Ma, Nick and the girls were sitting at the table playing dominoes. They were playing for matchsticks and for the fun of it.

'Oh, good evenin', Mr Loovakish,' said Ma.

'Ah, yes, how's your father, eh, Mrs Harrison?' said Mr Lukavitch. 'I am just asking if anyone has six pennies for my sixpence. My meter says no gas.'

'Oh, we can find you pennies,' said Ma, 'but now you're 'ere and I'm just goin' to make a pot of tea, would you like to sit down with us?'

'How bloody kind,' said Mr Lukavitch, and sat happily down with the family. 'Such a day, don't you think?'

'Corblimey foggy,' said saucy young Fanny.

'All right for Jack the Ripper,' said Nick.

'Ah, I have heard of him,' said Mr Lukavitch, 'he—'

'Not in front of me girls, Mr Loovakish,' said Ma, and got up to put the kettle on.

'No, you bet, missus,' said Mr Lukavitch, and looked as if the Ripper was a bit of a blot on the East End. 'But London in the fog is itself, eh, and famous, don't you think?'

'Ruddy 'orrible,' said Nick.

'But better than the bleedin' marshes of Poland, you bet,' said Mr Lukavitch.

'Language, Mr Loovakish,' said Ma from the scullery.

'Yes, I am proud I can speak ruddy fine London English. And how is your father, you young ladies? Across the world in his battleship, I think, eh?'

'Not half,' said Amy.

'Pa's a gent,' said Fanny.

'Yes, it's 'ard on a gentleman like my 'usband to have to fight pirates in the China Seas,' said Ma, 'specially when there's these common jewel thieves enjoying themselves robbin' people and not gettin' caught. It's them that ought to be in the China Seas. You've read about them, Mr Loovakish?'

'Ah,' said Mr Lukavitch, and sighed. 'Most unhappy, yes.'

'It is for Pa,' said Alice.

'I am corblimey sad for you,' said Mr Lukavitch, and sighed again. But he brightened up when Ma made the tea and poured it. He spent a pleasant hour chatting to the family about the attractions of London, and made it known that he thought the King and Queen were ruddy tophole. He informed Ma how delighted he was to be lodging with her and her family. Ma was visibly pleasured to have him say so. Fanny, however, looked as if she was thinking of telling Pa that the lodger was getting too sociable with Ma. Alice looked amused, Amy looked pretty, and Nick looked thoughtful. He was thinking about work and how silent the fourth floor had been, and how jumpy Mr Pollard was whenever they came face to face. The manager obviously wanted to ask him questions about what had given him entry to the fourth floor, but just as obviously he'd been told not to. It was a nervous time for a claims department manager faced with the fact that one of his junior clerks had once been summoned by God.

In the meantime, Nick occasionally thought of the girl who'd become the favourite young relative of her long-invisible great-uncle. She probably enjoyed toasted crumpets in front of the fire on Sundays.

Chapter Ten

Another weekend jewel robbery, this time at a country house in Kent, almost made Ma do her nut. She expressed herself bitterly on the matter of common thieving criminals and the unlucky misfortunes of Pa. She would have gone round to the police station and definitely complained if Alice hadn't said it would be best not to let the local arm of the law know Ma was the wife of Albert Harrison, a gentleman convicted for swiping an American woman's sparklers. It might make them pay Ma a visit, just to turn the house over in a hopeful search for the missing loot. Ma said yes, best to keep quiet.

While Alice's birthday was still a fresh and lively memory, Freddy celebrated his nineteenth in old-fashioned style with his family and closest friends. His best friend, Cassie, starred in a very pretty flowered dress with puffed sleeves. And she put a red rose in her hair. Mrs Brown said she'd never seen Cassie look more of a picture. You'd better buck up, Freddy, she said, or someone might come and carry her off. Freddy said if that happened he'd lose his keenest football admirer. You and your football, said his mum. Don't forget Cassie will be nineteen herself next year, she said. All right, I'll carry her off meself then, said Freddy. On a horse,

Freddy? No, on a tram, said Freddy, and to Brockwell Park for a walk round the football pitch.

A third birthday was on the way, Nick's twenty-first, and his manager, Mr Pollard, called him in during the morning to say his increment would commence the week of his birthday. Nick said thanks very much. Mr Pollard told him he was a junior clerk no longer and that office boys and their like would now address him as Mr Harrison. You're a promising employee, said the manager, and went on about his prospects with the company. Nick had a feeling he was being encouraged to say something about what had happened on the fourth floor exactly a month ago. He decided not to take the bait, being sure God expected him to keep his mouth shut.

'Let me see, weren't you out of the office for the latter part of an afternoon one day last month, Harrison?'

'Yes, I think I was, sir.'

'I'm not complaining, of course.'

'Nor am I, Mr Pollard.'

'I think that's all,' said Mr Pollard.

It wasn't quite all, however, because during the afternoon he again summoned Nick, who thought his eyes looked a little glazed.

'You wanted me, Mr Pollard?'

'Harrison?' he croaked.

'Yes, sir?'

His voice cracking, Mr Pollard said, 'Go up to the fourth floor immediately.'

'Pardon?'

'Immediately.'

Up Nick went, thinking it meant trouble of an uncomfortable kind. The large oak door was open, as it had been on the first occasion. He walked through the ante-room and knocked on the inner door.

'Enter, Harrison.' The deep voice reached his ears, and he went in. God was standing with his back to the window. Nick advanced under the piercing gaze of the bewigged City gentleman in the painting. God, his optics glinting in his broad craggy face, waited until Nick came to a halt before his desk. Then he turned and said, 'What d'you know about the human race, Harrison?'

'Nothing, sir,' said Nick, thinking what a peculiar start this was.

'Nothing? Nothing?'

'Well, not much, sir, except didn't it all start with Adam and Eve?'

'Adam and Eve?' God growled like an unbeliever of biblical stories, which Nick thought very odd. 'Are you an idiot, Harrison?'

'Well, I probably am, sir, about the human race.'

'The human race is burdened by its numeracy, Harrison. Do you know what that means?'

'Yes, sir, there's a lot too many of us. That's what I meant, how Adam and Eve ever managed to—'

'I noted your point, Harrison, and what I meant in return was that it's idiotic to suggest Adam and Eve should shoulder the blame for the errors and omissions of the entire world.' God was in his growling element. 'What is the answer to the fact that there are too many of us?'

What a question, coming from him, thought Nick.

'No idea, sir, except if the world was able to shake itself, a lot of us might fall off,' he said.

'Including yourself?'

'Not if I could find a lamppost to hang on to,' said Nick. The awesome chairman didn't look impressed.

'What if the wrong people fell off?' he said. 'What if we lost the world's finest brains, the finest doctors and most of our child-bearing women?'

'Well, rotten hard luck, sir, but if I might say so, I don't think it would happen like that. I mean, not everyone would be out in the streets or hanging out their washing. A lot would be indoors, in their houses or workplaces. They wouldn't be able to fall off, sir, they'd just rattle about.'

God's expression became pitying.

'What if those who just rattled about were the idiots of the world, or the parasites?' he asked.

'I suppose the world would feel sorry for itself, sir.'

'The human race, Harrison, began to make the world feel sorry for itself centuries ago. What do you consider is your value to civilization?'

'Just the value of a claims clerk, sir, although I can play football a bit.'

'H'm.' God might have rubbished that response, but didn't. 'Harrison, in the event of another flood, do you realize that the first people to be thrown off an overloaded ark would be the politician, the civil servant, the journalist, the banker and the insurance man? The carpenter, the engineer, the inventor, the builder, the doctor, the nurse and even the musician and diarist would all stay on. Either you or I would have to go. Now, tell me again what you consider to be your value to civilization.'

'Well, sir, I – um—'

'Get on with it.'

'Well, sir, if you mean that whichever of us was aboard would be chucked off, then I suppose my value would be the same as yours.'

'Which would be?'

'Nil, sir.'

'Exactly,' said God, 'though you're a damned impudent scoundrel to say so. However, the point is to make sure events don't give you an inflated sense of self-importance. Remind yourself from time to time that you'd be no loss to the world if you disappeared in another flood. Now, the time at the moment is just coming up to three-thirty. You are accordingly to be at the Exchange Teashop at not later than a quarter to four, where you will meet my niece, Miss Somers. Is that clear?'

'Yes, it's clear, sir, but—'

'Buts are not permitted in this office, Harrison. They're detrimental to the health of the company. Just one thing more. Don't speak of this conversation or of my niece. Wait. State the cost of the bill at the teashop a month ago.'

Nick saw what that meant, that it was against God's inclinations to allow his niece to be treated by one of his insignificant clerks. But Nick had his own ideas about what was right and proper.

'I forget, sir,' he said.

God vibrated.

'Oh, you do, do you, you pipsqueak?'

'It's not important,' said Nick.

'Dismiss,' growled God.

Down went Nick to inform Mr Pollard he had to go out. Mr Pollard, looking ill, informed him in turn that he was excused for the rest of the afternoon.

She was there, in the teashop, sitting at the same

corner table and wearing the same hat and coat. It was a horrible November day, damp and murky, but she looked vivacious and alive. Annabelle was indeed very much like Lizzy, her mother, in her young years. Lizzy had actually been only fourteen when Ned fell into her big brown eyes and drowned himself beyond recovery. Without knowing anything about Lizzy and Ned Somers, Nick might all too easily have fallen into their daughter's optical pools if he hadn't been on his guard. On his guard he had to be.

'Hello again,' he said, reaching the table.

'Well, I'm blessed,' said Annabelle, 'it's you. Have you been lying in wait? I'm flattered if you have. I mean, I don't think anyone's ever lain in wait for me before. Are you going to sit down?'

Nick, sitting down, said, 'Listen, what's going on?'

'Pardon?' said Annabelle. 'Oh, I've ordered, by the way. Same as before, pot of tea and two toasted crumpets each.'

The teashop was full of the tinkling sounds of spoons, cutlery and china as City gents and messengers enjoyed an old-fashioned break. Annabelle was full of seeming innocence and Nick full of suspicions that God's favourite young relative was having him on in some way or another. It didn't occur to him that far from having him on, Annabelle felt she had met a young man who was excitingly interesting. Being a very self-assured young lady, with an angelic gift for getting her own way, she hadn't had to work terribly hard to persuade her great-uncle to let her meet one of his clerks again. Uncle John had scowled, growled, rumbled and muttered, but was outdone by her feminine determination in a very short time. Of course, he'd said things like any girl who wants to hobnob with a petty clerk needs to have her brains examined, but that was only eyewash, because he'd been a petty clerk himself once.

'I'm scratching my head about you, Miss Somers,' said Nick.

'I told you last time, boo to Miss Somers,' said Annabelle. 'I don't know how you can be so stuffy when we're going to have tea and crumpets again. I can call you Nick, can't I?'

'Help yourself,' said Nick.

'Well, then. By the way, was Uncle John nice to you?'

'Not much. He spent ten minutes proving I was nobody.'

'But I told you, no-one can be nobody,' said Annabelle. 'Didn't you point that out to him?'

'What, and been struck by lightning? We don't have much, me and my family, but we're all alive, and none of us wants to disappear in a flash of fire and a puff of smoke. Did you come up to have lunch again with your uncle?'

'Yes, but I didn't have much lunch, so I'm sort of famished for tea and crumpets. Oh, famous, here they come.'

The same waitress brought the tray. The aroma of the hot buttered crumpets brought a sigh of bliss from Annabelle, which made Nick smile.

'Here we are,' said the waitress, a nice-looking girl.

'You're getting to be a favourite with me,' said Nick.

'Oh, a pleasure to see you and your young lady again, sir.'

'Don't tell God that,' said Nick.

'Beg your pardon?' said the waitress, having set everything out on the table.

'It's all right,' said Annabelle, 'he's having another of his funny days.'

The waitress laughed.

'I like his funny days,' she said, and departed.

'Well, I'm blessed,' said Annabelle, milking cups, 'I'll have to speak to Uncle John about you.'

'What for?'

'Trying your luck with a waitress when you're with me. It's very bad manners.' Annabelle passed him a cup of piping hot tea, then helped herself to a crumpet.

Nick took one, then said he supposed she had a very easy job if it allowed her to come up to the City once a month. Annabelle said it wasn't at all easy, it was a bookkeeping job, and that it was her immediate boss who gave her the time off. Well, he was her mother's eldest brother.

'Another uncle?' said Nick.

'Smashing,' said Annabelle, 'he's my Uncle Boots.'

'Who?'

'Oh, he's always been called Boots ever since being born a baby boy. Would you like to meet him one day?'

'Well,' said Nick, a young man with his social horizons limited by reason of certain family circumstances, 'if I ever get kicked out of insurance by your Uncle John, I might ask if your Uncle Boots could give me a job.'

'Oh, yes, shall I give you my telephone number?' said Annabelle.

'Not likely,' said Nick. 'If your Uncle John only

half suspected I had your telephone number, he'd chop me up on the spot. I can't afford to be chopped up, I'd have to give up work. Where'd you live, by the way, in a mansion?'

'What a daft question,' said Annabelle, enjoying not only her crumpet but the occasion as well. She was entirely pleased with herself, carried along by a belief that a girl could always get what she wanted if she went the right way about it. She twisted boys round her little finger with ease, and although she was aware that Nick wasn't a boy, but a young man, she was quite confident she could become his one and only within a few months. She had made up her mind about that during her time in this teashop with him a month ago. He was so much more grown up than boys. 'What makes you think I live in a mansion?'

'Well, you look like that and sound like it,' said Nick, who was fighting a battle while Annabelle was only indulging in whims and wishes. If he wasn't careful he'd start thinking about roses round the door. That wouldn't do at all. Ma would have fits. Ma needed the whole family to help keep the secret which, if it came out, would make it necessary for them to move again. Probably to Australia this time. She knew and they all knew that the only friends they could have were those who wouldn't do more than brush the surface of the family, like Freddy and Cassie, Dumpling and Danny. Nick could not afford a close relationship with any girl. Suffering sociability, he thought, why does this girl have to be gorblimey tophole? That made a little grin appear on his face. Annabelle didn't miss it.

'Are you pleased?' she smiled, and the smile

made her look like peaches and cream in Nick's eyes. Well, when a bloke was finding a girl so good to look at, that was the sort of phrase that came into his mind.

'Am I pleased about what?' he asked. They were on their second crumpets.

'That I look and sound as if I live in a mansion.'

'Is that my crumpet you're eating?' asked Nick.

'No, it's mine.'

'You ate mine last time.'

'Only half of it,' said Annabelle, 'and stop dodging the question. I'm not posh, nor's my family. My grandmother's an old-fashioned cockney, a wonderful lady. My mother's wonderful too. So am I, but we don't live in a mansion. Nick, where do you live?'

'With Ma and my sisters,' said Nick.

'I know that, you silly. I mean where, not who with. We're off Denmark Hill.'

'Well, that's pretty posh,' said Nick. The houses there had bathrooms. He and his family used Manor Place public baths. He and Alice paid for themselves, but it cost Ma one-and-six a week for herself, Amy and Fanny. It was an amount she always had to allow for. 'I suppose your Uncle John, not having any children of his own, is going to make you his heiress.'

'Crikey,' said Annabelle in good old family fashion, 'whatever gave you that idea? I don't come first. There's my dad and my dad's father and my dad's mother, who's Uncle John's sister-in-law. Look, you still haven't said where you live.'

'Walworth,' said Nick. Brown eyes opened wide.

'No, do you really? That's where my mother and

her family lived for years. Well, I think that's promising, don't you?'

'Promising for what?' asked Nick, deciding to take his mind off her and think about football.

'For being friends,' said Annabelle, not given to shyness or hesitations.

'I'll have to ask God about that,' said Nick.

'Uncle John? Blessed saints,' said Annabelle, 'I don't let him choose my friends for me, I just let him take me to lunch once a month because he doesn't have any granddaughters he can fuss and spoil. He's a gruff old thing, but his bark's a lot worse than his bite.'

'I'm glad to hear it,' said Nick, and Annabelle refilled their cups. 'D'you want any cake?' He had a little more money in his pocket this time.

'No, not really,' she said. 'Next time you see Uncle John, stand up to him. He'll like you if you do.'

'With any luck, I might be able to keep out of his way.'

'I told him it was disgraceful, you being a junior clerk,' said Annabelle.

'And what did he say to that?' asked Nick.

Annabelle laughed. Two crusty city gents turned their heads to look at her.

'He said he didn't make a habit of discussing pipsqueak employees with little girls.'

'Never mind,' said Nick, 'little girls are like Christmas decorations, nice to have around.'

'Are you looking at me?' asked Annabelle.

'Don't leave it too long before you're on your way,' said Nick, 'it's dark and murky outside. I'll settle the bill and walk you back to the offices, shall I?'

'Oh, yes, I want to leave a little earlier in case the fog comes down. But it's my turn to pay this time.'

'No, it's not,' said Nick, 'you don't have turns to pay, it's not what young ladies are for.'

'My, aren't you masterful?' said Annabelle. 'When did you say you were twenty-one?'

'Tomorrow week,' said Nick.

'Oh, famous,' said Annabelle, 'you'll be a man then, officially.'

'Well, at least I'm no longer a junior clerk,' said Nick, 'and what juniors there are around the offices have to call me Mr Harrison now.'

'Well, I'm not going to,' said Annabelle.

'You'd have to if you were a junior yourself with the company,' said Nick. 'Either that or sir.'

'Don't make me giggle,' said Annabelle. 'But I do wish you many happy returns for next week, Nick, and lots of congratulations. Shall we go, then?'

Nick paid the bill, raising a smile in the young waitress with the tip he gave her. When he left with God's young and fascinating niece, the day was dark and murky all right, but there was no yellow fog. They parted company when they reached Holborn. Nick opted for a lighthearted goodbye.

'So long, Miss Somers, it's been a pleasure,' he said.

'Oh, don't mention it, Mr Harrison,' said Annabelle. 'But thanks ever so much for treating me again.'

'Enjoy your life,' said Nick, and Annabelle smiled. If he thought he wasn't going to see her any more, he'd better think again.

''Bye, Nick,' she said and whisked away, disappearing into the murk.

Nick went home reflecting on the fact that a girl

of peaches and cream could make life difficult for him. Well, what bloke could introduce a girl like that to a family with an uncomfortable secret to keep?

'Uncle Boots?' Annabelle put her head into the office of her favourite relative.

'You're back?' said Boots, a man with a liking for young people.

'Yes, I'm here,' said Annabelle. The time was five-fifteen. 'I just have one or two little things to do. Uncle Boots, thanks ever so much for always giving me time off to have lunch with my Uncle John once a month.'

'Well, once a month doesn't make for problems,' said Boots, and noted Annabelle's little sparkle of excitement. 'Your flush isn't on account of the Growler, is it?' The Growler was how he saw Annabelle's great-uncle.

'What d'you mean?' asked Annabelle.

'Who's been kissing you?' smiled Boots.

'What a funny question,' said Annabelle. 'I've just come back to do one or two little things before everyone leaves.'

'Help yourself,' said Boots, and Annabelle went to her little office, where she checked that a certain slip of paper was safely tucked into her handbag. Yes, there it was, an address written on it. She'd wheedled it out of Uncle John, who'd had to use the internal office telephone system to get it from a department, which had made him growl a bit about pipsqueak clerks and misguided girls.

Annabelle smiled.

'Who's fencing the stuff?' asked Inspector Clark of Scotland Yard.

'That's it, guv'nor, who is?' asked Detective-Sergeant Plunkett. 'Not the usual villains.'

'I don't like hot sparklers vanishing overnight,' said the Inspector, 'it gives me heartburn. Harrison's loot has never come to light, either.'

'Harrison?'

'Knocker Harrison of Hackney.'

'Yes, I remember now. Didn't he say he dropped the swag when he did a runner out of the hotel?'

'Hackney advised me he specializes in fairy stories. His loot didn't get fenced, either. Start working on the usual sources and find out if any of them know anything about a Continental carrier, some Clever Dick who's taking sparklers directly out of the country.'

'Right, guv'nor.'

Over supper that evening, Alice said a feller at Galloway's had been giving her the eye lately. Ma asked what sort of feller. One with a lot of cheek, said Alice. Amy said she liked that kind best herself. Ma said you're not old enough to like any kind, so just keep your mind on your schooling and grow up a lady, like your Pa wants you to. Oh, said Amy, one that sells gold watches down Petticoat Lane? I'll put you over my knees you say something like that again, said Ma, and as for you, Alice, you can't stop young men looking at you, but you and Nick, well, like I've said before, it's best not to think about relationships till Pa's out of the Navy and doing hospital work. Hospital work, said young Fanny, what's that, Ma? Caring for the sick and wounded, said Ma, to make up for all the grief he's caused his family.

Nick said what wounded? People that's fallen

down the stairs, or been knocked down by one of them beer carts that go galloping about all over London, said Ma. There's not many horse-drawn ones left, Ma, said Alice. I don't want to be contradicted, said Ma. Amy said Pa had got to be a doctor before he could care for the sick and wounded. Ma said no-one could look more like a gentleman doctor than Pa, but as he wasn't one he could clean the wards and read books to the patients. That's caring work, she said, and I expect Nick knows how much the hospital might pay him for that. About ten bob a week, said Nick.

Ma gave that only a second's thought before deciding driving a coal cart would be best for Pa, after all. He'd earn a bit more than ten bob. Then she asked Nick if anyone had been making eyes at him, like someone had at Alice. Nick said no. Alice glanced at him, thinking it would be a surprise if he didn't get eyed by some girls. He was a bit like Pa in his looks, except he had grey eyes, not blue. But he did have Pa's smile. Fatal to some girls. Ma said well, you're still young, Nick, you don't have to think about a girl yet.

'Well,' said Amy, 'Freddy Brown's thinkin' about Cassie Ford, and Danny Thompson is thinkin' about Chrissie Evans, and they're not as old as Nick.'

'Yes,' said Fanny, 'but Freddy and Danny don't 'ave dads that are in the Navy.'

'Bless us,' said Ma, 'imagine you talkin' sense like that, Fanny.' And she went all perky at knowing her youngest knew how many beans made five.

Cassie turned up again at that evening's committee meeting. She'd come, she said, to support

Dumpling in a certain matter. If you're not careful, Cassie, said Nick, it'll go down in the rules that every time you turn up Danny has to open the parlour window and Jimmy has to chuck you out of it. Oh, what a kind thought, opening the window first, said Cassie, but I'm not seconding it, all the same. Freddy, she's your headache, said Nick, do something about her. Well, I ask you man to man, Nick, said Freddy, haven't I been trying to do something about her nearly all me life? And where's it got me? Up a ruddy gum tree.

I want to say something about the particular matter, said Dumpling. Read the minutes of the last meeting, said Nick. Yes, all right, Nick, said Dumpling, and read them. When they'd been passed, she said the committee ought to make a new rule about how the team should behave on foggy Saturday afternoons when matches had to be cancelled. Cassie said she seconded that. Nick said shut up, then asked Dumpling if she was feeling all right.

'No, I ain't,' said Dumpling, 'and nor's Cassie. I was 'aving a talk with 'er when I met 'er off the tram yesterday, and I found out that 'er and me both suffered 'orribly that Saturday afternoon when there was no match because of fog. What Freddy done to 'er and what Danny done to me don't 'ardly bear mentioning.'

'All right, keep it dark, then,' said Nick, 'and let's get on.'

Dumpling said she had to mention it for the sake of her honour as a footballer and a permanent member of the committee, and also to protect Cassie's honour as a respectable girl. Nick said if he knew Cassie at all, it was Freddy who needed protecting.

'But what about my blushes?' asked Cassie.

Danny looked at Freddy, Freddy looked at Nick, and they all looked as if they were hearing things.

'Who said that?' asked Nick.

'Some voice out of the fog, I reckon,' said Freddy.

Dumpling said that wasn't very funny, that she and Cassie were still suffering horrible. 'Yes,' she said, 'and when I told me dad what Danny done to me, 'e was so upset for me 'e nearly coughed 'imself into 'is grave.'

'I couldn't say a word to my dad,' said Cassie, 'I was too blushin'.'

'Someone give me strength,' said Nick.

Danny cleared his throat and said, 'There's been a sort of misunderstandin'.'

'No, there ain't,' said Dumpling, 'and I feel it's me duty to report to our captain and ask 'im what 'e's goin' to do about it. It's a shockin' slur on the reputation of me beloved Rovers.'

'Are you going to tell me something that's highly private and personal, Dumpling?' asked Nick.

'Criminal, more like,' said Dumpling. She was helping her mum with some baking in the kitchen on that particular Saturday afternoon, she said, and Danny was playing games with her brothers and sisters in the parlour. Anyway, her mum made the kids go up to their bedrooms on account of creating bedlam. So she went to keep Danny company in the parlour. She thought they could have a blokes' talk about football. Instead of which she had to put up with a lot of daft kisses and saucy cuddling, and what's more, Danny also took liberties with her best Saturday jumper. She had to yell several times for her mum, but her mum didn't seem to hear her, which she should have, as she was only doing some baking.

'I'm innocent,' said Danny, 'I wouldn't take liberties with Dumpling's jumper, I got too much respect for her person. I appeal to yer, Dumpling.'

'I ain't talkin' to you,' said Dumpling. 'As for Cassie and what Freddy done to 'er, well, she told me he behaved like he was married to her, and when she realized 'e wasn't, she fainted.'

'And I don't 'ave any recollection of what happened next,' said Cassie.

'Nor me,' said Freddy, 'I was unconscious.'

'Anyway, I second it,' said Cassie.

'Second what?' asked Nick.

'Everything Dumpling said.'

'Is this a football committee meeting or what?' asked Nick.

'Or what, that's what,' said Dumpling. 'I mean it's both. I want to propose that on foggy Saturdays when there's no match, the committee forbids any bloke to 'orribly aggravate girl supporters by doin' to them what shouldn't be allowed, and which is soppy as well. That's what upsets me most, Nick, footballin' blokes goin' in for all that daft stuff. Me and Cassie suffered a lot of it, and it's got to stop.'

'All right, seconded,' said Nick.

'Oh, bless yer, Nick, I knew me and Cassie could rely on our captain to respect our honour,' said Dumpling.

'All in favour?' said Nick.

They all raised their hands, Cassie as well.

'I'm naturally in favour of payin' respect to Dumpling's jumpers,' said Danny.

'All right, enter it in the minutes, Dumpling,' said Nick.

'What shall I put, Nick?' asked Dumpling.

'Oh, put down that on foggy Saturday afternoons the committee hereby forbids Danny Thompson from taking liberties with your jumpers, and Freddy Brown from doing things to Cassie that make her feel he's married to her.'

'Nick, can't I just put the committee 'ereby forbids any Rover to take advantage of us girls?'

'No, be more specific,' said Nick.

'What's specific?'

'More exact.'

'Well, you ought to say more exact, Nick,' said Dumpling. 'No-one minds you chuckin' yer weight about, but I don't like you showin' off. What d'you want me to write down that's more exact?'

'Well, to begin with you can put down what you suggested, that the committee hereby forbids any Rover taking advantage of any of our lady supporters. Then add that if Danny mucks about with your jumpers and Freddy makes Cassie faint, they've got to marry you.'

'Eh?' gasped Dumpling.

'I second that,' said Cassie.

'Oh, me gawd,' said Dumpling, 'you ain't serious, Nick, are yer?'

'Well, course 'e is, Dumpling,' said Danny. 'As captain, it's 'is duty to be serious. You get it entered, and I'll come round and see yer next time it's too foggy for football.'

'I'll break yer legs,' gasped Dumpling. 'Nick, I ain't—'

'Add further,' said Nick, 'that the committee lays down this rule for the honour of the Rovers.'

'No, I ain't goin' to,' said Dumpling. 'Blow that

for a lark, I won't be able to call me footballin' legs me own, nor me jumpers.'

'Mind you, Chrissie,' said Cassie, 'we've got to do something on foggy Saturday afternoons.'

'I think I'll go to the flicks meself and put me person and me honour out of harm's way,' said Freddy.

'Some hopes,' said Cassie.

'Anyway, I'm just goin' to enter the bit about the team bein' forbidden to take advantage of us girls,' said Dumpling.

'Dumpling,' said Danny, 'might I implore yer to believe I 'old yer jumpers sacred? It was all that fog, yer know. I couldn't see what I was doin'.'

'Well, it's all officially forbidden now,' said Dumpling.

'Only on foggy Saturdays,' murmured Cassie, 'not on foggy Sundays.'

''Ere, Cassie, whose side you on?' demanded Dumpling.

'Freddy's,' said Cassie.

'Cassie, you're confusin' me,' protested Dumpling.

'It's her clockwork brainbox,' said Nick, 'it's not the same as ours, Dumpling.'

'Can we get on?' said Freddy. 'Then I can treat Cassie to some fish and chips.'

'Crikey, he loves me,' said Cassie.

There were no items of great note, and the meeting came to a finish twenty minutes later, Saturday's team having been selected, and Dumpling having said a prayer that it wouldn't be foggy.

Freddy treated Cassie to plaice and chips, a penny more than cod and chips, and Cassie said she'd tell her dad what it meant.

'What'll yer tell him, then?' asked Freddy, as they sauntered along eating the meal out of newspaper.

'That you love me,' said Cassie. 'Is it a sort of mad love, Freddy?'

'It makes me feel I might get certified,' said Freddy.

'Oh, help, that's mad love all right,' said Cassie.

Freddy and Cassie, with their cross-talk, understood each other perfectly. Freddy knew there was no other girl for him but Cassie, and Cassie knew he knew.

Annabelle was out at a dance with a group of friends, and Lizzy and Ned were at home, seated beside the living-room fire like a long-established married couple who didn't need anything more than that. Bobby, Emma and Edward, their other children, had just gone up to bed.

'I think that girl's up to something,' said Lizzy, pausing in her needlework.

'Which one,' said Ned, 'Emma or Annabelle?'

'I'm surprised you have to ask,' said Lizzy, 'it's only Annabelle who gets up to things.'

'Just enthusiasms,' said Ned. 'They usually only last five minutes and they're always harmless.'

'Well, I think this one's lasting longer than five minutes,' said Lizzy. 'She's got a secret behind those smiles of hers, and I just wonder if it's anything to do with that young man I told you she'd met at her great-uncle's offices.'

'Well, if it is, I think she might have an interest in him,' said Ned. 'She's grown out of all the boys she knows, she's just of the age when a girl looks for someone older than boys.'

'She ought to tell us if she's up to something with this one,' said Lizzy.

'I don't think Annabelle would get up to something that would shock you, Eliza,' said Ned.

'She's very impulsive,' said Lizzy. 'And she likes havin' her own way.'

'Don't we all? But if there is a young man in the picture, he won't be a weed. Annabelle would never go for a drip. In which case, our young madam might have met her match.'

'Here, what d'you mean by callin' your own daughter a young madam?' said Lizzy.

'Well, she's a lot like you,' said Ned.

'Are you saying I was a young madam when I was her age?' demanded Lizzy.

'Not half,' said Ned.

'Well, I like that.'

'Yes, I liked it myself,' said Ned. 'Part of your young charm, Eliza.'

'Blessed cheek,' said Lizzy, sounding just like Annabelle.

'So, you see, Boots, it's inevitable that Germany under Hitler will go to war,' said General Sir Henry Simms, a spruce man not yet sixty and as fit as a fiddle. He and Boots were in the study of Sir Henry's handsome Dulwich mansion, and had just come to the end of an hour's discussion on Germany over coffee and brandy. The friendship that existed between Boots, eldest son of a cockney mother, and the aristocratic military-minded Sir Henry, was as unconventional as the relationship Polly had with Boots. Sir Henry's liking for Boots, and his daughter's love for the man, had been born of the fact that neither was prejudiced by the distinctions of class. If Polly had ever had any feelings of being different from the lower classes, they had been swept away early on during her years as an ambulance driver, when she found herself identifying with the earthy and bitter humour of the men of the trenches. The moment she met Boots and found out he was an ex-Tommy, he had immediate appeal for her. And if Boots had been free, Sir Henry would have had no objection whatever to Polly marrying him.

Boots, on the Officers Reserve list, said, 'This country will never be ready to take Germany on again.'

'Hitler has no plans to engage with us again, Boots, but as in the Great War, we may be forced into a new conflict.'

'Well, damn that,' said Boots, 'I'll be in it.'

'Yes, you and hundreds of other men like you, because of your Great War records,' said Sir Henry. 'You'll all be needed, and in positions of command.'

Polly entered the study then. She looked classically elegant in a black costume and dazzling white blouse.

'Have you finished with Boots, Papa?' she said. 'Only I'd like to show him something.'

'Have you time to be turned over to Polly, Boots?' smiled Sir Henry.

'Five minutes,' said Boots.

'God, what a miser the man is with his time,' said Polly. 'This way, if you please, Mr Adams.'

Boots, looking amused, followed her out of the study and up the handsome staircase, Polly showing stocking seams immaculate and straight. She took him into her bedroom. The lights were on, the bedroom a rosy pink. She closed the door.

'Is it the Crown Jewels you're going to show me, then?' asked Boots, his guard up.

'No, me,' said Polly. 'Look.' She took from a wardrobe a hanger, from which depended a semi-transparent black silk nightdress. 'There, wouldn't you like to see me in this? It won't take me more than a jiffy to slip into it. How about it, old darling?'

'And then what?' asked Boots.

'Sometimes, old thing, I can't believe the kind of questions you ask,' said Polly, holding the nightie up against her body.

'I fancy your father and stepmother know I'm up here with you,' said Boots.

'Darling, I'm over twenty-one,' said Polly, 'so let's make giddy love.'

'Here, with your parents down below?' said Boots. 'Polly, you're bluffing.'

'I'm not, I'm just reckless,' said Polly. 'I sometimes have crazy images of you doing it with me on top of an open bus.'

'With the rain coming down?' said Boots.

Polly laughed and threw the nightie on to the pink overlay of the bed.

'Do you know who I'd most like to be?' she asked.

'Cleopatra?' said Boots.

'No, Mrs Robert Adams. Divorce Emily. Marry me.'

'Time's up,' said Boots, 'I must get home to my family.'

'Hope you break your leg on the way,' said Polly.

184

'Bless you, Polly,' said Boots, 'you're a lovable woman, and a favourite friend of mine.'

'A friend? You stinker,' said Polly, but she was laughing when she saw him out.

Chapter Eleven

On Saturday, Nick arrived home just before one. Alice was already in, Galloway's being within easy walking distance. Five minutes later, Amy and Fanny came in. They'd been down the East Street market, shopping for Ma, as they often did on Saturday mornings.

'Here we are, Ma,' said Amy, putting the laden shopping-bag on the kitchen table. Ma was in the scullery, getting the midday meal ready on the gas cooker. She came into the kitchen.

'Yes, Ma, and look what I found,' piped up young Fanny. She produced a leather wallet. 'Mind, I dunno what's in it, I 'aven't looked yet.'

'Fanny!' Ma clapped a shocked hand to her bosom and nearly fell down.

'Oh, you little 'orror!' gasped Amy.

'But we're hard-up,' said Fanny, 'and Ma talked about havin' to sell the piano.'

'That was before we had a lodger,' said Alice.

'Wait a minute,' said Nick, 'what did you mean, Fanny, you found it?'

'Well, Pa used to find things, didn't he?' said Fanny.

'Oh, me failin' heart,' said Ma, sitting down to avoid collapsing, 'I don't know 'ow many times I've prayed none of you would inherit your Pa's findin' ways, and here's me youngest takin' after him when she's only eleven. Where's me smelling-salts and me ballroom fan?' Ma had never been to a ball in her life, but she did have a very pretty tortoiseshell fan given to her when she was a girl, and she always called it her ballroom fan.

'Now see what you've done, Fanny,' said Amy, fetching the smelling-salts from the dresser, 'given Ma a faintin' fit.'

Ma took the little bottle, removed the stopper and sniffed.

'Someone fan me,' she sighed, and Alice did so, using the folded daily paper.

'Come on, Fanny,' said Nick, 'explain exactly how you found that wallet.'

It lay on the table, looking accusingly at the family.

'It fell out of a posh bloke's overcoat,' said Fanny. 'Well, through it, like, as if he 'adn't put it back properly in his inside pocket. I saw it, and when he walked away from the stall it was on the ground.'

'And you picked it up?' said Alice.

'Yes, I found it where it fell,' said Fanny, 'and brought it 'ome.'

'You didn't tell me, you little 'orror,' said Amy.

'Well, you were buyin' veg at the time,' said Fanny, looking as if she couldn't understand what all the fuss was about. 'I bet Pa would've brought it 'ome, specially if we were hard-up.'

'I think I'm going to have to paste your bottom, Fanny, if you do any more of this kind of finding,' said Nick.

'Crikey,' said Fanny, 'I won't find anything, then, if everyone's goin' to shout at me. I'll just let the fam'ly starve.'

'If I get a heart attack,' said Ma faintly, 'don't call Dr McManus, just let me pass on peaceful.'

'Nick, what's in the wallet?' asked Alice, still fanning Ma.

Nick opened it. There were some unused postage stamps, two folded shop bills, a letter in its envelope, three pound notes and a ten-bob note.

'Lummy, look at that money,' said Fanny. 'Finders keepers, that's what Pa used to say.' Alice whacked her bottom with the folded newspaper, which made Fanny feel very hard done by.

'Well, bless me,' said Ma, sitting up, 'three pounds ten, would you believe. Well, I suppose—'

'Nothing doing,' said Nick, 'I'm taking the wallet to the police station.'

'But there's coppers in police stations,' said Fanny.

'Yes, d'you want to come with me?' asked Nick.

'Me?' said Fanny.

'You could explain how you found it.'

'Oh, couldn't you just say I found it accidental?' asked Fanny, preferring, like Pa, to keep police stations at a distance. 'I don't feel well enough to go with you.'

'I bet you don't,' said Alice, and Fanny dodged another smack.

While Ma was making a recovery and delaying the midday meal, Nick took the wallet to the police station. He informed the desk sergeant that his youngest sister had found it in the East Street market and brought it home. The sergeant, examining the contents, said he appreciated the girl's honesty.

'The owner's name is on the letter, with his Camberwell address,' said Nick.

'So I see. Well, if he doesn't call in for his

188

property, we'll get in touch with him. What's your sister's name and address, sir?'

Nick gave them. When he got back home, he informed Fanny of the conversation. Fanny quivered a bit.

'They're not comin' round to arrest me, are they?' she said.

'The sergeant didn't say so. I expect the owner might make a hopeful call at the police station, when he'll get the wallet back. How's your bottom?'

'Alice give it another one,' said Fanny, 'which ain't fair when I only found the wallet because we're hard-up.'

'You'll get another six in a minute,' said Alice.

When the family finally sat down to their meal, it at least meant Fanny kept her bottom safe from further punishment. Just as they finished the meal, there was a knock on the front door.

'Sounds like a copper's knock,' said Nick.

Fanny turned pale and scrambled up.

'That's it, answer the door,' said Ma.

'No, I'm not at 'ome,' gasped Fanny, 'I've gone somewhere.'

Nick answered the door. A man of about thirty was on the step.

'Excuse me,' he said, 'but does Fanny Harrison live here?'

'Yes, I'm her brother,' said Nick.

'Could I have a word with her?'

'What about?'

'She found my wallet down the market. I apparently dropped it there. I didn't expect to see it again, but I called in at the police station on the off-chance, and there it was. Are you the bloke who handed it in?'

'Yes. Fanny brought it home. Hold on a moment, and I'll get her.'

But Fanny had bolted into the backyard loo and locked herself in. So Ma went to the front door in her place.

'Oh, are you the gent that lost 'is wallet?' she asked.

'Yes, that's me,' said the bloke, a decent-looking character. 'I'd like to thank your daughter for having it taken to the police station.'

'Oh, Fanny can't come to the door just now,' said Ma, 'she's – well, she's not in a position to. But I'll tell her you called to thank 'er.'

'And to give her this for her honesty,' said the appreciative bloke, and handed Ma three glittering half-crowns. 'The police sergeant said if I wanted to reward the girl, ten per cent of what was in my wallet was reckoned to be right, so I'm happy for her to have seven-and-six.'

'My, 'ow kind,' said Ma. 'My 'usband that's in the Navy always says profit by good example, but of course Fanny didn't bring your wallet 'ome thinkin' about any profit.'

'I'm sure,' said the generous bloke. 'So long, and thanks again.'

'Oh, thank you too,' said Ma.

When Fanny was persuaded to come out of hiding, she was given a lecture on the benefits of honesty by Ma. See what it did, giving the wallet to the police, like honest people should, she said. The gent came straight round from the police station to show his gratitude, she said. Yes, he gave us a reward of five bob, she said.

'Seven-and-six,' said Nick.

'Oh, was it?' said Ma.

'Crikey oh blimey, I get seven-and-six for findin' a wallet?' said Fanny.

'No, the fam'ly gets it,' said Alice.

'I'll put it with me 'ousekeeping money,' said Ma, 'as a sort of reward for fam'ly honesty.'

'Don't I get nothing?' asked Fanny.

'Not a penny,' said Alice.

'Well, that's the last wallet I'm goin' to find for the fam'ly,' said Fanny.

'You never spoke a truer word,' said Alice, 'I'll see to that. It's bad enough that we have to think about—' She stopped. Someone was coming down the stairs. Seconds later Mr Lukavitch knocked and put his head round the kitchen door.

'Hello, yes, how are we?' he asked, smiling.

'Oh, good afternoon, Mr Loovakish,' said Ma.

'How's yer canary?' asked Amy.

'That is good, eh?' said Mr Lukavitch. 'I come to ask do Amy and Fanny like money for their pocket, Mrs Harrison?'

'Not half,' said Fanny, who felt she'd been diddled.

'Good,' said Mr Lukavitch, and came in. He gave Amy and Fanny a threepenny bit each. Amy said he was as nice as an uncle. 'Ah, yes?' he said. 'That is what you think I am like? A bleedin' nice uncle?'

'Not half,' said Fanny again.

'Ruddy tophole,' beamed the lodger. 'Nick, your mother is telling me you asked about my polishing.'

'A machine?' said Nick.

'That is right first time, Nick, a treadle machine. You know?'

'Like a sewing-machine?' said Nick.

'Buzz-buzz, eh?' said Mr Lukavitch, and laughed. 'How many girls you have, Nick?'

'Why, d'you want one?' asked Nick.

Ma giggled, the girls giggled, and Mr Lukavitch roared with laughter.

'Girl for me, Nick? No, no,' he said, 'I am too bloomin' old for girls. A fine woman, more like, don't you think?'

'One like Ma?' suggested Amy.

'Ah, a ruddy fine woman, eh?' said the happy lodger, smiling at Ma. Ma's perky looked arrived.

'Flattered, I'm sure,' she said.

'You'd better not be too flattered,' said Fanny darkly, 'or I'll tell Pa.'

'Alice, give that saucy girl another smack,' said Ma.

'Happy families, eh, that's the thing,' said Mr Lukavitch, and went on to say it was corblimey fortunate for them to have been born in England. He'd been born in Poland himself, he said, as an unwilling subject of the Russian Tsar. No bloody good, he said, shaking his head. After the war, when Poland was fighting the Bolsheviks, his wife dead because of them, he'd come to England and been allowed to stay. But now look, he said, there's a madman in Germany called Hitler, and one day Hitler will make war and Poland will be swallowed up again.

'Now you mustn't talk like that, Mr Loovakish,' said Ma kindly, 'we've 'ad all the wars we want, and nobody wants another one.'

'No, no, strike a light, no, Mrs Harrison. Have a fag, Nick.'

'Ta,' said Nick, 'then I've got to get ready to go to football.'

'And I must do more work,' said Mr Lukavitch.

Nick liked the Polish gent, but didn't think much

of his fags. They weren't Players, that was for sure. They tasted as if they'd been made from dog-ends collected by street kids.

The Rovers and their supporters were a happy band of people that afternoon. Their opponents were Charleston Street United, and the Rovers soon had them hopelessly disunited. The United's goalkeeper had a terrible first twenty minutes. Crash, bang, wallop. The Rovers put three goals past him. Dumpling quivered all over with hero-worship.

'What a team,' she enthused, 'I've never been more admirin' of all our lovely blokes in their jerseys and shorts.'

'Don't they 'ave lovely knees and legs?' said Julie Hurst, Ronnie Smith's girlfriend.

'They've got footballin' legs, that's what,' said Dumpling. 'I can't be admirin' of any blokes that don't 'ave footballin' legs.'

'Oh, yes, ever so sexy,' said Meg Miles, Charlie Cope's one and only.

'They're what?' said Dumpling, who didn't go in for knowing about that kind of word.

'Give a girl goosepimples, don't they?' said Meg.

''Ere, mind what yer sayin',' protested Dumpling, 'you don't want to get as soppy as some of the blokes. Crikey, look at Freddy goin' it.'

A frustrated opponent elbowed nifty Freddy in the ribs. In return, Freddy bowled him over. The ref blew for a foul, but Cassie yelled, 'Tread on 'im, Freddy, never mind the ref!'

The ref ran to the touchline in stern fashion.

'Who said that?' he demanded.

'Me,' said Cassie, angelic smile uppermost. The ref blinked.

'H'm, yes, well, best if you don't – um – well, I'll overlook it,' he said, and hastened back to the action.

'What come over him?' asked Dumpling.

'Cassie gave 'im goosepimples,' said Alice.

The Rovers ran out easy winners at full-time, and Dumpling treated Danny to a hearty slap on his back. Danny, caught off balance, went flying.

'Now then, clumsy,' said Dumpling, 'what's up with you?'

'I ain't hurt, Dumpling,' said Danny. 'Well, not much, and I treasure all yer lovin' touches.'

'I dunno what you're doin' down there,' said Dumpling, standing over him, 'you ain't lost use of yer footballin' legs, 'ave yer?'

'No, just me eyesight,' said Danny happily. 'That ain't 'alf a lovely red petticoat you're wearin', Dumpling.'

Dumpling gave a yell and fled blushing from the spot.

But she didn't half give Danny what for on the tram going home, telling him his soppy complaint was getting chronic and he ought to see a doctor. And so on. Danny didn't mind. He'd met her mum in the week, and she asked him how he was getting on with Dumpling. Well, I keep getting walloped by her tongue, he said. My, that's promising, that is, Danny, said Mrs Evans, and you're welcome to the use of me parlour any Saturday or Sunday when it's foggy.

Mr Lukavitch went out on Sunday morning, as he always did, carrying his black bag. He was going, he said, to some Sunday markets, including Petticoat Lane, to sell his little gifts to stallholders who could always find customers for them.

Ma and her family wished him luck.

'Many thanks, not half, eh?' smiled Mr Luka-vitch.

Nick's twenty-first birthday arrived, and so did a number of greetings cards. There was a very attractive one with suitable lines of doggerel.

> 'Now that you have come of age
> It's time that you said, "Please,
> Tell me, Daddy, if you will,
> About the birds and bees."'

It was signed, 'With my best wishes, Annabelle.'

The monkey, she'd found out his address. He slipped the card into his jacket pocket before any of the family had seen it.

Ma insisted he had a slap-up tea party, and Nick said he felt like one. It might cure his headache, he said. He'd been given a headache by Gran Emerson, who'd told him that her son Wally's sailor friend had come up with the news that the *Iron Duke* had gone for scrap years ago. Nick said kind of the sailor bloke to find out, but actually his Pa changed ships a lot, and Ma actually wrote her letters to the Navy's address in Hong Kong. Oh, I see, said Gran, only Wally's friend won't be able to find out if your Pa's got a chance of coming home soon unless he knows the name of his ship. Ma won't mind his arrival being a happy surprise, said Nick, so Wally can tell his friend not to bother. Oh, it won't be no bother, said Gran. It might be to us, said Nick, but only to himself.

Cassie and Freddy, together with Dumpling and Danny, were invited to the party, and so was Mr Lukavitch. Ma had bought new dresses for Amy and Fanny out of the reward money for family honesty, which delighted the younger girls. And she put on a spread that was enjoyed by one and all. Then Amy, quite talented, played some good old music hall songs on the parlour piano. After which, Mr Lukavitch asked if he might have a turn on the piano, as at Alice's party, and Ma said she'd be pleasured. Fanny said, in a dark aside, that there was too much pleasuring going on considering Ma was a married woman. Only Alice heard her, so only Alice gave her a pinch.

Mr Lukavitch said he'd play some Polish music, which he did, and the music galloped. It brought all the girls to their feet for a knees-up, and the parlour floor trembled. What floor wouldn't when Dumpling was going it in a knees-up?

'No, no,' laughed Mr Lukavitch at the piano, 'a Polish mazurka, not a bleedin' London knees-up.'

'Language, Mr Loovakish,' called Ma, 'specially as we got company.'

'Yes, ruddy good, eh? But a mazurka, that is it, don't you think?'

It was a rousing party, Amy and Mr Lukavitch taking turns at the piano, Amy playing with enthusiasm, her feet thumping the pedals, and Mr Lukavitch doing his best to introduce everyone to Polish party frolics.

It was Alice who noticed a little something loosely flapping under the right pedal of the piano, and she drew Nick's attention to it.

'What d'you think it is?' she whispered.

'All I know is that the joanna is Pa's heirloom,'

Nick whispered back. 'But leave it, Alice, and we'll have a look later, unless it falls off. So keep watching it.'

When the celebrations were finally over and all the guests gone, Ma saw to it that Amy and Fanny went to bed. Alice and Nick said they'd do some clearing up in the parlour, where Nick went down on one knee, fished about under the right pedal of the piano and detached the loose little something. It was a brown envelope, folded into a small shape with dried glue still adhering to it. There was something in it. He unfolded it and opened it up. He carefully spilled the contents on to the table, and the flash of sparkling diamonds leapt to the eye.

'Crikey,' breathed Alice, 'I bet Pa knows something about them.'

'They're his insurance,' said Nick.

'Oh, you think he kept these for 'imself, Nick?'

'He told Ma not to sell the piano, and that he had some confidential savings.'

'That's right, so he did.' Alice watched as Nick counted the perfectly matching jewels. Twenty-four. 'I bet they were once a diamond choker, Nick. They're Pa's now, he's doin' his time for them. Lor', what's Ma goin' to say?'

'Ma's going to have several fits if she knows this lot is on the premises. Don't tell her, let Pa decide what he wants to do with them when he comes out.'

'D'you think we ought to make 'im post them anonymous to the police?' asked Alice.

'Well, you're not going to take them round to the police station, and neither am I,' said Nick, 'otherwise they'll think we might have the rest of the loot here. You're the apple of Pa's eye, so you keep them and tuck them safely away in your bedroom. Pa's got to have the responsibility of making an honest move or a dodgy one.'

'Yes, that's best,' said Alice. 'Mind, I won't stand for a dodgy one, even if he has done time for them.'

'We're going to opt for honesty?' said Nick.

'We've got to, you know we 'ave,' said Alice.

'That makes sense,' said Nick, 'so let's think about posting them to Scotland Yard ourselves. We can take our time.'

'Crikey, but what a terrible shock for Pa if when he comes out there's no insurance under the piano pedal.'

'He'll have to do what Ma wants him to,' said Nick.

'And what's that?'

'He'll have to drive a coal cart.'

When Saturday arrived, damp and misty, the Rovers were sadly off form. They played like wet celery. Well, that was what Fanny said, and young though she was, Fanny knew her stuff as a critic. The Rovers lost for the first time this season. Dumpling was devastated, and her dad, who'd refereed the match, could only say cheer up, Dumpling me pet, Christmas is coming. I'll be dead by Christmas, said Dumpling – of a broken heart.

She spoke her mind on the tram going home.

'Ain't you blokes ashamed?' she said. 'I could've beat that lot from Deacon Street playin' on me own with Fanny in goal. I never thought I'd live to see the day when Browning Street Rovers would perform like a left-over rice pudden.'

'I'm hurtin' down to me boots, Dumpling,' said Starving Crow.

'Yes, but you ain't near to dyin' of mortification like I am,' said Dumpling.

'I'm sufferin' with yer, Dumpling,' said Danny.

'So you should be,' said Dumpling, 'and Nick as well. Oh, me sad 'eart, imagine our captain playin' like the mornin' after the night before.'

'Must be in love,' said Charlie Cope.

''Ere, mind what you're sayin',' admonished Dumpling, 'it's bad enough our captain playin' like a drain, without 'im gettin' as soppy as the rest of yer. Nick, you ain't thinkin' about daft kissin' and cuddlin', are yer, when you still got years of football in front of yer?'

Regrettably, Nick's mind had wandered a bit during the game. A soccer match usually made him forget everything outside of football, but this afternoon that girl had kept creeping into his thoughts. Her colourful image had taken no notice of the occasion, it simply leapt over the doorstep of his mental dwelling and presented itself repeatedly to his imagination. It hadn't even knocked. It entered uninvited.

'What's that you said, Dumpling?' he asked.

'Oh, me gawd, 'e just ain't with us this afternoon,' said Dumpling.

'Never mind, Dumpling, I'm 'ere,' said Danny.

'Don't talk to me,' said Dumpling, 'I ain't in the mood. Blimey, eleven blokes, and not one pair of footballin' legs among the lot of yer this afternoon. I might just pass away in bed tonight from the shame of it.'

'Can I come and pass away with yer, Dumpling?' asked Danny.

'My life, in her bed?' said Starving Crow.

'What a way to go,' said Charlie Cope.

Dumpling ignored the daft lot.

She was not only disgusted with her beloved Rovers, she was cross as well. When Danny came round that evening to ask if he could take her to the pictures or sit in the parlour with her, she said no, you can't, and bashed the door shut. It nearly did irreparable damage to his good-looking hooter.

On Sunday morning, Nick was in the passage when Mr Lukavitch came down, complete with his black bag. Nick asked him if he was actually doing a carrying job for a doctor too busy to do it for himself.

'Eh?' said Mr Lukavitch.

'Well, is there a baby in your bag?' grinned Nick.

'Eh?' said Mr Lukavitch, and Nick explained that English kids were brought up to believe babies arrived in doctors' black bags. Or were found under gooseberry bushes. Mr Lukavitch roared with laughter. 'You're a funny young man, Nick,' he said. 'No, no, I carry my beads and other little gifts in my bag, as I have told your family.'

'To markets like Petticoat Lane?'

'Ah, I like Petticoat Lane, yes, that's the place, Nick. I have said I don't get rich, but I get happy meeting fine cockney women. Cockney women are ruddy tophole, don't you think, eh?'

'As good as Polish women?' said Nick.

'Ah, Polish women all bloody Catholics,' said Mr Lukavitch.

On Wednesday evening, at the committee meeting, Dumpling spoke her mind once more about the Rovers' first defeat when the match came up for discussion. I don't know that any of the team deserves to be picked for next Saturday, she said, but we can't just field the reserve and me. I suppose you all know what the street kids have been saying about the Rovers, she said. They've been saying you all ought to go in for knitting.

I second that, said Cassie. She was in attendance again, as the supporters' official representative and as a girl who was dead against being on the outside edge of anything that interested her.

'Cassie, if you don't stop seconding and proposing,' said Nick, 'I'll get Freddy to take you out into our backyard and dump you in our dustbin.'

'Some hopes,' said Cassie, 'he'd go home with a leg torn off. Besides, I'm not here to do a lot of proposin', I'm here to give you some 'elpful criticism. I've been asked by Alice and all the other supporters to tell you that after the way you played last Saturday, you ought to be pensioned off. Fanny said it's your age, that you're a bit past it. She said you were all right while you were still twenty, but since you've been twenty-one you've got a bit old in the legs.'

'Gawd 'elp us,' said Danny, 'yer own sister and all, Nick. That's serious, that is.'

'It's serious all right,' said Dumpling, 'specially as you looked past it yerself on Saturday.'

'Me?' said Danny.

'Yes, you,' said Dumpling, whose bouncy cheerfulness had taken such a beating over the defeat that even her jumper had a deflated look, which posed the possibility that gloom had actually made her lose weight. 'It seems to me, Danny, that all that daft cuddlin' and kissin' you go in for 'as put years on you. I've 'eard that that sort of thing can make a bloke old before 'is time. I noticed on Saturday that yer legs 'ad gone a bit stringy, like me grandad's.'

'Turn it up, Dumpling, I ain't Nick's age yet,' said Danny.

'Well, something made you play as if you was ninety,' said Dumpling. 'Nor was Freddy much better.'

'Yes, we ought to think about droppin' Freddy from the team,' said Cassie, 'only I like 'im in his shorts and showin' his knees. You do 'ave quite handsome knees, Freddy.'

'Nice of yer to say so, Cassie,' said Freddy. 'I'll admit I'm old before me time meself, but not on account of kissin' and cuddlin'. More on account of certain problems I'm always up against.'

'Well, I notice you're not up against me much,' said Cassie. 'I was only sayin' to me dad yesterday that I could die of neglect sometimes.'

'All cough,' said Nick, and all coughed except Cassie and Dumpling.

Dumpling said, 'What's Cassie mean?'

'Don't look at me,' said Freddy, 'I'm tryin' to believe this is a committee meetin'.'

'Well, it is,' said Dumpling, 'and it's all about some of the Rovers playin' like my grandad, only I don't think that's the trouble with Nick. I mean, look at 'im. You can 'ardly say 'e's got whiskers.'

'It's love,' said Cassie, 'he's got a girl somewhere.'

'Yes, that's what's so 'orrible,' said Dumpling gloomily, 'our captain gettin' this chronic complaint. He could've waited till 'e was forty. At that age, any bloke could be past it.'

'Past what?' asked Freddy, grinning.

'Football, of course,' said Dumpling.

'Thanks for that bit of relief,' said Freddy.

''Ere, Nick, who's the girl?' asked Danny.

'Search me,' said Nick, and brought the meeting to order. At least, he tried to, but last Saturday's defeat and Dumpling's conviction that it was caused by too many of the blokes doing too much soppy stuff with girls, kept intruding. However, when he announced that neither Ronnie Smith nor Frankie Hughes could play on Saturday, on account of family commitments that included a burial, Dumpling sat up straight – well, roundly straight – and her jumper that had looked deflated filled out.

'Oh, crikey Moses,' she said, 'that means we're one man short, Nick, and that you've got to give me a game.'

'Yes, so be a good bloke, Dumpling,' said Nick, 'and stop gnawing at old bones. Get your footballing legs ready for Saturday. You're taking Ronnie's place.'

'What, centre forward?' gasped Dumpling.

'That's it,' said Nick.

'I second it,' said Cassie.

'I'll 'ave a lie down meself,' said Freddy.

'Might I congratulate yer, Dumpling?' said Danny, nobly putting aside trepidation.

'Oh, I never been more complimented,' beamed Dumpling. 'Oh, 'elp, though, I don't 'alf feel sick at all I been sayin' about you, Nick. I can't 'ardly believe the honour you've just done me. Me, centre forward for Browning Rovers, it's me dream come true. I'll be grateful to yer till me dyin' day.'

'Granted,' said Nick.

The die was cast. Dumpling was going to play centre forward against Rodney Road United, another of the Rovers' deadly rivals.

*   *   *

Over breakfast the next morning, Nick asked Ma if she could remember exactly what Pa had done after arriving home on the day he'd gone in for a jewel snatch. Ma said she didn't like Nick using common words about Pa, and what did he want to know for? Out of interest, said Alice. Well, said Ma, Pa didn't do anything special, and he certainly didn't say anything about what he'd been up to. After a while he went into the parlour to write a letter, and he didn't have time to do much else because suddenly the police knocked on the door just when he was enjoying a nice cup of tea with her.

Alice glanced at Nick. Nick winked. Alice winked back. They didn't think Pa had spent his time in the parlour just writing a letter.

Brother and sister were one in keeping the secret of Pa's insurance policy under their hats.

Boots took some invoices along to Annabelle for posting. His sister's eldest daughter jumped a little as he walked into her own cosy office.

'Sorry,' he said.

'What for?' asked Annabelle.

'For waking you up,' smiled Boots.

Annabelle, assistant bookkeeper in the busy concern run by Boots and his brother Sammy, said, 'Uncle Boots, that's almost a libel, I wasn't asleep.'

'Slander,' said Boots.

'Well, slander, then, which sounds worse.'

'What's on your mind?' asked Boots.

'Oh, help, is it showing?'

'Something is,' said Boots, 'but I don't know what.'

'I suppose I ought to tell someone in the family,'

said Annabelle. 'Mum and Dad both suspect I'm up to something.'

'And what are you up to?' asked Boots.

'You're not to laugh,' said Annabelle.

'Promise,' said Boots.

'I've met someone.'

'Well, who's going to laugh about that? It happens to all of us all the time.'

'Once in a lifetime, you mean,' said seventeen-year-old Annabelle.

'I see,' said Boots, looking solemn. 'That's different, of course. I think you mean fate has struck.'

'It could have,' said Annabelle, 'but I'll make allowances for not knowing everything yet.'

'I've got five minutes unless my phone rings,' said Boots.

'Well, bless you, Uncle Boots,' said Annabelle and told him about Nick in rather extravagant detail. It brought in her doting great-uncle, of course.

If Boots could hardly believe his ears at this recounting of Annabelle's precocious goings-on, his good-humoured expression did not change. He knew how self-assured Annabelle was, and how she could twist infatuated boys around her little finger, treating none of them with any seriousness. Life and boys were a game to her, which wasn't unusual with some girls. Some girls of sixteen or seventeen saw boys of their own age as friends, not prospects, and probably had an instinctive preference for young men. Annabelle had found one very much to her liking and was having a game with him. What it was doing to him, Boots could imagine, for Annabelle was as lovely as Lizzy had been at her age.

Lizzy's looks and personality had fascinated Ned. But she had never played a game with him, he had been her one and only real boyfriend, the one who put dreams and stars into her eyes. Annabelle was using the awesome authority of her great-uncle to bring this young man, Nick Harrison, within range of her whims and impulses, most of which were playful five-minute wonders.

'You like him, do you, Annabelle?'

'Yes, of course, he's grown up,' said Annabelle, 'and he's fun.'

Boots felt fun was exactly what she had in mind. Well, life should be fun for young people, but sometimes a game of fun could be played in the wrong way and with the wrong person. The young man Nick, knowing she was the great-niece of the company chairman, would probably be feeling slightly dizzy about Annabelle's attentions. Annabelle had him at a complete disadvantage. Boots believed in a more open and natural development of a relationship.

'Why don't you tell your parents about him so that you can simply invite him to Sunday tea and dispense with this business that ends up in the teashop once a month?'

'Oh, I couldn't be as forward as that,' said Annabelle.

'Not much,' said Boots.

'But I couldn't,' protested Annabelle. 'A girl can't make the first move.'

'Who's making all the moves now, then?'

'That's different,' said Annabelle.

'I see,' said Boots, 'you're waiting until he's head over heels and is begging to show himself to the family, are you?'

'Crikey,' said Annabelle, 'd'you think such a smashing young man could fall for me head over heels, Uncle Boots?'

'If he does, treat him gently,' said Boots.

'What d'you mean?' asked Annabelle.

'Well, you might find it's no longer fun to him,' said Boots, 'you might find young men can be serious.'

'I'll be thrilled,' said Annabelle. Boots shook his head at her and went back to his office.

Annabelle talked to her parents about Nick that evening, and when Lizzy learned that he lived in Walworth, she thought immediately of down-at-heel scruffs, street corner characters and headlice. She'd always had a horror of the lice that could infest the heads of Walworth schoolchildren and emigrate to the heads of adults. She expressed doubts about Nick. Annabelle laughed, and said he was a clean-looking young man who couldn't ever have been a street urchin or a ragamuffin. Lizzy said well, she and Ned would like to meet the young man and see for themselves what he was like. Lizzy felt he couldn't be as good a prospect for Annabelle as a doctor. Ned felt that he and Lizzy should base their reactions first of all on Annabelle's feelings, although, like Boots, he suspected Annabelle was simply enjoying one of her enthusiasms.

Annabelle said that as soon as the young man was obviously madly keen on her, he'd want to be invited to meet her family, and she'd encourage him to ask.

'You'll just make do with having tea and crumpets with him until then?' smiled Ned.

'It's fun,' said Annabelle.

'We didn't do things that way when I was a girl,' said Lizzy.

'I bet you still had fun,' said Annabelle.

'So we did,' said Ned, and Lizzy laughed.

Mrs Emily Adams slipped into bed. It received her kindly. They were old friends. She stretched blissfully, her hair flooding the white pillow with dark fiery auburn.

Boots, undressing, said, 'I think Annabelle's found a young man.'

'What, on top of all the boyfriends she's collected?' said Emily.

'I think she's gone off boyfriends in favour of the young man,' said Boots.

'Well, unless he's a bit clever,' said Emily, 'he'll still get twisted round her little finger.'

'I've a feeling from what she says that she's playing games with him but isn't having matters all her own way,' said Boots.

'Well, we all know Annabelle,' said Emily, 'everything's a game to her. But she's a lovely girl, just like Lizzy was at her age.'

'I'm intrigued,' said Boots, looking comfortable in his dark-blue pyjamas. 'I think Annabelle's smitten. I'd like to meet this young man.'

'Well, I suppose Lizzy and Ned will invite 'im to Sunday tea some time,' said Emily.

'It's the usual thing in this family,' said Boots. He turned out the light and slid into bed beside Emily. The bed and his wife both received him kindly. His wife turned and cuddled up. He smiled in the darkness, knowing what cuddling-up meant.

Chapter Twelve

Alice, Amy and Fanny had been sisterly enough not to send their brother barmy by having hysterics about Chrissie Dumpling playing centre forward in her own jersey and shorts.

'He's not a bad old bloke,' said Amy during a chat on the matter with her sisters.

'Yes, 'e can't help bein' our brother,' said young Fanny, 'he was born that way, poor old codger.'

'And he did take us to the pictures,' said Alice.

'And treated us to choc'lates when he 'ad his rise,' said Amy.

'Besides, if we start laughin',' said Fanny, 'he might do one of his tickling jobs on us.'

'He takes his borin' old football very serious,' said Amy.

'It's not borin',' said Alice, 'it's manly.'

'Oh, chase me, Charlie, what a thrill,' said Amy.

'Besides, not bein' able to have a girlfriend on account of Pa, Nick's got to have a serious interest like football,' said Alice.

'Molly Palmer's sister Ethel wouldn't 'alf like to be his best interest,' said Amy. Molly Palmer was a school friend of hers, and her eighteen-year-old sister Ethel was a notable Walworth female cuddle.

'Well, she's not goin' to be,' said Alice. 'She'd eat him as soon as she got 'im on her parlour sofa.'

'Anyway,' said Amy, 'I think I'll come and watch Chrissie playin' centre forward.'

'Well, mind your giggles don't get hysterical,' said Alice. 'I don't want to tell Ma you had an accident in Brockwell Park.'

'Here, d'you mind?' said Amy.

In the quarry on Saturday morning, a whisper arrived at Pa's shoulder. That was the usual arrival point for whispers, the shoulder, from where they travelled up to the ear in quick time.

'Bein' a good boy now, are yer, Knocker?'

'I pride myself on not being an aggravating man,' said Pa, swinging his pickaxe.

'Yer bleedin' pretty as well, ain't yer? But Tiny Angel ain't goin' to spoil yer looks pervidin' you stay a good boy. Thought I'd tell yer.'

'Very obliging of you,' said Pa, who had stopped passing complaints through the grapevine about the reductions in Ma's allowance.

'Yer a ponce, Knocker.'

And sod you too, thought Pa.

The Rovers had accepted Dumpling as centre forward for the critical match against Rodney Road United, as well as the dread fact that she was going to play in her jersey and shorts. And it came to pass. She took off her coat, and in her jersey, shorts and football boots, she joined in the pre-match kick-about. She looked exactly like a sporting edition of Billy Bunter's sister.

Amy fell about. The other girl supporters held themselves in check. The Rodney Road team rolled in the aisles like ruddy hooligans. Their captain bawled for Nick, and Nick arrived ready for the confrontation.

'What's that plum puddin' doin' on the pitch?' asked the Rodney Road captain.

'Watch your manners,' said Nick, 'that's our centre forward.'

'Yer what?'

'You heard, Claud.'

'I 'eard all right,' said Claud, whose name wasn't his own fault, 'but I ain't believin' it. Eleven Browning Street cissies, well, that can't be 'elped, but a fat girl centre forward and ten cissies ain't what we've come to play. Nor ain't it allowed.'

'Who said?' asked Nick.

'Me,' said Claud, with his team looking as if they were all wetting themselves. 'I said it, Nick.'

'Well, strike a light,' said Nick, 'you're scared. I don't mind you all feeling a bit nervous, but scared, well, who's going to tell your mums?'

'Scared? 'Ere, do us a favour,' said Claud, 'put your bonce in a sack, eh? You ain't seriously expectin' us to play against Fat Floradora, are yer?'

'You better had,' said Nick, 'or you'll get known as the Rodney Road dummy-suckers.'

'That's done it,' said Claud, 'we'll play all right, but she ain't goin' to get no quarter, she'll get tripped, barged and bleedin' murdered same as if she was a bloke. Fair?'

'It's your funeral,' said Nick, sounding a lot more confident than he felt.

When the teams began to line up, Freddy said to Nick, 'Regardin' Dumpling, I've got to tell yer I've never seen as much as that in a football jersey before.'

'Nor have Rodney Road United,' said Nick, 'so

cheer up, Freddy, we couldn't have let her flap about in her dad's overcoat this time.'

Dumpling kicked off for the Rovers, wobbled about a bit, then charged forward in the hope of the ball coming back to her. She cannoned into an opponent and he bounced on his back. The ref blew for a foul. Dumpling gave him a hurt look.

'Wasn't my fault 'e fell over,' she said, 'ain't 'e got any muscles in 'is legs?'

'No arguin'.'

The free kick was taken. Nick met the flying ball with his head and it soared back into the United's half. Dumpling bounded in pursuit. What a performance she gave. Cheered on by Alice, Cassie and the rest of the Rovers' supporters, she rushed about here, there and everywhere. Claud ordered his men to flatten her. Flatten Dumpling? Some hopes. They just bounced off her. Periodically, she fell over, either because she was overweight or overenthusiastic.

To Dumpling, the ball was there to be booted, and she aimed ferocious kicks at it whenever she was near the opposing goal, and generally threw the Rovers' dangerous rivals into confusion. They didn't seem to know what to do when she came bearing down on them, robust chest to the fore, curly hair dancing. Her energy was inexhaustible. From his position at right back, Danny watched her with fond admiration, and took silent umbrage when he heard an opposing supporter say he'd never seen a balloon playing football before.

The Rovers scored twice in the first half, Rodney Road once. Sucking her slice of lemon at half-time, Dumpling let it be known she was heartbroken that she hadn't scored herself.

'Never mind, Chrissie,' said Alice, 'everyone's got their eyes on you.'

'Crikey, 'ave they really?' said Dumpling, her football shirt rising and falling from her exertions. 'Well, I don't 'alf feel proud, then. I just 'ope we win and that I don't let me beloved Rovers down.'

'All the blokes are praying for you,' said Nick.

'Ain't that nice of them?' said Dumpling.

'I'm greatly admirin' of yer, Dumpling,' said Danny, 'and willing to sit in yer parlour with yer tomorrow, if it's foggy.'

'No, it's forbidden,' said Dumpling.

'Only on Saturdays,' said Danny.

'True,' said Nick.

'That's right,' said Cassie.

'Oh, me gawd,' gasped Dumpling, 'I forgot about Sundays.'

'I didn't,' said Cassie.

'Nor me,' said Danny.

'Time's up,' said Nick, 'back to the battle, blokes.'

Dumpling swelled with pride at being included as one of the blokes, and her football jersey took the strain manfully. She was soon in the thick of things again, bursting with a heartfelt desire to score a goal. But midway through the second half, the Rodney Road idiots levelled the score at two-all, not realizing how much pain and anguish this caused Dumpling. It upset her as well, and she committed a bit of mayhem among the opposition.

'Ruddy 'ell,' said Claud, 'can't someone tie 'er to a railway line?'

It was ding-dong all the way during the final minutes, and still Dumpling never stopped bouncing, charging and ballooning about. While she wasn't the best footballer in the world, she could boot a ball and she never gave up.

A miracle happened. She scored the winning goal three minutes from the end. Never for a moment had Nick thought they were going to be able to record anything like that for posterity. The whole team wanted it to happen, so that Dumpling could pass away blissfully when her time came, but everyone reckoned it was asking too much of the Almighty.

But it did happen, and it came about like this. Starving Crow, the team's long and bony left winger, who received special family dispensation for playing on their Sabbath, did one of his fast runs and dribbles, then performed his favourite trick of cutting in. Dumpling, joggling about in front of Rodney Road's goal, yelled at him to pass to her. But Starving Crow tried a shot. The ball hit the crossbar and rebounded. It sailed down towards Dumpling's robust chest.

'Oh, 'elp!' she gasped, and her chest arched in defence. Smack. The ball hit it, bounced off and flew at speed past the gaping goalkeeper. Browning Street Rovers whooped. Their supporters shrieked. Rodney Road United sagged. Their captain, Claud, made a fast recovery and bawled an appeal.

''Andball, ref!'

''Andball me foot,' yelled delirious Dumpling, 'where's he think I keep me 'ands, then, up me jersey?'

'Goal,' said the ref, and pointed to the centre spot. Dumpling fell over in ecstasy. The supporters did a touchline knees-up. Starving Crow and Herbert Briggs brought Dumpling to her feet and took her back to the centre circle, where Nick slapped her on her shoulder and told her she was a corblimey ruddy hero, the kind of complimentary language she understood.

'I can die 'appy now,' she said breathlessly, 'and wasn't it lucky I'd got new whalebones in me stays? They make me chest even more robust, yer know.'

'I'll get the team to autograph them,' said Nick, as the flummoxed opposition began to line up again.

'Would yer really?' Dumpling glowed. ''Ere, what'm I talkin' about? Me stays are private.'

Rodney Road put the ball into desperate play, but their cause was lost. The ref blew for time not long after, and the Rovers smothered Dumpling with kisses and cuddles. She said she didn't mind as long as no-one was actually being barmy.

'Well, I can't tell a porkie, Dumpling, not right now I can't,' said Danny, 'I'm barmy all over for yer.'

'Yes, ain't I 'eroic?' said Dumpling, and in her rapture was reckless enough to tell Danny he could join her in her mum's parlour tomorrow afternoon. Mind, on the tram going home, she did add a rider, saying they could have a lovely football talk about how she scored the winning goal.

'All right, Dumpling, we'll do that as well,' said Danny.

'What d'yer mean, as well?' asked Dumpling in alarm.

'Sort of in addition, like,' said Danny.

'I'll saw yer daft 'ead off,' said Dumpling.

When, on the morrow, Mrs Evans heard Danny had been invited, she made sure the parlour was left exclusive to him and Dumpling, and she also made sure Dumpling wore her best Sunday blouse and skirt.

Some time during the afternoon, the kids, banned from the parlour, came pouring into the kitchen from their horseplay on the stairs.

'Mum, Mum, Dumpling's shoutin'.'

'No, she's not,' said Mrs Evans, sharing the kitchen fireside with her husband.

'Yes, she is, Mum, she's shoutin' for 'elp.'

'Well, me and your dad don't want any of you tryin' to rescue 'er,' said Mrs Evans.

'Not till teatime,' said Mr Evans, who'd had the pleasure of seeing Dumpling score the winning goal yesterday.

'That's it, not till teatime,' said Mrs Evans.

That meant Dumpling endured the soppiest Sunday afternoon of her life.

'Oh, me gawd,' she gasped once, 'if you don't give over messin' about, I'll get me dad to bash yer brains out.'

'I ain't secondin' that,' said Danny, re-engaging.

'Mum! 'Elp! Dad! 'Elp!'

No answer was the parental reply.

Ma nearly blew her top on Monday morning when her daily paper reported another big jewel robbery, this time at a house in St John's Wood. What made it all the more aggravating was that an Inspector Clark of Scotland Yard admitted the police didn't have a single clue about the identity of the miscreants.

'They soon found clues that brought them after your Pa,' she said. 'They must've 'ad a real grudge against him considerin' what a gentleman 'e was to everybody. Fancy comin' after 'im on the very day 'e was daft enough to get above 'imself, and now lettin' these real criminals go around 'elping themselves whenever they like. It's just not lawful, allowing common burglars to get away with it. I've a good mind to write to Mr Pierpoint.'

'Who's Mr Pierpoint?' asked Alice.

'The public hangman,' said Ma.

'Who'd you want hanged, then?' asked Nick.

'Inspector Clark,' said Ma.

Inspector Clark, in fact, felt even more aggravated than Ma did, and he made his feelings clear to Detective-Sergeant Plunkett. Sergeant Plunkett said patience was a virtue, and that enough of it would help them cop the crooks. Inspector Clark told him to drop himself into the nearest lav and pull the chain. He didn't have any patience, he'd used it all up, he said, especially as nothing had come of his hopeful theory that the missing loot of the first two burglaries might have landed in the lap of a Continental fence.

* * *

Mr Pollard coughed.

'Ah – everything all right, Harrison?' he asked.

'I've no complaints, sir,' said Nick.

'Ah – um – quite so.' Mr Pollard, of course, was hoping that an inviting mumble would bring forth some information from Nick concerning his relationship with the fourth floor. It brought forth nothing except a question.

'Is that all, Mr Pollard?'

'Yes – no – ah, I merely wished to say that since your rise your work has been excellent.' Mr Pollard coughed again. 'One might have thought the increment has given you the incentive to apply yourself most efficiently to your work.'

'Well, half a crown extra a week can do wonders,' said Nick. But not as much as five bob, he thought, especially as it's December and Christmas is coming.

'I see. Yes. Very well, Harrison, that's all.'

I'm no wiser than he is about the reason for what's been happening, thought Nick as he went back to his desk. All I know for certain is that I'm a bit gone on God's great-niece. That's a fact, that is, and it's something that shouldn't have happened to me. Boring as it was, it all came back to Pa being the skeleton in the family cupboard. Now, if Annabelle didn't happen to be related to God, but was just the girl next door and one of our football supporters, I could invite her into Ma's parlour on a foggy Sunday afternoon and chance having her ask awkward questions about when did I last see my father.

'Harrison, what are you doing with that piece of blotting paper?' The voice of Mr Clewes, senior clerk, interrupted Nick's musings.

'Pardon?'

'Are you eating it?'

'My mistake,' said Nick, coming to, 'I thought it was lunchtime.'

'Off his rocker,' said a saucy junior clerk.

Well, I'm not myself, thought Nick, and that's another fact. And will I see Annabelle again? A lot better if I don't.

The bell tolled for him that afternoon. That is, Mr Pollard called him in and in a hollow voice told him to go up to the fourth floor immediately. Up Nick went, remembering it was just four weeks since he had last seen Annabelle.

God was in his usual heaven, seated at his desk. His mane of iron-grey hair made him look a bit like Lloyd George, except that his features were broader and craggier. He watched Nick's advance in silence. Nick, coming to a stop, felt he was required to stand at attention and salute, but decided he'd be a right Charlie if he did. So he simply waited for God to speak.

'I see you've survived, Harrison,' said the awesome person.

'Survived, sir?'

'I presume you realize that since I last saw you, the world has witnessed the demise of thousands of people? Many thousands. Some by natural causes, some by violence, some by suicide and some by accident. You, I see, weren't one of them. You've survived.'

'Yes, sir, so have you.'

The glint entered the searching eyes.

'Is that a deliberate impertinence, you scoundrel?'

'No, sir,' said Nick, 'I just thought that as so many people have passed on since you last saw me, you and I could count ourselves lucky.'

'Damn my soul,' said God, 'you are being impertinent. Business customs and practices being what they are, Harrison, pipsqueak clerks may exist, but not for the purpose of speaking out of turn. Or speaking at all. However, there are other people in the world, people of a worthy kind. One of them is my great-niece. Therefore, reluctant though I am to give you further time off, I am acceding to her request for you to meet her in the usual place. God knows what gets into the minds of worthy young ladies, but there it is. You will arrive at the Exchange Teashop in twenty minutes, at a quarter-to-four precisely. You will take no liberties, nor suppose yourself to be of any importance. You are merely to give her polite company and due respect.'

'Sir, that might sound all very fine—'

'What? What?'

'Well, so it might, sir, but it's labelling me as a nobody. If I'm to give Miss Somers company, I don't want to arrive feeling I've just been let out of a box, and that I'm only to say yes or no.'

'You young bugger,' said God.

'Is that it, then, sir? Am I getting my cards?'

'You're more likely to get your infernal neck broken if you're not out of this office and back at your work in ten seconds. Wait,' he growled as Nick made for the door. 'Damn it, very well, I accept you're another human being no better and no worse than most of us, so go and meet my niece.'

'Right, sir, I'm on my way.'

'You'd better be,' said Annabelle's great-uncle.

'My God,' said Nick in apt fashion, as he slid into a chair at the corner table, 'I don't know what you say to your great-uncle about me, but he gives me a feeling I'm only six inches tall.'

'Oh, hello,' said Annabelle, 'how nice to see you again.' Her smile curved her lips, showed her white teeth and found its way into her eyes. Her dark lashes fluttered. She's a minx, thought Nick, she's playing games, but who couldn't like her? 'What was that you said about my respected Uncle John?' asked Annabelle, wondering just a little why her pulse rate felt jumpy. She simply never suffered from that kind of thing.

'Never mind,' said Nick, 'it's not your fault he was born of thunder and lightning.' He looked around. The teashop was nearly full. The young waitress, catching his glance, smiled and nodded. Nick gave her a little wave.

'Well, I'm blessed,' said Annabelle, 'what's the idea?'

'Friend of mine,' said Nick. 'Have you ordered?'

'Yes,' said Annabelle, 'I was sure you'd be on time, but I don't know what Uncle John would think about you waving to waitresses as soon as you come in.'

'Feed me brimstone, I expect,' said Nick, and Annabelle let a little soft laugh escape. She had a brown velvet hat on today, its brim almost as low as an eye-shade, and she looked very much a fashionable young lady alive with amusement.

'You do like sharing tea and crumpets with me, don't you?' she said.

'It's a lot better than running to catch a tram,' said Nick.

'I should jolly well hope it is,' said Annabelle.

'You sent me a birthday card,' said Nick.

'I always send my friends birthday cards, and your birthday was your twenty-first,' she said. Their waitress arrived and set out their order. The hot buttered crumpets gave off the usual welcome aroma.

'Thanks,' said Nick.

'Always a pleasure, sir, and nice to see you again.'

'Mutual,' said Nick.

'Hope so,' said the waitress, smiling as she left them to themselves.

Annabelle, pouring the milk, said, 'Did you have an uproarious birthday party?'

'Well, we had a knees-up and a mazurka,' said Nick.

'What's a mazurka?'

'Search me,' said Nick, 'but we've got a Polish lodger who can play the piano a bit and thinks a mazurka's an improvement on a knees-up.'

'I bet it isn't,' said Annabelle, 'there's nothing as lively or as much fun as a knees-up. There, there's your tea, now let's enjoy the crumpets. You can talk to me while we're eating. Why d'you have a Polish lodger?'

'Well, he was Polish when he turned up,' said Nick, 'and we didn't think we ought to upset him by changing to a Spanish one.'

'Aren't you funny?' said Annabelle. 'Oh, listen, Nick, as you live in Browning Street—'

'Yes, that reminds me,' said Nick, 'thanks for the birthday card, but where did you get my address from?'

'Uncle John. He gave it to me very growlingly, he said something about me making an office boy of him, and that I was out of my mind in wanting the address of a pipsqueak clerk. I told him that if he talked that way again, I'd stop coming up to have lunch with him.'

'I think you've a way of running things,' said Nick.

'I'm actually very sweet,' said Annabelle. 'Anyway, as you live in Browning Street, I wanted to ask if you know the Brown family of Caulfield Place. Do you, Nick?'

'Freddy Brown's a close friend of mine.'

'Well, isn't that interesting? His sister Susie is married to my Uncle Sammy. Don't you think that's interesting, a bit like destiny being at work?'

Nick said he hardly ever thought about destiny. Usually, on his way to work in the mornings, he said, he thought about processing funeral claims for poor old deceased widows like Mrs Potter of Clapham. Going home in the evenings, he said, he thought about what he was going to get for supper, and after supper he thought about going round to see friends like Freddy.

Annabelle said she didn't believe a word of that. No-one simply thought of insurance claims and suppers every day. Wasn't he thinking now of what a coincidence it was that they both knew Freddy? Nick said he did sometimes think it was a small world. Annabelle asked if he also knew Freddy's lovable girlfriend, Cassie Ford. Everyone knows Cassie, said Nick. Well, the world's getting even smaller, then, said Annabelle, and asked if he knew the residential area of Denmark Hill. Nick said he knew it well, and that he also knew the Tower of London, Hyde Park and Hackney Wick.

'Blessed saints,' said Annabelle, 'how did Hackney Wick get a mention?'

'We used to live there,' said Nick, 'we're Hackney Wick cockneys.'

'Oh, we're Walworth cockneys mostly,' said Annabelle. 'My mother and her brothers are Adams'. Have you heard of the Adams' of Walworth?'

Nick, working an enjoyable way through his crumpets, gave that thought. Annabelle eyed him in amusement. She was getting to know him now. He didn't really have to think about her question, he was working up to some kind of joke.

'Yes, I think I've heard Freddy talk of them,' he said. 'Well, he would, I suppose, seeing that his eldest sister is married to one of them. Of course, I don't know any of them. I know most of the market stallholders, some of the assistants in Woolworths, and the manager of the Maypole in the Walworth Road, but no, I don't know any of your Adams'.'

'Oh, dear, what a shame.' Annabelle's colourful smile showed itself. 'Do you go to Ruskin Park sometimes? I've played lots of tennis there with my Uncle Boots and his daughter Rosie. Do you play tennis?'

'No, football,' said Nick, 'on Saturday afternoons in Brockwell Park.'

'Honestly?'

'Well, there's the occasional foul or a dirty trip—'

'No, you silly, I don't mean that and you know I don't. I mean, do you really play in Brockwell Park?'

'Yes, honestly,' said Nick.

'You look as if you could be good at open-air games,' said Annabelle. She thought then that it was a bit silly waiting for him to take the initiative, especially as her mum wanted to meet him and look him over. Quite certain he liked her, she said in her self-assured way, 'Look, if you've never played tennis I could book a court in Ruskin Park one Sunday afternoon and teach you. Then you could come back home and have tea with my family.'

That's done it, thought Nick. It's put the ruddy cat among the poor old pigeons. I've got to get out of this before I get in really deep. I'm already up to my knees. Who wouldn't be with a dream of a girl, even if she does like playing games? Pa, you're a problem to your family.

'Well, that's a nice offer, Annabelle,' he said, 'but I don't think my girlfriend would go for it.'

Annabelle's belief in herself suffered a sharp shock. Somehow, from the moment she had developed an unusual interest in him, it had never occurred to her that he might have a steady girlfriend. She hadn't allowed the thought to enter her head. Her interest had been such that she instinctively excluded any idea of a rival. All the boys who were madly keen on her didn't have other girls in the wings. Dismayed and disconcerted, she bit her lip. Unhappiness lodged itself, unhappiness of a kind totally foreign to her. She swallowed.

'Oh, I see,' she said, and Nick felt a twinge of conscience about having summoned up a girl who didn't exist. But he felt he knew more than enough about this girl's background to be certain none of her family would jump over the moon if she brought home the son of a felon doing hard labour. It wouldn't be snobbery or anything like that, it would be natural family reaction, and quite understandable. All the same, he wished he hadn't made her look visibly unhappy.

'I expect you've got a close friend or two,' he said.

'Yes, lots, of course.' Annabelle felt utterly down in the dumps. Worse, she felt awful about the way she had contrived to get him into this teashop every month. Uncle Boots hadn't liked it, and she ought to have thought about that, because Uncle Boots was usually so good-natured about everything. People's sins and omissions usually made him smile or laugh. 'Oh, look, you must think me pretty awful about all this.'

'About tea and crumpets with you?'

'Yes, getting you here the way I have.'

'Nothing awful about it,' said Nick, 'nor about you. You're a lovely girl, and I mean that. I think you've pulled my leg a lot, but I do that sort of thing myself. The bloke who gets you in the end can look forward to all kinds of fun and games, seeing you'll never be dull or boring. Well, that's my opinion, an honest one. It's been fun and games spending time in this teashop with you, never mind if your Uncle John has growled about it.'

'Oh, don't,' said Annabelle. Everything was upside-down. Sure that she could make him fall for her, it hadn't happened. He'd already fallen for someone else. She herself was the one who had ended up with suffering feelings. 'No, I really am so sorry I've behaved stupidly.'

'I don't agree,' said Nick, 'it hasn't been like that at all. Well, how could it have been when it's been so enjoyable, and a lot better than being stuck at my desk?'

'I think you're trying to be very nice about it,' said Annabelle. 'Shall we go now?'

They parted a little later in Holborn, as usual. Nick, realizing it was a final parting, wished her the very best of luck. Annabelle couldn't think of anything to say except goodbye. Nick, going home, wondered if there wasn't some way round his predicament, for he hated the thought of never seeing her again. Annabelle, going her way, thought she'd never be happy again. At seventeen, of course, that was what any mortified young lady would think.

She told her parents that evening that she had changed her mind about Nick Harrison, so they didn't have anything to worry about now. She had an over-bright smile on her face. If Lizzy thought it was the end of one more girlish enthusiasm, Ned wasn't so sure.

Annabelle later phoned her cousin Rosie, adopted daughter of Boots and Emily. Rosie, who had been brilliant at school, was due to enter Somerville College, Oxford University. Meanwhile, she was studying at home, as well as being a help to her mother and grandma.

'Hello, Annabelle.'

'Rosie, I – oh, how's everyone?'

'Same as usual, I'm happy to say,' said Rosie, a fascinating young woman in her nineteenth year and devoted to the adoptive parents who had given her such a lovely life.

'I'm glad someone's happy. I'm not, I've come a terrible cropper, and I'm so humiliated.' Annabelle recounted her tale of woe.

'Well, bless you, my child,' said Rosie. 'Didn't I ever tell you that she who runs ahead of the tiger has a terrible time when it catches her up?'

'I don't think that's a bit funny.'

'Sorry, lovey, rotten of me. Is it hurting?'

'No, of course not.'

'It's just your pride, lovey?'

'I feel so stupid.'

'And a bit jealous?' said Rosie.

'Jealous? Me? Who of?'

'His girlfriend.'

'Oh, her. Hope she catches measles.'

'Oh, dear, I think it's serious. Well, look, I can't talk a lot now, but come round tomorrow evening and we'll work something out. It's ridiculous, any suggestion of parting for ever, when you don't know if his feelings for his current girlfriend are really deep or not. You're not pining away at this minute, are you?'

'Of course not. I'm stupid, but not as stupid as that.'

'Well, good. Come round tomorrow evening. Shall I tell your Uncle Boots that disaster has struck?'

'Don't you dare.'

'All right, lovey, chin up.'

Nick, trying to put Annabelle out of his mind, had popped in on Gran Emerson and Ivy on his way home from Holborn. They had customers. He waited his turn, and when it came, Ivy grabbed his attention.

''Ello, me dear, what can I do for you in private?'

'You saucebox,' said Gran, 'you'll get me shop a bad name.'

'Can I 'elp it if I fancy showin' Nick me picture postcards?' said Ivy.

'I'll make do with you selling me a sixpenny bar of Cadbury's milk chocolate,' said Nick.

'Don't get me too excited,' said Ivy, placing the bar on the counter.

'Any news about yer Pa's ship, Nick?' asked Gran.

'Only that whatever ship it is, it's still in the China Seas,' said Nick, paying for the chocolate and making for the door before Gran could ask other questions.

'See yer some time, 'andsome,' called Ivy.

'Not in private yer won't,' said Gran with a larky giggle.

Dumpling arrived early for the evening's committee meeting just to give herself time to say hello to Ma and the family. Ma told her she was looking a nice healthy girl.

'Yes, ain't I?' said Dumpling. 'It's me footballin' that does it, Mrs 'Arrison. Oh, did yer hear about me scorin' the winning goal last Saturday week?'

'Yes,' said Ma, 'I 'eard a lot about it from Nick and me girls.'

'I headed it, yer know, with me robust chest,' said Dumpling proudly. That was double Dutch to Ma, and so it was to Amy, but Nick, Alice and Fanny had an acquired understanding of what Dumpling meant.

'I'm sure it's a myst'ry to me,' said Ma, 'and it still don't sound natural, girls playin' football. And I don't know that a girl's chest ought to be anywhere near a football.'

Fanny giggled. Alice and Amy struggled to keep their faces straight and just about won.

'Oh, I'm one of the blokes when I'm in the team,' said Dumpling cheerfully.

'Dumpling,' said Nick, 'in appreciation of your winning goal, accept this with my compliments.' And he gave her the large bar of milk chocolate. He had bought it thinking that because he'd been unkind to Annabelle, he ought to be kind to someone else. There were few people in Walworth who didn't think a sixpenny bar of Cadbury's a real treat. Dumpling gazed at it in rapture.

'Oh, yer a lovely captain, Nick,' she said, 'I dunno I'll ever come up against one as sporty as you.'

'They'll know it if you do,' said Amy wickedly. It had no effect on Dumpling, touched by her captain's gesture of appreciation.

'I dunno that I won't keep this choc'late for ever

instead of eatin' it,' she said. 'I mean, well, it'll always remind me of me winning goal and 'ow the captain of me beloved Rovers give it to me in appreciation of me footballin' gifts.'

'Tell you what, Dumpling,' said Nick, 'you eat the chocolate and I'll give you a signed certificate about the goal. How's that?'

'Oh, would yer, Nick?' breathed Dumpling, beaming mistily.

'Half a tick, and I'll rough it out,' said Nick. Annabelle was on his mind and he was in the mood for doing good deeds. 'We've got ten minutes before the others arrive.' He lifted a sheet of notepaper from a drawer in the dresser and sat down at the table. He used a pencil to scribble the tribute, then asked Dumpling if she'd like him to read it out.

'Not 'alf,' she said.

'Corblimey, you bet,' said young Fanny.

'How's yer canary, Alice?' said Amy.

'All ears,' said Alice.

'Go on, read it out, Nick,' urged Dumpling, and Nick did so.

'This is to certify that on the third Saturday of November, 1933, at the age of eighteen, Miss CHRISSIE EVANS in capital letters played centre forward for Browning Street Rovers against Rodney Road United, known as the demons of Walworth soccer. It's also certified that despite the rough-house tactics of the demons, Miss CHRISSIE EVANS in capital letters burst courageously through their defence and scored the winning goal three minutes from time. It's finally certified that her fearless chest played a noble part in this historic act of footballing valour. Signed, Nicholas Harrison, Captain.'

'Crikey,' breathed Dumpling, 'fancy all that bein' certified, Nick.'

'That's not the only thing round 'ere,' said Alice.

'Nick, could yer do it in yer best writin' with no crossings out?' asked Dumpling.

'I'll do it during the committee meeting,' said Nick, 'and the committee can sign it too.'

'Oh, Mrs 'Arrison, ain't yer got a kind son?' said Dumpling. 'I don't 'old with some of the blokes callin' 'im a bit lah-de-dah on account of 'im talkin' like a bank manager sometimes. If you could see 'im when he's performin' 'eroic for the Rovers, well, anyone would take 'im to be as manly as any navvy.'

'Chrissie, I'll 'ave you know Nick's like 'is sailor Pa, a gent,' said Ma.

'Certified,' said Alice.

'Oh, Nick's a gent all right, Mrs 'Arrison, and none of us mind that,' said Dumpling.

The front door knocker sounded then, and so did a voice calling through the letter-box.

'Coo-ee, Nick, it's me and Freddy and Danny.'

Irrepressible Cassie had turned up again.

The committee's discussion of recent results and form took in Dumpling's winning goal against the Rodney Road lot. Dumpling herself, apart from admitting she'd made history, played a modest part in the discussion. Then Nick wrote out the certificate of merit, with Danny looking proud, Freddy grinning, and Cassie showing her sweetest smile. Everyone signed, and Dumpling clasped the completed certificate to her jumper.

However, she then brought up the subject of what footballers didn't ought to do to each other. She hadn't mentioned it last week, she said, but she just couldn't help herself tonight, because it was playing on her mind. Danny had been at it again last Sunday week in her mum's parlour. He'd as good as turned her best Sunday blouse inside-out, she said.

'Now look here, Dumpling,' said Nick, 'what goes on between you and Danny in your mum's parlour is just between you and him. It's nothing to do with the team or the committee. Speak to your mum about it.'

'But I did speak to 'er,' said Dumpling, 'and I showed 'er what Danny 'ad done to me blouse, and she said well, it couldn't be 'elped and that Danny could stay to tea. Of course, when me dad 'eard, 'e nearly 'ad a fatal seizure, but somehow 'e can't bring 'imself to tell Danny never to darken our doorstep again. Nick, can't the committee lay down a sort of law of be'aviour? Otherwise, me mum says she might 'ave to ask Danny to marry me.'

'I second that,' said Cassie.

'But what about me footballin' career?' protested Dumpling.

'Some time or other, Dumpling lovey,' said Nick, 'we've all got to chuck our footballing careers out of the window.'

'I second that as well,' said Cassie, giving Freddy a pointed look.

'So do I,' said Danny.

'Oh, me breakin' heart,' said Dumpling, 'I won't 'ave anything to live for.'

'Course you will, Dumpling,' said Danny, 'you'll 'ave me.'

''Ere, I ain't goin' to live soppy ever after, not while I've still got me powerful footballin' legs,' said Dumpling.

'Never mind, me darling,' said cheerful Freddy, 'you'll always 'ave yer signed certificate.'

'And Danny'll promise to love and honour your footballing legs,' said Nick. 'What's the next item on the agenda?'

Chapter Thirteen

Mr Lukavitch continued to be no trouble at all. He didn't get drunk, he worked quietly away in the upstairs top, while treating himself occasionally to the pleasure of sharing a pot of afternoon tea with Ma. Now and again he visited the East Street market to do a bit of shopping, becoming a familiar figure to neighbours. Sometimes a neighbour would stop Ma in the street and mention him.

''Ello, Mrs 'Arrison, me and me old man 'eard you'd got a lodger. I must say 'e seems a respectable gent to look at, but of course I ain't been forward enough to ask 'im 'is name.'

'It's Mr Loovakish,' said Ma.

'Well, I never, is that foreign? It sounds remarkable like Russian. He ain't one of them Russians that come over years ago to save their 'eads bein' chopped off by them bloodthirsty Bolsheviks, is 'e, poor man?'

'No, he's a Polish gent,' said Ma, 'and 'e came over just after the war.'

'My, yer don't say. I thought all Polish gents 'ad black whiskers. Or p'raps that's Russian, I'm never sure. Anyway, it's not 'is fault 'e was born Polish, nor your worry, I 'ope. I mean, 'e don't look the kind that'll murder you and yours in yer beds.'

'Oh, I wouldn't 'ave any lodger in me house that 'ad them kind of looks, Mrs Williams,' said Ma.

'Mr Loovakish is a very kind and pleasin' lodger.'

'Well, a pleasin' lodger must be real pleasin' to a woman whose 'usband's away like yours is, Mrs 'Arrison. Is 'e still in China, like?'

'There's no end to 'is labours,' said Ma. 'Nor to them Chinese pirates,' she added.

'It's 'ard on yer, Mrs 'Arrison.'

'Don't I know it,' said Ma.

'Never mind, I'm sure yer kind lodger won't stop bein' pleasin','

'How kind,' said Ma.

On Friday afternoon, Mister Horsemouth made one of his so-called helpful calls on Ma and asked about the lodger. Ma said she'd got no complaints about Mr Loovakish, it was that man Tosh Fingers she objected to, so she'd be obliged if he'd see to it that Mr Fingers didn't come round again. Mister Horsemouth had the sauce then to say he didn't take any orders from tuppenny-ha'penny females, and she was to remember she was costing him money. Ma told him in return to kindly note she knew where it was coming from, and that there was no such thing as a tuppeny-ha'penny female, that they were all worth a sight more than he was. Mister Horsemouth said bugger me or something like that, and he also said that in future he'd just be paying the rent for her and no extra. That's still costing me, he said. Ma went stiff with umbrage. Anyway, said Mister Horsemouth, Nick could earn a lot more oof than he'll ever earn in insurance, so if he wants to better himself, tell him to come and see me.

'I told 'im not likely,' said Ma to Nick later that day. 'Mind you, 'e was very compliment'ry about you, sayin' you could be turned into a smart young swell favourable to ladies that 'ad got more money than sense. I told 'im to show 'imself out, that he wasn't goin' to 'ave the chance to lead you astray like 'e led your Pa.'

'If I'm here next time he calls,' said Nick, 'I'll knock his head off, shall I, Ma?'

'No, best not to do any damage to him,' said Ma, 'or 'e might not give us any allowance at all. Best to put up with 'is sauce and them big teeth of his.'

Ma was very practical.

It was the Saturday before Christmas, and as a newspaper weather expert had aptly forecast, the day was bright and crisp and even. Boots stopped his car outside the entrance to Brockwell Park, and two young ladies alighted.

'Thanks, Daddy,' said Rosie.

'Yes, thanks, Uncle Boots,' said Annabelle.

'I'm not asking what it's all about,' smiled Boots, and drove away.

'Well?' said Rosie, clad in a belted blue coat and a woollen hat. The blue of the coat emphasized her fairness. Willowy and naturally elegant, she was, at five-feet-seven, an inch taller than Annabelle, whose strawberry-red coat enriched her brunette colouring.

'Well what?' said Annabelle.

'Shall we take a look?'

'Yes, come on,' said Annabelle, 'it was your brainwave, so you're the last one who should hang back.'

They walked through the open gates into the park, making for the football pitch.

'Are you sure he'll be here?' asked Rosie.

'I only know he said he played here on Saturday afternoons. Oh, lor', I still can't see exactly how it's going to help.'

'Oh, you simply wait for inspiration to strike,' said Rosie.

'Supposing his girlfriend is here watching him?'

'There, that's inspirational, my chicken,' said Rosie. 'Simply put yourself next to her and outshine her. You do have quite a fatal beauty, and all's fair in love and war. Oh, Romeo, art thou here, Romeo?'

'Rosie, I'll bite you.'

'Sorry, lovey.'

They passed the netball arena and took the path to the football pitch. The time was twenty minutes past two. In the distance, a match was in progress. The kick-off time in mid-winter was two o'clock. They noticed spectators standing close to the touchline. There were two separate groups, one of a few young men and a solitary girl, the other of six girls together with a man and his dog.

As Annabelle and Rosie approached, they heard one of the six girls yell.

'Freddy, get up! Break his leg!'

Rosie and Annabelle stopped on the path. The six girls had their backs to them. The yelling girl, in a maroon coat, had long raven black hair tied with a red ribbon.

'Rosie, that's Cassie, Cassie Ford,' said Annabelle.

'And there, sweetie, is Freddy himself, Uncle Sammy's young brother-in-law,' said Rosie. 'Heavens, the excitement, can Romeo be here too? Didn't you tell me that Freddy's a close friend of his?'

'If you're going to keep on talking about Romeo, Rosie Adams,' breathed Annabelle, 'I'll send you home. It's bad enough – oh, there he is.' Her eyes ran about, tracking a long-legged figure down the pitch at a little distance behind Freddy and to his left. Freddy was moving forward, the ball at his feet. A burly opponent came charging at him, and Freddy slipped the ball sideways and forwards, giving Nick the chance to run straight on to it. One of the girls, young-looking, shouted at him to shoot. Nick picked up speed, ran at the ball and struck it with his right foot. He ballooned it high over the opposing goal. The six girls yelled in disgust.

The young-looking one shouted, 'Rubbish! Go home!'

And Rosie and Annabelle heard a plump girl say, 'I just don't know what's come over Nick recent, he plays 'eroic one week and like a fairy on a rockcake the next.'

'He's in love,' said Cassie.

'Oh, me gawd,' said Dumpling, 'it don't bear thinkin' about, the captain of me footballin' Rovers goin' in for all that soppy stuff.'

'It's not all that soppy,' said Cassie, watching the action while unaware of the presence of Rosie and Annabelle at a little distance behind her. Rosie was killing herself at what she was hearing. Annabelle, watching Nick, had a jumpy pulse rate.

'Annabelle,' whispered Rosie, casting a glance at Nick, 'is that your beloved?'

'Oh, you Rosie, I'll really biff you in a minute,' breathed Annabelle.

Rosie took a longer look at Nick, who was helping Danny at the moment to ward off an attack by the opposing forwards. She understood Annabelle's romantic interest a little better then, for Nick was very much a young man, tall, vigorous-looking and with fine straight legs. All the boys contemporary with Annabelle and who competed for her favours would seem no more than boys to her compared to this healthy young man. Rosie watched him as the ball came sailing over from the wing. He used his head to meet it, but his head miscued and the ball angled limply away and fell at the feet of an opponent, who booted it straight at the Rovers' goal. Charlie Cope, much to the relief of temporarily agonized supporters, got a gallant hand to it and turned it round the goal for a corner.

Young Fanny expressed her feelings again.

'Wake up, Nick, can't you!'

The man's dog barked in sympathy with her disgust.

'Oh, me failin' 'eart,' groaned Dumpling, ''e nearly gave a goal away there. Alice, what's up with 'im?'

Rosie and Annabelle heard a slim, attractive young lady say, 'I don't think he knows if he's out of bed yet, Chrissie.'

Oh, thought Annabelle, that's his girlfriend, I suppose. Alice. Oh, blow that, she looks nice. What am I doing here?

'Annabelle,' whispered Rosie, 'shall we let Cassie know we're here?'

'No,' whispered Annabelle, 'I'm going home.'

'No, you're not, sweetie, this is all too exciting,' murmured Rosie.

The corner had been taken, and Nick broke free with the ball. If he'd known Annabelle was present and watching, he'd have probably fallen over his feet. As it was, her image kept intruding all too often, as it had ever since he'd seen the look of dismay on her face. However, his footballing skill took over now, and he hit a splendid pass to Starving Crow out on the left wing, and away went the likeable follower of Moses. Nick ran at speed down the field, and Starving Crow saw him coming in his role as attacking centre half. He angled the ball through the opposing defence, and Nick, coming up at a rushing pace, made full amends. He hit a beauty.

The six girls leapt in delight.

'Goal! Goal!'

'Oh, me 'ero!' Dumpling bounced about in joy. 'What a goal. Ain't you proud of yer brother now, Alice?'

Annabelle didn't miss that remark. She supposed one of the others had to be his one and only. Not Cassie, of course, and not the plump girl, or the very young one.

'My goodness,' said Rosie, 'that really was magic, Annabelle.' Rosie knew something about football. She and her brother Tim, together with Boots, sometimes went to see the local amateur team, Dulwich Hamlet, play. 'Did you see it? A dream of a goal, and he's not bad himself, either. He's the one, is he, the light in your eyes?'

'Blessed saints, will you stop laughing at me, you horror?'

'Sorry, sweetie.' Rosie simply couldn't help being tickled by Annabelle's leap into the giddying whirlpool of romantic confusion. Having had boys at her feet from the age of fifteen because of her fascinating looks, Annabelle had suddenly lost her head and her composure. Oh, poor love. Rosie herself was immune to all that. All her deepest affections were directed at her family, especially at her adoptive father.

'Perhaps we should say hello to Cassie,' said Annabelle.

'And meet the other girls to see which one is your rival?' said Rosie.

'No, you thing, I'm not going to be so stupid. Come on.' Annabelle braced herself, and she and Rosie left the path and walked over the turf towards the six girls. 'Hello, Cassie, surprise, surprise,' said Annabelle.

Cassie swung round. She stared for a moment at the two girls, nieces of Freddy's brother-in-law, Sammy Adams. She knew Rosie and Annabelle as well as Freddy did. Her face, tingling in the crisp cold air of the December afternoon, broke into a delighted smile.

'Crikey, where did you two come from?'

'Oh, through the gates five minutes ago,' said Annabelle. 'We were just enjoying a walk in the park.'

'My, don't you both look nice and posh?' said Cassie.

'I don't mind looking nice, Cassie,' said Rosie, 'I hope I don't look posh.'

'Oh, you don't 'ave to be ashamed of it,' said Cassie, 'it becomes you. And my dad says I look a bit posh meself on Sundays, and Freddy says so too.'

'Why are you watching football?' asked Annabelle, resolutely keeping her eyes off Nick.

'Well, Freddy's playin',' said Cassie, 'it's our own local team and all us girls are supporters. If they didn't 'ave us, they'd just be any old team.'

'Oh, yes, I can see Freddy,' said Rosie.

'Yes, isn't he smashin' in his jersey and shorts?' said Cassie.

Rosie, teasing-eyed, pointed and said, 'And so's that one, isn't he?'

Cassie turned. Following the pointing finger, she said, 'Oh, that's Freddy's captain, Nick Harrison. He's just scored a marvellous goal, and we're winning two–one. Would you like to meet our supporters?'

'Oh, we won't stop,' said Annabelle. She was having a very trying time attempting to be her normal composed self. For a seventeen-year-old, she could be very composed. Now she actually felt nervous in case Nick caught sight of her. Oh, lor', he'd think she was running after him. She'd feel a lot better if she left.

But the other girls were all looking now, and Cassie, a happy character, liked to bring people together.

'Look,' she said to the other supporters, 'here's two of Freddy's relatives, they're like 'is cousins, really. That's Rosie and that's Annabelle. And this is Chrissie, and these are Nick's sisters, Alice and Fanny, and this is Meg and this is Julie.'

'Oh, pleased to meet yer, I'm sure,' beamed Dumpling, 'I'm one of our team meself, yer know, I've played in goal and centre forward.'

'Crikey,' said Annabelle in astonishment, 'you haven't, have you?'

'Not 'alf,' said Dumpling, proudly, 'I'm one of the blokes mostly. You can ask Alice, she's got a high standin', bein' our captain's eldest sister.'

Rosie, killing herself again, but able to hide it, said to Alice, 'Is that right, then, is she one of the blokes mostly?'

'Not mostly,' said Alice, liking the looks of these well-dressed girls, 'just all the time.'

'Oh, yer couldn't 'ave been more compliment'ry, Alice,' said Dumpling happily. The ref blew a long blast on his whistle. 'That's 'alf-time,' said Dumpling to Rosie and Annabelle, 'you can meet our beloved Rovers now, they're easy the best team in Walworth.'

The Rovers were heading for the touchline. Annabelle, glimpsing Nick among them, panicked.

'Oh, we've got to go now, we're in a hurry,' she said.

'Oh, are we?' said Rosie.

'Yes, come on,' said Annabelle. Too late. The sweaty Rovers were swarming in search of their half-time lemon, engaging in boisterous chat with the young girl, the one called Fanny. Annabelle's sixth sense warned her that someone had picked her out, and the next moment that someone was beside her, exuding the warmth that came from physical exercise.

'Jumping crackers, it's not you, is it?' It was a whisper in her ear. Annabelle could have stuck pins in herself for being so tongue-tied. Helplessly, she turned her head. There he was, a young man of the outdoors in his jersey and shorts, knees slightly muddy, hair a little awry and a wondering smile on his face. Annabelle felt like making a complaint. Well, he was so in control of himself, while she was all confusion. It shouldn't be allowed to happen to a girl. Inherited courage came to her aid.

'Oh, hello,' she said brightly. Dumpling came further to her aid, although unconsciously.

'That's Freddy's cousin Annabelle, Nick,' she said, 'we've all just met her and Rosie. That's

Rosie, she's a cousin too. Well, that's what Cassie said. Oh, Nick's our captain, by the way.'

'Fascinating,' said Rosie, 'I don't think we've ever met a football team captain before, have we, Annabelle?'

'Well, if you don't mind me sayin' so,' said Dumpling, 'it's a bit of an honour to meet the Rovers' captain. Mind, I won't say he don't chuck 'is weight about sometimes. Other times 'e gets it into his 'ead to keep sayin', "Now look 'ere, my girl." But 'e can't 'elp it, it's on account of him 'aving a clerkin' job in the City.' With the other girls mingling with the rest of the team, Dumpling had this particular stage to herself. 'Nick, you 'aven't said 'ello to Freddy's cousins.'

'I've been listening to you, Dumpling,' said Nick, giving away nothing of the fact that the appearance of Annabelle out of the blue was the most welcome event of the week, never mind if it posed complications. In the crisp afternoon light she looked stunning. 'Pleasure to say hello,' he said, 'but don't take too much notice of Chrissie, she's known for going over the top. So you're Freddy's cousins.' As Alice was within earshot, Nick had said nothing so far to indicate he knew Annabelle. 'Lucky old Freddy.'

'Did someone call?' Freddy inserted himself into the group. 'Well, look who's here, Sammy's favourite nieces. Might I say you're both lookin' like Christmas presents? 'Ave you met Nick?'

'Oh, yes, we've had the honour,' said Annabelle.

'Does he give autographs?' smiled Rosie.

'Crikey, Nick, what a thought,' said Dumpling, 'you could sell yer autograph for a penny a time for the team kitty.'

Nick laughed.

'All right, Dumpling, get the street kids lined up, and I'll sign at seven for sixpence or fourteen for a bob,' he said. 'But let them know photographs will be extra.'

Rosie thought then that he was utterly right for Annabelle. He really was a fine-looking young man with grey eyes like her father's. Her adoptive father's. No wonder Annabelle had lost all interest in her many boyfriends. And no wonder some girl had already laid claim to the young man. Heavens, how was Annabelle going to cope with that?

'Shall we put our names down for a photograph each, Annabelle?' she said. 'Signed, of course.'

Annabelle, recovering some of her normal poise, said, 'I'll be thrilled.'

'I'll be surprised,' said Nick.

'I'll have a banana,' said Freddy.

'Signed?' said Rosie.

'I never 'eard of anyone signing a banana,' said Dumpling.

'What brought you two girls to the football pitch?' asked Nick, taking a slice of lemon from Fanny as his young sister entered the group.

'We were just strolling,' said Rosie, 'and we saw Cassie.'

'What's the name of your team?' asked Annabelle.

'Browning Street Rovers,' said Dumpling. 'Everyone knows the Rovers in Walworth. Nick's well-known too, bein' our famous captain.'

'When he's not playin' rubbish,' said Fanny.

'Excuse Fanny,' said Nick, 'she's one of my sisters.'

'Well, don't tell ev'rybody,' said saucy Fanny,

'it'll make it harder to live with for me and Amy and Alice.'

The referee's whistle sounded again.

'Half-time's up, Nick,' said Dumpling.

'Come on, Freddy,' called Cassie. She arrived at his back and pulled him away from Rosie and Annabelle. She also delivered a warning little kick. Freddy accepted it manfully, knowing it was for standing too close to Rosie.

Nick, not quite sure what to say to Annabelle, made do with, 'Well, have a nice Christmas.'

Annabelle gave him a slightly scornful look, supposing the reason why he'd acted as if he'd only just met her was because he didn't want his girlfriend to know, whichever girl it was. It had to be either the girl called Meg or the one called Julie. It couldn't be that jolly plump girl, could it? She was the one who'd monopolized him these last several minutes. Help, could it possibly be her? She was jolly all right, but a pumpkin of a girl.

'You're getting left behind,' she said.

'So I am,' said Nick, and smiled at both young ladies. 'So long,' he said, and followed his team back on to the field.

'Rosie, are you and Annabelle goin' to stay and watch?' asked Cassie.

Rosie looked at Annabelle. Annabelle was in a dither.

'Well, just for a few minutes,' said Rosie and she and Annabelle watched as the Rovers kicked off for the start of the second half. Rosie, still highly tickled about everything, put the question that Annabelle wanted to ask. 'Is Nick's girlfriend here?'

'Pardon?' said Cassie, and Alice, next to her, gave Rosie a look of curiosity.

'Your captain, Cassie, is his girlfriend here?'

'Oh, Nick doesn't have a girlfriend,' said Cassie. 'He knows lots, but he doesn't 'ave anyone special. Mind, he's a bit gone on Norma Shearer.' Norma Shearer was a Hollywood film star. 'But I don't think he's got hopes. Well, I don't suppose he could afford her, not Norma Shearer.'

Annabelle wanted to spit. She'd been lied to about him having a girlfriend. Rosie, however, was smiling.

Alice, suspecting that this striking fair girl had developed an interest in her brother, said, 'Nick's funny about girls. He doesn't believe in gettin' seriously attached till he's earnin' quite a bit more than he is now. He says a feller shouldn't go steady with a girl till he can treat her to something more posh than a seat in a cinema.'

'Crikey, Alice,' said Cassie, 'I didn't know Nick 'ad those kind of principles.'

'They're not principles,' said Annabelle in an impulsive outburst, 'they're rhubarb.'

'Yes, who wants something more posh than a cinema seat?' asked Rosie.

'I've just said, Nick's funny about that sort of thing,' remarked Alice, 'and I can't see him gettin' serious about any girl yet. Not for a couple of years, anyway, and not with the pride he's got in his principles, even if they are a bit funny.'

Oh, the rotten devil, we'll see about that, thought Annabelle. I'll give him principles. I'll give him fib to me about having a girlfriend. How could he do that? Crikey, I'm a woman scorned. Oh, you wait, Nick Harrison, I'll make you wish you'd never been born.

'Rubbish!' yelled young Fanny. Herbert Briggs

had missed an open goal. 'Call yerself a footballer?'

Annabelle laughed. Rosie looked at her. Aunt Lizzy's eldest daughter seemed to have made a recovery.

They left after a few more minutes, saying goodbye to Cassie and the other girls.

'Well, ducky?' said Rosie.

'He doesn't have a girlfriend,' said Annabelle.

'Just principles,' smiled Rosie.

'I bet,' said Annabelle. 'No, I think he's just scared that he'll get the sack if he starts walking out with me. He's scared that Uncle John will demolish him with thunder and lightning. D'you know what he calls Uncle John?'

'Tell me,' said Rosie.

'God,' said Annabelle.

Rosie shrieked. 'God? But he's just an old growler.'

'Rosie, what did you think of Nick?'

'Dishy, lovey,' said Rosie.

'But what a rotten devil, telling me he had a girlfriend.'

'Well, I suppose that's what comes of being scared of God,' said Rosie. 'Come on, let's go to Brixton now and buy some Christmas presents for our nearest and dearest. You can think about the best method of slaying your devious Romeo on the way.'

The match ended in a draw. Dumpling said that was what came from not picking her as centre forward. Fanny said, typically, it was just the result of playing like a lot of rubbish boxes. Cassie said she'd have something to say to a certain right half with two left legs, and Freddy moved quickly out of her way. Danny asked Dumpling if he could sit next to her on the tram home. Not likely, said Dumpling, not after what's been happening in me mum's parlour just recent. Suppose it happened on the tram, she said, and the conductor came up and saw? I suppose we'd have to invite him to the wedding, said Danny. Stop getting barmy ideas about weddings, said Dumpling.

Alice, on arrival home, informed Ma that two girl cousins of Freddy Brown had turned up at the match, and that they'd interested themselves in Nick. Well, said Ma, I don't care whose cousins they are, we don't want them interesting themselves in your brother, and you all know why. It's enough, she said, that we have to tell certain stories to all your friends, and our neighbours too, without having to tell the same stories to new friends that might get a bit special to you and Nick. Still, never mind, she said, perking up, we won't have the shadow of sorrow hanging over us for ever, just for one more year and a bit, and perhaps not as long as that if Pa gets good conduct marks.

Ma could get a bit repetitive about the shadow of sorrow, but if repetition was boring it always had a wise edge to it. Nick knew that, because he'd had to tell stories to Annabelle, a girl whose peaches and cream look had suddenly reappeared in Brockwell Park. He wondered if a similar reappearance would happen. He didn't think so. Not only was the meeting accidental, but she had given him a very cutting look just before the start of the second half.

What a lovely girl, though.

Chapter Fourteen

Ma took a good look at Sunday morning's newspaper before sitting down to breakfast. Not a word about the jewel robberies caught her eye, and she might have expressed loud disgust that the cops hadn't nabbed the robbers if the day had been other than a Sunday. As it was, they all went to church later that morning, which gave Ma a chance to ask the Lord to think of Pa, much more of a gentleman than a common burglar.

In the afternoon, they went to see Pa. On the way, Amy said old Mrs Munton, a neighbour, was being buried tomorrow. Nick said not before time, she'd been dead a week.

'I think I might just go to the funeral,' said Ma.

Ma liked a good funeral, especially a royal one. Pa had taken all of them to see the funeral of Queen Alexandra in 1925. There were thousands on the streets, Queen Alexandra having been beloved of the people, according to Ma, but Pa managed to get his family as far as the Mall. There, the people were six deep on either side. When the cortege came in sight, a deep hush settled on the crowds, and even young Fanny, four at the time, stopped fidgeting. Soldiers lining the route bowed their heads, their arms reversed. Pa took his hat off and held it reverently against his chest. Ma had her handkerchief out. Drums beat the Funeral March, and the cortege with its coffin rolled slowly by, pulled by bluejackets. Women cried and Ma blew her nose as respectfully as she could. The late Queen's sons followed the coffin.

What a lovely funeral, said Ma, now let's go and have hot pie and mash somewhere. Pa said he didn't think they'd get any at Buckingham Palace, only black pudding because of the funeral. Ma said don't make that kind of a joke on a sorrowful day like this, so Pa took them to Joe's Pie and Mash Shop off Covent Garden. He paid for the meal with a ten-bob note, which he extracted with a flourish from a very posh-looking leather wallet. Ma asked him in a whisper where he'd got it from. Pa said that's funny, my love, just where did it come from? Ma knew all right, and she also knew why Pa had got them through to the Mall. It was where a lot of posh and well-heeled mourners would be. Ma gave him a whispered earful about it being the most disgraceful thing he'd ever done, considering he'd done it at Queen Alexandra's funeral. Pa said his hand must have slipped, and that, anyway, the dear old biddy had probably been too busy settling down in heaven to have noticed. Just wait till I get you home, Albert Harrison, said Ma. Still, she enjoyed her pie and mash. So did everyone else.

The prison warders in the main looked as tough and hard-bitten as most of the convicts, but some could show a bit of humour. Inside the gates, the warder inspecting the contents of Ma's large cake tin said, ''Ello, 'ello, what've we got 'ere, Mrs Harrison, goodies for yer naughty ole man?'

'Excuse me,' said Ma, 'it's not your place to be disrespectful.'

'Beg yer pardon, I'm sure, missus.'

'So you should,' said Ma, always on her dignity in this place.

In the visitors' room, the convicts present looked grey and put-upon. When Pa came in, he looked bright and breezy. He bowed to Ma before he sat down.

'How's your royal self, queen of me heart?' he said.

'Sufferin',' said Ma, 'specially as I've been thinkin' of the funeral of poor Queen Alexandra and how you committed what you shouldn't 'ave.'

'Water under the bridge, old lady, water under the bridge,' said Pa, taking affectionate stock of his daughters. Up came one of the watchful warders to see if the cake tin was lethal or innocuous. Nick, holding the tin, took the lid off to disclose a Christmas fruitcake baked by Ma. The warder informed her that if her better half had taught himself to go in for baking cakes as good as hers, he'd have made a different name for himself.

Ma said, 'I'll thank you not to make them kind of remarks about Mr 'Arrison, who's only here on account of bein' unfortunate. He's never been a common criminal in all 'is life. And where're you goin' with that cake, might I ask?'

'Well, you know the rules, Mrs Harrison,' said the warder. 'We'll have to cut the cake open. There's a chance a hammer and chisel might've accidentally fell into it when you were doin' the mixin'.'

'I hope you're not casting aspersions, Mr Lorrimore,' said Pa.

'I hope so too,' said Ma, 'I've never let anything fall accidental into any of my bakin'.'

'Well, we'll take a look,' said the warder, and off he went with the cake.

'It's upsettin', what you have to put up with, Pa,' said Amy.

'Good on you, Pa, for not letting them get you down,' said Alice.

'Serve 'em right, Pa, if you pinched their watches,' said young Fanny.

'You Fanny,' whispered Ma in outrage, 'that's aggravatin' talk, that is, and I don't want any more of it.'

'Bless your heart, Fanny,' said Pa, 'your appropriate speech was bravely spoken, but slightly upsetting to Ma.'

'There's something else I don't like,' said Ma, and lowered her voice to tell him that in future that kind friend of his was only going to give her enough to pay the rent. If she hadn't been getting ten bob a week from the lodger, she wouldn't be able to feed her family properly. Pa's cheerful look lurched a bit, and he seemed very put out. He glanced at Nick. Nick said not to worry, they'd manage somehow. Yes, up to you, Nick, to see Ma doesn't get too worried, said Pa. Ma said she was thinking about selling a few things, including the piano. Pa looked shocked.

'I'll have to make a firm request to you not to do that, Mabel,' he said. 'Didn't I mention before that the family joanna's a valuable heirloom and antique?'

'With a Queen Anne birthmark,' said Alice.

'More like my birthright,' said Pa.

'Part of the family, Pa?' said Nick.

'Quite so,' said Pa. 'So I put it to you, my son, should a man's family birthright be sold when it's dear to him? I'll rely on you to see Ma doesn't slip

253

it to some rag and bone merchant who might come knocking. There's its valuability to consider, d'you see.'

'Valuability, right,' said Nick.

The warder brought the cake back then, in its tin. The tin looked larger on account of the cake looking smaller. It was in quarters neatly fitted together.

'Passed all correct for consumption, Harrison,' said the warder.

'It doesn't look all correct to me,' said Ma, 'it looks all shrunk.'

'Have to inform you, Mrs Harrison, that hard labour convict 43789 ain't allowed a cake all to himself.'

'It's a pleasure, Mr Lorrimore, to concur,' said Pa, 'and in any case, I've never been one to keep the good things of life all to myself, apart from Mrs Harrison, of course.'

'What a caution,' said the warder, departing with a grin. Alice and Nick were positive the prison staff really did like Pa. Well, the Hackney coppers had never shown any hard feelings at failing to nab him when his hand was in someone else's pocket.

The visitors' room was now full of gaunt bony convicts talking to their next of kin out of the corners of their mouths.

'Albert,' whispered Ma, 'what did you mean about our piano's valuability?'

'Keep it in the family, Mabel old gel, that's what I mean,' said Pa. 'It's my birthright and my hope for the future.'

'Crikey, Pa,' said Amy, 'you're not goin' to spend your future playin' the piano in the streets like an organ-grinder and 'is monkey, are you?'

'That he's not,' said Ma firmly, 'he's goin' to drive a corporation water-cart or a furniture van. Or a coal cart.'

'Lord love you, Mabel,' said Pa, 'didn't I tell you I was thinking of forming a business partnership with Alice and Nick?'

'What sort of partnership?' asked Ma, suspicion writ darkly on her brow.

'I'm working on it, if you get me,' said Pa.

'I've got you all right,' said Ma, 'and you can forget it. There's not goin' to be any business partnerships, nor sellin' old baskets like you mentioned before.'

'Old Masters,' said Nick.

'Same difference, if I know your Pa. As for the piano—'

'Don't sell it,' said Pa, 'use these fivers to keep you going.'

Talk about quickness of the hand deceiving the watchful eye of authority. Without either of the warders spotting even a glimmer of movement, two folded white fivers suddenly came into being, only to disappear as Pa slipped them under the biscuit tin. Ma then put on an act of inspecting the pillaging job that had been done on the cake, and another disappearing trick took place, inside the waistband of Ma's skirt.

'Lovaduck, good old Pa,' said Fanny.

'Wait a bit,' whispered Ma, 'where'd you get them from, Albert?'

'Ah,' said Pa, and winked.

'Now, Pa,' said Alice.

'Good as the real thing, Alice my pigeon,' murmured Pa.

'Lord give me patience,' breathed Ma, 'they're duds.'

'Pa, you shocker,' said Alice.

'Crikey, and we went to church this morning,' said Amy.

'Lord bless you,' said Pa.

'You need a cure, Pa,' said Nick.

'He'll get one when he's home,' said Ma. 'I suppose you made them, did you, Albert 'Arrison?'

'That's a very hurtful remark, Mabel, considering they cost me four fags,' said Pa.

'Don't answer me back,' said Ma. 'That's been half the trouble, me lettin' you answer me back and also lettin' you have your own way a lot too much. Well, let me tell you, Albert 'Arrison, when you come out, everything's goin' to be done my way, not just for your own sake, but for the sake of your son and daughters that want to live honest lives.'

'Mabel, who could want that more than me, their affectionate dad?' said Pa. 'Don't the girls look souls of honesty, and doesn't Nick look a young man born to make an honest name for himself? Haven't I slipped you a little oof so that you can buy them some honest Christmas presents? All I'd like to say is that I don't want their honesty to leave them poverty-stricken.'

'Crikey, no, I don't want to end up poverty-stricken, Ma,' said Fanny, 'I'll probably only 'ave one pair of shoes and one pair of knickers.'

'You Fanny,' breathed Ma, 'd'you want a clip, talkin' about knickers in 'ere, you saucy girl? As for you, Albert, look what your kind of honesty's done for your fam'ly. If it wasn't for Alice and Nick earning wages, we'd been in the workhouse, specially now your so-called 'elpful friend is 'ardly bein' 'elpful at all.'

Pa's cheerful look took another lurch.

'I can't take kindly to that,' he said.

'Don't fret, Pa,' said Alice, 'we're managing, and at least while you're in here the law knows you've got nothing to do with these jewel robberies.'

'Yes, that's nearly a blessin',' said Ma, 'it makes Pa nearly look honest and 'ard done by.'

'A kind of alibi for your integrity, Pa,' said Nick.

'Well, my son,' said Pa, 'I can fairly claim I've got integrity.'

'And your family piano,' said Nick, and Pa gave him a glance.

'Yes, we'll make sure we keep the piano,' said Alice, and Pa slipped her a glance too. Alice smiled. Pa coughed.

'Bless you, my children,' he said.

'Bless you too, Pa,' said Amy.

'H'm,' said Ma.

When the family left a little later, they wished Pa a merry Christmas and a happy New Year. Pa said with a bit of luck it might turn out a very happy New Year. Pa was cooking something up.

When the family arrived home, Nick had a good look at the fivers. They seemed all right to him. So Alice also had a good look. She couldn't find any fault.

'Not that I know much about what's dud and what's genuine,' she said.

'Nor me,' said Amy.

'Lovaduck,' said young Fanny, 'if no-one knows much, Ma, we could be rich for a bit. Well, till they're spent.'

'I don't want to 'ear any talk about us passin' dud notes over a counter,' said Ma. 'Mind, I won't say they couldn't be useful if we ever got poverty-stricken.'

257

'Yes, if me and Amy and Alice 'ad to go about all ragged,' said Fanny.

'I was thinkin', Ma,' said Alice, 'if Pa had told the police where the jewels were, he might not have got hard labour, nor as much as five years.'

'Alice, not in front of the children, if you don't mind,' said Ma.

'Ma, you don't have any children,' said Alice, 'you've got three growin' daughters and a grown-up son.'

'Never mind that,' said Ma, 'just be careful what you say.'

'Ma, none of us would ever say what we shouldn't,' said Amy.

'Not about Pa we wouldn't,' said Fanny. She and Amy were as solid as the Rock of Gibraltar in their reliability.

'The point is,' said Nick, 'if Pa had told the police where the jewels were, that would have landed his accomplices deep in the murky soup.'

'What's murky soup?' asked Fanny.

'It's one you make with thick turnips,' said Amy.

'Crikey, I didn't know that,' said Fanny. 'Here, did Nick say accomplices?'

'Frankie says our brother gets them kind of words from 'is insurance company,' said Amy.

'It's funny Frankie can say anything at all with that gobstopper stuck in his neck,' said Fanny.

'I don't like anyone talkin' about accomplices,' said Ma, 'it's a word that don't sound honest.'

'But if Pa had spilled the beans,' said Nick, 'his life wouldn't have been worth living.'

'Old Horsy would've got him,' said Alice.

'We won't 'ave any more of this kind of talk,'

said Ma, 'or 'ave you got something to say, Amy?'

'Yes, Ma,' said Amy, 'how's yer canary?'

Christmas Day arrived. The kitchen, the parlour and the passage were all decorated with colourful paper chains made by Amy and Fanny. A home-made Chinese lantern hung from the centre of the kitchen ceiling, and the range fire burned and glowed, warding off the chill that was hanging about in the backyard. The coal bunker was well-stocked, Nick having paid for a delivery of three hundredweight. Christmas was a time when the kitchen and parlour fires were generously refuelled, and the kids of hard-up families sneaked about beforehand nicking any kind of fuel for the occasion. A housewife might say to her old man, ''Ere, where's that broken chair gone that you was goin' to mend?' 'Search me, me old Dutch, it was out on the doorstep five minutes ago, where I was goin' to do the mendin'.'

For dinner, Ma did roast beef with Yorkshire pudding and veg, followed by Christmas pudding and hot custard. Mr Lukavitch accepted an invitation to sit down with the family, and by the time the meal had come to an end, his slightly hollow chest seemed to have filled out, and his eyes seemed to reflect the moist brightness of the hot custard.

'Strike a light,' he said, 'never have I known such a bleedin' lovely Christmas dinner, ain't I? Don't you think? Yes, I do think. What a fine bloke I am to be among you. Bloody good, eh?'

'Now now, Mr Loovakish,' said Ma, 'it's Christmas Day, remember.'

'Yes, we're all corblimey tophole cockneys,' said Mr Lukavitch.

'No, you're Polish,' said young Fanny.

'Polish cockney, you bet,' beamed Mr Luka-vitch. He spent the rest of the day with the family, and in the evening they introduced him to Christmas card games played for matchsticks, and to chestnuts roasted on the fire. In return, he produced a large box of chocolates for the whole family. Ma said he shouldn't have done it, not when he wasn't making a rich living. Mr Lukavitch said it was a ruddy pleasure and that receiving kindness was worth a lot more than being rich.

Annabelle had a lovely Christmas with her family and with the Adams families, everyone meeting up on Christmas evening at the house in which Anna-belle's maternal grandmother known as Chinese Lady lived with her husband, and with Boots, Emily, Rosie and Tim.

For her part, Chinese Lady would not have considered Christmas properly ordered if any of the individual families had not been present. Everyone knew that, of course, and so everyone attended. So did Vi's parents, Aunt Victoria and Uncle Tom. It gave Chinese Lady pleasure to note how her family had multiplied. There were Lizzy and Ned's four children, Annabelle, Bobby, Emma and Edward, and there were Rosie and Tim, belonging to Boots and Emily. Tommy and Vi had produced Alice, David and Paul, while Sammy and Susie were the parents of Daniel, Bess and Jimmy. Of all her granddaughters, Chinese Lady thought Anna-belle at seventeen quite lovely, and Rosie at eighteen such a striking young lady. Rosie was not an Adams by birth, only by adoption, yet of all the younger generations, Rosie was the one who was dearest to Chinese Lady, although she would never have said so.

The young people made themselves heard above the adults, although it couldn't be said that any of the adults had become quiet and retiring. Everyone contributed something to the revelry, and Boots, as usual, put himself in charge of most of the party games, which made Chinese Lady say, as usual, that he had a disreputable habit of turning every game into one for hooligans. And Rosie, as she always did, said a little hooliganism at Christmas parties was very allowable.

That didn't apply so much to Postman's Knock, always a must. During the course of this, Annabelle received a lovely smacker from Sammy who, in turn, received one from his wife Susie who, in her turn, received one from Boots. Rosie, called out next, regarded her dad critically.

'She's left lipstick.'

'Your Aunt Susie has? Well, it's a nice flavour,' said Boots, and wiped it off.

'You shouldn't kiss her on the mouth,' said Rosie.

'All in the rules, Rosie.'

'Never mind that, don't do it again, she's your sister-in-law,' said Rosie.

'It's Christmas,' said Boots.

'No excuses,' said Rosie, teasing him.

'Postman's Knock isn't an excuse, it's an opportunity,' smiled Boots.

'So's Christmas,' said Rosie.

'Bless you, my child,' said Boots, and Rosie laughed and gave him a Postman's Knock kiss on his cheek.

*   *   *

Miss Polly Simms, the long-standing friend of the Adams family, was one of several guests at a country house in Sussex. She would have preferred to be with the Adams families, who enjoyed Christmas in uninhibited Dickensian fashion. She had enjoyed it with them on two occasions, but no invitation had arrived this year. Polly suspected Emily had put her foot down. Well, Emily had a case for doing just that, as Polly frankly admitted to herself. So she accepted an invitation from the Mannering family in Sussex. The Mannerings owned a brood of sons, daughters, nieces and nephews who had been among the Bright Young Things of the Twenties, as Polly had herself. Alas, while Polly had eventually found more useful things to do, the Mannerings' brood hadn't. The women had remained flappers, and the men still thought they weren't living unless they charged around the countryside in noisy sports cars at midnight. By the time she retired to bed at two in the morning, Polly had had more than enough of what she considered their boring inanities. As far as interesting people were concerned, the men and women of Chinese Lady's extensive family were high on her list, Boots in particular, of course. She always felt Emily failed to appreciate what an exceptional man her husband was. The idiocies of the human race irritated and even enraged many people. They only amused Boots. Polly asked him once why idiot politicians didn't make him swear. I'm an idiot myself, he said. Join the club, said Polly, so am I.

In some extraordinary way, Polly, born of the upper classes, identified completely with the Adams' and all that their cockney antecedents had given them, a great love of life and a great capacity to enjoy it.

Slipping into bed in a guest room, she lay thinking about Boots and why Emily was his wife and not herself. That was always a bitter thing in her mind.

The door opened, and with her bedside light still on, she saw Gregory Mannering, the divorced son of her hosts. He had a smile on his face, and a bottle and two glasses in his hands. A dressing-gown covered him. Quietly, he closed the door, using his slippered foot.

'Don't mind, do you, Polly? Thought we could share a nightcap.'

He'd been at the vintage port most of the evening, and was about the only person present whom Polly hadn't found tedious. Forty years old, he was a chunky, amiable man with a fine war record, having served with the British forces in Mesopotamia and Salonika. He'd collected a scar on his forehead. It didn't mar his looks as far as Polly was concerned. She was war-hardened, and battle scars on men did not upset her in the least.

Gregory Mannering advanced to the bed and sat down on the edge of it. Polly eyed him without offence, her attractively piquant looks making her look much younger than her thirty-seven years. She knew, of course, that he was here in the hope of being invited into her bed.

'Is that more port, old bean?' she asked.

'Only the best, old girl.'

'And then what?'

'Up to you, old darling.' Gregory poured a measure of port into each glass and offered her one. Polly sat up and took it. Her breasts, much to be admired for

263

their still pouting firmness, glimmered behind the semi-transparent silk of her black nightie. 'I hear you're considered the only virgin in London these days, Polly.'

Polly, sipping port, said, 'And what else do you hear?'

'Well, dear old chum, I hear on quite good authority that you're carrying a torch.'

'I'm always fascinated by good authority,' said Polly, her brittle smile showing. 'It has the astonishing ability to listen at a thousand keyholes at one and the same time. I'm sometimes sensitive about whether or not it can also look through bathroom windows without ever falling off the ladder. Oh, well, if it can I must learn to live with it. Thanks for the nightcap, Greg old cheese, sorry you can't stay.'

'Fond of you, Polly, damned if I'm not, but up to you.'

Polly knew what would happen. Once he was in bed with her, she'd close her eyes and make every attempt to imagine he was someone else. Boots. It was bound to be traumatic, imaginatively striving to turn him into the one man she had ever genuinely wanted for her very own. On the other hand, Gregory belonged to that never-to-be-forgotten breed of men who had known the great sound of the guns, and was her body so inviolate that she could not give it except to Boots?

'Well, don't just sit there, old sport, come and join me,' she said.

Horrors, once he was about to slip in with her she changed her mind, which was damned hard luck on Greg, who was naturally as keen as mustard.

'Come on, play fair, old girl,' he said.

'Can't,' said Polly, 'I don't go in for that kind of cricket. Sorry, old sport.'

'That's it, knock my wicket down,' said Greg, but he took her refusal like a game old soldier and a gent. One didn't force a woman like Polly Simms, decorated for her outstanding record as a wartime ambulance driver. He left her bed and her room, taking his port with him, giving her a fond good night.

Polly thought why the hell do I let that frustrating swine Boots spoil me for all other men? God, love is the very devil.

The Rovers always played a special Christmas match on Boxing Days against their deadliest rivals, Manor Place Rangers. It counted as a lighthearted fixture, with no honour at stake, and both teams usually fielded scratch sides because of absentees spending Christmas with relatives. The Rovers had to bring in Dumpling, her willing dad, and young Fanny. Dumpling was overjoyed, Fanny keen as mustard, brushing aside Ma's feelings of horror and Nick's warning that she might get trodden on. He found shorts, shirt and socks for her, and Starving Crow lent her his young brother's football boots.

Good old Bonzo Willis, the Rangers' beefy captain and centre half, decided he needed to have a word with Nick before the kick-off.

'Oi, Nick, come 'ere,' he called.

'What's up?' asked Nick, arriving for the confrontation.

'What's up, what's up? You mean what's that, don't yer?' said Bonzo, pointing to Dumpling. Dumpling was taking part in the kickabout around the Rovers' goal area. 'What is it, might I ask?'

'That's Evans, our scratch inside right for today,' said Nick.

'Don't gimme that,' said Bonzo, 'she's a ruddy female. Get 'er orf. She ain't natural.' That was a bit unfair. Dumpling was perfectly natural. All she had was her own, and she'd fitted it tidily inside her shorts and jersey. Certainly, she looked a dumpling, but no-one could have justifiably called her not natural. 'Get 'er orf, Nick, and we'll lend yer one of our supporters, seein' it's a friendly.'

'Sorry, Bonzo, can't be done,' said Nick.

'Now listen, mate, we 'ad to play against a fat goalie when we last met yer, and it upset us. We ain't playin' against no fat female. 'Ere, and 'oo's that titch?' He'd spotted Fanny darting about.

'That's my youngest sister,' said Nick, 'we're very scratch today, but as it's Christmas, does anyone mind? We don't.'

'Listen, yer cockeyed lemon,' said Bonzo, 'I don't care if it's Christmas, Easter or bleedin' pancake time, you expectin' us to play against a fat female and yer titch of a sister?'

'Well, if you don't, we'll claim the match, then, as a walkover,' said Nick. 'Pity, really, when it's the festive Boxing Day friendly. I'll tell my team you're packing up and going home to your mums.'

'Nick, I ain't got nothing against you personal,' said Bonzo, 'but can't yer stop talkin' like a bleedin' sugar plum fairy? All right, we'll play the match, but tell Fatty and Titch it ain't goin' to be as friendly as all that.'

'Right, got you, Bonzo.'

So the game began, the Rangers cackling a bit at the sight of Dumpling as inside right, and young Fanny out on the right wing, where Nick thought

266

the enemy could do her the least harm. The first thing that happened was when Dumpling was given the ball by Ronnie Smith as he kicked off. She dribbled round formidable Bonzo and left him so much off balance that he fell over like a drunken elephant. Supporters Alice, Cassie, Julie and Meg nearly died laughing.

Dumpling enjoyed herself from then on. No-one, not even her loving dad, who was at left back in place of Frankie, could have said she was the brains of the forward line. But she was certainly the engine. She'd said she'd feed Starving Crow on the left wing, he being a headache to any opposition, but she didn't seem to know where he was most of the time. Fanny received the ball more often than she was supposed to, and on each occasion she seemed to disappear inside the opposition. She made up for that by kicking every enemy ankle within reach of her right boot.

It hardly mattered that Dumpling was more of an engine than a skilled tactician. She was such a bother to the Rangers that Bonzo copped her once with a shoulder charge that bundled her off her feet and sent her rolling. Dumpling, never one to be discouraged, had her own back a few minutes later by tripping him up and treading on him. Bonzo, the marks of her studs on the seat of his shorts, bawled for her to be sent off.

The ref, having blown for a foul, admonished Dumpling.

'Me, what've I done?' she said. 'And what's 'e cryin' about, ain't he 'ad 'is Christmas puddin'?'

All the same, it was still a lighthearted game, with plenty of goals. Fanny, shutting her eyes and giving a squeal as she kicked the ball in a goalmouth scramble, found she'd scored. Bonzo grinned.

'Well done, Titch,' he said.

'Crikey, was that me?' gasped Fanny in delight.

At half-time the score was three each. Nick took his team off, patting the backs of Fanny and Dumpling.

'Ain't we 'eroic, me and Fanny?' beamed Dumpling.

'Well, you're both still alive,' said Nick, and noticed then that four girl supporters had become five. A strawberry-red coat caught his eye, the wearer chatting animatedly to Freddy and Cassie. Alice put herself beside Nick and whispered to him.

'Freddy's brunette cousin's just turned up again,' she said. 'Who's she after? It had better not be you.'

'Would a gorgeous girl like that be after me, a pipsqueak clerk?'

'What d'you mean, a pipsqueak clerk? Where'd you get that from, you dope?'

'Fair question, Alice me girl. Just a thought.'

'Some thought, I don't think,' said Alice. 'Anyway, how would she know if you were a pipsqueak clerk or not?'

'Who's she?'

'Her.'

'Freddy's ravishing cousin?'

'Don't come it,' said Alice. 'But oh, 'elp, wouldn't you just like to be able to try your luck with her? She really is luvverly.'

Dumpling ballooned in.

'Crikey, Alice, ain't it an excitin' match? Fancy Fanny scorin' a goal. I'm 'oping to knock in one or two meself in the second 'alf. Mind, I dunno 'ow Nick come to let the Rangers score three. I know

268

it's only a friendly, but I don't like to see 'im gettin' careless. I got a special place for Nick in me album of football memories, yer know. 'Ere, Freddy's cousin Annabelle 'as joined us again. Ain't that compliment'ry? Of course, I told 'er last time that our team's the best in Walworth.'

Nick glanced. Annabelle was taking absolutely no notice of him, she was immersed in her dialogue with Freddy and Cassie. Freddy was wearing a good-looking grin. Nick helped himself to a slice of lemon, moving away from Alice and Dumpling. Danny joined him.

'What d'yer think of Dumpling's performance, eh, Nick? Gettin' to be a reg'lar in the side, ain't she?'

'It looks that way, Danny.'

'Of course, I ain't too sure girls ought to play a lot of football.'

'I'm sure myself that they shouldn't,' said Nick. 'Can't you marry Dumpling and make her bake cakes and cook the Sunday dinner?'

'Now 'ow can I if she won't let me?'

'Well, make her let you.' Nick put the sucked lemon slice into his mouth, ground it up and swallowed it. Its sharpness gave his brains a lift, which distracted him from Annabelle. 'Get her in her parlour and do what you can to pull her jumper off.'

''Ere, turn it up,' said Danny. 'She won't like that, and nor will 'er dad. 'E'll boot me out.'

'Wake up,' said Nick. 'Tell him first, and at the right moment make the kind of noise that'll bring him running into the parlour.'

''Ere, 'old on, Nick, that ain't first thing decent,' said Danny, turning quite dusky. Cassie, Freddy and Annabelle were joined by Dumpling and Fanny, and the dialogue grew more animated, and Annabelle hadn't taken even a single glance at Nick. Nick, of course, didn't know whether to be relieved or miffed. 'Now listen,' said Danny, 'I ain't goin' to get anywhere near Dumpling's 'ighly personal female wear, let alone pull it off.'

'Would you like me to have a private word with her dad on your behalf? I think—'

The ref's whistle interrupted Nick.

'Come on, blokes, back on the field,' called Dumpling, who had the makings of a captain able to chuck a lot of weight about.

'Goodbye, Cassie,' said Annabelle. ''Bye, Freddy, happy New Year to your team.' She smiled, waved and left, and still without acknowledging Nick.

'What was all that about?' he asked Freddy, as they went back on to the field.

'All what?' said Freddy. 'Oh, with Annabelle, d'you mean? Just a chat about Christmas and football.'

'Fanny, come here,' said Nick, and his saucy-eyed young sister skipped up to him, looking a slim tomboy in her football outfit. 'Keep away from the Rangers' goalmouth,' said Nick, 'I don't want to have to tell Ma you got swallowed up and disappeared for ever. She's fond of you. Stay out on the right wing, and if big Bonzo does get anywhere near you, fall over and yell for a foul.'

'No, I want to score another goal,' said Fanny.

'Do as you're told,' growled Nick.

'Some 'opes,' said saucy Fanny.

As it turned out, the second half was a genuinely friendly affair, even if the competitive instinct occasionally made itself felt. It was only Dumpling who put some fearsome heart and soul into all she did, so Bonzo plonked her on her bottom a couple of times and told her it was still Christmas. Dumpling took a bit of umbrage at that, and in the dying seconds, with the teams equal, she did her best to lay the Rangers' goalie out by booting the ball straight at him from only six yards out. He punched it clear. Up it sailed and down it came. Up bounced Dumpling in an attempt to head it, and up leapt a group of Rangers with her, she in the middle of them. All heads missed the ball. Down came the mêlée of players, Dumpling still in the middle. She shrieked. The Rangers peeled away from her, and there she was, her football shorts down around her knees, and a pair of very fetching rose-pink drawers decorating her middle and giving some charming colour to the grey afternoon.

'Oh, yer rotten 'ooligans, who done that, who pulled me shorts down?' she yelled in outrage.

Both teams had a good look and then fell about.

'Oh, corblimey,' gasped young Fanny, 'I'll 'ave an accident.'

The ref blew for time. Dumpling pulled her shorts up.

'Where's me dad?' she yelled.

Her dad was fading into the distance, trying to reach the changing hut before he coughed himself to death on the field.

'Cheer up, Dumpling,' said Freddy, 'you played a treat.'

'Where's Nick, where's me captain?' demanded Dumpling.

'Right behind you,' said Nick, and Dumpling swung round.

'Did yer see what they done, Nick? Pulled me shorts down just to stop me scorin' the winning goal.'

'Honest accident,' said beefy Bonzo.

'I 'ope it was,' said Danny, feeling for Dumpling's embarrassment, but even more gone on her on account of the pretty colour of her personal and private whatsits.

'I can tell you one thing, Dumpling,' said Nick, 'if it stopped you scoring the winning goal for us, it also stopped them scoring it for themselves. They all fell over.'

'Honest?' said Dumpling, and her beam arrived. 'Oh, well, I don't mind, then, I'd always do anything to stop me beloved Rovers gettin' beaten.'

'What a performance,' grinned good-hearted Bonzo. 'Christmas drawers on, eh?'

'Course not,' said Dumpling, 'Christmas is nearly over.'

Chapter Fifteen

Ma went potty the day after Boxing Day. The paper reported another jewel robbery. Nick handed her the smelling-salts and Alice fanned her. Ma said in a faint voice that she'd go early to her grave if common criminals didn't stop being dishonest. Then there's all the expense we've suffered from having to celebrate Christmas, she said. It's lucky we've got them two fivers your Pa was good enough to give us.

'But wouldn't it be a bit dishonest to use them if they're duds?' said Alice.

'Well, I wouldn't except in an emergency,' said Ma, 'and I'd only spend about five shillings, say, just to show I'm in favour of honesty.'

'You'd get four pounds, fifteen shillings change,' said Nick.

'My, so I would, and all good money,' said Ma, and perked up a treat.

A scorned woman struck.

She arrived in company with Cassie and Freddy for the next committee meeting.

Nick nearly fell down on opening the door to her and the others.

'Is this the house, Cassie?' she asked.

'Yes, it's where our captain and secretary lives,' said Cassie. 'That's him, Nick Harrison.'

'Good evening,' said the scorned woman.

'You met Freddy's cousin Annabelle at that other match, Nick, didn't you?' said Cassie. 'Well, she's come to—'

'Wait a minute,' said Nick, 'what's going on? Take care how you answer that, Cassie, or you'll be out before you're in.'

'Well, I don't think that's very nice,' said Annabelle, done up to look like the answer to a starving bachelor's prayer. 'What a brute. He doesn't bite as well, Cassie, does he?'

'No, he's just showin' off a bit, like some fellers do,' said Cassie. 'Freddy's the same. Nick, you're not goin' to keep us standin' in the passage, are you?'

'Freddy, would you like to say something?' asked Nick, shot to pieces at actually having Annabelle in his house, where every wall secreted the echoes of family whispers. 'What's this all about?'

'In short,' said Freddy, 'Annabelle's taken a fancy to the Rovers and the supporters' club.'

'She's what?' said Nick.

'She's taken a fancy—'

'I heard you,' said Nick.

'What a rude man,' said Annabelle, 'and so aggressive. Are you sure he's captain and secretary and everything else, Cassie?'

'Oh, it's nothing serious,' said Cassie, 'he just likes to be in charge. My Uncle Patrick's the same. He's a police sergeant. Nick, can't we go in your parlour?'

'Let me get this straight,' said Nick, who was trying to work out what had hit him. 'Have you brought Annabelle along to the committee meeting for some reason or other? If so, what?'

'To elect 'er to the supporters' club,' said Cassie.

'What supporters' club?'

'Oh, Dumpling's goin' to propose it,' said Cassie, 'and me and Freddy's goin' to second it.'

'Freddy, are you off your flaming rocker?' asked Nick.

'Genuine case of enthusiasm, Nick,' said Freddy. The door knocker sounded, the latchcord was pulled, and in came Dumpling and Danny.

'Oh, 'ello, Annabelle,' said Dumpling, 'glad you could come, but what's everyone standin' in the passage for?'

'Your captain's a bit fussed,' said Annabelle.

'What's 'e fussed about?' asked Dumpling.

'I'm sure we don't know,' said Cassie.

'I don't think he's in a very good temper,' said Annabelle.

'Who, Nick?' said Dumpling.

'Ain't 'ad some aggravatin' news, 'ave yer, Nick?' said Danny.

'Well, at the moment I'm aggravated up to my eyebrows,' said Nick, 'but all right, in you go. The parlour fire's alight.'

The parlour, in fact, was warm and welcoming, the fire radiating a glowing heat. Annabelle thought it a cheerful and tidy-looking room, an old piano in one corner. The Victorian terraced houses of Walworth weren't unknown to her. She'd been to Freddy's home more than once, and had heard so many family stories about the house in which Chinese Lady had brought up her sons and daughter that she could easily picture it in her mind. Annabelle was actually proud of how her grandma, her mum and her uncles had not only survived every kind of hardship, but had gone on to do wonders for themselves and their sons and daughters, including herself and Rosie.

Nick put six chairs around the table in the middle of the room, and they all sat down. He glanced at Annabelle, who had placed herself between Cassie and Dumpling. She looked as cool as a cucumber. What was she up to?

'I've done the minutes of the last meetin', Nick,' said Dumpling, 'd'you want me to read them, as usual?'

'Go ahead,' said Nick, 'then perhaps we can sort out who's playing games.'

'I thought all this was going to be pleasant and friendly,' said Annabelle.

'I don't know very much about it myself,' said Danny. 'Dumpling only told me that—'

'Shut up,' said Nick. 'Let Dumpling read the minutes before I go off bang.'

Freddy grinned. Danny scratched his head. Cassie smiled, Annabelle kept her face very straight, and Dumpling read the minutes. When they were passed, Nick said perhaps someone would let him know what was going on.

'Well, it's like this, Nick,' said Dumpling. The supporters, she said, were important to the Rovers, and they all thought they should form an official club, especially as Annabelle wanted to join.

'Oh, she does, does she?' said Nick, fighting on shifting ground.

'Does he mind?' asked Annabelle of Freddy.

'No, of course he don't,' said Freddy, 'the more the merrier.'

'If I'm not wanted—'

'Course you're wanted,' said Dumpling, 'it's compliment'ry to us.'

'Your captain doesn't look complimented,' said Annabelle.

You terror, thought Nick, you're deliberately giving me a headache.

'He's not been 'imself lately,' said Cassie. 'Some of us think he's in love, only 'e won't say, will you, Nick?'

'Just get on with it,' growled Nick.

Dumpling said she'd had a nice talk with Cassie and Annabelle at half-time on Boxing Day, after Cassie and Annabelle had already talked about the team and the supporters, and that it was Annabelle who'd said they ought to form an official supporters' club, which she'd like to join herself, as she was keen on football and was very admiring of the Rovers.

'Oh, she is, is she?' said Nick.

'Why does he keep saying things like that, Chrissie?' asked Annabelle.

Chrissie, is it? So she's already bosom chums with Dumpling, thought Nick. What's her game? If she knew she was in the house of a family whose old man was doing hard labour, she'd faint.

'Oh, don't take 'im serious, Annabelle,' said Dumpling blithely, 'Nick's got nice ways when 'e ain't lordin' it a bit.' Anyway, she said, she and Cassie thought what a smashing idea, an official supporters' club, with all the supporters wearing knitted blue and white scarves, and having round metal clip-on brooches printed with the name of the Rovers.

'Do what?' said Danny.

'Scarves and brooches?' said Nick. 'Who thought that lot up?'

'Annabelle,' said Cassie, who'd let Freddy's

brunette cousin know about the Boxing Day fixture and other things as well. 'She's got lots of ideas, and Dumpling's goin' to propose her as an official supporter and as a member of the committee.'

'I'm going barmy,' said Nick.

'I ain't far behind,' said Danny.

'I'm tryin' to keep me nose in front,' said Freddy. 'If I don't, I'll be all behind like the cow's tail for evermore. So I'd better ask, can we 'ave another member on the committee?'

'No,' said Nick, in a rare old panic at the thought of Annabelle entering his home week after week.

'There, I thought I wasn't wanted,' said Annabelle to Cassie.

'Oh, don't mind Nick,' said Cassie, 'Chrissie'll put him right, she knows about the rules.'

Dumpling said yes, there was one rule that allowed the committee to elect another member if they needed one, which they did on account of Nick being the only member that had had a posh education and could use big words. The committee ought to have another member like him, one that could talk like he did and do some educated arguing with him, like Annabelle could.

'Me meself, and Freddy and Danny, we get argued out of things by Nick,' she said. 'Well, 'e uses words sometimes that we've never 'eard of, and it sort of makes us speechless. I been speechless I don't know 'ow many times.'

'Pardon?' said Freddy.

'Dumpling, much as I admire yer,' said Danny, 'I can't recollect you was ever short of sayin' something. I said to yer dad once, I said one more admirin' thing about you was 'ow you could speak up, even if you was gagged and bound like Pearl

278

White used to be in them old film serials.'

'I'm talking about not bein' able to always understand Nick's clerkin' talk,' said Dumpling.

'You're talking about getting another female on the committee,' said Nick.

'Well, did you hear that, Cassie?' said Annabelle. 'Did you hear him call me a female as if I was just anybody?'

'It's all right, he's just a bit grumpy this evenin',' said Cassie.

'He's muttering too,' said Annabelle.

'I'm scratchin' me head about all this,' said Danny.

Dumpling said everyone had got to remember there were four members of the committee, and only one was a girl, herself. It wasn't asking much to have another girl, especially one that was educated as good as Nick. Anyway, she'd got some proposals to make. She proposed first that the supporters should form an official club.

'I second that,' said Cassie.

'As usual, you're out of order,' said Nick.

'All right, I'll second it,' said Danny. 'Can't do no 'arm.'

'I'm going to bed,' said Nick, 'to stuff my headache under the pillows.'

'What about all in favour?' asked Dumpling. Danny, Freddy, Cassie and herself raised their hands. 'Yes, thanks ever so much, Cassie, but you ain't actu'lly entitled to vote. Nick, you votin' against?'

'I'm incapable,' said Nick.

Dumpling said he'd soon be better, he wasn't the most famous Walworth football captain for nothing. Anyway, she said, her proposal had been passed.

She then proposed that Annabelle be elected to the supporters' club, and Freddy seconded on the grounds that his brother-in-law, Sammy Adams, might have something to say to him if he shirked it, never mind what Cassie would do to him. Dumpling asked who was in favour, and she, Cassie, Freddy and Danny all showed their hands again.

'What about you, Nick?' asked Danny.

'I'm paralysed,' said Nick. 'If I'm not, then I'm ruddy well dreaming. Supporters don't have to get elected, you mugs. If they want to come and watch, they can, so stop carrying on like a lot of Alices in Wonderland.'

'My, Mr Harrison does growl, doesn't he?' said Annabelle.

'Annabelle, what're you callin' 'im Mr Harrison for?' asked Dumpling.

'Well, he sounds very important,' said Annabelle.

'Important?' said Danny.

'Yes, a bit like God,' said Annabelle, and glanced at Nick for about the first time. One could have said thunder was writ large on his brow, and that she showed the glimmer of a demure smile.

'I want a few words with you some time, young lady,' he said.

'The proposal's passed, Nick,' said Dumpling, 'you don't 'ave to 'ave any words with anyone.'

'Now look here, Dumpling,' said Nick, 'if you don't stop running this show, I'll set Mr Johnson's dog on you.'

''Ere, steady on, Nick, Johnson's dog'll make mincemeat of Dumpling,' said Danny.

'Well, corblimey good,' said Nick, 'we'll all have shepherd's pie for Sunday dinner.'

'With dumplings?' said Freddy.

'Oh, I can't believe me ears,' said Dumpling, 'I never 'eard Nick speak like that before.'

'Like a cannibal?' said Annabelle.

'Is there any more rubbish to come?' asked Nick.

Dumpling said there was more to come, but it wasn't rubbish, it was to propose the election of Annabelle to the committee. Danny seconded, and all hands went up again except Nick's.

'There,' said Dumpling, 'you're in now, Annabelle, and we're ever so pleased to 'ave yer as one of us.'

'Yes, one of the blokes,' said Cassie.

'I'm thrilled,' said Annabelle.

'I'm under the doctor,' said Nick.

'There, he's cheered up now,' said Cassie, 'he's made a funny joke. D'you want to sort of speak a welcomin' address, Nick?'

'Not without having a fit,' said Nick. He scowled at Danny and Freddy. 'Talk about female cunning and dragoonery hitting you two chumps over your fat heads and rendering you as daft as backward parrots.'

'Eh?' said Danny.

'What was that 'e said?' asked Freddy.

'Drag what?' said Danny.

'Dragoonery,' said Annabelle. 'It means being compelled by force.'

'There y'ar,' said Dumpling, 'it's one of Nick's educated clerkin' words. Ain't it 'appy for us girls that Annabelle knows what it means and can argue the toss with 'im on our be'alf when he's chuckin' 'is weight about in committee? I'll always fight to me dyin' breath to stand up for Nick as the best football captain in Walworth, but I've got to admit he don't 'alf lord it at committee meetings. Still, there's never any 'ard feelings, 'e's a sport most times, like I am meself.'

'D'you get that, you two twits?' said Nick to Danny and Freddy. 'See what you've done? You've landed us with two female committee members, and what with Cassie slipping craftily in every week on the pretext that she's a spokesman for the supporters, we're going to be knocked for six. No wonder I've got to see the doctor. You listening, Danny?'

'Well, Nick, I got to say—'

'Shut up,' said Nick. Annabelle sat enthralled and thrilled. Crickey, what a lovely evening, what gorgeous fun, and what a way of getting her own back on Nick. 'How'd you think we can run a serious football team with a committee stacked with petticoats and knitting? Mark my words, we'll be voting every week on having to buy blue and white bloomers and funny hats for the supporters and probably rattles as well.'

'Excuse me,' said Cassie, 'did I 'ear bloomers?'

'I did,' said Annabelle, 'he came right out with it.'

'Nick, I'm blushin' for yer,' said Dumpling.

'I like yer rose-pink ones best, Dumpling,' said Danny. 'Still, I won't say blue and white ones in the team's colours wouldn't look a treat on yer. I could be very admirin' of 'em.'

''Ere, d'you mind?' said Dumpling.

'I'll knock a hole in your head in a minute, Danny,' said Nick. 'D'you realize we've already heard some up-the-pole talk about knitted scarves and metal brooches? Where's the money coming from?'

'Oh, we could organize raffles and run dances,' said Annabelle. 'We could run the dances at Browning Hall. I know about Browning Hall. My mum and uncles used to go to dances there when they were young.'

'Oh, aren't you bright, Annabelle?' said Cassie.

'Yes, don't she 'ave helpful ideas?' said Dumpling. 'She could be ever so valuable to us, and I 'ope the Rovers will come to be 'er life's work till she's about forty. We don't mind you don't live in Walworth, Annabelle.'

'Oh, thank you, Chrissie, how kind,' said Annabelle.

Nick growled. Annabelle smiled.

'I give up,' said Nick. He reported on the team's finances, pretty rocky with only a few bob in the kitty, and on a letter he'd had from the secretary of Portland Street United, whose team had fallen apart and wouldn't be able to play any more matches. They never did have any stuffing, said Dumpling. As for the Rovers' match on Saturday, said Nick, did anybody want to suggest that Dumpling played centre half, Cassie in goal and Annabelle centre forward?

'Is 'e serious?' asked Cassie.

'Sarky, more like,' grinned Freddy.

'Are yer bein' sarky, Nick?' asked Dumpling. 'Only I'd be joyful to play centre 'alf. Course, I wouldn't be as good as you, but I'd do me best for the honour of it.'

'Like to put it to the vote, would you, Dumpling?' said Nick.

'Oh, ain't yer generous, Nick?' breathed Dumpling.

'Sarky, more like,' said Freddy.

'All in favour?' said Nick, and they all eyed him. One could have said thunder was writ large on his brow again.

'Er, well,' mumbled Danny.

Freddy coughed. The door opened, and Ma looked in.

'Well, I never, no wonder I seemed to be 'earing a lot more voices than usual,' she said, 'there's six of you. Still, you've got a nice fire to keep you warm.' She spotted Annabelle. 'My, you're new,' she said. What a lovely girl, she thought, who could she be?

'Oh, 'ello, Mrs 'Arrison,' said Dumpling, 'Freddy's cousin Annabelle's come among us this evenin'. She's a new supporter, and she's on the committee now.'

'Pleasure to meet you, Annabelle, I'm sure.'

'That's Nick's mum,' said Cassie.

Annabelle took in the neat appearance of the perky woman and her friendly smile. So she's his mother, with her husband in the Navy. Well, she looks nice.

'How'd you do, Mrs Harrison, it's a mutual pleasure.'

'We're just goin' to vote on me takin' Nick's place at centre half on Saturday,' said Dumpling.

'Beg pardon?' said Ma, blinking.

'Yes, me at centre 'alf, would yer believe,' beamed Dumpling.

'Chrissie, it's not natural,' said Ma, 'and what's Nick going to do?'

'See a doctor,' said Nick.

'You and Chrissie both better see one,' said Ma, and left them to it.

The vote went against Dumpling. She took it

sportingly, just like one of the blokes, while Cassie and Annabelle declined to be considered for any match. The team picked itself then, and the meeting came to an end, leaving Nick with the peculiar feeling that he'd been turned inside-out.

'Me and Cassie'll take you 'ome now, Annabelle,' said Freddy.

'No, I expect Nick wants to,' said Cassie, 'him bein' in charge and Annabelle a new supporter.'

'Thanks, but my dad's picking me up at nine,' said Annabelle, and Ma came back then, carrying a tray on which were six cups of steaming tea and a plate of rockcakes baked in the afternoon.

'Here we are,' she said, 'I thought as there was six of you I'd make a nice pot of tea for you,' She placed the tray on the table. ''Ave you 'ad a nice committee meetin'?'

'Thanks ever so much for the tea and cakes, Mrs 'Arrison,' said Cassie, 'and we've enjoyed an awf'lly fruitful meetin'.'

'Yes, we've got an official supporters' club now,' said Dumpling. 'Annabelle's been elected to it nearly unanimous, and she's on the committee as well. She's got lots of ideas for raisin' funds.'

'That's nice,' said Ma, thinking the girl just a bit too attractive for Nick's good. Well, a young man like him, and a girl like that, Lord knows what might come of it if Nick went weak in the head about her. 'Well, enjoy the tea, there's sugar in the bowl for anyone who wants it.'

'Mrs 'Arrison,' said Freddy, as Ma departed, 'you're a woman after me own heart.'

'No, she's not,' said Cassie, 'I am.'

Nick silently passed the cups and saucers around. His eyes met Annabelle's. Hers were clear and innocent. The tea was drunk and the rockcakes eaten while she chatted away with Cassie and Dumpling. She's going to send me permanently barmy, thought Nick.

Someone knocked on the front door.

'That could be my dad,' said Annabelle, looking at her watch. It was just after nine. Nick answered the door. A man in an overcoat and trilby smiled at him.

'Have I got the right house?' asked Ned. 'Is my daughter Annabelle here?'

'Come in,' said Nick, 'she's in the parlour.'

He took Ned in, and Ned made a brief survey of the young people. They all looked pleasantly healthy, even the girl burdened with plumpness.

'Hello, Dad,' said Annabelle, 'thanks for being on time. We've finished the meeting. This is my dad, Chrissie. He knows Cassie and Freddy, of course, but not you and Danny.'

'Hello,' said Ned.

'Oh, and this is Nick Harrison, Dad,' said Annabelle.

'Pleasure,' said Ned, and shook hands with Nick. So this is the bloke she says she's not interested in any more, is it? Well, I should think some girls are. Looks a fine young man. 'Are you the one who runs this football team I've heard about?'

'I helped to run it until I fell ill,' said Nick.

'When did that happen?' asked Ned.

'About an hour ago,' said Nick.

'Uncle Ned, don't take any notice,' said Cassie, 'he's not ill, he's just been a bit peculiar all evenin'.'

'Yes, you 'ave been a bit growlin', Nick' said Dumpling.

'A bit like God,' murmured Annabelle.

Nobody quite heard that, so Freddy said, 'What was that, Annabelle?'

'Oh, nothing much,' said Annabelle, coming to her feet and picking up her coat from the sofa. Silently, Nick took the coat and held it out for her. She slipped into it, fastened the belt, then put her hat on. 'Thanks ever so much for such an interesting evening, everyone, and I'll see you all at the match on Saturday and here again next week, when we can talk about organizing raffles and so on. Oh, and do thank your mother for the tea and cakes, Mr Harrison. Shall we go now, Dad?'

'I'm ready,' said Ned, 'good night, all. Perhaps I'll come and watch your team in action one Saturday.'

'Oh, you'd be ever so welcome,' said Dumpling.

Nick saw father and daughter out.

'Good night, Nick,' said Ned.

'Yes, good night,' said Annabelle.

'I'll be at the doctor's tomorrow, if I'm needed,' said Nick. He watched them walk to a car. He watched them enter it. He heard the engine fire, and then away they went up Browning Street towards the Walworth Road, headlamps lighting the way for them.

'Annabelle, you pickle,' said Ned, as they turned left into the Walworth Road, 'what're you up to with that young man?'

'Dad, I told you, I'm just interested in the football team, especially as Freddy's a member and it's got so much to do with where Grandma brought her family up. It's like going back to my maternal roots.'

'Can't think why you went off Nick Harrison,' said Ned, 'he seems a fine-looking bloke to me.'

'Bless me, d'you think so? I thought he was a bit ugly myself.'

Ned, motoring past a lighted tram, said, 'I find that a suspect remark. You are up to something, aren't you? Your mother is having a job convincing herself you're only interested in a football team. So am I. Three times you had tea in the City with Nick, and then suddenly it was just "oh, him."'

'You can go off some people, you know,' said Annabelle.

'So why, with the help of Cassie and Freddy, have you got yourself elected to Nick's football committee?'

'It's not his committee.'

'Come on, pet, out with it, what's it really all about?'

'Fun,' said Annabelle.

'Well, watch out that fun doesn't turn serious one day and knock you for six,' said Ned.

'Oh, I shan't lose my head, Dad.'

'I've a feeling you might have already lost it without recognizing it's gone missing,' said Ned. 'Never mind, pet, I'll stand with you in all your trials and tribulations.'

'Good old Dad,' said Annabelle, thinking about the variety of stunned expressions on Nick's face all through the hoot of a meeting.

'She's an official supporter, she's been elected to the official supporters' club and she's on the committee as well?' said Alice. 'Who's gone barmy?'

'All of them,' said Nick, 'and it's time I had a word with Freddy and Danny. Cassie's got Freddy by his nose, and Danny's besotted with Dumpling. Cassie and Dumpling performed a put-up job in getting this girl Annabelle on the committee, and Freddy and Danny got sucked in.'

'Well, I don't like it,' said Ma, 'I've got a feeling about 'er.'

'So have I,' said Alice.

'D'you mean she might be after Nick?' asked Amy.

'Alice feels she might be,' said Ma. 'I wouldn't mind about it if Pa was home and out of the Navy. I wouldn't mind Nick takin' up with 'er then. I've never seen a nicer girl, nor a prettier one.'

'What about me?' said Amy.

'And me?' said young Fanny.

'Yes, you're both pretty pictures,' said Ma. She sighed. 'It don't become a mother to discourage 'er eldest daughter and 'er only son from 'aving special friends, except I know there'd be awkward moments about Pa. It's gettin' embarrassin' with Gran Emerson and Ivy, with them askin' after Pa so much, and that friend of Ivy's 'usband sayin' he's never 'eard of a sailor bein' away from home for years on end. I wish people wouldn't get so interested in Pa's whereabouts. This girl Annabelle now, if she gets interested in Nick, she'll get interested in Pa as well, and 'is whereabouts.'

'I've got that in mind, Ma,' said Nick, who had.

'It's a shame, Nick,' said Ma, 'when she looks such a nice, kind girl. I'd be very approvin' of you walkin' out with one like 'er.'

'Yes, I think she'd suit you, Nick,' said Alice, 'but it can't be done, can it? Well, not yet it can't.'

'I've got so many reasons for feeling ill,' said Nick, 'that it's a wonder I don't need an operation.'

Talk about women being like a Chinese puzzle, he thought, and talk about girls being like women well before they were. What was that ravishing young beauty up to if not trying to send him cuckoo? I'll go grey if she keeps coming here to haunt me.

'I just don't understand,' said Lizzy when Ned and Annabelle had arrived home. 'Annabelle, you've never been interested in football before.'

'Oh, I am now,' smiled Annabelle.

'You'll get me really worried one day with the way you carry on,' said Lizzy. 'Are you sure you just want to share Freddy and Cassie's interest in this football team, and that it's nothing to do with that certain young man?'

'What certain young man? Oh, him,' said Annabelle.

'Your dad has just said he seems a very nice young man.'

'Oh, well, never mind,' said Annabelle.

'Never mind what?' said Lizzy, while Ned stood by with a little smile on his face.

'That he might be very nice,' said Annabelle.

'I wish you'd make sense,' said Lizzy.

'It's an effort sometimes when you're only seventeen,' said Ned.

'I'm goin' to take a look at this Nick Harrison,' said Lizzy. 'If you mean to go and watch his team on Saturday, I think I'll come with you.'

'Mum, no,' said Annabelle.

'Why not?' demanded Lizzy.

'I'd feel soppy.'

'Soppy?' said Lizzy.

'Yes, six years old,' said Annabelle.

'I'm gettin' a headache,' said Lizzy.
'He said that.'
'Who did?'
'He did,' said Annabelle, and laughed.

Chapter Sixteen

'Well, well,' said the Governor.

'Spoiled his looks a bit, as you might say, sir,' said the chief warder.

'Very unfortunate fall of an accidental kind, Governor,' said Pa, who had an ugly bruise on his forehead, another on his jaw and a graze on his cheek. He'd done what he'd known he shouldn't, he'd delivered a complaint about Ma's severely cut allowance into the grapevine. 'Might I suggest some carpet treads on the iron stairs?'

'I didn't have you brought to my office to get my goat, Harrison,' said the Governor, 'but to ask you who knocked you about. I don't allow that kind of thing in my establishment.'

'Believe me, Governor, I'm not in favour myself,' said Pa, 'but when you trip on a stair, down you go, and that's it. Very hurtful. However, Governor, now I'm here might I put a proposition to you?'

'No fancy talk, Harrison, you hear me?' said the chief warder.

'Give you my word, Mr Saunders,' said Pa.

'That's funny talk. Cut it.'

'What's the proposition?' asked the Governor, and Pa put it to him with admirable clarity, even if he made use of a few unnecessary adjectives. The chief warder blinked, the Governor eyed Pa impassively.

'Well, well,' he said again.

'Glad to have you consider it, Governor,' said Pa.

'I'll consider it if you mention a name or two,' said the Governor.

'Now, Governor, I ask you fair and square, could I do that without first getting a guarantee of goodwill?' asked Pa, gently rubbing his bruised jaw.

'He's a caution, this one,' said the chief warder.

'Harrison, if you can deliver, I can guarantee your almost immediate release,' said the Governor. 'Note, Mr Saunders, how carefully the official reason for release must come about.'

'Come about, sir, right,' said Mr Saunders.

'Proceed, Harrison,' said the Governor.

Pa spilled the beans, and not about the American lady's jewels alone. The Governor, satisfied, and not unaware that results would add further to the distinguished nature of his record, gave Pa the order to dismiss.

'Thank you, Governor,' said Pa, 'but first might I be awarded two days solitary on account of having been obstreperous?'

'Ah, yes,' said the Governor, 'I take the point, Harrison. Make it three days, Mr Saunders.'

Word soon got round, of course, that Knocker Harrison, far from having split on whoever roughed him up, had been so aggravated at being asked for a name that he gave the Governor a basinful of lip. It put him in the hole of Calcutta for three days. Well, said some hard cases, Knocker ain't such a ponce, after all.

Annabelle, the woman scorned, was at Saturday's football match. Naturally gregarious, with an engaging personality, she mixed in effortlessly with the other girl supporters. Alice couldn't help liking her, and young Fanny thought her not a bit stuck-up. Fanny also thought she wasn't really very interested in Nick, she didn't say one word about him, not even when he scored one of his cracking centre half goals. And at half-time, when the Rovers came off the field, she talked mostly to Freddy and Danny, turning her back on Nick.

Nick accepted it was all just as well. The more he saw of her, the more he wanted to carry her off to somewhere private, smack her bottom, tickle her silly and then eat her.

During the second half, she cheered all Freddy's efforts, clapped when Ronnie Smith scored, and said oh what a shame when Charlie Cope failed to prevent a goal by the opponents.

The pitch was slippery from rain. Nick, attempting a sliding tackle close to the touchline, missed completely and slithered several yards forward to finish on his back at the feet of the official supporters' club.

'Now then, clumsy,' said young Fanny.

'Thanks very much,' said Nick. 'You got anything to say, Miss Somers?'

'Yes, utter rubbish,' said Annabelle.

And that was all she said to him during the entire match. She'd gone by the time the team had changed.

I'll get her, thought Nick, I'll get her. Ruddy hell, though, what do I do with her when I do get her? Ask her to come and visit Pa with me?

Mr Lukavitch didn't go out with his bag of beads on Sunday. He'd caught flu. Ma said you couldn't trust flu, it was one of them sly diseases that sneaked up on people when it should have been hibernating. Ma could say hibernating. She often said she'd heard Mrs Clancy of Revesby Street was hibernating again. What she meant was that Mrs Clancy had taken to her bed with a new bottle of gin and wouldn't be seen for a couple of days. In regard to flu, Nick said it didn't hibernate in the winter, anyway, only in the summer. Ma said well, it ought to.

She did her best for the likeable Polish lodger. Feed a cold, starve a fever, that was how she went about it. It was what she and most women in Walworth believed. So she didn't take up any solid foods for Mr Lukavitch, but she did supply him with mugs of hot tea and Bovril. He was poorly, she said, but not chronic. She didn't want anyone to go up and see him in case the germs sneaked up noses and took hold. Nick and the girls asked what about her nose, then? Ma said that having had the flu twice herself in her lifetime, her nose had got immunity.

She went round to the doctor's on Monday morning to tell him about Mr Lukavitch, and the doctor called later, confirmed it was flu, told him to stay in bed and left him a bottle of medicine. Ma was present, and she noted the fact that the lodger was ailing but doing his best to be cheerful. He asked the doctor how his bleedin' canary was. Still singing, said the doctor, and Mr Lukavitch said corblimey, ruddy good, eh? Mind, it was in a bit of a weak voice, said Ma, and you've got to forgive him for using language to the doctor. The girls said all right, we forgive him. Corblimey, course we do, not half, said saucy Fanny. Yes, but don't keep copying him, said Ma, or you'll all get a clip. Don't forget you're Pa's daughters, she said, and your Pa's a gent at heart, remember.

In the evening, Nick was in the parlour with Danny, helping him to compose a letter to the head office of the London and South Eastern Railways. It was an application for a job in railway workshops. Danny wanted to better himself, saying he was desirous of marrying a certain party in about a year. Nick said a certain rotund party? No, Dumpling, of course, said Danny. I told you, you'll have to force the issue, said Nick, so have a quiet word with her dad about getting her into her parlour and getting her jumper off.

'Make sure her dad comes in at the right time—'

'You've said all that once,' complained Danny, 'and I ain't doin' it. I ain't been brought up to get any girl's jumper off, least of all Dumpling's, which I kind of cherish.'

'Granted,' said Nick, 'but you've got to show her you mean business, and when her dad comes in on cue and finds you waving her jumper about, he'll order you to marry her or take his shotgun to you.'

'He ain't got any shotgun, yer daft haddock, and even if he 'ad, I ain't interferin' with Dumpling's personal clobber. Now, would yer mind if we got on with doin' this important letter?'

They were getting on with it when Nick heard the front door open. Someone had used the latchcord. It couldn't have been any of the girls. They were all in the kitchen with Ma, Alice at the sewing-machine, Amy knitting herself a woolly hat, and Ma doing her best to put a wave in Fanny's hair with the help of the curling tongs. Ma's three girls had always looked well cared for. Even in Hackney

Wick, when Pa had been an irregular provider, due to the unreliable returns of his profession, Ma had seen to it that none of her offspring ever left the house looking a thing of rags and patches.

'Hold on a tick, Danny.' Nick went into the passage, and there was slinky Tosh Fingers already halfway up the stairs. 'Wait a minute,' said Nick, 'what's your game?'

Tosh turned, his permanent grin spreading to become an invitation to a waltz, if Nick cared to.

''Ello, Nick me young friend, 'ow's yerself this 'appy New Year? I won't be more'n 'alf a jiffy, I'm just goin' up to see 'ow the guv'nor's acquaintance is. Toby, yer know. Well, I was passin' by, and the guv'nor said while I was doin' that, I could look in on the gent and see if 'e's lodgin' nice and comf'table with Mrs 'Arrison. 'Oo I 'old in regard, 'e said.'

Since no-one with any sense would trust Tosh Fingers to even serve a bun to an elephant without trying to nick the animal and sell it as horsemeat to a pie and mash shop, Nick said, 'Yes, I heard all that, but what're you after?'

'After? I just told yer, Nick, it's a goodwill call.' Tosh resumed his climb of the stairs. Nick went up after him and cut him off on the first floor landing. He blinked hurtfully. 'Yer in me way, Nick,' he said.

'You can't go up,' said Nick, 'Toby's down with the flu.'

Tosh scratched his chin.

'Well, ain't that a cryin' shame, Nick, a nice bloke like 'im? I tell yer, matey, flu don't 'ave no respect, not even for archbishops. A church-goin' aunt of mine caught it once at the end of July, would yer believe, just as she was lookin' forward to knockin' down a few coconuts at the Bank 'Oliday fair on 'Ampstead 'Eath. We had to bury the poor old girl the day after the Bank 'Oliday, and 'er old man, me Uncle Jim, put a coconut in 'er coffin to send 'er 'appy to the Lord. 'Ope it ain't goin' to be likewise fatal for Toby. That would upset the guv. Well, I'll go up and extend me condolences and see how 'e is, eh?'

'Not till I've been up first to ask him if he wants to see you,' said Nick.

'All right, Nick, you do that,' said Tosh.

Nick went up to the top floor, knocked on the door of the lodger's bedroom, opened it and put his head in. Mr Lukavitch was in bed, looking wan, his eyes closed.

'Toby?'

His eyes opened.

'Ah, Nick,' he said, his voice a bit husky.

'There's a bloke called Tosh Fingers wanting to see you.'

'Him?' Mr Lukavitch sighed.

'He's called to see how you are.'

'How bleedin' kind, eh?' Mr Lukavitch dragged the words up. 'Let him come up.'

'Well, keep an eye on your belongings or they'll disappear,' said Nick. 'Are you feeling a bit better?'

'I think so, don't I? Yes, I think.'

'Hope so,' said Nick. He went down and told Tosh he could go up.

'Well, I'm a warm-'earted bloke, Nick, and it comes natur'lly to me to cheer up a sufferin' friend,' said Tosh, and up he went. Nick returned to the job of trying to help Danny make a name for himself with the General Manager of the LSER.

If Nick hadn't closed the front door, he probably wouldn't have heard Tosh leave. But he had, so he did hear him. The front door always made its own little noise when it was opened and closed. He got up from the table and looked through the bay window. Mr Lukavitch might not have owned any family silver, but he also might have. One could never tell with some of the characters to be found in London.

By the light of the lamp just across the street, Tosh Fingers was visible, going like Springheeled Jack towards the Walworth Road. He was carrying Mr Lukavitch's black bag.

Up went Nick to look in again on the lodger. He didn't want to worry him when he was obviously aching all over with flu, but he felt he had to.

'Toby, that bloke has gone off with your bag.'

'Ah, yes. Yes. Don't worry, Nick.'

'Oh. Right. If you say so. Sorry to have woken you up again. Hope you have a good night.'

'Thank you.'

Nick liked the Polish lodger, but not his friends, Mister Horsemouth and Tosh Fingers.

On Wednesday morning, there was a paragraph on page four of Ma's daily paper relating to a dramatic incident at one of His Majesty's prisons. A warder on duty in the nearby quarry narrowly escaped being crushed to death by a boulder which, having become dislodged, hurtled precipitately down from the lip. A prisoner performed an act of heroism by flinging himself at the warder and pushing him clear in the nick of time, although at great risk to himself. Warder and prisoner both fell. The warder escaped unharmed, the prisoner broke an arm. The prison Governor intended to approach the Home Office with a view to securing parole for the convict in question. The man had undoubtedly saved the warder's life.

Ma missed the paragraph.

The Governor thought it said just enough. He called Pa into his office, and Pa, his left arm in plaster and a sling, arrived accompanied by the chief warder.

'Convict 43789 present and correct, sir,' said Mr Saunders smartly.

'Complete with plaster and sling, I see,' said the Governor. 'Is it uncomfortable, Harrison?'

'Not uncomfortable, Governor, no,' said Pa. 'More inconvenient, you might say.'

'I might,' said the Governor, 'but I prefer to point out it looks convincing. You'll have to make your own arrangements to have the plaster removed. If you go to a hospital to have it done, they'll want to know who plastered a perfectly sound arm.'

'Well, Governor,' said Pa, 'I do happen to know—'

'I'm sure you know all the quacks in London,' said the Governor. 'You'll be released Monday week, but God help you if Inspector Clark of Scotland Yard draws a blank, and God help you too if you break any conditions of your parole. You'll be back inside before you can turn round. My compliments to you, Mr Saunders, for arranging the incident so well, and I trust Warder Brinkley has got over his near heart attack.'

'No worries, sir, all in the line of duty,' said the chief warder.

'It had to take place before and not after the law has made its move,' said the Governor.

300

'Understood, sir,' said Mr Saunders. Pa understood very well himself. It had been his idea to contrive a convincing reason for his release before the law took action on the information he'd supplied. Otherwise, certain sensitive people might think he'd blown the gaff, and that it was this and not a subsequent life-saving act that had secured his release. In which case he might become the victim of a fatal accident. As it was, the law was lying low at the moment, waiting to pounce on the gang and its leader. Scotland Yard had agreed to make Pa's release look exclusive to his act of heroism. The Governor and the law were taking a chance on his information being correct. Pa was much obliged for their belief in him, and said so.

'Our belief, Harrison, is in the fact that an excuse can be found to hang you if the law draws a blank,' said the Governor.

Pa assured him he was dead against being hanged.

During the afternoon, Nick was summoned to the fourth floor, much to the renewed agitation of his manager, who had hoped all this unheard-of stuff had blown over. Nick, of course, wondered if the summons meant a renewal of tea and crumpets with Annabelle.

God received him with a searching look, as did the bewigged bevy of City merchants.

'H'm,' said the almighty chairman.

'Sir?'

'You're still among us, Harrison.'

'Yes, I'm still alive, sir.'

'Something we must all put up with, would you say?'

'Well, I do have a few friends who don't mind.'

'Life is full of surprises,' said God, 'and some are more surprising than others. However, that is by the way. I have to tell you, Harrison, that at the end of next month the company will be dispensing with your services.'

Nick, in shock, could only say, 'Pardon?'

'I think you heard me, Harrison.'

'Well, so I did, sir, but that doesn't mean I find it easy to believe. No-one's complained to me about my work, and if I'm getting the sack, I'd like to know why.'

'It's enough for you to know your department manager will be advised this afternoon that you're leaving us.'

'I don't think that's very fair,' said Nick.

'Don't be impertinent.' God scowled.

'I don't see it's impertinent to ask for a reason,' said Nick.

'The reason, Harrison, is that this is not a suitable place for your employment.'

'Sir?' Nick was incensed, particularly as he knew he simply couldn't afford to lose his job. New ones didn't hang about on trees. 'Why isn't it?'

'Because I say it isn't, you whippersnapper.'

'Blow that for a lark,' said Nick, 'I don't like the smell of it.'

Thunder creased God's brow.

'Damned if I ever heard such impudence,' he said.

'Yes, I know, sir, but I can't believe you think this is fair,' said Nick.

'I haven't finished yet. Stand still and listen. First, as far as being fair is concerned, you're being given exceptionally good notice. Secondly, on the first Monday in March you will commence work with the firm of Parker, Rawlings and Gregson Ltd in St Mary Axe. They deal in imports and exports. Mr Gregson's assistant will be leaving in March, and you'll take his place. Your salary will be one hundred pounds a year.'

'Sir?'

'Yes?' said God. Nick groped. 'Lost your tongue for once, have you, Harrison? I find that a pleasant change.'

Nick was still groping. Hundred pounds a year? Two quid a week? Ma would do a knees-up and the girls would dance on the table. He could give Ma a pound a week for her housekeeping and put ten bob a week into a savings account. Wait a minute, how had this happened?

'Excuse me, sir, is this anything to do with Annabelle?'

God's scowl reappeared.

'Are you referring to my great-niece, Miss Somers?' he asked threateningly.

'Yes, I am, sir. Has she—'

'Hold your tongue,' growled God. 'You can forget Miss Somers, you pipsqueak. I think we agreed weeks ago that you are of very little importance to civilization, or to any young lady deserving of sound prospects. I am merely advising you, Harrison, that having studied your record with this company, I have decided to give you a chance to make more of yourself than you will here. If you have anything worthwhile to offer commerce, and you'd better have something, you will give Parker, Rawlings and Gregson the benefit of it. When you commence your job with them, do so in the knowledge that you are no more and no less than any young man of twenty-one. But I won't have you getting above yourself, do you understand?'

'Yes, sir.' Nick was certain this was a warning not to get fanciful ideas about Annabelle. Actually, of course, he had very fanciful ideas about her. What bloke wouldn't? But he simply wasn't in a position to do anything about it. 'Mr Douglas, can I at least thank you?'

'If you attempt to bow and scrape, Harrison, you'll disappoint me.'

'No, just thank you, sir.'

'Very well. That's all, Harrison.'

'Goodbye, sir.'

'Oh, I'll have my eye on you, Harrison,' said God. He failed to mention he held the majority of shares in Parker, Rawlings and Gregson Ltd. Nor did he give any indication he liked the young man in whom Annabelle was so interested.

A little while after Nick had returned to his desk, the manager called him in again.

'Harrison, I understand from the company staff manager that you're leaving us at the end of February, that you've obtained a new job.'

'Yes, that's right, Mr Pollard.'

'We shall be sorry to lose you, of course,' said Mr Pollard, failing to look the part. He seemed visibly relieved.

'Kind of you to say so, Mr Pollard.'

'Not at all. Good luck, Harrison.'

'Thank you, Mr Pollard.'

Nick blew most of the money in his pocket on his way home by buying two boxes of chocolates from Gran Emerson's shop. Ivy served him and wanted to know if he'd met a young lady who was so alluring that one box wasn't enough for her.

'Funny you should ask that,' said Nick.

'Oh, yes?' said Ivy, avid with interest.

'Yes,' said Nick.

'Well, then?' said Ivy, larks in her eyes.

'That's all,' said Nick.

'Oh, yer teasin' bugger,' said Ivy.

''Ere, I 'eard that, you baggage,' said Gran.

'Slip of me tongue,' said Ivy. ''Ere, listen, Nick, Wally's sailor friend says the Navy ain't fighting Chinese pirates, that they sorted them out years ago.'

'They must have popped up again,' said Nick.

'Must they?' said Gran.

''Well, you know what the Chinese pirates are like,' said Nick, 'if they're not popping up again, they're multiplying. So long, girls.'

Ma didn't actually do a knees-up when she heard the good news, but she came close, especially when she received a box of chocolates. The girls all gave Nick a kiss and a cuddle, and performed encores when the second box was presented to them.

'Now what d'you think of havin' a brother, you Fanny?' said Amy.

'Oh, I ain't sufferin' half as much now,' said Fanny.

'Well, I'm pleased to hear it, Fanny,' said Nick. 'Like a tickle would you?'

Fanny, putting herself behind Ma, said, 'Ma, don't let him.'

'Oh, I liked a nice tickle meself when I was young,' said Ma. 'Your Pa tickled very romantic.'

'What's a romantic tickle?' asked Alice.

'It's – well, never mind that,' said Ma, 'but I daresay when Nick does get a young lady, he'll know just 'ow to do it in a way she'll like.'

'How to do what, Ma?' asked Amy.

'Tickle 'er romantic, of course,' said Ma.

'Oh, that,' said Amy. 'Never heard of it.'

'Will that girl Annabelle Somers be comin' to the committee meetin' tonight, Nick?' asked Alice, enjoying a chocolate caramel.

'I'm trying not to think about it,' said Nick, and then went to answer a knock on the front door. He found Tosh Fingers and his permanent grin standing on the step.

'Well, 'ere we are again, matey,' said Tosh, hat down almost to his eyebrows.

'Nice of you to knock this time,' said Nick.

'Kind of yer to mention it, Nick. I've just come to see 'ow the guv'nor's acquaintance is, not 'aving 'ad a postcard from 'im.'

'That's his bag you're holding,' said Nick.

'Course it is, Nick, course it is. Didn't I take it with me last time so's I could sell 'is little 'ome-made gifts for 'im? It's 'is livin', yer know, and it's an 'ard livin'. But 'e keeps cheerful, and 'e's nicely tucked away 'ere.'

'What's that mean?' asked Nick.

'Well, ain't I admirin' of yer Ma's 'andsome residence? There ain't many such-like places in the East End that a bloke can tuck 'isself nicely away in. You ain't said 'ow Toby is, by the way. He ain't passed on, 'as 'e?'

'No, he was up this morning,' said Nick.

''Eaven be praised,' said Tosh. 'I'll nip up and give 'im the guv'nor's best wishes and return 'is bag to 'im, shall I?'

'Don't pick his pockets while you're up there,' said Nick.

'Me?' said Tosh. 'Course I won't, Nick, course I won't.' Up he went like an oiled machine. He was there for fifteen minutes. When he came down, Ma was waiting for him in the passage. 'Well, 'ello, Mabel. 'Ow's yer dear old self, eh?'

'I'm not old yet,' said Ma, 'and I'll thank you when you leave this 'ouse not to let me friends and neighbours see you. If you keep callin' like this, I'll get a bad name.'

'I like yer jokes, Mabel, always did,' said Tosh. 'The guv'nor sends 'is regards, and 'e's still keepin' a friendly eye on Albert, yer know. I expect 'e'll pay yer one of 'is 'elpful visits soon, bein' attached to yer welfare like 'e is.'

'Goodbye,' said Ma.

'See yer, Mabel,' said Tosh, and eased himself out of the house as if all his joints were well-greased cogs.

Pa, lining up to collect his evening meal on his enamel plate, was in his usual cheerful frame of mind, even though the chief warder had told him that official approval of his parole wouldn't come through until Monday week.

Too much haste to release you won't look good. These things take time, said the warder. Understood, said Pa, I'll arrive at me dear wife's door like an unexpected surprise. Don't sell any gold watches on your way home, said the chief warder, or you'll have an unexpected surprise yourself, a nasty one.

'Knocker?' A whisper arrived at his shoulder.

'I'm listening, old man,' murmured Pa.

'Ain't they givin' yer no favours for savin' Brinkley's life?'

'Doesn't look like it.'

'Bleedin' ungrateful sods. All you're gittin' is a broken arm? Might as well 'ave let that boulder do for Brinkley.'

'I share your feelings,' murmured Pa.

'Knocker, yer still a ponce, ain't yer?'

'Good luck to you too, old man,' said Pa.

Chapter Seventeen

'Annabelle, I want to meet this young man,' said Lizzy.

'Oh, he'll turn up one day, Mum,' said Annabelle, putting her hat and coat on.

'Turn up?' said Lizzy. 'D'you mean all casual like?'

'I'm not sure,' said Annabelle.

'Now listen, my girl, first you're interested in him, then you're not, now you are—'

'No, it's Cassie and Freddy and the football team, Mum.'

'You must think I'm simple,' said Lizzy. Despite Ned having said he liked the look of Nick Harrison, she was far from happy about what Annabelle was up to. 'You haven't joined that team just because you like Cassie and Freddy, it's all to do with that young man, and don't think I don't know it. Annabelle, I'm not havin' you finding ways of running after him, it's not becomin' for a girl. Now if you want to be respectable friends with him, you just bring him here to tea one Sunday, d'you hear?'

'Yes, Mum. One Sunday. Right-ho, Mum. Yes, I'm coming, Dad.'

Ned dropped her off at the house in Browning Street, and said he'd be back at nine to drive her home.

'You're a good old dad, Dad,' said Annabelle.

'You couldn't, I suppose, get yourself elected to a local committee for something or other instead of having to come here every Wednesday evening?' said Ned.

'Dad, I hate committees.'

'This one as well?'

'Oh, this one's by itself,' said Annabelle, 'it's fun.'

Ned smiled and drove away. Annabelle knocked on the door of Ma's house. Nick opened it almost at once.

'Good evening, Captain Harrison,' said Annabelle, 'am I a bit early?'

What a caution. Cool as you like and saucy with it. Nick couldn't remember a time when he'd felt as frustrated and aggravated as now. I've a good mind to do a tickling job on her, he thought.

'Yes, you are a bit early, you minx,' he said, 'but come in and I'll sort you out on the quiet.'

'On the quiet? Oh, is your girlfriend somewhere around, then?' asked Annabelle, stepping in.

'I went off her at Christmas,' said Nick.

'Oh, dear, what a shame,' said Annabelle, 'is she heartbroken, or have you been telling me lies?'

That, of course, hit Nick on his raw edge. The whole family lived on a lie.

'Never mind that, come this way,' he said, and took her into the warm parlour, where she divested herself of her hat and coat. He placed them on the sofa. Annabelle, a delight to the eye in a warm sweater and skirt, fluffed her hair and smiled. Bless the girl, thought Nick, what a gorgeous creature.

'Now look here,' he said, 'what's the big idea?'

'Big idea? I don't know what you mean,' said

Annabelle. 'I hope you're not going to be all growling again. Just because you're the captain and everything else doesn't mean I'm going to stand for being bullied and scowled at.'

'That's done it,' said Nick and went for her. Annabelle, exhilarated, hared around the table and chairs. Nick, having gone off his rocker, legged it in pursuit.

'Coo-ee, Nick, we're 'ere,' called Dumpling, opening the front door by its latchcord.

'Consider yourself saved by the gong,' said Nick to Annabelle.

'I didn't know you were a hooligan as well as a growler,' said Annabelle.

Dumpling and Danny came in, and were followed almost immediately by Cassie and Freddy, and Nick had no option but to see them all seated and to open the meeting.

Everything went to pot again as far as Nick was concerned. A discussion on last Saturday's match was a three-way performance by Dumpling, Cassie and Annabelle. The Rovers had just scraped home by three goals to two, and it was Dumpling's opinion that the blokes were still suffering from too much Christmas pudding. Yes, said Cassie, they all looked a bit over-fed to me. Annabelle said she thought their knees had a feeble look. Mind you, Danny didn't play too bad, said Dumpling.

'Well,' said Danny, 'nice of you to—'

'He still looks a bit like the mornin' after, though,' said Cassie.

Dumpling said she'd sort him out by making him run round the block ten times tomorrow evening. Still, she said, he could have played worse, and Nick hadn't done too bad, neither. Annabelle said yes, she thought Mr Harrison hadn't looked quite as full up with Christmas pudding as the others and had played quite a good captain's game as the middle half back or whatever it was.

'Centre half,' said Nick, 'and we don't need to discuss what we all had for Christmas dinner.'

'Here, we 'ad turkey, would you believe, Annabelle,' said Cassie. 'Me dad brought it 'ome from his work on Christmas Eve. He said it dropped off the back of a goods train. He couldn't put it back because the train was goin' too fast, and as he didn't want to leave it lyin' about on the line, he brought it 'ome, and we cooked it.'

'Downright sensible,' said Freddy, 'it's always best to do a bit of cookin' with a—'

'Freddy, we don't want to talk about turkey,' said Dumpling, 'more about why we nearly could 'ave lost the match last Saturday. You ought to keep to the point at a committee meetin'.'

Annabelle said she supposed some changes ought to be made to the team for next Saturday, but didn't feel she knew enough about them yet to offer any suggestions herself. But she'd been thinking about running a profitable raffle, and went on to detail how to organize it cheaply and effectively. The profit could be used to buy the wool for the proposed blue and white scarves for the supporters, which could be knitted by volunteers.

'Don't look at me,' said Freddy.

'No, I suppose not, Freddy,' said Annabelle graciously, 'and I suppose our captain doesn't do much knitting, either, does he?'

'Chuck her out,' growled Nick.

''Ere, steady on, Nick,' said Dumpling, 'I don't know what's up with you lately.'

'He was under the doctor last time,' said Cassie. 'It simply must be love.'

'Oh, gawd,' sighed Dumpling, 'not our captain, it could ruin 'is football. Worse, it could ruin the Rovers.'

It was like that all through the meeting, and it drove Nick barmy. Ma brought tea and cake in again, saying they needed something hot as it was cold outside. She gave Annabelle an inquisitive look. Annabelle smiled.

'Nice to see you again, Mrs Harrison,' she said, 'and thanks ever so much for thinking of us.'

'My, you're a nice girl,' said Ma, ''ave you got a nice young man?'

'Oh, yes,' said Annabelle, who had made up her mind ages ago that Nick was the one, never mind the dismaying moments he'd given her. 'Yes, I have.'

'That's good,' said Ma, thinking it was an escape for Nick, and went back to the kitchen to tell the girls it was all right, that Annabelle Somers had a young man and wouldn't be a danger to their brother according.

'What a very nice mother you have, Mr Harrison,' said Annabelle, as Nick handed round the tea.

'Annabelle, what d'you keep callin' 'im Mr 'Arrison for?' asked Dumpling.

'Oh, I like to show respect,' said Annabelle without batting an eyelid. 'I mean, he is the captain and everything else, isn't he?'

'Oh, yes, some blokes do like to be that and everything else as well,' said Cassie. 'Freddy's the same. Still, it does show they're kind of manly. I feel sort of weak and feeble when Freddy's doin' a real manly act.' Freddy coughed, and Danny almost

313

fell off his chair. ''Ave I said something?' asked Cassie.

'I didn't 'ear anything special,' said Dumpling, 'it 'appens in a lot of parlours. Mind I don't call it manly, just daft and aggravatin'.'

'Dumpling,' said Danny, 'might I say I don't feel aggravated meself when I'm in yer parlour?'

'That's it, Danny,' said Nick, 'get her in her parlour and do a thorough job on her. Get 'em all in their parlours and do a thorough job on the lot of them.'

'What a coarse brute,' said Annabelle, 'and doesn't he get into foul tempers?'

'He's got a point, though,' said Freddy, 'I never met any girls that carried on more than you three – 'elp, who did that?'

'Me,' said Cassie, 'I kicked you.' She went on to say she had to address the meeting on behalf of the official supporters' club, that everyone approved of having knitted blue and white scarves, that they'd knit them themselves when the wool was bought out of the raffle profits. Dumpling proposed the raffle, and that Annabelle be put in charge of it. Danny seconded it. Nick glowered at him.

'You want to say something, Nick?' asked Dumpling.

'No, I just want to go home,' said Nick.

'Oh, the poor bloke,' said Cassie, ''e doesn't know he's already home.'

A few minutes later, just as the meeting ended, a car horn tooted outside. The time was a minute after nine.

'That's my dad,' said Annabelle, 'come to pick me up again.'

Nick helped her into her coat and saw her out

314

after she'd said good night to the others. The car was there, Ned waiting at the wheel.

'So long, no hard feelings,' said Nick from the doorstep.

'Oh, by the way,' said Annabelle, 'my mother wants you to come to Sunday tea. She hasn't met a football captain before.'

'I'm sorry, I can't,' said Nick, more fed-up about Pa than he'd ever been.

'Don't be silly, of course you can,' said Annabelle.

'I can't,' said Nick, 'for personal reasons. Ask me again in about eighteen months.'

'My mother won't wait for eighteen months,' said Annabelle, and gestured to her dad, a gesture asking him to wait just a bit. 'I don't know why you're being so silly. You haven't got a girlfriend, I know you haven't, and I simply don't see why you can't come and have Sunday tea with us.'

'I can't take you on as my girlfriend, if that's what you mean,' said Nick. 'In any case, you mentioned to my mother that you've got a young man.'

Annabelle stiffened.

'Well, I haven't,' she said, 'and do you have to be so unkind?'

'Yes, if that's what you think it is,' said Nick.

'I hate you, then,' said Annabelle. 'Goodbye.'

That made Nick wince. Annabelle walked to the car and got in. Ned waved to Nick and drove off.

Annabelle was so quiet that Ned asked, 'Anything the matter, pet?'

'I've made a mistake,' she said, 'he's a rotter.'

'Is he? You sure?' said Ned.

'Yes, and I don't want to talk about him.'

'Come on,' said Ned, 'what went wrong?'

'I made a mistake about him, that's all, Dad. Just don't ask me to talk about it.'

When they arrived home, she went straight up to her bedroom. Lizzy asked what the matter was.

'She's in love,' said Ned.

'And that's sent her straight up to bed?' said Lizzy.

'No, not that,' said Ned. 'She won't say, but I think it might be she's just discovered there's someone else, someone he hasn't mentioned before. Well, you know how it is, a feller can have all kinds of faults, including being a crook, without getting the push from a girl. But having someone else in the background, that's bound to turn him into a stinker. Annabelle's opinion of him now is that he's a first-class one.'

'Well, if she's in love with him,' said Lizzy, 'the sooner she falls out of love the better. Mind you, I didn't like the way it all started up in the first place, and you have to have suspicions about a young man who's not polite enough to come and introduce himself to a girl's parents. No wonder this one didn't. He couldn't look us in the eye, I suppose. Still, I'm sure she'll soon get over it, she might be a bit impulsive, but she's got a strong will. We'd best not say too much to her, or ask a lot of questions. Best to let her get over it in her own way.'

'Well, I'm not going to worry her with questions,' said Ned, 'and I'll only give her any advice if she asks for it.'

'It's a shame, a girl havin' her first serious feelings and bein' let down by someone who's a friend of Freddy's,' said Lizzy.

'On the other hand,' said Ned, 'it's only what I

think. I could be wrong about there being someone else.'

'No, you're probably right,' said Lizzy. 'Unless – lor', you don't think he tried to get fresh with her, do you, Ned? I don't think Annabelle would've liked that, she'd have been really upset.'

'Well, she might just tell us the real reason if we leave her to herself and don't bother her,' said Ned.

'Yes, all right,' said Lizzy, who felt she could now go back to thinking about Annabelle marrying someone like a doctor later on. She'd make a very nice doctor's wife.

Annabelle woke up the next morning feeling that Nick Harrison ought never to have been born.

Midway through the afternoon, Boots asked her what was wrong.

'Nothing,' she said.

'Out with it,' said Boots.

'Life's rotten,' said Annabelle, 'and so are some people.'

'One particular specimen?' said Boots.

'I'm ever so busy,' said Annabelle, keeping her head down. 'Oh, blow, why can't some men be more like you?'

'Lucky for them they're not, sweetie, I'm a shocker,' said Boots.

'No, you're not, but he is.'

'He?'

'My lips are sealed about him,' said Annabelle, 'and for ever.'

'I see,' said Boots. 'Well, let me know when all is forgiven.'

'Never,' said Annabelle, a woman doubly scorned.

Boots smiled. His endearing niece was having her

first real emotional problems. She liked to be in control of the games she played, and he wondered if she'd gone about this one in the wrong way.

As for Nick, at this moment he wasn't very fond of himself.

Annabelle was an absent spectator at Saturday's match, Dumpling was a suffering one, hardly able to believe what a feeble game Nick played. Fanny said she'd never seen him so dozy. The Rovers only drew the match, and that against a side Dumpling said they should have beaten hollow. It was such a blow to her pride that when Danny said he'd meet her in her parlour tomorrow afternoon, she weakly said oh, all right. Her dad, who'd refereed the game, said Danny was welcome in the parlour any time he liked.

Dumpling had recovered a bit by Sunday afternoon, and was well able, in her own estimation, to keep Danny away from her jumper. Mind, it was a bit foggy outside, which sort of gave her an uneasy feeling. Well, fog outside and a cosy parlour inside had shocking memories for her. However, since she was in her nineteenth year, she reckoned she was old enough to handle Danny, fog or no fog.

'Sit there,' she said, pointing to one of the fireside armchairs.

'Pleasure, Dumpling,' said Danny, seating himself.

'And I'll sit 'ere,' said Dumpling, and sat down on the sofa. What a mistake that was, because Danny undermined her immediately by presenting her with a collection of pristine cigarette cards of famous footballers. Dumpling went swoony over them. 'Oh, yer couldn't 'ave pleased me more, Danny,' she said in a sort of fainting voice.

'I bet yer'll like the one of Jimmy Dimmock of Spurs,' said Danny, moving to sit beside her.

'Oh, me rapture, it's overcomin' me,' sighed Dumpling, so seeing just how overcome she was, Danny put an arm around her waist and kissed her. When Dumpling came up for air, she gasped, ''Ere, what d'you think you're doin' of?'

''Ave yer seen the one of Billy McCracken of Newcastle United?' asked Danny.

'Oh, me 'appy 'eart,' moaned Dumpling, so seeing she was in no condition to break his leg or damage his hooter, Danny kissed her again. From then on, Dumpling endured another terrible time.

The kids, playing in the kitchen, informed their mum they could hear Dumpling yelling for help. Mrs Evans said no-one was to worry, Danny was with her and giving her all the help she needed.

'I'll go in a bit later and see if the fire's all right,' said Mr Evans.

'That's it, a bit later,' said Mrs Evans.

So a bit later, Mr Evans went in, by which time the cigarette cards were all over the rug, and Dumpling's skirt and jumper were all over the place.

''Ere, what's goin' on?' asked Mr Evans, looking like a father in shock. 'Or what's comin' off would be more like it.'

'Oh, me blushes,' gasped Dumpling, 'thank gawd you're 'ere, Dad. Get 'im off me.'

'Is that you there, Danny?' demanded Mr Evans sternly.

'Yes, it's me, Mr Evans,' said Danny.

'Blowed if I ever saw the like,' said Mr Evans, 'you're compromisin' me own daughter. I'm afraid

I'll 'ave to ask you to do what's right and honourable.'

'I'll be pleasured to, Mr Evans,' said Danny fervently, 'it's me life's wish to do what's right and honourable by Dumpling.'

'Well, though I'm shocked to me core at seein' me own daughter 'alf-undressed,' said Mr Evans, 'yer a gent, Danny, at acceptin' responsibility for 'er condition. Easter weddin' suit yer?'

'Not 'alf,' said Danny, 'and I've got a bit of money saved up.'

''Ere, wait a minute,' panted Dumpling, 'I ain't—'

'Easter Saturday, I reckon,' said Mr Evans.

'Fine,' said Danny.

'But, Dad,' gasped Dumpling, 'what about me football?'

'That's a point,' mused Mr Evans. 'Tell yer what, Dumpling lovey, Danny'll let you out of the kitchen on Wednesday evenings for yer committee meetings, and on Saturday afternoons for the matches. I'll ask 'im to play fair with yer on that.'

'But, Dad, what about all that daft married stuff in between?' asked Dumpling faintly.

'Oh, I reckon we can both rely on Danny to see that you get to like it,' said Mr Evans. ''E was doin' fine when I come in. There y'ar, Dumpling, you're fixed up fair and square now for bein' wed and still keepin' yer football goin'. All right, Danny, you can get off her now.'

*　　*　　*

'It's not actually hurting, is it?' said Rosie. She was with Annabelle in the latter's bedroom.

'Yes, it is,' said Annabelle.

'All over?' said Rosie.

'Certainly not,' said Annabelle, 'it's just my pride, that's all. I never felt so small in all my life.'

'You're not madly gone on him, then?' said Rosie.

'Madly gone?' said Annabelle. 'Rosie, be your age, I'm not a twelve-year-old schoolgirl, I'm a working woman.'

'Working woman, oh, yes,' said Rosie. 'Sorry, ducky. I see now, you just wanted him as a good friend. You know, there's nothing going on between us, we're just good friends, just two workers of the world.'

'I'll hit you,' said Annabelle.

'Only trying to cheer you up, lovey,' said Rosie. 'What could he have meant when he said ask him again to Sunday tea in eighteen months?'

'I don't know, do I? And I'm not interested. I wouldn't have him for a friend now even if he went down on bended knees and said prayers.'

'Oh, poor Nick,' said Rosie.

'What d'you mean, poor Nick?'

'I liked him. He seemed such a healthy-looking young man. Listen, lovey, I think you ought to try to find out what the mention of eighteen months means.'

'I know what it means,' said Annabelle, 'a lifetime. Eighteen months is nearly two years. The cheek of it, expecting me to wait nearly a lifetime for the pleasure of his company at Sunday tea. He's got a hope.'

'Oh, dear,' said Rosie.

'What d'you mean, oh dear?' demanded Annabelle.

'You're ever so flushed, ducky, for a working woman,' said Rosie.

Annabelle grabbed a pillow and went for her best friend. Rosie caught the pillow, cradled it and winked at Annabelle over the top of it.

They burst into laughter.

Nick spent most of his Sunday wondering if there was some way to let Annabelle know he hadn't meant to put her off in such an unfriendly fashion. What would happen if he came clean with her, if he told her the truth about Pa? She just might say well, you're not a convicted felon yourself, so let's go to the pictures next Saturday. But would she? One thing was certain, her parents wouldn't be in favour, nor want him to go to tea one Sunday. And if God ever got to know, his prospective new career would never get off the ground.

Mr Lukavitch at least had a good Sunday, having recovered enough to go out with his bag during the morning and to share a pot of tea with the family in the evening. Back to his agreeable self, he expressed his gratitude to Ma for all she had done on his behalf while he was ill, and told her she was a corblimey tophole woman. How kind, said Ma. Don't mention it, old dear, said Mr Lukavitch. Ma said she wasn't old yet. No, not ruddy likely, beamed Mr Lukavitch, and went back up to his lodgings to do a little more work before going to bed.

'He's forgotten his fags,' said Fanny a few minutes later.

'Someone take them up to 'im,' said Ma.

'All right, I will,' said Fanny. When she came down again she said the lodger had been ever so pleased to get his packet of fags back. He'd got a glass eye fixed and was working on some beads, which she didn't think as attractive as coloured ones. They were little glass beads, she said. Ma said she supposed some people liked glass beads. Nick said if they were strung together, Pa could probably sell them as five-bob diamond necklaces. Ma said she'd be obliged if no-one talked that way about Pa, not when walls had several ears.

Pa at this moment was looking forward to being released on parole, particularly as the Governor had told him there was an honest job waiting for him at Woolwich Arsenal. Pa hadn't been too sure about that at first.

'Well, Governor, I—'

'You'll take it, Harrison, for the sake of your family.'

'Of course, Governor. Ah, in the stores?'

'Not in the stores.'

Pity, thought Pa, there were pickings in stores.

'No, Governor, right, not in the stores.'

'One step out of line, Harrison, and you'll be back here.'

Frankly, thought Pa, I'm not keen on that. It looks like I'll have to go along with Ma's ideas, and earn an honest living.

'You can rely on me, Governor, not to let you down.'

'That had better be true,' said the Governor.

When the day was drawing to its close, Rosie said to Boots, 'Mum's gone to bed with her Ethel M. Dell novel.'

'Hope it won't come between us,' said Boots.

'Oh, you'll win,' said Rosie. 'Anyway, Daddy,

about Annabelle, with all the brains you're supposed to have and all your experience of what makes people tick and go off bang, you must have some idea of what eighteen months could mean.'

'You've got the wrong bloke,' said Boots, raking the dying ashes of the living-room fire, 'I'm still what they call an innocent abroad.'

'Yes, and I'm Queen Elizabeth,' said Rosie. 'No, come on, think of some reason why Nick Harrison should have to wait eighteen months before he can accept an invitation to tea from Annabelle.'

'Let's see,' said Boots, 'he's an insurance clerk, I believe, working for the company headed by Annabelle's fearsome great-uncle.'

'Yes, poor bloke,' said Rosie, 'it takes an insurance clerk years to get to a really decent wage, doesn't it?'

'And probably makes him think twice about whether or not he can afford to get married,' said Boots. He finished raking the ashes, sat down and filled his pipe. Rosie lit a taper from the glowing ashes and applied the flame to his tobacco. The familiar aroma pleasured her sense of smell. Eyes met through little spirals of blue smoke. Rosie smiled. There were no two people who were more compatible than Rosie and Boots. 'Your works are ticking,' she said.

'I'm thinking,' said Boots, 'that perhaps young Mr Harrison is coming into money in eighteen months.'

'Sorry, old darling, that's a feeble thought.'

'Is it?'

'Yes, of course,' said Rosie. 'Waiting to come into money wouldn't be any reason at all for not accepting an invitation to tea.'

'Unless at the moment he doesn't have a Sunday suit,' said Boots.

'That's even more feeble,' said Rosie.

'Well, perhaps he's got a catching complaint,' said Boots, 'the kind that needs another eighteen months to be cured.'

'That's not even feeble, that's a washout, a dud,' said Rosie. 'You're letting me down. Can't you have a flash of inspiration?'

'Is this life or death stuff?' asked Boots.

'I'm not sure,' said Rosie. 'I mean, I don't know if Annabelle's really keen or if she's just miffed that the young man hasn't fallen at her feet. All her boyfriends have.'

'Well, perhaps she's suddenly met her match,' said Boots. 'Don't you think it would be a good idea to let her work it all out for herself?'

'Yes, I do think,' said Rosie. 'I'm just curious about the meaning of eighteen months.'

'Count up to a hundred and see if that'll help,' said Boots.

'That's very inspirational, I don't think,' said Rosie.

Chapter Eighteen

Dumpling and Danny called on Monday evening. They wanted to talk to Nick, so Nick took them into the parlour. He noted that Danny looked highly pleased with himself, while Dumpling was having trouble with her expressions.

'What's on your minds?' he asked.

'I've got worries I never thought I'd ever 'ave durin' me footballin' career,' said Dumpling.

'What worries?' asked Nick.

'Dumpling, I keep tellin' yer, they don't 'ave to be worries,' said Danny.

'Never mind what you tell me,' said Dumpling gloomily, 'I got 'orrible feelings me footballing's goin' to be interfered with. Me dad's done it on me, Nick.'

'He's pawned your football?' said Nick.

'Course not,' said Dumpling, 'me dad wouldn't do that. No, he's gone and arranged for me and Danny to get married. I ain't ready for it.'

'Well, I am, Dumpling, gawd bless yer,' said Danny, 'and I'll look after all yer worries, which ain't worries, really.'

'What happened?' asked Nick.

'I ain't sayin',' said Dumpling, 'except I was in me mum's parlour with Danny yesterday when me dad came in. I was never more embarrassed.'

'Why?' asked Nick, keeping his face straight.

'Well, it was accidental circumstances, like,' said Danny. 'I was showin' Dumpling a set of cigarette cards of footballers, and 'aving a bit of a cuddle as well, and some'ow we fell over and Dumpling – well, um – Dumpling finished up underneath just as 'er dad walked in. Well, of course I 'ad to do what was honourable, and me and Dumpling's goin' to get churched on Easter Saturday. D'you mind keepin' these details confidential, Nick?'

'Of course,' said Nick. 'Congratulations, Dumpling, I'm tickled for you.'

'Oh, me sad 'eart,' said Dumpling mournfully. 'I mean, me, one of the blokes, 'aving to live soppy ever after. But me dad's mind is made up, 'e says it's for the honour of the whole fam'ly, and me mum said that as long as Danny's doin' right by me, she'd forgive 'im for what 'e might 'ave done in the parlour. Mind, I don't remember it 'appening while we was lookin' at the cigarette cards.'

'I'm a bit hazy meself now,' said Danny. 'I just remember that some'ow or other I fell on top of Dumpling accidental, like, just as 'er dad come in.'

'Well, accidents can sometimes serve a good purpose,' said Nick.

'I don't call livin' soppy ever after a good purpose,' said Dumpling, sighing at what it was all going to do to her football.

'It'll work out, Dumpling,' said Nick, 'so best of luck to both of you.'

'Thanks, Nick,' said Danny, 'and might I ask yer to be me best man?'

'Pleasure,' said Nick.

'Crikey, will yer really do that, Nick?' said Dumpling, looking a bit happier. 'We couldn't be more complimented, our captain as our best man.'

'I couldn't be more complimented myself,' said Nick.

'Oh, I'll bet you'll make a smashin' speech,' said Dumpling.

'I'll work on it,' said Nick, 'and perhaps include a wish that all your troubles will be little footballers.'

Dumpling blushed rosy red.

'Oh, crikey,' she said.

'Well, it's a thought,' said Nick.

'I ain't against it meself,' said Danny.

'Oh, Lord 'elp me footballin',' said Dumpling.

'Hello, Daddy love,' said Rosie over the phone the next day, 'could I speak to Annabelle?'

'She's working,' said Boots.

'Oh, yes, I know she's a working woman, she told me,' said Rosie, 'but I've just thought you were right, after all, when you said eighteen months was probably the amount of time Annabelle's Romeo felt he needed before he could afford to take up with a steady girlfriend. Weren't you clever?'

'Not specially,' said Boots, 'it was only a guess.'

'Telepathy, more like,' said Rosie. 'I remembered it was what his sister Alice said when Annabelle and I met her at one of the football matches. I wondered if Annabelle has remembered too. Of course, I could phone her tonight instead of speaking to her now—'

'Hold on,' said Boots. A smile on his face, he called Annabelle from her office and put the phone in her hand. 'Rosie wants to talk to you,' he said.

'Well, I just hope she isn't going to give me a hard time,' said Annabelle, and Boots left her with the phone, knowing girls preferred not to have adults listening in. 'Hello? Rosie?'

'Good morning, working woman,' said Rosie.

'Good morning, layabout.'

'Listen, lovey, it's just a question of poverty between you and Nick,' said Rosie.

'Nick?' said Annabelle. 'Oh, him. What d'you mean, poverty?'

'Don't you remember his sister Alice telling us he didn't think he'd be able to afford having a girlfriend for a couple of years?' said Rosie. 'Well, eighteen months is almost as good as two years. He's too proud, it seems, to ask a girl out while his pockets are lined with poverty.'

'But our mums and dads and aunts and uncles all had to live with poverty, yet they weren't too proud to take up with each other,' said Annabelle. 'What sort of a world is he living in, for goodness sake?'

'You can ask him that when you go to the football committee meeting tomorrow evening,' said Rosie.

'I'm not going.'

'Oh, dear,' said Rosie.

'If you don't stop saying oh dear every time we have a conversation,' said Annabelle, 'I'll fall out with you, Rosie Adams.'

'Sorry, lovey, but you could still ask Nick—'

'I'm not going to ask him anything,' said Annabelle.

'But why?'

'Hate him, that's why.'

'Oh, dear,' said Rosie.

'There you go again,' said Annabelle, 'and I've got work to do. Rosie, you don't really think someone would be too proud of his poverty to come to Sunday tea, do you?'

'He might be,' said Rosie, 'but as you hate him,

we can drop the subject. Who wants to invite a hated young man to tea, anyway.'

'I'm going to hate you as well in a minute,' said Annabelle. 'No, I must ring off now. I'll see you some time. 'Bye.'

'Well, that's rich,' said Boots, and laughed. He was enjoying a light lunch with Annabelle in Lyons teashop, Camberwell Green, and his niece had been confiding in him.

'I don't think it's at all funny,' said Annabelle.

'Not a little amusing even?' said Boots.

'No, certainly not,' said Annabelle. 'How would you like it, Uncle Boots, if you felt your life had been blighted?'

'Blighted?'

'Well, to suffer disappointment in someone is a bit blighting,' said Annabelle.

'Let me see,' said Boots, 'you met him through lift gates, then three times in a City teashop, then by way of his football team. You then wangled yourself into the supporters' club and onto his committee, turned him inside-out, I imagine—'

'Uncle Boots,' protested Annabelle.

'And finished up hating him,' said Boots.

'Well, he's a stinker,' said Annabelle.

'Yes, very amusing,' said Boots.

'Oh, yes, a hoot, I don't think,' said Annabelle.

'Never mind, sweetie, all over now,' said Boots, who knew it wasn't.

'What d'you mean, all over?' said Annabelle.

'Isn't it, then?'

'Yes, but I've still got the scars of my wounds,' said Annabelle.

'I see,' said Boots with suitable gravity, 'you're

330

now thinking up ways to push young Mr Harrison over a cliff, are you?'

'Uncle Boots, how can you say a thing like that? I'm surprised at you. Don't you love me any more?'

'Treasure you,' said Boots, 'you're my sister's first-born and my mother's first grandchild. However, if it's not all over between you and the stinker, will you be going to the committee meeting in Walworth this evening?'

'Certainly not,' said Annabelle. 'Well, perhaps I might, but only to resign. After all, when a young lady doesn't want a certain person ever to darken her doorstep, she can't sit on the same committee as him. Uncle Boots, it's the worst case of stuck-up pride I ever heard of, not wanting me for his one and only girlfriend just because he doesn't earn very much.'

'So that's it,' said Boots.

'Pardon?' said Annabelle.

'I thought it was all to do with him refusing to accept an invitation to Sunday tea.'

Annabelle turned pink.

'What did I say, then?' she asked.

'That he's refused to have you as his one and only lady love.'

'Oh, I didn't say that, and I wouldn't, it's too corny.'

'Have some coffee,' said Boots, and ordered two from the Nippy who'd served them. The teashop was fairly full, but he and Annabelle were tucked nicely away. 'Tell me, young lady,' he said, 'is this all still a game to you, or do you have your first serious feelings?'

'Oh, help, must I say?' asked Annabelle.

'Not if you don't want to,' said Boots.

331

'It's just that – oh, blow, I don't like saying so, but I'd hate not to see him again, Uncle Boots, even if he is a rotten case of stuck-up pride. D'you think that means serious feelings?'

The Nippy brought the coffees, and a smile as well.

'There we are, Mr Adams.'

'Thanks, Molly,' said Boots.

'Anytime, Mr Adams.'

'Springtime's favourite with some people,' said Boots, and the Nippy giggled herself away.

'Uncle Boots, you're a shocker,' said Annabelle, 'she'll expect you to meet her in the park on Easter Sunday.'

'Not if I can help it,' said Boots, 'she's six months engaged to a bloke who's seven feet tall. Where were we?'

'Oh, it was did I know if my feelings were serious,' said Annabelle.

'Are you going to the committee meeting this evening or not?' asked Boots.

'I suppose I should,' said Annabelle, 'I suppose it would be the polite thing to do, to tell them in person that I'm resigning.'

'Well, instead of your dad driving you there, I will,' said Boots. 'Then I'll be able to meet the stinker and let you know what I think of him.'

'Oh, yes, I'd value your opinion,' said Annabelle. 'Uncle Boots, you're not still laughing at me, are you?'

'Perish the thought,' said Boots.

He arrived with Annabelle well before the meeting started that evening, which gave him a chance to sum up the young man. Like Ned, he thought there was nothing to quarrel with in respect of Nick's vigorous and wholesome looks, nor with the fact that he was unmistakeably adult compared to the boys Annabelle had been going around with during the last few years. Further, his sense of humour was immediately apparent, and Boots valued a sense of humour in people. It helped them put up with those who took life too seriously.

Boots noted that Nick and Annabelle were wary with each other, Annabelle still suffering from being a woman scorned, and Nick, without Boots knowing it, still sure that he was in no position to court a girl as lovable and respectable as Annabelle. He'd have to tell too many lies.

Boots said he'd heard of the famous football committee meetings. Nick, of course, said he didn't know they were famous. Boots said that was the impression he'd formed from talking to Annabelle. Nick grinned and said they'd lately turned into hen parties. Blessed sauce, said Annabelle, looking gorgeous in her sweater and skirt. Boots asked just how they'd turned into hen parties, and Nick said there were three blokes and three females, and the blokes accordingly were outnumbered.

'Did you hear that, Uncle Boots?' said Annabelle. They were in the warm and cosy parlour, the fire burning. 'Did you hear him call us females as if we're just anybody?'

'A slight gaffe on your part, Nick,' said Boots, the room reminding him of Chinese Lady's well-kept parlour in the old family house in nearby Caulfield Place. They all looked similar, Walworth parlours. As in most, this one had an aspidistra in the bay window, a table in the centre surrounded by upright chairs, a piano in the corner, and a sofa and

333

armchairs suitably placed. If there was a difference, it was that some parlours, like this one, looked cosier and more welcoming than others. 'I presume you're thinking about the accepted fact that two girls are always the equal of three blokes, and that three outdo them?'

'It's a losing battle,' said Nick, 'but we take it like men. Hope it won't offend you if I tell you your niece always leads the charge.'

'I can't believe this,' said Annabelle, 'he's talking as if I'm not here.'

'I think you'll win', said Boots, and Nick thought him a man very much at his ease, a man one immediately liked. Annabelle's dad had had a similar air. 'Well, shall I get out of the way before the rest of the committee members arrive?'

'If you're not in any hurry,' said Nick, 'you can meet my family, and once you're in the kitchen, Ma will make a pot of tea.'

'Your father's not home on leave yet?' said Annabelle, who'd been waiting ever since she arrived to have Nick say something that would tell her he wanted to walk with her into a summer sunset.

'No, I'm afraid not,' said Nick, 'but you're welcome to meet my mother and sisters, Mr Adams.'

'Yes, I'd like to,' said Boots.

What happened then, of course, was that he spent the whole time in the kitchen getting to know Ma and the girls. He rarely had problems mixing with people, any more than Sammy did. People meeting Sammy for the first time felt after ten minutes that he'd been waiting all his life to get acquainted with them. Those meeting Boots for the first time thought what a decent bloke he was. Ma thought exactly that. Alice and Amy wished they'd put their best Sunday dresses on, and Fanny wished she had an uncle like him . . .

While Boots was being entertained by the family, and was entertaining in return, the committee meeting hardly touched on football. Well, who would have expected it to when there was so much to say following Dumpling's complaint that she was going to have to live soppy ever after with Danny come Easter Saturday? Danny, of course, said it didn't have to be soppy, that Dumpling had the wrong idea concerning conjugal rites. He didn't actually use that phrase, he simply said she had the wrong idea about what happened, but he knew what he meant. Cassie said she didn't know much about what happened herself, as she'd never been married, but she'd heard it was swoony. Same as fainting, I suppose, said Freddy. I've had some of that personally, he said.

'Freddy, what d'you mean?' asked Annabelle.

'Well,' said Freddy, 'I was sittin' on our parlour sofa with Cassie one foggy Saturday, and playin' cards with 'er. Our knees touched and we both fainted. Funniest feelin' I'd ever had, it was.'

'Well, I've got nice knees, they'd make anyone faint,' said Cassie. 'Of course, I fainted meself out of shock.'

'Cassie, you scream,' said Annabelle.

'Might I point out we haven't yet got as far as reading the minutes?' said Nick.

'Well, fancy anyone worrying about the minutes when Chrissie and Danny have just got engaged,' said Annabelle witheringly.

'Now look here,' said Nick, 'this—'

'He's off,' said Dumpling. 'I told you 'e gets like

this sometimes, Annabelle. Then it's all now look 'ere, you lot, and so on. Still, 'e can't 'elp it, bein' our captain—'

'And everything else,' said Annabelle. 'Chrissie, I'm sure you'll love getting married, and if you're going to buy a lovely bridal gown, I could get a generous discount for you in one of my Uncle Sammy's dress shops.'

'Oh, I thought one of me Sunday frocks would do,' said Dumpling, 'so's that I could change out of it quick, as there's always a football match Easter Saturday afternoon. Mind you,' she said gloomily, 'if Danny plays as usual, I've got a feelin' 'is mind won't be much on the football. I just 'ope that won't mean he'll let me beloved Rovers down on 'is weddin' day.'

'But, Chrissie,' said Annabelle, wanting to shriek with laughter, 'you and Danny will go on honeymoon after the wedding, won't you?'

'What, and miss the football match?' said Dumpling. 'I'd never forgive meself. Besides, I don't know I want any 'oneymoon. I'll be all alone with Danny, and Lord knows what 'e'll get up to. It's bad enough sometimes in me mum's parlour.'

'Read the minutes,' said Nick.

'There he goes again,' said Cassie. 'Freddy, can't you do something about Nick always wanting to talk about the minutes and 'ow much money there is in the kitty?'

'Well, it's like this, Cassie,' said Freddy, 'it's what we're actu'lly gathered 'ere together for.'

'Freddy, stop bein' a spoilsport,' said Cassie, 'Chrissie and Danny gettin' engaged is a lot more excitin' than reading some old minutes.'

'Yes, of course it is,' said Annabelle.

'Still,' said Danny, 'proud and 'appy as I am that Dumpling's consented to be me better 'alf, we ought to get on with the meetin'.'

'It was me dad that consented,' said Dumpling.

'You sure?' said Freddy. 'I mean, who's Danny engaged to, then, you or your dad?'

'Freddy, you barmy or something?' said Dumpling.

'We all are,' said Nick. 'At least, I know I am. I'll need locking up soon.'

'All right, I'll read the minutes, shall I, Nick?' said Dumpling.

'Not if it's going to interfere with the wedding,' said Nick.

'My word,' said Annabelle, 'isn't the captain an old stickler, and a bit sarky as well?'

'Yes, it's not every day two of us get engaged to be married,' said Cassie.

'Don't keep remindin' me, Cassie, I still ain't over me gloom,' said Dumpling.

'Dumpling, if you don't read the flaming minutes, I'll pull your football shorts down myself next time you wear them,' said Nick.

'Well, what a brute,' said Annabelle, 'I wouldn't like to come face to face with him on a dark night.'

'Freddy, chuck her out,' said Nick.

'Chuck who out?' asked Freddy.

'All of 'em,' said Nick, 'then let's have a committee meeting.'

'Nick, I don't know why you're carryin' on so alarmin',' said Cassie, 'you never used to have a bad temper. You ought to be singing the 'appy Weddin' March on behalf of Chrissie and Danny's engagement.'

'You'll be singing in a minute,' said Nick, 'but it

won't be the Wedding March, it'll be with your head tucked underneath your arm after I've chopped it off.'

'Cassie, hit him,' said Annabelle.

'Oh, he don't mean it,' said Cassie, 'he likes me really. He 'ad a last waltz with me once at a dance at Browning Hall, didn't you, Nick?'

'How thrilling,' said Annabelle. Nick muttered.

'That reminds me,' said Dumpling, 'I 'ope you'll all come to me weddin'. I told me mum and dad I'd like all the football committee there, that it might 'elp to cheer me up a bit, specially now Nick's goin' to be best man, bless 'im.'

'I'd love to be there, Chrissie,' said Annabelle.

'I'll be in a corblimey asylum,' said Nick, 'and if they won't let me out for the day, Freddy'll have to take my place.'

'Oh, dear,' said Annabelle, 'he is in a state, isn't he?'

'I've said it all along,' remarked Cassie, 'he's in love. It gives you funny turns. Freddy's the same. He's always 'aving funny turns.'

'Meeting's over!' bawled Nick.

'Eh?' said Dumpling.

'What's he shouting for?' asked Annabelle, who had given up on her intention to resign.

'Yes, what yer shoutin' for, Nick?' asked Danny. 'The meetin' ain't properly started yet.'

'It's not started at all,' said Nick, 'it's just another hen party natter so far.'

'Oh, lor', you do sound upset, Nick,' said Dumpling, 'I'd best get on.' She read the minutes, Nick reported on the parlous state of the finances, and then on the fact that the fixture list was now full all the way to the end of April. The loss of the

Portland Road team's fixture had been taken care of with a new one. He was happy to announce that, he said.

'He's feelin' better now,' said Cassie.

'I didn't know he could feel better,' said Annabelle.

'Oh, Nick 'as lots of nice moments,' said Dumpling. 'It's the weight of all 'is responsibilities that sometimes makes 'im out of sorts.'

'And bein' in love,' said Cassie.

'Perhaps it's unrequited,' said Annabelle.

'Beg yer pardon?' said Danny.

'Is that something to do with movin' the goalposts?' asked Freddy.

'Course not,' said Dumpling, 'goalposts are sacred. It's one of Annabelle's educated words.'

'What I mean,' said Annabelle, 'is that perhaps the girl our captain's in love with doesn't return his feelings. Perhaps he shouts at her like he does at us.'

'Crikey,' said Dumpling, 'if I can put up with all Danny's daft cuddling and kissin', she ought to be able to put up with Nick shoutin' a bit. All the Rovers put up with 'im chuckin' his weight about, it's for the sake of the team.'

'Yes, and who is this girl that's upsettin' Nick?' asked Cassie.

'Yes, what yer keepin' her dark for, Nick?' asked Danny.

Nick did a bit of hard breathing before opening up a letter lying on the table in front of him.

'We've had an application from a bloke called Johnny Richards,' he said. 'His family's just moved into Walworth from Peckham. He used to play for a team called Peckham Albion. He'd like to join the Rovers.'

'All right, tell 'im we'll give 'im a trial game,' said Freddy.

'Nick, you 'aven't mentioned who this girl is,' said Cassie. She had a good idea herself who it was.

'Freddy, bash Cassie's head in with the coal shovel,' bawled Nick.

'He's shouting again,' said Annabelle.

'I'm sure I don't know what's come over 'im,' said Cassie.

The door opened, and Alice looked in.

'Is anything wrong?' she asked. 'We keep hearin' someone hollering.'

'Oh, it's all right, Alice,' said Dumpling, 'Nick's just a bit out of sorts again.'

'Well, keep your voice down, Nick,' said Alice, 'Annabelle's uncle thinks someone's breakin' up the furniture. Good evenin', Annabelle, Nick's not hollering at you, is he?'

'No, at everyone generally,' said Annabelle.

'Nick, what's up with you?' asked Alice.

'Don't ask,' said Nick.

'I'll be bringing you all cups of tea in a tick,' said Alice.

'How's my uncle getting on?' asked Annabelle.

'Just like one of the fam'ly,' said Alice, 'and Fanny wants to keep him. Won't be a minute with the tea.'

She brought it in not long after, and at a moment when Nick was having to put up with more chat about Dumpling's forthcoming marriage to Danny. Everything had gone to pot again. But the hot tea and slices of homemade cake were welcome and civilizing. The meeting came to an end ten minutes later, and Dumpling, Danny, Cassie and Freddy departed. Nick saw them out and took the opportunity to buttonhole Freddy and Danny on the doorstep.

'Listen, you two, now that you're full members of the petticoat brigade, wear jumpers and skirts at all future meetings.'

'Eh?' said Freddy.

'Beg yer pardon?' said Danny.

'You heard,' said Nick. 'Those girls are taking the committee apart, and you're helping them. You'll both look pretty in jumpers and skirts, and I'll know where I stand, one bloke against five jumpers.'

'What's Nick sayin'?' asked Cassie from the gate.

'Search me,' said Freddy, ''e sounds as if he's gone off his chump.'

'Oh, 'e'll be all right tomorrow,' said Dumpling.

'There y'ar, Nick, you'll be all right tomorrow,' said Danny, and he and Freddy left with their girls. Nick closed the door and went back into the parlour, where Annabelle had donned her hat and coat. Nick gave her a challenging look.

'You're a monkey,' he said.

'Well, thanks very much,' said Annabelle. 'But at least I don't bawl and shout at people.'

'I think you've been playing games with me ever since we met,' said Nick.

'I haven't, really I haven't.'

'By the way,' said Nick, 'I'm starting a new job with a firm of exporters and importers at the beginning of March.'

'You're what?' said Annabelle.

'Your great-uncle arranged it, did you know?' said Nick.

'No, of course I didn't,' said Annabelle. 'Is it a better job?'

341

'Much,' said Nick.

'Well,' said Annabelle, 'if he'd known that you bawl and shout at people and knock their heads off, he'd have given you the sack, not a much better job. I never dreamt, when I first met you, that you were actually a hooligan.'

'How would you like a smacked bottom?' asked Nick.

'How would you like your face pushed in?' countered Annabelle.

'Call it quits,' said Nick. 'I've been wondering if you've any idea why your great-uncle put me in the way of this new job.'

'Well, he said nothing at all to me about it,' said Annabelle. 'Will it make any difference?'

'To what?' asked Nick.

'Oh, come on, you blessed stick-in-the-mud,' said Annabelle, 'you know what I mean.'

'I'll talk to you later on,' said Nick.

'How much later on?' demanded Annabelle. 'I'm only asking to be friends with you.'

'Well, in a year or so—'

'Don't make me laugh,' said Annabelle.

Boots made himself heard then.

'Ready to go, Annabelle?' he called.

'Yes, ready, Uncle Boots.'

Boots came into the parlour, coat on, hat in his hand.

'Had a good committee meeting?' he asked.

'Famous,' said Annabelle.

'Good,' said Boots. He'd thanked Ma and the girls for putting up with him and making him feel at home. He'd made use of the time to sum up the family, and he'd come up with one or two interesting conclusions. It was all on account of being intrigued by what was happening to Lizzy's elder daughter

'Thanks for bringing Annabelle, Mr Adams,' said Nick. 'Would you know what it was that turned her into a terror?'

'Oh, they're all terrors by the time they're five, Nick,' said Boots.

'Oh, don't mind me,' said Annabelle.

'Still,' said Nick, 'she's a very entertaining terror.'

'Oh, how kind,' said Annabelle, 'it's such a pleasure to meet a gentleman. Good night.'

'So long, Nick,' said Boots, 'you lost, did you?'

'I'm lucky I survived,' said Nick, and watched them walk to Boots's car.

'So,' said Boots, as he turned into the Walworth Road with the evening misty, 'that's the young man you can't make up your mind about.'

'Yes, did you notice what a stinker he is?' said Annabelle.

'What's the answer?' asked Boots. 'Boiling him in oil?'

'Oh, come on, Uncle Boots, what did you really think of him?'

'I think your mother will like him,' said Boots.

'Oh, help, I think I do have serious feelings,' said Annabelle.

'Sure?' said Boots.

'Well, it's no joke, I can tell you.'

'Right, no joke,' said Boots.

'I'm not actually desperate,' said Annabelle.

'Right, not actually desperate,' said Boots.

'Uncle Boots, I'll hit you.'

'Understood,' said Boots.

'He's so funny,' said Annabelle, 'and I teased him dreadfully. He looked once or twice as if he was going to blow up. Well, he shouldn't have told me I couldn't be his one and only. I mean, why can't I? All that business about not wanting to be asked to tea for eighteen months, that was just a way of telling me to hoppit. I don't know how anyone can be like that when I'm so sweet and lovable – oh, what d'you think, growling old Uncle John has put Nick in the way of a much better job, which he's starting in March.'

'Is that a fact?' said Boots. 'Now why would he do that?'

'I'm sure I don't know,' said Annabelle. What she did know was that just before Christmas she had told her great-uncle to stop calling Nick a pip-squeak, and that if he didn't she'd never come up and have lunch with him any more. He asked her why she had to say a thing like that. Because Nick's going to be my young man, said Annabelle. A muted roar was her great-uncle's response to that. It was a little later, in the teashop, that Nick shocked her by telling her he had a girlfriend.

Boots mused at the wheel. If there was one thing he'd found out during the evening, it was that Nick's dad had never been in the Navy. Just a few questions, asked out of interest alone, had brought replies that would have told anyone with any knowledge of the Services that Mr Harrison had never been an able seaman. Fighting pirates in the China Seas for years on end? Not a chance. And Mrs Harrison had said something very odd, she'd said her husband wouldn't be home for nearly another eighteen months. That amount of time rang a bell. Something wasn't quite as it should be with

344

the Harrison family, something that could be seen as the reason why Nick was holding back from committing the best part of his social life to Annabelle. A pity, for his mother was a typically perky and resilient cockney woman, his sisters likeable and engaging.

If there was a skeleton in the family cupboard, they could keep it to themselves as far as Boots was concerned. His own family had something to hide, the fact that his stepfather had been a German spy during the war. The secret wasn't too difficult to keep, for only he and his stepfather knew it.

'I don't think Nick was telling you to hoppit, Annabelle,' he said, 'I think you should ask him again.'

'Uncle Boots, I can't,' said Annabelle, 'I just can't let him feel I'm running after him.'

'Fair point,' said Boots. 'Did you resign from the committee?'

'No, I didn't. I thought, why should I?'

'Well, of course, if you did you couldn't turn his committee meetings upside-down, could you, you tease?'

'It's fun,' said Annabelle. 'We nearly drove him potty this evening, Chrissie, Cassie and me, by talking about Chrissie having become engaged to Danny. It made him bawl at us. And the more he bawled, the more I wanted to—' Annabelle checked.

'Wanted to what?' smiled Boots, as they crossed the junction at Camberwell Green.

'Oh, you know,' said Annabelle.

'I think you'll win,' said Boots, not for the first time that evening.

'I've got to,' said Annabelle, 'or I'm sure my life will be ruined.'

Boots laughed. He took her home and had a word with Lizzy on the side, telling her not to worry about the bloke in question, that Annabelle's first serious feelings were directed, in fact, at a very likeable young man with a very acceptable family.

'Well, why doesn't he come and show himself?' asked Lizzy.

'I've a feeling he thinks he's too hard-up to see himself as a prospect for a girl like Annabelle,' said Boots.

'Oh,' said Lizzy, who frankly wasn't in favour of Annabelle being kept in rags as a wife. 'Oh, that's very awkward, Boots. I mean, we're not stuck-up, but we wouldn't want Annabelle to live a poverty-stricken life.'

'Well, that's only the present position,' said Boots. 'He's starting a better job in March.'

'Look,' said Lizzy, 'I'm not too sure exactly what Annabelle's real feelings are. D'you know what they are?'

'Yes, serious,' said Boots.

'Oh, lor',' said Lizzy.

'Keep smiling, old girl,' said Boots.

Chapter Nineteen

Annabelle intended to go to Saturday's football match, since everything relating to Nick's team was fascinatingly funny. Further, there was the ongoing little war she was conducting with Nick, something that was exhilarating in its way, even if she did feel like kicking him at times. But a phone call from one of her boyfriends on Friday evening was a reminder that she had a previous engagement, a Dutch auction at her old primary school near King's College Hospital. She and a whole group of friends had committed themselves a month ago. The proceeds were for the hospital, which existed mainly on voluntary contributions.

So instead of watching Nick and his team, in company with her new friends, Annabelle spent the afternoon at the school, helping to make a success of the event. It upset her just a little to find that her new interests were making her grow away from old interests. The boys of seventeen or eighteen years were all as much fun as they'd ever been, but they simply didn't quicken her pulse rate, which had got into the habit of jumping about each time she saw Nick.

Oh, blessed saints, she thought, I'm not done for, am I? Of course I'm not. How could any young working woman of seventeen be done for, just because someone excites her a little? I'm not going to fall in love until I'm twenty, when I'll be old enough to put up with the pangs.

All the same, although the Dutch auction was a lively and successful affair, she kept wishing she was with her new friends, watching the footballers and listening to unbelievably comic stuff from Cassie, who was a scream of a girl, and from Chrissie, whom the team called Dumpling. Most of all, of course, she wanted to be in the same place as Nick.

Oh, help, is it really serious with me?

If Annabelle's thoughts were all mixed up that weekend, Dumpling's were very clear, and fixed on the certainty that married life with Danny really was going to muck up all her footballing interests. He came round on Sunday afternoon to sit in the parlour with her, this being his automatic privilege now that he was engaged to her. Mrs Evans saw to it that none of the kids disturbed the happy couple. The happiness, of course, was all on Danny's side, and he was keener than ever on a cuddle, and so on. If a cuddle was soppy enough, so on was even worse. But Dumpling didn't yell for help. She knew it was no use to, not now Danny had official entitlements.

However, she did appear in the kitchen after a little while looking slightly flushed.

'Chrissie, you 'aven't left Danny to 'imself, 'ave you?' said Mrs Evans.

'No, I've just come out for a bowl of cold water and a flannel,' said Dumpling, going into the scullery.

'What d'you want cold water and a flannel for, love?'

'Danny's 'ad an accident,' said Dumpling.

''Ow could he 'ave an accident in me parlour unless 'e fell over the fender?' asked Mrs Evans.

'No, 'e didn't fall over the fender, Mum, and it's nothing fatal,' said Dumpling, 'it's just that 'e's got a black eye.'

'How'd he get that?' asked Mr Evans.

'I give it to 'im,' said Dumpling, carrying the bowl of water and the flannel through the kitchen and on to the parlour.

'That girl,' said Mrs Evans to her old man, 'don't she know girls don't start givin' black eyes to their fiancés till they're married to them?'

'Never mind, she's got the right instincts,' said Mr Evans, 'she's doin' a bit of minist'ring just like a wife already. That cold water'll keep Danny's eye from swellin' up too much.'

'Bless 'er, we'll give 'er a nice weddin',' said Mrs Evans.

'And a fair drop of the best port,' said Mr Evans. 'That'll 'elp.'

'It'll make 'er drunk,' said Mrs Evans.

'That's what I mean,' said Mr Evans, 'it'll 'elp Danny, save 'im gettin' two black eyes on 'is weddin' night.'

Monday

Pa, feeling as free as the air and wearing a suit for the first time since he'd arrived at Marsham Gaol, reached Charing Cross Station at eleven in the morning. All he needed now to get him home was a bus. Hold on, he thought, I'm supposed to be in the Navy. Ma's been working on that one for over three years. It's a shop in the Caledonian Road for you, Albert Harrison. You can't go home in a suit, you need a uniform and a kitbag. And you need to get this plaster off.

Off he went to Finsbury, watering place of a bloke he knew well, a struck-off doctor. He caught him before he went out to enjoy his liquid lunch. For the price of a couple of whiskies, he obliged Pa by removing the plaster, using a fearsome-looking pair of cutters that were out of the Ark. He congratulated Pa on the healthy look of his arm. Pa paid up and there were no further comments. Then he made his way to the Caledonian Road, whistling as he went.

The shop in the Caledonian Road was like a cavernous emporium. It was stocked to the ceiling with second-hand clothes of every kind. Pa, with a few quid in his pocket, found exactly what he wanted, an able seaman's uniform in excellent condition that fitted him perfectly. The cap, however, was one size too large, and he was against sartorial sloppiness. No problem, said the proprietor, there's several more in the basement, if you'll hang on a tick. As soon as he disappeared, Pa thought a lining of newspaper would make the cap fit, and after all, the whole lot could be chucked away in a day or so. A quick exit would relieve him of the necessity of paying. With the uniform and cap bundled into a kitbag the proprietor had also supplied, Pa made for the door. He stopped halfway.

'One step out of line, Harrison, and you'll be back here.'

Pa did the wise thing. He changed his mind. The proprietor reappeared with four other sailor caps, one of which fitted as if it had been made for Pa's noble head. Its band bore the name 'HMS ARETHUSA'. He settled the bill and departed, taking himself by public transport to Waterloo Station. The day was cold but bright, and the London scenes exhilarated him. He made use of the Gents in the station to change into the uniform. Out he went with his kitbag, and he bought a bunch of flowers from a straw-hatted lady vendor, telling her she ought to be on the stage because she was the image of Chili Bouchier, the revue star. The flower lady said you're a one, you are, Barnacle Bill. Pa gave her a wink, then caught a bus to Walworth.

Into the shop run by Gran Emerson he went to buy boxes of chocolates for his girls, all three of whom never failed to show their fondness for him.

''Ello, sailor,' said forward Ivy, ''ow's yer luck, then?'

'Not bad,' said Pa, 'how's yours?'

'Dunno yet,' said Ivy, 'but I've got 'opes. I like sailors.'

'You like anything 'andsome in trousers,' said Gran. 'What can we do for yer, Captain Nelson?'

Pa bought three boxes of chocolates, which made Gran and Ivy give him second looks, especially as he had a kitbag and a bunch of flowers.

As he placed the chocolates in the kitbag, Gran said, 'Excuse me askin', but might yer name be 'Arrison?'

'I'd be surprised if it wasn't,' said Pa genially, 'seeing it's my born monicker.'

'Well, I'm blessed,' said Gran, 'we know yer fam'ly, yer wife, son and daughters, and they're a lovely lot. 'Ome on leave at last, are yer?'

'Home for good,' said Pa, 'my time's up.'

'I see yer been servin' on the *Arthusa*,' said Gran, making the best attempt possible to pronounce it.

'My, all them Chinese pirates and all, they been a real 'eadache to Mrs 'Arrison.'

'Ruddy treat, missus, I can tell you, getting away from them,' said Pa.

'See yer around,' said Ivy, giving him a wink, and Pa left smiling.

Dumpling's mum was standing at her gate, a warm shawl over her shoulders. She was talking to a neighbour about Dumpling getting married at Easter, and that the lucky bloke was Danny Thompson.

'Does 'e know 'e's lucky?' asked the neighbour.

'Danny's 'ighly appreciative of our Chrissie,' said Mrs Evans, 'which 'e should be. Well, there's a lot more of Chrissie than there is of most other girls – 'ello, who's this sailor comin' down the street?'

The neighbour, taking a look, said, 'Well, 'e don't belong to anyone I know.'

'He's got a kitbag and flowers,' said Mrs Evans. 'Bless us, could 'e be Mrs 'Arrison's sailor 'usband, the one that's been out in the China Seas? There, look, 'e must be, 'e's turned in at 'er gate.'

'My, my,' said the neighbour, 'she'll be over-come.'

'She'll be that all right,' said Mrs Evans, ''e's been away for years, and you know what sailors are.'

Pa, at Ma's Walworth abode for the first time, entered by using the latchcord and went through to the kitchen. It didn't take him long to realize Ma wasn't at home, which was a mite disappointing to him. Someone was in the house, however. The lodger. Pa heard him moving over the landing on the top floor. Introducing himself could wait. Ma was probably only doing a bit of shopping.

Meanwhile, the grapevine had long been busy spreading the news that Knocker Harrison had got parole on account of saving the life of a screw. Knowing that, Pa went out and used a public phone box to call Mister Horsemouth at his office in Hackney, where he conducted a moneylending business that meant worry and sorrow for borrowers who fell behind with their weekly cash repayments. He also ran a bookmaker's business. Both businesses had been an effective cover for his other activities over a period of several years. The local coppers reckoned they might get him one day for stepping out of line as a moneylender or for proving he used illegal runners to collect bets. It never occurred to them he was frying bigger fish. Well, he was friendly to every copper in the district, and contributed to police charities.

He expressed himself happy to know Pa was home. Welcome back, Knocker, he said, just heard you were out, having done a life-saving job. You're a bleedin' hero, he said. Something like that, said Pa, except it was a bit against the grain. Well, there was a lot of weeping, I heard, said Mister Horsemouth, on account of the screw not finishing up as flat as a pancake. Forgot myself for a sec, said Pa. Don't apologize, said Mister Horsemouth, I'd have done the same meself if I'd known it was going to open the gates for me. Kind of you, said Pa, and then asked if he was now due for his cut in respect of the job he'd been sent down for. Mister Horsemouth said of course, except there's a large deduction on account of all the advances made to Mrs Knocker, and also it wouldn't be wise to divvy up the balance yet. You don't want word to get about that you've suddenly come into a useful lump of oof, Knocker, it'll land the cops on your doorstep. All right, said Pa, I'll wait a while. Three months, say, said Mister Horsemouth. Oh, and get Toby out of your place immediate, he said, because now you're home the flatties might decide to see if you've got the loot stuffed up your bedroom chimney. In any case, they'll be watching you, to see if you start getting flush. Tell Toby to pack up his stuff and to meet me this evening in the Black Bess, you know where.

Suits me, said Pa, which it did, very much. He didn't say Scotland Yard knew now that the American woman's sparklers had landed in Mister Horsemouth's mitts. But he did say he was much obliged for the way Mister Horsemouth had looked after his better half. Glad you mentioned it, said Mister Horsemouth, seeing it was upsetting hearing about all the complaints you had. Pa said he was upset too, hearing about you cutting down on my missus. Don't give me any sauce, said Mister Horsemouth, you just keep your nose clean until I'm ready to use you again. Right, said Pa, I'll wait for you to let me into some jobs that'll be financially lucrative, and I'll also wait for the rest of my cut. Yes, say in about four or five months, said Mister Horsemouth, also known as Brains.

What a crook, thought Pa, but he said a cheerful and friendly goodbye before hanging up. He knew he'd covered himself. He'd established an excellent reason for his release and made himself look innocent of what was about to befall Mister Horsemouth and his gang of what Ma called common criminals. Pa had always been touched that Ma hadn't seen him as one of them. He didn't like to feel he was common in any way.

Returning home, with interested neighbours noting his jaunty sailor's walk, he found Ma was still out, so he went up to see the lodger and to say hello to him. Mr Lukavitch was most happy to meet Ma's better half.

'Corblimey tophole, so you are the friend of our friend,' he said. He was working, but not at bead-polishing. He was a naturally talented jewel-cutter and polisher, but not a law-abiding one. Being law-abiding kept a Polish immigrant poor. Being the other way about meant he had money in the bank. 'You are out, you have been set free? Bloody good, eh? Pleased to meet you, I think. How did it happen?'

Pa told him. He knew all about the lodger and what he was doing here. He was altering the shapes of stolen jewels and handing them to Tosh Fingers every Sunday. Tosh got worried the Sunday when flu kept Mr Lukavitch in bed, which was why he'd appeared the following day to collect the stuff. Pa hadn't been able to make much of a protest about Polish Toby using Ma's upstairs top to carry on his work, not without risking being done up very painfully. The consolation was that Toby's rent was very welcome to Ma.

'Ah, you saved the life of a warder?' said Polish Toby. 'Most unusual, I believe, eh?'

'Temporary fit of insanity,' said Pa, who rarely sounded like a Hackney-born cockney. 'I forgot what he was at the time. Still, it came in useful. Now, a message from Brains. You're to get out. Right away. Now. This afternoon. Meet him in the Black Bess pub this evening. Take everything with you. You won't be coming back.'

'How bloody sad,' said Polish Toby, 'I've had tophole lovely kindness from Mrs Harrison.'

'I trust she didn't overdo it,' said Pa.

'Excuse me, old cock?'

'Never mind, just get packed.'

Polish Toby said a taxi was necessary, because of the largeness of his trunk, into which he had to fit his folding machine. Pa said he'd go and find a taxi while Toby was doing his packing. First, however, he went down to the parlour and inspected the right pedal of the piano. Ruddy horrors, the little packet wasn't in place. Some crook's half-inched it, he thought. I think I'd better have a word with Nick, he's the best one to talk to. It'll be sad if I've been done down by my own family. No, wait a bit, I think Nick and Alice tipped me the wink when they said they'd make sure the piano wasn't sold, that it had valuability. I think that was a way of telling me they knew where my investment was. But where is it now? If Nick and Alice are looking after it, I can compliment myself for having brought up a reliable son and a caring daughter. Ma, of course, can take some of the credit. No doubt about it, a good woman's worth her weight in gold watches.

Now where's Ma got to?

Ma had gone up West. Well, she still had those two fivers Pa had slipped to her out of the goodness of his heart, and it was just possible they weren't duds. She could try changing one. Not in a bank, of course, nor in any of the local Walworth shops, nor down the market. An honest woman couldn't land a local shopkeeper or stallholder with a banknote that might be a bit dubious. It wouldn't be right. But a West End shop, well, that was different. West End shops were made of money.

So, dressed in her best coat and hat, and putting on the style, Ma entered a shop that wasn't too posh and chose some very nice hair ribbons and hankies for the girls. She tendered one of the fivers in a casual and ladylike way, and the assistant didn't even hold it up to the light. She gave Ma change of four pounds, fifteen shillings and ninepence with no questions asked, would you believe.

Wisely, however, Ma decided not to use another shop to get the second fiver changed. She instinctively felt it wasn't a good idea to scatter dubious banknotes around in the West End. Of course, hers might be genuine, but it was as well to remember that Pa, unfortunately, still had a little bit of the devil in him when it came to chancing his arm. In any case, she could buy lovely frocks for Amy and Fanny and a broderie anglaise blouse for Alice in a quite fashionable dress shop in the Walworth Road. And they'd be a lot cheaper than in the West End. Still, Ma did stay around long enough in Oxford Street to use some of the change in a Lyons teashop. She'd had a sandwich before leaving home at twelve-thirty, and in Lyons she treated herself to a pot of tea and a currant bun. She thought about Nick and that lovely girl, Annabelle Somers, and she felt what a pity it was that Nick couldn't get serious about her, or about any girl until Pa was home. Mind, Annabelle Somers dressed and talked very posh, and might not want Nick to take up with her. Just as well, thought Ma. Lordy, when Pa does get out, he's got to do the right thing by his son and daughters, he's got to go straight. If he doesn't, I'll knock his head off with me stew saucepan, the iron one.

Ma finally arrived home at ten minutes past three. When she walked into the kitchen she found a sailor waiting for her. She stared and gaped.

'Hello, my old darling,' said Pa, 'is that your best itfer you're wearing? Dash me if you don't look like an Ascot filly.'

Ma went weak at the knees and fell down. Fortunately, Pa caught her halfway to the floor and sat her on his lap, where he gave her a kiss and a bit of a saucy cuddle. Ma gasped a request for her smelling-salts. Pa told her she didn't need those, that he'd bring her round himself. Whereupon, in due regard for his promise, he gave her several loving smackers, which not only brought her round but made her tell him to remember they weren't alone in the house, that Mr Lukavitch, the lodger, was upstairs. Then, of course, she asked him what he was doing here in a sailor's uniform, he hadn't escaped from the Navy, had he? She said Navy because of the walls having ears.

Pa told her a story about saving a warder's life. He didn't tell her it was a put-up job, that another warder had sent a huge boulder crashing down on a given signal. Nor did he tell her it would have missed Mr Brinkley, anyway. Not that old Brinkley was confident it would. Pa also refrained from telling Ma the real reason for his release was because he'd blown the gaff on Mister Horsemouth, the brains behind the jewel robberies. No, he convinced Ma he'd earned parole on account of his life-saving act. He explained how and why he'd acquired the able seaman's uniform. He'd wanted to look the part to any of Ma's friends and neighbours who might be about when he reached Browning Street.

Ma was most touched by that bit of loving thoughtfulness, and felt more overwhelmed than ever by happy events. She was also quite faint. So

Pa, a handsome and manly gent, and still young at heart, carried her into her bedroom and began a different kind of overwhelming, just as Mrs Evans had thought he would. Ma, bless her, became so faint she didn't know what to do about his devilry.

She could only gasp, 'Albert 'Arrison, oh, I never knew the like in all me born days. I can't 'ardly believe this.'

However, Pa, despite being set on re-establishing himself as her living breathing husband, was more loving than hurried. Ma, accordingly, didn't feel she could actually complain.

'Well, yo-heave-ho, Mabel, dashed if you aren't still a pretty woman.'

'Albert 'Arrison, oh, in me own house in the middle of the afternoon and the lodger upstairs, where's your respect?'

'I've got it with me, Mabel, and the lodger's left. He had to go in a hurry, to join a Polish relative.'

Ma, lovingly overwhelmed, gasped faintly a minute later, 'Albert, oh, I've still got me best hat on.'

'Don't worry,' murmured Pa, 'it's not in the way.'

Nick and the girls were overwhelmed themselves by the reappearance of Pa in the bosom of his family. They listened to the story of his act of bravery, an act that had resulted in his release on parole. He also told them that sometime during the week he had to go to Woolwich Arsenal where, according to the Governor of Marsham, a job was waiting for him.

'Crikey, Pa,' said Amy, 'd'you mean an honest job?'

'He better had mean just that,' said Ma.

'Well,' said Pa, his paternal cheerfulness spreading over his family, 'being on parole, as I am, and having promised your Ma to be the soul of honesty, I'll postpone going into business for myself until—'

'You're not goin' into business for yourself now or ever,' said Ma, fully recovered from his act of devilry.

'No, Pa, you're not,' said Alice.

'I second that,' said Nick.

'So do me and Fanny,' said Amy.

'We don't want you goin' out and findin' wallets any more, Pa,' said young Fanny, 'it upsets Ma. I found a wallet down the market once and we took it to the police station and got a reward for being honest, didn't we, Ma?'

'It made me very appreciative of what honesty can do for a fam'ly,' said Ma, 'and I 'ope your Pa's learned to be appreciative too. He's goin' to take the job at Woolwich Arsenal and stick to it, or else.'

'Or else what, Ma?' asked Alice.

'Boil you in oil, Pa,' said Nick.

'Pa, you've just got to be good,' said Amy.

Pa studied his family. He couldn't say he still didn't have a feeling for using his natural talents, but no more could he say he wasn't remarkably happy at being back with his wife, son and daughters. Perhaps holding down an honest job wouldn't actually hurt him, and there was always the chance of being transferred to the stores once he'd discovered the best way of going about it.

'Well, I'd not be your Ma's favourite gent if I couldn't count me blessings,' he said. 'I'll take the job and stick to it. I wouldn't want to commit the mortal sin of being ungrateful to Warder

Brinkley for having his head in the way when that boulder was coming down. You can inform all your friends and neighbours I've been granted an honourable discharge from the Navy for saving an officer from drowning and for downing my fair share of Chinese pirates.'

The girls laughed. Ma smiled. Nick looked as if a new world was dawning. Pa out of clink and doing an honest job was all he could have asked for at this particular stage in his life. He thought of Annabelle, a tease, a minx and a delight.

'It's funny our lodger movin' the very day you come 'ome, Pa,' said Amy.

'Oh, I had the pleasure of meeting him before he left,' said Pa, who hadn't mentioned the bloke to the Governor or the law. 'He asked me to give all of you his regards. He seemed a very sociable cove.'

'Yes, he was very sociable with Ma,' said Fanny, 'and her teapot.'

'Alice, give that girl's bottom a smack,' said Ma, 'then let's all give thanks that although your Pa misfortunately got above 'imself when he shouldn't 'ave, he made up for it by doin' a life-savin' act that got 'im out of the Navy. I must say 'e looks very 'andsome in 'is battleship uniform.'

'He ought to have some medals,' said Amy.

'He could buy some down Petticoat Lane one Sunday,' suggested Nick.

'Well, we'd all be proud to see your Pa wearin' medals,' said Ma.

'I'd wear them with modesty on the right occasions,' said Pa.

'But would it be honest to wear bought ones?' asked Alice.

'Well, perhaps it wouldn't be genuine honest,'

said Ma, and frowned a little. Then she perked up. 'Still, it would be very deservin',' she said.

Ma was never too proud to stretch her principles, especially when she had change in her purse from a dud fiver.

After supper, a bit of a scratch meal because Ma was happily disorganized, Pa spoke to Nick in the parlour.

'About the family piano, Nick, I wonder—'

'Enough said, Pa.'

'I haven't said anything yet, my lad.'

'No need to, Pa, and might I point out I'm now twenty-one and addressed as Mr Harrison at the office?'

'Don't come it,' said Pa, 'just tell me if you know that something's gone missing from the piano.'

'I suppose you mean your confidential savings,' said Nick. 'Yes, Alice and I found them. The glue came unstuck.'

'Ah,' said Pa. 'Well,' he said breezily, 'if you'd let me have them—'

'That's all, Pa,' said Nick, 'except that Alice had a little talk with me ten minutes ago, and we decided that if you go back to picking pockets or selling gold watches, we'd take the little packet to the police station and tell them where we found it.'

''Ere, 'old on,' said Pa, shocked into Bow Bells dialect, 'am I 'earing me own flesh and blood layin' down the law?'

'Something like that, Pa.'

'Ruddy 'ell,' said Pa, 'you'd shop your own dad?'

'Something like that, Pa.'

'I ain't believin' it,' said Pa. 'You mean them confidential savings of mine are goin' to sit around

362

not doin' anything useful for me and your Ma?'

'No, they're going to do something,' said Nick, 'just as soon as you go back to your old ways.'

'It's blackmail,' said Pa.

'Yes, I know, Pa, and so does Alice,' said Nick. 'But we need this family to be fairly respectable to help us have a reasonable future. Alice would like to meet a decent bloke and I'd like to qualify for reasonable prospects. If you get me.'

Pa blinked. Then his cheerfulness surfaced.

'Strike a light,' he said, 'I'm over a barrel.'

'Better than being in the Navy fighting Chinese pirates,' said Nick.

Pa roared with laughter.

Nick opened the door to visitors later. Cassie, Dumpling, Freddy and Danny sort of poured into the passage.

'Yer dad's 'ome,' said Dumpling.

'So we 'eard,' said Danny.

'We've come to share your happiness,' said Cassie imaginatively.

'Pleased for yer fam'ly, Nick,' said Freddy.

Nick took them into the parlour for the moment, where they let him know how pleased they were for his Ma. Cassie said a striving mother who was husbandless had to be a joyful woman when he turned up out of the China Seas. Dumpling said good on yer, Nick, and slapped his back, which nearly put him down for the count.

'Me mum saw 'im, yer know,' she said. 'She was at the gate and she saw 'im comin' down the street in 'is uniform and kitbag.'

'How did he get in his kitbag?' asked Freddy.

'Freddy, you daft or something?' said Dumpling.

'I only asked,' said Freddy.

'Talk to 'im, Cassie,' said Dumpling. 'He's all right when 'e's playin' football, but when he ain't 'e's a bit like Danny, daft as a broom 'andle that's lost its 'ead.'

'Now, Dumpling,' said Danny in a proprietary way, 'there ain't no cause to suggest me and Freddy's—'

'Don't answer me back, or I'll sit on yer,' said Dumpling, who was going to fight like the clappers to get the upper hand as Danny's better half. 'We ain't 'ere to argue the toss, but to compliment Nick and 'is fam'ly on 'aving his dad 'ome on leave.'

'He's not on leave,' said Nick, 'he's home for good, having served his time.'

'Oh, what a remarkable happy feeling,' said Cassie, and gave him a kiss.

'Nick, does yer dad play football?' asked Dumpling.

'Come and meet him,' said Nick, 'and we'll find out if he'd like to put some dibs into our kitty, and I daresay Ma will boil the kettle for a pot of tea.'

'Crikey,' said Dumpling, 'I'm so overcome for yer Ma, Nick, that I 'ardly mind at the moment about livin' soppy ever after with Danny.'

Chapter Twenty

Tuesday evening

The law had been trailing Tosh Fingers since the hour of Pa's release. The law knew Tosh as an ingratiating and slippery customer who'd been fined a few times for taking street corner bets on behalf of a character called Monty Cooper, otherwise known as Mister Horsemouth, a moneylender and bookmaker. Tosh was also known for collecting loan repayments on behalf of Cooper, but the local police had never suspected he was capable of serious infringements of the law, or that Cooper had nefarious interests outside his moneylending and bookmaking business.

Inspector Clark was after both men, consequent on Knocker Harrison spilling the beans. Monty Cooper, he'd said, was the brains behind the jewel robberies, including the old job relating to the American woman. Cooper had taken possession of the loot from that, said Knocker, but you won't find it on his premises, nor will you find any sparklers from the recent jobs. And when you do get him to cough up with what he does have somewhere or other, you won't recognize most of it. He gets it altered by a pro. I don't know which pro, said Knocker. Your best bet is to tail Tosh and his guv'nor, Monty Cooper, until one of them leads you to the sparklers, or better still, to catch Tosh and the accomplices on their next job. There'll be a next one. Ask your men not to wear loud hobnailed boots or bowler hats while they're following Tosh. He's got very fine-tuned ears for the sound of boots, and an eye for the law's bowler hats.'

Inspector Clark had put men on Tosh and Cooper. Tosh hadn't done anything or gone anywhere out of the ordinary so far, but a note had been made of the fact that a well-dressed bearded gentleman in an Ulster and Homburg had made a call on Cooper at his office.

'Now why should a cove looking like King Edward the Seventh call on Horsemouth?' asked Inspector Clark of Detective-Sergeant Plunkett.

'Needs a loan, havin' lost a packet on the gee-gees?' suggested Plunkett.

'Could be. On the other hand, what about the fact that the burglaries have all taken place at houses and suchlike owned by people high up on the social register?'

'And when said owners weren't at home, guv.'

'Glad you're following me,' said Inspector Clark.

'Closely, guv.'

'So I notice. You'll be treading on my bleedin' foot in a minute. Well, I'm not displeased, I've got certain feelings about Cooper now, and I favour Knocker Harrison's informative help. And we've got the address of King Edward the Seventh. Could be useful, that.'

Ma, her erring better half back in her life, made sure on Wednesday morning that he took himself off to Woolwich Arsenal to apply for the job the Governor had said was available. Ma made sure by going with him. He carried a letter from the

Governor in his pocket. He got the job all right, but his sangfroid took a cruel blow. It was a dungaree and broom job, along with a large dustbin on wheels, entailing sweeping workshop floors and collecting waste. The pay was thirty bob a week. But he had to take it. Ma was adamant. She said the captain of his battleship would charge him with mutinous ingratitude if he didn't. She meant the Governor of Marsham Gaol, of course. Pa's philosophical nature helped him to recover by the time he and Ma got back home, when he told her he reckoned he could work his way up from sweeping floors to a job in the stores within a year. Ma said if he got that kind of quick promotion she'd be proud of him. Pa said a stores job could prove lucrative. Ma said yes, it ought to be good for more than thirty bob a week. My feelings exactly, said Pa.

That same day Nick received a letter from Annabelle.

'Dear Captain, Secretary and Everything Else, I'm dropping you a line to let you know I can't get to Wednesday evening's committee meeting. I expect you'll be bitterly disappointed at not having me there, but it's our monthly dance at our local church, which I always go to with my friends. Anyway, if Chrissie wants to make any proposals, ask Cassie to second them for me, as Chrissie's proposals are always brilliant. I trust the team is prospering, and by next week's meeting I'll have all the details ready for running a successful raffle in aid of our supporters' scarves and so on. Yours truly, Annabelle Somers.'

PS. Can you foxtrot to syncopated music?'

What a girl. Nick grinned over the letter, which had arrived by the midday post. Something had to be done about Annabelle now that Pa was out and had accepted an honest job. All thoughts of what Pa's dubious accomplishments had done to the family had to be put behind him. Now was the time for a bloke's fancy to lead him to a serious talk with the young lady who was standing him on his head at committee meetings.

'Daddy, about Annabelle and Nick,' said Rosie.

'What about them?' asked Boots.

'D'you think it's going to be bliss in the making because he's moving to a better job?' asked Rosie.

'You'll have to ask Annabelle,' said Boots.

'I don't think I'll risk that,' said Rosie, 'she'll throw something heavy at me. Does Nick know what a state she's in about all his dilly-dallying?'

'Young love's a bit traumatic,' said Boots, thinking of his feelings for Elsie Chivers when he was Annabelle's age.

'Painful, I'm sure,' smiled Rosie.

'Well, you could say that, poppet.'

'D'you think Nick is right for Annabelle?'

'If he turns out to be right in the eyes of your Aunt Lizzy,' said Boots, 'he'll be right for Annabelle.'

'Crikey,' said Rosie, 'you're so wise you could be another King Solomon.'

'Hope not,' said Boots, 'I'd have to cope with two hundred concubines.'

Rosie shrieked with laughter.

Friday night

'Saucy buggers,' murmured Detective-Sergeant Plunkett. The January air was as cold as charity in a freezing mood, frost whitening the cobblestones of this mews in Knightsbridge, which backed on to handsome town houses of the rich and noble. Moonlight put a glitter on the frost.

Two men wearing rubber-soled shoes had gone over the wall, leaving a third man keeping watch. Sergeant Plunkett, with colleagues, had followed Tosh Fingers all the way from Hackney, for Inspector Clark had ordered a night tail on him until further notice. Tosh had joined up with two men when he reached Brompton Road. It was now nearly one in the morning, and Knightsbridge was asleep. Plunkett whispered to one colleague, telling him to go round to Prince's Gardens and watch the front of the house in question. He didn't know it, but it was the town house of Lord and Lady Kettlesborough, who had left for the South of France fifteen hours earlier, taking their servants with them.

Round to the front of the house went the CID man. Plunkett and two other colleagues waited, watching Tosh Fingers, a dim figure lurking about in the shadows of the wall. It was an hour before his accomplices reappeared. Over the wall they came, one dropping a Gladstone bag into Tosh's arms. He took it back once he'd landed, much as if the bag would feel safer out of Tosh's clutch. The three of them began a noiseless scarper. Very unfortunately, while temporarily exposed by the moonlight, they found their progress suddenly impeded by the materializing figures of three burly plainclothes men.

'Hello, Tosh,' said Sergeant Plunkett, 'out collectin' bets, are you?'

Tosh did a slippery one-two, and the other men executed a quick turnabout. Not a chance. Plunkett tripped Tosh, and his colleagues jumped on the other men.

'Fair cop,' said one.

''Ere, what's the game?' protested Tosh, as he was hauled upright.

'Let's find out, shall we?' said Plunkett.

It all led to Mister Horsemouth being divorced at three in the morning from the bed he shared with Mrs Horsemouth, and that led to the arrest of the gentleman who looked like King Edward the Seventh. He was charged with being an accessory to the burgling of various residences owned by noble friends of his. He had laid information with Mister Horsemouth as to when the owners and their servants would be away.

A hoard of stolen sparklers and other valuables was brought to light the following day. The hoard was a residue, for much had been sold. Polish Toby, responsible for the alteration of a large amount of the jewels, had a nose for safety-first tactics, and he vanished on news of the arrests.

Pa was not required to bear witness. He had already played his helpful part. The Governor was very pleased with him, and so was Inspector Clark.

Just after Nick arrived home on Saturday morning, Fanny answered a knock on the door. A nice-looking feller in a cap and overcoat asked if he could speak to Nick.

'Hold on a tick and I'll get 'im,' said young Fanny. Taken with his looks, she asked, 'Excuse me, but would you 'ave a brother about thirteen or fourteen?'

'Funny you should ask,' said the bloke, 'only I've got one who's fourteen.'

'Well,' said saucy Fanny, 'if 'e's like you, I wouldn't mind if he came round to see me.'

'Aren't you a bit young?' said the bloke.

'Yes, but I don't want to be late startin',' said Fanny, 'I might get left at the post. Anyway, stay there and I'll get Nick.'

She went through the passage and called her brother. Nick came out of the kitchen and said hello to the bloke.

'What can I do for you?' he asked.

'I'm Johnny Richards. You wrote to me in answer to me letter about your football team, tellin' me you'd be pleased to meet me and that I might like to see the Rovers in action.'

Nick looked him over. He seemed an upright bloke, with good square shoulders and the kind of looks that Walworth girls admired. Sort of manly and fearless.

'Glad to meet you, Johnny,' he said, and shook his hand. 'Come in for a tick.' He took him into the parlour, and Johnny showed he was a bit of a gent by removing his cap. 'If you're free this afternoon, you can come and watch our match with Old Kent Road Hotspurs.'

'Fine with me,' said Johnny.

What an agreeable bloke, thought Nick, and about my age. Alice might like him.

'Excuse me a couple of secs, Johnny, while I get our chief supporter to come and talk to you about how we run the team. Hold on.'

He went back to the kitchen. Alice, looking as nice as always in a crisp white blouse and blue skirt, was slicing bread to be eaten with the midday meal. Nick told her she was wanted.

'What for and who by?' asked Alice.

'Bloke called Johnny Richards.'

'Yes, he's smashin',' said Fanny.

'Give it a go, Alice,' said Pa, due to start his job on Monday.

'He'd like to talk to you about the supporters' club,' said Nick.

'Don't make me laugh,' said Alice, but she went. Johnny Richards blinked a little when she entered the parlour. Well, Alice always had a ladylike look.

'Hello,' he said, 'are you the chief supporter of Browning Street Rovers?'

'Who are you?' asked Alice.

'Johnny Richards, hopin' to get a place in the Rovers. Is that a good start?'

'Start to what?' asked Alice.

'To goin' to see the Rovers together this afternoon,' said Johnny.

'My, you're in a hurry, aren't you?' said Alice.

'Well, I'm disengaged at the moment, y'know,' said Johnny, 'and short of a best friend.'

'Can't you make a best friend of your grocer?' asked Alice.

'Our grocer's my grandad,' said Johnny.

'Well, that's not my fault,' said Alice. 'Why'd you want to talk about the supporters' club?'

'Are you Nick's sister?'

'Yes, he does 'appen to be my brother,' said Alice.

'I like him bein' your brother,' said Johnny.

'Why?'

'Well, he could've been your feller,' said Johnny.

'I think you're comin' it a bit,' said Alice.

Nick reckoned he'd put his eldest sister on the path to her first romantic walk in a park because she was still talking to Johnny fifteen minutes later, and

372

because when she and Fanny left for the afternoon's football match, Johnny met her on the corner of the Walworth Road and sat with her on the tram all the way. And he was beside her most of the time during the match.

Annabelle turned up and stood between Cassie and Dumpling, listening to them as they alternately praised and rubbished their team. Nick came in for a lot of rubbishing.

'Look at 'im,' groaned Dumpling, 'I just don't know what's come over 'im just recent. What with me bein' promised to Danny in daft wedlock and Nick fallin' over 'is feet lately, me life's taken a sad turn, Annabelle, I can tell yer.'

'Cheer up, Chrissie,' said Annabelle, 'I'm sure Danny's going to make you a loving hubby, and as for Nick, well, there's a remedy, isn't there? At next Wednesday's committee meeting we can tell him that if he doesn't pull himself together, we'll do it for him. And we'll do it by proposing that Danny should be captain in his place.'

'Crikey,' breathed Cassie, 'Nick'll fall off 'is chair and likely never get up again.'

'Oh, dear, poor bloke,' said Annabelle.

As for Dumpling, her roundly plump face, usually healthy with colour, showed the paleness of horrendous shock.

'Annabelle, we can't do that,' she gasped, 'we can't vote for Danny to be captain in place of Nick. Nick's our hero.'

Well, he's not mine, thought Annabelle, and I could spit.

'Still, something's got to be done to bring him to his senses,' she said. She didn't, however, mean his football senses. 'There, now look.' Nick had been floored by an Old Kent Road player as wide as a backyard coal bunker. 'We can't have a captain who can't stay upright.'

'But Danny won't do as captain,' said Dumpling earnestly. 'I know 'e's me future husband, but if he was captain and the Rovers was losin', 'e'd just cuddle them in sympathy. Nick would knock their 'eads together, like a good captain should.'

'It's love that's done it to him,' said Cassie.

'Oh, gawd, I 'ope not,' said Dumpling.

'It's only the first pangs,' said Cassie. 'Freddy had a lot of first pangs, which sort of made 'im cross-eyed, but he's all right now, I pulled him together.'

Annabelle laughed.

Nick was collared by Alice and Johnny at half-time, Johnny commenting on the match and Alice saying that although she couldn't keep up with his cheek, it would only be fair for Nick to give him a trial. Nick said he thought he could fix it. Alice smiled. She'd found a young man. It was one of those instant things, like a flash of lightning.

Annabelle, watching Nick, fidgeted in frustration. That made her cross with herself. Why should she let anyone give her the fidgets?

Nick was suddenly in front of her then, smiling at her.

'Hello, committee member,' he said, 'thanks for your letter and apologies for absence. We missed you.'

'Pardon?' she said. 'Oh, yes, you're the captain and secretary. I forgot for a moment that we'd met.'

Nick laughed.

'I'd like a few words with you,' he said.

'What sort of words?'

'I'll think of some,' said Nick, 'but watch out if you play up.'

'Oh, are you thinking of making an appointment, might I ask?'

'Well, I mean to see you,' said Nick, 'but not now, it's back to our sporting labours.'

You better had see me, thought Annabelle, or I'll send you another letter, with a bomb in it.

The Rovers won the match, despite Nick being in love. Annabelle left to go home, and Freddy, when he was washed and changed, walked along the path with Cassie.

'I've got a funny feeling Nick's a bit gone on Annabelle,' he said.

'Oh, you do surprise me,' said Cassie. 'I'll faint in a minute that your penny's dropped at last.'

'Well, don't faint here,' said Freddy, 'not in Brockwell Park.'

'No, I'll do it on the tram,' said Cassie, 'and you'd better sit next to me so's you can revive me.'

'What, loosen yer coat and blouse?' said Freddy.

'No, not on the tram, wait till we get 'ome,' said Cassie.

'All right,' said Freddy, 'I'll do it for you in yer parlour.'

Cassie giggled.

'Freddy, you'll 'ave a faintin' fit yourself,' she said.

'Yes, I know,' said Freddy, 'but it can't be 'elped, and in a way I'm looking forward to it.'

Annabelle's brother Bobby, thirteen, having answered a knock on the front door on Sunday morning, mounted the stairs and called to her. She was in her bedroom, having just returned from church with her parents.

'Hi, sis, you're wanted.'

'Who by?' Annabelle came out on to the landing of the family house in Sunrise Avenue, off Denmark Hill.

'A feller,' said Bobby.

'Do I know him?'

'Well, he knows you,' said Bobby, 'because he asked for you.'

'What's his name?'

'Harry something, he said.'

'Harry something? Oh, was it Harrison?' Annabelle didn't wait for an answer, she swept past Bobby on her quick way down the stairs. Nick was on the doorstep. 'Well, I'm blessed, where did you come from?'

'Home,' said Nick.

'Well, I don't know what my brother was doing, leaving you stuck on the doorstep on a cold morning,' said Annabelle. 'Would you like to come in?'

'I'd like to have a word,' said Nick.

'In here,' said Annabelle, and took him into the front room. There was a Sunday fire going, and she wanted to have him to herself for the moment. 'Go ahead,' she said. Nick took his hat off and examined it. 'Excuse me,' she said, and took it away from him. 'I mean, you're not going to have a few words with an old hat, are you?'

'No, I hardly ever talk to hats,' said Nick. 'The fact is I said one or two things to you a little while ago that I want to apologize for. Yes, sorry and all that, Annabelle. Well, when I start me new job I'll be able to afford a social life instead of just football.'

'Well, bless me, have you woken up at last?' asked Annabelle.

'I haven't been asleep, I—'

'I don't want any excuses,' said Annabelle. 'I just want to know if I'm going to be your one and only.'

'What a nice thought,' said Nick.

'Oh, d'you think so?'

'I like the sound of it.'

'Well,' said Annabelle forthrightly, 'if I come to the pictures with you on Saturday evenings and help you to learn to play tennis, you've got to forsake everything except treating me as special. I'm not anybody, you know.'

'I do know,' said Nick, 'I've been under the doctor since I met you.'

'How kind,' said Annabelle. 'Well, then?'

'Well what?' asked Nick, slightly off balance.

'Oh, come on, you blessed thickhead,' said Annabelle, 'I don't actually have to ask for a kiss, do I?'

'Should I ask your parents first?'

'Certainly not,' said Annabelle, 'you can kiss me first, and then if I like it, I'll take you to meet my mum and to say hello again to my dad. But if I don't like it, you'll have to try again.'

Nick kissed her, on her warm moist mouth. Annabelle closed her eyes and went a bit faint, as Ma did last Monday afternoon.

'How was that?' asked Nick, who'd liked it himself.

'I don't know, I can't remember,' said Annabelle faintly. 'You'll have to do it again.'

Nick did it again, very willingly, and Annabelle came out of the encore with her eyes still closed and her knees weak.

'Have I passed?' asked Nick.

Annabelle opened her eyes.

'Has the train gone?' she asked. Nick laughed. She smiled. 'Now, come and talk to my parents,' she said, 'and talk nicely to them. Don't tell my mum you were ever a ragamuffin, an urchin, a street corner boy or a hooligan. Tell her you've got a prosperous new job and a certificate for being respectable.'

'I could tell her other things, I could tell her my sisters drive me up the wall, that Ma did the dance of the seven veils when she was eight, and that Pa's done time for doing a Charlie Peace job.' Charlie Peace was a man who'd made a name for himself years ago as London's craftiest and most successful burglar. 'How about that?' said Nick.

'Oh, you daft thing, be your age,' said Annabelle, 'you've got to be serious, not barmy. You can't make jokes like that about your dad in front of Mum, specially not when everything's all about you and me.'

'It's serious, everything about you and me?' said Nick.

'Yes, of course. I—' Annabelle had an unusually reticent moment. It induced a little flush. 'I mean, it's not a game any more, is it?'

Well, thought Nick, if it gets critical and I start thinking about wedding bells, I'll have to tell her about Pa or it might all blow up in my face at the wrong moment. No, that's no good, I've got to tell her now, otherwise there'll still be times when I'll have to come up with lies.

'Listen, Annabelle,' he said, and he told her everything about Pa. Annabelle listened, dubious at first, then disbelieving, then round-eyed and astonished. But it didn't change the way she felt about him. He ended up by saying, 'Now you can see why I tried to keep my distance.'

Annabelle drew a long breath, then released a slightly shaky smile.

'Nick, you silly, you should have told me before,' she said. 'What kind of a girl d'you think I am? How could anyone blame you for your dad not being brought up right? You seem to have been brought up right yourself, your mum's made a smashing job of you, and I'd trust you with my life's savings.' She smiled again. 'Nearly thirty pounds, let me tell you,' she said. 'I know you chuck your weight about a bit – look how you've chucked it at me – but you're still my best bloke. Besides, all our families are as cockney as yours is, and cockneys don't take any notice – well, not much – of what some of our relatives get up to. Mind, you and I will have to take a lot of notice of what your dad might get up to now he's out, we've got to make sure he stays in his honest job. I'll talk to him if I have to, you see if I don't. We won't let him spoil things for us, we're going to have lovely times together, and at committee meetings I promise not to make you bawl and shout. You're funny when you bawl and shout, did you know that?'

'Annabelle—'

'Oh, you silly,' she said again, and gave him an impulsive hug. 'You should have told me all this when we first had tea and crumpets together. Well, you must have known then that I'd made up my mind I was going to be your one and only. Nick, you do want me for your one and only, don't you?'

'Yes, I seriously do,' said Nick, thinking her

support made her his favourite bet for the kind of future that had roses round the door.

'Then that's all that matters,' said Annabelle. 'So now we'd better go and tell my mum and dad. It's best not to keep these things secret. Secrets sort of fall out of locked cupboards. Dad will be nice about it because he's like my Uncle Boots, but Mum will have fifty fits and one more. Still, when she's recovered she'll see what a nice lovely bloke you are yourself, and after all your dad did save a warder's life and earned himself a medal.'

'I don't think there was any medal,' said Nick.

'Well, we won't say so to Mum. Actually,' said Annabelle, 'you'll like my mum when you get to know her, she's got lovely looks. But don't go dotty about her because, as my Uncle Sammy says, she's my dad's married wife. Let's see, your hair looks nicely brushed, your tie's straight, and you only need to stick your chest out – Nick!'

Nick was doing his first tickling job on her. But because she was a peach of a girl in every sense, the tickling was of the kind recommended by Ma, and it made Annabelle decide she'd come back for a bit more later on.

Yes, after they'd talked to her mum and dad, and her mum had recovered from her fifty and one fits.

THE END

MISSING PERSON
by Mary Jane Staples

The house in Caulfield Place, off Browning Street in
Walworth, was haunted, or at least that's what the street
kids said. So when two men, a woman, and a parrot moved
in, everyone was very interested, especially fourteen-year-
old Cassie Ford, who was particularly fascinated by the
parrot.

And it was just about this time that Mr Finch, Chinese
Lady's husband, and Boots's stepfather, began to get
mysterious telephone calls. Mr Finch had never told the
rest of the Adams family – except for Boots – the secrets of
his past, or what kind of work he did for the government,
and he decided not to tell them about the slightly sinister
telephone calls either.

It was when he took Chinese Lady on a summer's day
jaunt in his Morris motorcar that things began to happen.
For, in the Hog's Back Hotel, Chinese Lady went to the
cloakroom, and when she came back Mr Finch had
vanished. It took all of Boots's ingenuity to finally discover
what had happened, and Cassie's knowledge of the
Caulfield Place parrot was to prove a vital clue in
unravelling the mystery.

Here again is the Adams family from *Down Lambeth Way*,
Our Emily, *King of Camberwell*, *On Mother Brown's
Doorstep* and *A Family Affair*.

0 552 14230 1

THE TRAP
by Mary Jane Staples

When Jamie Blair, twenty-four, unemployed, and back from the trenches, took lodgings at Larcom Street in Walworth, he had no idea he was walking into a trap.

The house was owned by Henry Mullins, big, burly, and a hard drinker. Henry made life hell for his four step-children who looked half-starved and frequently got bashed. Seventeen-year-old Kitty was the one Jamie felt most sorry for. She took the brunt of Henry Mullins' bad temper whilst trying to protect her sisters and brother.

When Mullins suddenly died – in somewhat suspicious circumstances – Kitty realized they could be in trouble. If she wasn't careful the authorities would take the younger children away – split the family up. She wasn't having that, not after all they'd gone through, and nice, kind Jamie Blair was the one to save them.

Too late Jamie found himself with a ready-made family and a stubborn and fiery young termagant called Kitty who was determined not to let him go.

0 552 14106 2

TWO FOR THREE FARTHINGS
by Mary Jane Staples

Horace was ten, Ethel seven, when Jim Cooper, home from the trenches, minus an arm and just about managing on his own, found them huddled in a doorway on a wet night in Walworth. Slightly against his better judgement he took them in, fed them cocoa, and put them to sleep in his bed. A few days later he found that – somehow – he had become the unofficial guardian of Horace and Ethel. It was him, the orphanage, or separation for the gutsy little pair who would have to be farmed out to anyone who would take them, and Jim felt a sudden affinity for the two cheeky cockney kids. The first thing he had to do was find fresh lodgings for them all.

Miss Rebecca Pilgrim was a woman of strict Victorian principles, eminently respectable, and determined to keep her privacy intact. She had reckoned without her new lodgers – Horace, Ethel and, above all, the irrepressible Jim Cooper. And thus began the humanizing of Miss Pilgrim, who turned out to be younger, prettier, and far gentler than any of them had suspected.

0 552 13635 2

A SELECTED LIST OF FINE NOVELS
AVAILABLE FROM CORGI BOOKS

THE PRICES SHOWN BELOW WERE CORRECT AT THE TIME OF GOING TO PRESS.
HOWEVER TRANSWORLD PUBLISHERS RESERVE THE RIGHT TO SHOW NEW
RETAIL PRICES ON COVERS WHICH MAY DIFFER FROM THOSE PREVIOUSLY
ADVERTISED IN THE TEXT OR ELSEWHERE.